#murderfunding

II

Gretchen McNeil

ff FREEFORM BOOKS

Los Angeles   New York

First Edition, August 2019
10 9 8 7 6 5 4 3 2 1
FAC-020093-19172
Printed in the United States of America

This book is set in AGaramond, Arial, Compa, Helvetica, Melior, Tahoma, Times-Roman/Monotype; Badhouse Light/House Industries
Designed by Marci Senders

Library of Congress Cataloging-in-Publication Data

Names: McNeil, Gretchen, author.
Title: #MurderFunding / by Gretchen McNeil.
Other titles: HashtagMurderFunding • Hashtag murder funding • Murder funding
Description: First edition. • Los Angeles ; New York : Freeform Books, 2019.
    • Sequel to: #MurderTrending. • Summary: Seventeen-year-old Becca
    auditions for a new, non-lethal reality show featuring Painiacs, hoping to
    prove that her deceased mother was not Alcatraz 2.0 executioner Molly
    Mauler.
Identifiers: LCCN 2018034810 • ISBN 9781368026277 (hardcover)
Subjects: • CYAC: Survival—Fiction. • Murder—Fiction. • Social
    media—Fiction. • Reality television programs—Fiction. • Love—Fiction. •
    Lesbians—Fiction.
Classification: LCC PZ7.M4787952 Aab 2019 • DDC [Fic]—dc23
LC record available at https://lccn.loc.gov/2018034810

Reinforced binding
Visit www.freeform.com/books

To the Wolfpack: Nadine, Julia, James, Jen, and Brad

"Let them eat bread and circuses."
—THE POSTMAN

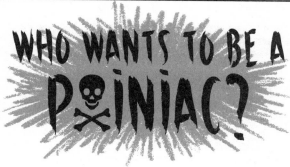

WHO WANTS TO BE A PAINIAC?

645,982 likes

tristan_mckee Hey, The Postman fans—are you missing your number one app? Does your day feel incomplete without updates from your favorite Painiac? If so, then this is your lucky day!

Merchant-Bronson Productions and FundMyFun.com announce the newest television sensation: Who Wants to Be a Painiac?, a game show version of The Postman set to air on the Reality Network. Go to www.FundMyFun.com/whowantstobeapainiac to show your Postmanticity!!!! If we raise $250,000 by December 15, open call auditions will take place on the 17th, 9 a.m., at Stu-Stu-Studio in Burbank, California. MAKE YOUR DREAMS COME TRUE! Donate now! #Painiacs #WhoWantsToBeAPainiac #Auditions #RealityTV #MerchantBronson #RealityNetwork #ThePostman #Postmantics

1 HOUR AGO

RECENT ACTIVITY

capedcapuchinghost *immediately checks flights to LA* SO THERE! Excited AF!!!!!!
#ThePostmanForever

wolfgang_collins Is this a Postman Enterprises, Inc. affiliated show? Cuz I thought the FBI shut the whole company down. #IzConfused

ellen_enchanted2 Hold up. Good taste aside, how is this legal?

mcdonnelson @ellen_enchanted2 Who cares! The Painiacs are coming back! I've been in withdrawal.

....

phoebe_temptressta Putting together my costume as I type. With one hand. #SoundsDirtyButIsnt

....

ihate_snailmail @ellen_enchanted2 I'm reporting this to the authorities ASAP and I suggest you do the same. With the manhunt for The Postman under way and PEI under federal indictment, there is absolutely no way this should be allowed to happen. ESPECIALLY considering the actions of these morally corrupt Postman "fans" in recent weeks trying to hunt down #CinderellaSurvivor...

....

eltonjohn4evzz @ihate_snailmail Oh, like the Postmantics are the only ones to blame? You anti-Postman activists are just as bad. Those witch hunts for the former Painiacs' families? Not exactly legal, asshole.

....

splendour420 #FundMyFun just hit $35,000 in less than an hour. #PostmanticPower

....

judy_kline @ihate_snailmail A certain SECRET message board is already organizing a protest at Stu-Stu-Studio for December 17. Message me if you want an invitation to join the group.

....

snowqueenwinter Painiac auditions? This is my dream!!!! I need a costume, right? We should all come in costume? Like with a persona and everything? Right, of course we should. HAHAHAHAHA. I'm such a spaz. Just so juiced!

....

wicked_josh Do you think my Gucci Hangman cosplay would be okay to audition in? Or should I do something original?

....

skullcrusherchic @judy_kline Oh yeah? Well there's another SECRET message board (you're not the only one, dickhead) and we'll be at auditions to protect the auditioners. Postmantics? Feel free to DM me to get an invite. Freedom of speech, bitches.

....

eureka_sammy150 @judy_kline Messaged you

....

squirrelwoman @skullcrusherchic ME ME ME

pqe_bachmann @skullcrusherchic DM sent

ihate_snailmail @skullcrusherchic You're disgusting. Reported you to Instagram for violation of its policies.
#FreedomOfSpeechBitches

maiv_moms @judy_kline DM'd you

jiwoo_s @wicked_josh Def something original.

thegriff If ever there was evidence that The Postman was a multi-conglomerate conspiracy aimed at controlling the masses through coordinated entertainment ventures, THIS WOULD BE IT!
#DontTrustTheFeed #WideAwakeEyesOpen #FakeNews #ThePostmanAlive

skullcrusherchic @ihate_snailmail Yeah, and we're coming for you next.
#WitchHunt #FedxersMustDie

darkness_falls @judy_kline There's a special place in Hell reserved for harassing supposed Painiac family members. I heard you people are showing up at funerals across the country, accusing every old lady in a closed coffin of being D.I.Ynona. With no proof, no evidence. Do you realize how fucked up that is?

fedx_delivery @skullcrusherchic Not if we get you first...

ADD A COMMENT

BELTWAY BULLETIN

POLITICS—US Edition

November 23, 08:32 am ET

The Battle for the Presidency
by Adrienne Quiñones

In case you've been living in a cave for the last two weeks, let me get you up to speed.

It has been thirteen days since the House of Representatives passed H.Res. 1334, adopting six articles of impeachment against the president of the United States on grounds of high crimes and misdemeanors, as well as the highly controversial charge of treason, in accordance with Article II of the United States Constitution.

Despite the urging of his closest advisers, the president has not resigned from office à la Richard Nixon to avoid trial and probable conviction by a two-thirds Senate vote, which could, in the estimation of several hundred legal pundits, lead to criminal charges. Instead, sequestering himself inside the West Wing like a child who refuses to accept punishment, the president stubbornly clings to what little power he retains.

While there is little doubt that the current presidency won't survive the impeachment trial, several key facts in the Alcatraz 2.0 investigation remain nebulous. Authorities still have not released the identity of The Postman, Alcatraz 2.0's mastermind, ringleader, and presiding warden, fueling speculation that no one—not even the NSA—knows who he really is. Or was. Because no one can confirm whether The Postman is actually dead or alive.

Internet theories on The Postman's identity are as vast and numerous as the stars in the cosmos. Every media billionaire who hasn't been seen in the last two weeks has been tapped as the potential mass murderer. As of yet, no credible evidence has been produced in favor of any one individual.

Who might know The Postman's real name? The president, for sure, but he's probably not spilling the beans anytime soon. The former attorney general refuses to name names until his demand for immunity has been accepted, but most insiders think the ex-AG is bluffing. But the House managers who will be prosecuting the impeachment trial seem pretty confident in their case, as evidenced by the inclusion of the treason charge. Could it be they have a couple of surprise witnesses up their congressional sleeves?

And then there's Dee Guerrera, along with fellow "Death Row Breakfast Club" survivors Nyles Harding and Griselda Sinclair. Could the Alcatraz 2.0 whistle-blowers know the identity of The Postman? The trio *did* have access to sensitive information during their final hours on the prison island, but far from being forthcoming with the media, the Alcatraz 2.0 survivors have gone into hiding as legions of The Postman's rabid fans, self-dubbed the "Postmantics," attempt to hunt them down.

To complicate matters, another group of anti-Postman activists are gaining in number, and while the Postmantics' goal is to make the Death Row Breakfast Club pay for their supposed crimes, the Fed-Xers (get it?) are stalking funerals across the country, searching for the real identities of the deceased Painiacs.

One thing is sure: between the impeachment, the Postmantics, and the Fed-Xers, the American people are going to learn more about Alcatraz 2.0 than they ever wanted to know.

Set your DVRs and stock up on salty snacks. This doozy of an impeachment trial is set to begin December 17.

Please send feedback to the author @TheRealaquinonesBB.

ONE

BECCA WINCED, SQUINTING AGAINST THE BRIGHT FLASH OF midmorning sunlight as it reflected off the impossibly shiny surface of her mom's coffin.

There should be some kind of law against sunny days and funerals.

Ten feet away, Reverend Hamlin's understated monotone droned on and on about God and servants and souls, and though Becca should have been grieving or mourning or at the very least recalling all the cherished memories of her dead mom as the polished brown casket was lowered into the ground, all she could think about was how stupid it was.

Why bother polishing the casket? That thing was literally getting buried in the ground where no one would ever see it. And the plush interior? Did the bloody, mangled remains of her mom's body give even half a shit that they'd splurged for the tufted velour lining over the base-model crepe?

"Earth to earth," Reverend Hamlin recited. "Ashes to ashes, dust to dust."

To her left, Becca's younger brother, Rafa, sniffled and swallowed while he gazed woefully at the giant hole in the ground, attempting to conceal his sorrow behind a mask of self-imposed manliness, which was probably what he thought dudes were supposed to do at their mom's funeral, even though he was only ten. Becca reached down and grabbed his hand, giving it a squeeze. She wished she could shield him from this misery.

Behind them, Becca could feel Rita's convulsive yet silent sobs as she watched her partner of almost twenty years laid to rest, her hand gripping Ruth's sapphire-and-white-gold wedding ring, which now hung around Rita's neck on a chain.

Her mom and brother were mourning. Because that's what normal people did at funerals. They cried.

Meanwhile Becca was trying not to stare at Reverend Hamlin's nose hairs as they fluttered in and out of his nostrils with every breath.

What the hell was wrong with her?

It wasn't that Becca didn't love her mom or miss her mom or desperately wish the car crash that took her mom's life hadn't happened. She had no idea why she was unable to cry, which only added to her guilt. Because Becca had looked forward to her mom's semi-regular trips to Arizona to help take care of her best friend Tabitha, who was battling cancer. It meant three days indulging in the things Ruth didn't approve of, namely plaid miniskirts and ripped tees, nacho cheese sauce eaten straight from the jar, and uninterrupted access to The Postman app. Her mom's number-one pet peeve.

Can.

Not.

Hang.

Ruth loved to lecture Becca on the dangers of violence and young minds and yada yada yada. Becca would smile and pretend to listen . . . and keep watching. In secret.

Which is exactly what she'd been doing—alone in her bedroom, obsessing over the fallout of the Alcatraz 2.0 shutdown—when the phone had rung with the news of her mom's accident.

Guilt burrito, anyone?

"When our earthly journey is ended . . ." Reverend Hamlin's nose hairs quivered dramatically as he brought home the final prayer. "Lead us rejoicing into your kingdom, where you live and reign forever and ever. Amen."

Amen, Becca mouthed.

The mourners began to disperse, voices low and mumbling as they offered final condolences to Rita, then picked their way around the granite slabs that marked the uniform rows of graves. Becca's best friends, Jackie and Mateo, arms wrapped around each other for comfort, flashed Becca a tight smile before disappearing hand in hand down the hillside. Becca recognized other faces in the crowd—people from church, people from her school, parents who had known Ruth from the PTA. It looked as if most of Marquette, Michigan, had turned out for the funeral.

"Your mom loved you both very much," Rita said, her voice steady.

Rafa heaved. "I miss her."

"I miss her too," Rita said, pulling Rafa to her side and squeezing his shoulders tightly. "But she'll always be with us. I promise."

Becca reached out and tousled Rafa's wavy black hair. She may have been crappy at this mourning thing, but she was good at being a big sister. And Rafa needed her right now.

Rita smiled as she watched her children. Her warm brown eyes, though red-rimmed from crying, lit up her face. Her dark skin was luminous, her curly hair bounced around her ears, and Becca was struck by how beautiful her mom was, even in the face of tragedy.

"You look so much like her," Rita said, eyes fixed on Becca's face.

Becca fought the urge to cringe. Secretly, Becca had always wished she'd gotten Rita's genes like Rafa, instead of the pasty white skin and plethora of freckles she'd inherited from Ruth. No such luck.

"Believe it or not," Rita continued, reading Becca's mind, "you're more like her than you realize."

Don't call your mom crazy. Don't call your mom crazy. "Really?"

Rita nodded. Her eyes drifted to the open grave, glassy and unseeing, and when she spoke again, her voice sounded far away. "There was more to Ruth Martinello than you knew."

Becca wasn't about to contradict her mom five minutes after she'd buried her wife—even her penchant for deflective sarcasm had its limit— but she couldn't bring herself to agree. *There was more to Ruth Martinello than you knew.* For reals? If there was one person on this planet who was exactly what you'd expect her to be, it was Ruth Martinello. From her warm, ever-present smile to her sensible L.L.Bean cropped chinos and buttoned-up pastel cardigans, Ruth was the epitome of the friendly, supportive stay-at-home mom. She was the kind of person who helped everyone—neighbors, strangers, even her high school best friend in Arizona, who was dealing with chemo treatments for breast cancer. Ruth was always the first one to reach out with selfless altruism, which made Becca embarrassed of her own snarky edge and self-serving attitude.

While Becca was pondering Rita's comment, she caught movement out of the corner of her eye. Just a quick flash, like sunlight glinting off the side of a coffin. She turned as her mom led Rafa to the car, and saw a figure standing near a sprawling oak tree about fifty yards from the grave site.

It was a girl, Becca could tell by the outline of her body against the bright blue sky, even though she was wearing pants and a boxy black jacket. Her dark hair was cut into an asymmetrical bob—the left side shorter than the right—which hung loosely in front of her face, and she was holding a video camera in her hand.

Why was this pervy chick filming at a cemetery? Who gave her permission to document Ruth's funeral? And who still used a video camera? What was this, 2009?

Before she could even speculate as to the answers to these questions, the girl slipped behind the tree and hurried off down the hill.

"What the hell?" Becca said out loud. She took a few steps toward the rapidly departing girl and shouted, "Hey! Stop! What are you doing?"

"Becca?" Rita called from the car. "Come on. We need to get home. People will be arriving for the reception."

Becca paused. She desperately wanted to sprint across the lawn after the weird chick with the lopsided hair and demand to know why she'd been filming Ruth's funeral, but as she stood indecisively, a car rounded the cemetery drive. Becca saw the long side of the girl's hair flick toward her as she turned her head from the driver's seat. Their eyes met for a split second; then the girl made a hard left at a fork in the path and disappeared down the hill.

TWO

GOING BACK TO SCHOOL AFTER YOUR MOM DIED WAS THE fucking worst.

"Hey, Becca. Sorry for your loss."

"Becca, I am *so* sorry about your mom."

"It's Becca, right? Hey, tough break."

Can.

Not.

Hang.

Becca hardly knew these people, didn't believe the sincerity of their comments for half a freaking second, and it took literally every ounce of self-control not to answer with "Fuck off!" each time. Like the true asshole she was.

The only thing that would get her through this day from hell was her friends.

"Hey," Jackie said the moment she saw Becca in the hall. Her bright smile contradicted the concern in her eyes. "How are you?"

Becca shrugged. "Fine, I guess."

Mateo, always by his girlfriend's side, folded his arms across his chest. "You guess?"

"That's less 'typical teenage avoidance strategy' and more 'I honestly don't know,'" Becca replied. "Emotions are hard." She appreciated that her friends were worried about her, but they should know her well enough by now to realize that a main course of genuine emotion with a heaping side of sincerity was not on the Becca menu.

Jackie's smile relaxed. "Hard for *you*."

Becca rolled her eyes as she dialed in her locker combination. Jackie had been studying psych books ever since her parents' divorce and loved nothing more than "helping" her friends with nonprofessional diagnoses. "Yeah, yeah. I'm stunted. We know."

Mateo gave his girlfriend a look that said *Maybe not right now, Jackie?* "You don't have to talk about any of it. We're just here to support you."

"Of course." Jackie nodded in agreement. "You know we love you."

Becca was grateful for her friends. Grateful that they'd offered to come over the second she'd told them about her mom's accident, even though it was the night Jackie's mom worked the late shift at the hospital, which meant she and Mateo had most definitely been in some stage of sexy times when Becca had texted. She was grateful that they'd both been at the funeral, and she was grateful that they hadn't made her talk about any of it. Until now.

"Okay, Dr. Phil," Becca said with a sly grin. She needed to nip all this sincerity in the bud. "I'll let you know if I feel anything less than one hundred percent supported. Or maybe ninety percent? I think I could probably handle only feeling ninety percent supported by you guys. But if we drop to eighty-five, I'm fucking out of here."

Jackie shook her head, her long blond ponytail swinging across her back like a pendulum. "Smart-ass."

"Always." Becca clicked her locker door closed. "Come on, tell me something fun on the way to Bio."

Jackie slipped her hand into Mateo's as they threaded a path through the horde of students. "Apparently, Kasie McInerney's boyfriend brought a new girlfriend home with him from college for Thanksgiving break."

"Ouch."

"Yeah," Jackie said. "He never even broke up with Kasie. They were together three years and he's only been down in Madison for three months."

Becca tried not to glance at her friends. Would their relationship survive the trip to college next fall? Becca doubted it. And then what, would she be forced to choose between them a year from now when Jackie brought a new boyfriend home from college? *This is why I don't date.*

But Jackie clearly didn't see the potential parallel as she barreled on with the post-Thanksgiving-break gossip. "And Darlene Ahlberg has been telling anyone who'll listen she's visiting her aunt in LA for winter break again."

Becca arched an eyebrow. "What agent supposedly wants to sign her this time?"

"Worse than that," Jackie said. "She wants to audition for that new game show *Who Wants to Be a Painiac?*"

"Becca!" some rando sophomore boy in an oversize flannel shouted as he passed her in the hall. "I feel you, girl!"

"I could have you arrested for that," Becca called out in response, then turned back to her friends. "What's this about Painiacs?" she said, feigning ignorance.

"I forgot you've been unplugged," Mateo said. "Some production company is crowdsourcing a game show based on the Painiacs from Alcatraz two-point-oh."

"Oooh," Becca said. Only she didn't need Mateo to explain *Who Wants to Be a Painiac?* to her. She knew exactly what it was. The members of her Postmantics Facebook group had been discussing it nonstop since the Instagram post went live Saturday morning.

The day of your mom's funeral.

She really didn't want to admit to her friends that she'd been obsessing over her Facebook group feed instead of processing her grief, so it was easier to just pretend she had no idea what they were talking about. "Interesting."

"Disgusting is more like it," Jackie said, sounding as if she was about to vomit. "I can't believe someone thinks that's a good idea."

"Thankfully, we'll be up the mountain over winter break when it airs," Mateo said, then smiled expectantly at Becca. "You're still coming with us, right?"

Becca hesitated. A couple of weeks ago, she'd jumped at the chance to spend a week with Jackie, Mateo, and his family at their cabin near the ski resort at Keyes Peak, but now she wasn't sure if she should leave her mom and Rafa alone so close to Christmas.

"It'll be good for you," Jackie said, sensing her uncertainty. "You need to do something fun. What's the point of having two weeks off from school if all you do is stay home?"

"I don't know," Becca said. "Sleeping for two straight weeks seems kinda exciting right now."

"You're coming," Jackie said. "That's final."

"Fine," Becca said with a grin as she ducked into the bio lab. "But I won't like it."

The rest of the day was a blur. Bio to Calculus. English to Humanities. Government to Art History to study hall. Becca was on autopilot for most of it, moving from classroom to cafeteria to hallway like she'd done for days and months and years. For the most part, everything was the same: the same people, the same lessons, the same hallway chatter, though the daily conversations had shifted from The Postman's most recent kills to the latest police reports about vigilantes hunting down the Painiacs' families or reports on the whereabouts of the Death Row Breakfast Club. Still, the same fevered pitch of pop culture enthusiasm infected the halls of Marquette Senior High School, and yet somehow, today felt different.

It wasn't just the stream of "Sorry, Becca" or her friends' attempts to keep their conversations buoyant and substance-free that was weird. An out-of-body sensation haunted her. For a few moments, here and there, Becca almost forgot that her mom had died. She'd be laughing at one of Mateo's jokes or internal-monologue-ing about how boring Mr. Cartwright's lectures were, and in that instant, her life was exactly the same as it had been two weeks ago. It was as if she were floating above the tragedy that was her life, gazing down upon it with an objective eye. Then a memory would come flooding back, punching Becca in the gut and momentarily knocking the breath from her. She'd be graveside again, her mom and brother weeping, while Becca did nothing.

By the time the final bell rang, Becca had a throbbing headache. All she wanted to do was go home and collapse into bed.

Usually—which meant every single day—she went to Jackie's after school, but today Becca couldn't handle two hours of good-natured gossip and animal memes on YouTube. She dashed off a quick text of explanation to her best friend, then headed for the parking lot.

Becca stomped across the asphalt toward Rita's old Ford Explorer, a beat-up hulk of non-ecologically-friendly SUV, and practically ripped the door off the hinges as she opened it, angry that school hadn't offered her a complete escape from reality. She tossed her backpack across to the passenger's seat, then climbed behind the wheel. But she didn't start the car. She just sat there, panting, waiting for the tears to stream down her face.

They never came.

What the hell was wrong with her? Why couldn't she cry?

The lot began to empty out. The furor of post-school chaos crescendoed, then dissipated, leaving Becca alone in her car. But as stillness settled around her, Becca became keenly aware of someone standing in the trees, watching her.

There was a sharp sound, a foot snapping a dried twig in half that Becca could barely hear through the cracked car window, but it was enough for Becca to look up into the trees. Standing much as she had at the cemetery, half-obscured by the thin trunk of a white pine, was the girl with the camera.

THREE

SHE WORE THE SAME BOXY BLACK JACKET, THE SAME JEANS, but she'd added a pair of sunglasses, which obscured most of her face. Her dark, asymmetrical hair was tucked behind her ear on one side and hung down across her face on the other, and her hands, partially covered in purple fingerless gloves, held the same camera.

The girl stood frozen, the camera shoulder-high with the lens aimed at Becca, and even though they were close enough for Becca to discern the jeweled stud of a nose ring in the girl's left nostril, the girl didn't move, didn't speak, didn't make any attempt to explain why the hell she'd been following Becca around.

Following me around. On Saturday, Becca had just assumed the girl was filming her mom's funeral. Some kind of death fetish maybe. But now here she was at Becca's school. It wasn't the funeral this chick was interested in—it was Becca.

Becca had seen a movie like this once—a sociopath stalks his coworker, taking video footage of her, which ends with him filming her murder . . . as he was murdering her.

Yeah, that was *so* not going to happen.

Throwing open the car door, Becca squared her shoulders and marched to the end of the asphalt.

"Who the fuck are you and why the fuck are you following me?" She tried to sound tough, just in case this girl had any ideas about dragging Becca back into the woods and decapitating her.

The girl continued to stare, seemingly dumbfounded.

"Hey!" Becca snapped. It had been a long day. She didn't have any patience left. "I asked you a question."

"Two," the girl said slowly, finding her voice.

"Your name is Two?"

"No. You asked me two questions."

Great. A fellow smart-ass. "Are you going to answer or am I going to have to call nine-one-one and report a psycho stalker in the Marquette High parking lot?"

Instead of getting angry or defensive, the girl merely smiled as she clicked off her camera, then pushed her sunglasses up onto her forehead. "You can if you want, but I'm not actually doing anything illegal."

Becca felt something catch in her stomach. It was the first clear look she'd gotten at the girl's face, and even though five seconds ago she was thinking that this chick might try to murder her for a snuff film, she had to admit the face smiling back from the pine grove was stunningly beautiful. Unlike Becca's thin, crooked mouth, this girl's lips were full and plump, like one of those makeup models in a Sephora ad. She had high cheekbones, illuminated as if she were wearing a shimmery highlighter though Becca was pretty sure the girl wasn't wearing a whit of makeup. Her skin was supple, a luminous light brown, and her eyes were a surprisingly deep greenish hazel, bright and shining beneath hooded lids.

Becca was 100 percent positive she'd never seen this girl before Saturday. Marquette, Michigan, wasn't exactly a bastion of gorgeous cool chicks with awesome hair and nose piercings, and despite Becca's small social circle, she definitely would have noticed this girl around town.

As much as Becca was instantly attracted, it didn't change the fact that this stranger had been following her around with a video camera. "I'm pretty sure videotaping me and my family without consent isn't legal."

"Only if I sell it," the girl replied, glancing at the camera, which now hung limply at her side. "Or distribute it for public consumption."

"Seriously?"

"I'm Stef," the girl said. "Stef . . ." She paused, as if trying to decide what last name she was going to use. "Stef Ybarra."

Becca wondered if that was actually her name. Doubtful. "Funny, I was just calling you Creepy Stalker Girl in my head."

"You can if you want." Stef looked as if she didn't give a shit what Becca thought. "You sound just like her, you know."

Record scratch. "What are you talking about?"

"Your mom. You have the same voice."

Aha. So this was one of Rita's zoology students from NMU. That . . . still didn't make any sense. "I'm pretty sure Dr. Martinello wouldn't appreciate you filming her wife's funeral."

"I was gathering evidence."

Full stop. "You were gathering evidence about my mom's funeral? News flash, she's still dead."

Stef tilted her head to the side. "Um, no. About your mom."

Ruth? Couldn't be. She must mean Rita. "If you want to interview my mom about her research, you're supposed to go through the university to set up an appointment."

A crease formed between Stef's eyes. She looked confused, as if not entirely sure what Becca was talking about. "Not that mom."

"Clearly I'm hallucinating," Becca said.

Stef stared at Becca for a moment, greenish eyes scanning her face. The crease deepened, a wrinkly chasm between her eyebrows. "Oh my

God. You don't know!" Stef's voice was breathless, shocked, and the shift in tone accompanied the return of the camera, pointed at Becca's face. The red power light indicated that Stef was filming again.

"Know *what*?" The pounding in Becca's temples intensified, cranked up by Stef's weirdness. She wanted to go home, crawl into bed, forget this day ever happened. She literally had no clue what this chick was hinting at, but cute or not, Becca was officially tired of the conversation.

Stef's green eyes flicked up from the camera's view screen. "Your mom Ruth Martinello . . ." She turned her head sharply as if unsure how to continue, then cleared her throat and started again. "Ruth Martinello had another life."

Becca rolled her eyes. "Please. Are you going to try and tell me that my mom was what, a secret stripper? A CIA operative? An escaped convict with a price on her head?"

"No."

"Then what?"

Stef stood very still as she continued to film. "Your mom was the Alcatraz-sanctioned executioner known as Molly Mauler."

FOUR

EVERY TIME DEE GUERRERA HEARD A HELICOPTER BUZZ OVER the twentieth-floor condo she now called home, she was sure a news crew had found her.

The sound of chopping rotor blades was such a normal, everyday part of growing up in Los Angeles that Dee had rarely noticed them before. But now, as she sat propped up in an unfamiliar bed, her mangled right leg a crisscrossed mess of surgical scars and healing wounds, every single helicopter outside her window was a potential harbinger of doom.

Ironically, just two weeks ago it had been a helicopter that had been her savior when the Coast Guard landed on Alcatraz 2.0 and lifted her, Nyles, and Griselda to safety. Then, the dull roar of the approaching chopper had given Dee a sense of release, signaling the end of her struggles and pain. But the joy of their rescue, and of Dee's reunion with her dad, was short-lived, as the realities of "Life After Alcatraz 2.0" became all too real.

Her dad had tried to shield her from it, pasting a bright smile on his face from the moment they left San Francisco General Hospital a few days after her first surgery, but Dee could see the frayed edges of the smile, the deep circles beneath his eyes that betrayed sleepless nights and days fraught with worry. Dee's first hint of what was in store for them came when she was discharged from the hospital through a subterranean garage, and not into her dad's Prius or her stepmom's minivan or even a rental car of some generic make and model. Nope, her wheelchair was pushed up to the side door of a massive black SUV, with darkly tinted windows and driven by a burly man she'd never seen before.

Turned out, his name was Javier, and he, along with three colleagues, were the Guerreras' new bodyguards, accompanying Dee and her dad back to Los Angeles.

And not to the cheerful bungalow in Burbank that had been Dee's home before the Barracks on Alcatraz 2.0, but to a massive, high-security condominium complex near UCLA where Javier and his team could keep Dee and her dad safe.

Because, apparently, a lot of people wanted Dee dead.

Her dad never directly told her what was going on, but some careful eavesdropping and clandestine googling had painted a pretty grim picture of her reality. Their Burbank home? Besieged by news trucks. Her whereabouts? Hunted for, every day.

Just as Nyles had predicted, Dee was suddenly the most famous girl in the world.

The media was benign in comparison to the death threats. Former fans of The Postman blamed Dee and her friends for the app's demise, just as the dwindling supporters of the president held her responsible for the impending impeachment trial, and as speculation about the identity and whereabouts of The Postman himself continued to spiral out of control, the anger and frustration of the Postmantics were focused on the Death Row Breakfast Club. Websites, Twitter feeds, and entire Tumblr accounts were dedicated to fantasizing about their deaths, sharing dubious information about their pasts, and trying to piece together where they were hiding.

At the Guerrera compound, Javier inspected every piece of mail that arrived, and only a short list of people were allowed access to the condo. According to the news, Dee's location had yet to be discovered, but every time she heard a helicopter, she was sure that the legion of Internet stalkers and paparazzi hunting for her had finally made the discovery of a lifetime.

And Dee was terrified to think what that might mean, not just for herself but for her friends, and for her dad.

"Good morning, sleepy face!" Dee's dad slipped into her room, grinning from ear to ear. "How is the patient feeling?"

Dee smiled back. "It's three o'clock in the afternoon, Dad."

"I know," he replied as he fretted around her bed, opening and closing the venetian blinds to achieve the perfect balance of light and shadow. "Just teasing. Do you need another pillow? How about some water? With a bendy straw, like when you were little."

"Dad, I'm fine."

He inched the pull cord down, moving the parallel slats a nanometer, before turning back to his daughter. "How's the pain?"

"I think it's a little better today, actually." And for the first time in two weeks, Dee wasn't even lying.

"I don't believe you." Her dad dragged a chair to the side of her bed.

"I swear. I haven't taken a pain pill since breakfast. Been getting a little bit better every day."

Her dad's dark brown eyes were bloodshot when he looked up at her, his face weary. "I guess we all have."

Unlike Dee, he *was* lying. She knew he didn't want her to see the toll the last few months had taken on him, but it wasn't as if Dee didn't notice the white hairs poking out at kinky angles from his black waves.

Nor could she ignore the deep creases on his forehead or the fact that his clothes hung limp on his body.

Silence fell between them, thick and murky, and her dad's eyes trailed to the partially open window. She knew exactly what he was thinking about: her stepmom. It was bad enough that her daughter had been murdered, worse that Dee had been convicted of the crime. But discovering that Monica's death was all part of some crazy girl's plot against Dee? It was too much. Her stepmom had gone to stay with her sister in San Diego. She hadn't even seen Dee since her release from Alcatraz 2.0.

Not that Dee blamed her. Monica's death, though not by Dee's hand, was still on Dee's head, and not a moment went by that she didn't miss her stepsister. She'd had so little time to mourn Monica, to process her loss, as she'd been immediately put on trial and whisked away to Alcatraz 2.0. But as she sat in her new bedroom day after day, barely able to hobble from room to room on her crutches, she had nothing *but* time. Time to remember, and time to grieve.

The chime notification on Dee's cell phone pinged, and she was saved from the oncoming wave of melancholy by a text.

"Nyles?" her dad asked. He was smiling again, as he always did when Dee mentioned Nyles. It definitely wasn't the reaction Dee had been expecting from her overprotective father when faced with his daughter's first boyfriend. *I guess when your daughter almost dies, like, a million times, her first boyfriend doesn't seem so dangerous anymore.*

Dee nodded. "Martin's about to pull him into the underground garage."

"I'll have Javier escort him up." Her dad disappeared down the hallway with a wink as Dee pushed herself upright in bed. Her right leg, immobilized from the knee down after her second reconstructive surgery, was purple and swollen beneath the brace and bandages, her toes looking more like miniature eggplants than digits. Which was pretty disgusting. Dee flung a blanket over her leg to hide the aftermath from Nyles.

A few minutes later, Dee's dad ushered Nyles into her room. He was smiling his toothy grin, his blue eyes bright with excitement, and it was only the potential pain in her leg that prevented Dee from throwing herself into his arms the moment she saw him.

Nyles, meanwhile, all British and proper, waited respectfully until Dee's dad pulled the door closed before he leaned over the bed and kissed her.

It wasn't the first time Nyles had pressed his lips to hers—far from it—but for Dee, the thrill hadn't worn off.

"The thing that I hate," Nyles said, pulling away slowly as he eased into the bedside chair, "is that our first kiss was under less-than-romantic circumstances."

Dee smiled, remembering the first time he'd kissed her, which had been entirely a tactic to shut her up when he knew they were under surveillance. "True," she said playfully. "But just think of how many chances you have to make up for that."

"Myriad." He threaded his fingers through hers, gripping them tightly. "A lifetime. Now if only we could get you out of this bloody room."

Dee sighed. She was desperate for a change of scenery. "Any trouble getting here?"

He shook his head. "Child's play. Those brutes your father hired know their business. Picked me up in two cars and drove around for an hour before they made their way here." He chuckled to himself. "Ironic since I could basically walk here if I chose."

"If it was *safe*," Dee said, eyeing him closely. She didn't want Nyles doing anything rash that might get him killed. Like walking down the streets of West LA in broad daylight. Her dad had managed to find him a guesthouse to rent nearby on the property of someone he knew from work. Someone he trusted. But Dee wasn't sure how far trust would stretch when half the country was looking for Nyles. How long before a reward for information on his whereabouts was offered? Before a neighbor recognized him? Or a plumber working on the main house?

"Yes, yes," he said, flashing his toothy grin. "Don't fret about me. I'm fine."

They hadn't talked much about what would happen now, other than that they wanted to be together. Technically, Dee was still a senior in high school, and Nyles, a freshman at Stanford. Dee had it easy, to some degree. She still had her dad around to take care of her. But with his parents dead, and their estate in some form of probate since Nyles's conviction, money wasn't readily available. And though both she and Nyles realized that their futures were utterly up in the air, they'd made a tacit agreement to live in the moment and try not to think about what tomorrow would bring. A promise Nyles was holding her to.

"How's Griselda?" Dee asked, changing the subject.

"You'll be shocked to hear she's had offers to appear in *Playboy* and *Hustler*," he said, laughing through his nose. "Neither of which she's accepted. But her interview in *Wired* should be out soon."

"That sounds like Griselda."

"Doesn't it, though?" Nyles paused, as if debating something in his mind, then slowly pulled his cell phone from his pocket. "She sent me this today."

Dee took the screen from Nyles's outstretched hand and watched as a video began to play. It looked like a commercial for a new television show, complete with slick blood-splatter graphics, a catchy theme song, and a polished announcer who stepped immediately into the shot. He was young, judging by his smooth skin and baby face, though his noticeably spray-on tan aged him, as did the shiny gray suit with boxy shoulders.

"Hello, America! I'm Tristan McKee," the announcer began, in the rounded tones of a British accent. Unlike Nyles's inflection, which had a Jane Austen charm to it, this guy sounded as if he was about to pitch you a variety of As Seen on TV products.

"Do you miss your daily fix of crime and punishment?" Tristan continued. "Are you yearning for another live installment of murder and mayhem? Then, this December, the Reality Network has got just the thing for *you*."

Tristan swung his arm across his body to point at something out of shot. The video jump-cut to the title graphic, designed to look like an old-fashioned neon sign.

Tristan's voice rang out from off screen. *"Who Wants to Be a Painiac?"* Each word lit up as he spoke it.

At the mention of the word "Painiac," Nyles's nickname for the government-sanctioned serial killers who had hunted down the inmates of Alcatraz 2.0, a chill slithered down Dee's spine.

"What is this?" she asked, her voice shaky as panic began to ripple through her body.

"Keep watching."

Tristan McKee, looking smugger and more self-satisfied than before, panned back into view. "That's right, The Postman fans. The app may be gone, but the fun certainly is not. We're casting an all-new lineup of Painiacs for cable television! Without the actual bloodshed, of course." He winked at the camera and flashed a knowing grin. Dee could have sworn a ray of light glinted off Tristan's impossibly white teeth.

A web address flashed on the screen. "Pending our FundMyFun.com campaign goals, auditions will be held in Los Angeles on December seventeenth. Go to FundMyFun.com/whowantstobeapainiac now and make a cash donation so you don't miss your chance to get in on all the Painiac action!"

The title treatment for *Who Wants to Be a Painiac?* slid back into view with some additional text beneath it, including an address for some place called Stu-Stu-Studio in Burbank, while a different voice chimed in, talking about a million miles an hour like a cattle show auctioneer. "*Who Wants to Be a Painiac?* is a registered trademark of Merchant-Bronson Productions and shall not be copied, disseminated, or displayed without the express written consent of Merchant-Bronson. Any unauthorized use of the image seen here or of the term 'Painiac' may be in violation of trademark and will be prosecuted to the fullest extent of the law. Funds raised by FundMyFun.com shall be used at the sole discretion of Merchant-Bronson Productions."

Dee couldn't believe what she'd just seen. "This is a *joke*, right? There's no way the FBI's going to allow this."

"It's not a joke, I'm afraid." Nyles's calmness wasn't comforting. "Supposedly, the show won't have actual violence or, you know, murder. Just a game-show competition of some kind." He wrinkled his nose. "Although how they had the goolies to claim a trademark on 'Painiacs,' which they *blatantly* stole from me . . ."

Nyles had been incredibly proud of his made-up words—"Painiacs," the killers who hunted them on Alcatraz 2.0, and "Postmantics," The Postman superfans who bought Alcatraz 2.0 merchandise, paid extra money for private camera access, and populated the cesspools that were The Postman message board and comments feed.

Nyles took her hand. "Postman Enterprises, Inc. is on the verge of collapse, between the government canceling their contracts, the Justice Department freezing assets, and all the wrongful-death lawsuits. I wonder if they're somehow getting a cut of this."

"Merchant-Bronson Productions," Dee mused. She'd heard the name before. They produced reality television. *Just like The Postman . . .*

"A game show based on a prison that was based on a reality show." Nyles shook his head. "Only in America."

Dee was pretty sure that the Brits had their fair share of crappy, tasteless reality TV programming, but now wasn't the time to point that out. She was worried. The Postman was dead. Kimmi, who'd taken over for him, also dead. Dee was pretty confident on those two points, considering that she was the one who'd killed them both. But someone was trying to resurrect The Postman and all its murderous associations. Was it just a tasteless though innocent attempt to cash in on The Postman's popularity?

Or was *Who Wants to Be a Painiac?* more closely associated to Postman Enterprises, Inc.?

And then there was the million-dollar question that nagged at her long after Nyles had left.

Why?

💀 ○ ◁

seen by 152,124
💀 **by** Squirrel Woman, Haru Tanaka, **and 103,885 others**

Darkness Falls   is feeling naughty

This is a secret group for all the displaced "fans" of The Postman. It is
absolutely private. Posts will not show up on your wall, and none of your
friends will know you are a member unless they are also a member. Potential
members must have verified login IDs from The Postman, and must be
submitted to the moderators for approval. Screen grabs of the contents of this
group are prohibited and will result in your immediate removal from the
group and incur the eternal wrath of the Postmantics.
Like   Comment

NOVEMBER 15
....

RECENT ACTIVITY

Skullcrusher Chic   REWARD
seen by 24,390
💀 **by** Darkness Falls, **and 14,007 others**

I'm tired of this bullshit. How many weeks has it been since the Death Row
Breakfast Club destroyed Alcatraz 2.0? I'll tell you—TOO FUCKING MANY.
        Where the hell are they? There have been rumors, photos taken
through zoom lenses, erroneous manhunts everywhere from Anchorage to
Orlando. But I've yet to see one shred of actual evidence to prove where Dee
Guerrera, Nyles Harding, and Griselda Sinclair are hiding.
        And I, for one, am tired of it.

The authorities are protecting them, of that I think we're all pretty damn sure. To help their precious impeachment hearing? To protect the secrets of what really happened on Alcatraz 2.0? Or is it all a massive government cover-up?

I think it's time we found out.

I'm not ashamed to admit that Who Wants To Be a Painiac? has inspired me. If Merchant-Bronson can fundraise a goddamn TV show, surely we can fundraise a reward. And that's exactly what I'm proposing: a reward for any information that leads to the positive identification of Dee Guerrera, Nyles Harding, and Griselda Sinclair, and outs their hiding places. We can split the pot in thirds and put each as a bounty on the three of them.

I've already set up an account at FundMyFun.com/pounty (yeah, I know that's kind of lame, but "Postmanticism Bounty" might get us kicked off the site, and no one's going to guess what "pounty" actually means) and started things rolling with $1,000. Let's see how high we can push this, huh?

NOVEMBER 25

Vince Heinz This is completely brilliant. I wish we'd thought of it two weeks ago when the DRBC might have been easier to track down. Still, I bet if the pot gets up to $40–$50K we'll start getting some legitimate hits.

10d   Like   Reply

Skullcrusher Chic I know, dude. Kicking myself. But at least we've got the ball rolling now!

10d   Like   Reply

Tamara Gucci Literally the best thing I've seen all day. #CinderellaSurvivor needs to have her justice served.

10d   Like   Reply

Professor Xtant How are we going to verify leads?

10d   Like   Reply

Mac McDonnelson We should have three administrators in charge of collecting and following up on leads for each member of the DRBC.

10d   Like   Reply

Tom Ecklestein Good idea. I volunteer to coordinate Griselda.

9d   Like   Reply

Mac McDonnelson Is that too big of a job for one person? I'm picturing thousands of leads here.

9d   Like   Reply

Joel Whittman Tom, OF COURSE YOU WILL. Weren't you the #HottieGriselda's fan club president back in the day?

9d   Like   Reply

Tom Ecklestein If by "back in the day" you mean LAST MONTH, then yes. Besides, that just makes me more qualified. I know more about #HottieGriselda than anyone else.

9d   Like   Reply

Genesis "Jen" Galarza My husband is a detective with the LAPD. I'll take #CinderellaSurvivor, if no one objects. I might be able to use some insider knowledge.

8d   Like   Reply

Ajay Vaulted Genesis—do you think your husband can help? Let's not forget, #CinderellaSurvivor has at least eleven deaths on her head right now. If anyone ever deserved Alcatraz 2.0, it's her!

6d   Like   Reply

Zinglebert Bembledack I'll take the Brit if no one else wants him.

21hr   Like   Reply

Johnson Tyne Just added $100 to the pot.

8d   Like   Reply

Skullcrusher Chic Johnson Tyne Awesome!

8d   Like   Reply

....

Peggy Bachmann $50 from me. I wish it could be more, but maybe I can add to it on payday.

10d   Like   Reply

....

    Skullcrusher Chic Every bit helps!

    10d   Like   Reply

....

Onyekachi Eze My ten-year-old wants to contribute his piggy bank savings to the cause. $32.18. How amazing is my kid? Future warrior for justice here!

9d   Like   Reply

....

    Josh Wickham I'll double that.

    9d   Like   Reply

....

    Tamara Gucci I'll quadruple it.

    9d   Like   Reply

....

    Haru Tanaka What's his name? I want to make my contribution in his honor!

    8d   Like   Reply

....

Peggy Bachmann Hey, does anyone know if the Fed-Xers are doing something similar? Like offering a reward for information that leads to the Painiacs' families?

1hr   Like   Reply

....

    Skullcrusher Chic Don't give them any ideas.

    1h   Like   Reply

....

FIVE

BECCA STARED AT STEF THE STALKER IN DISBELIEF. "YOU think my mom was a cutesy serial killer dressed like a circus clown?"

"She *was*."

"She was *not*." Becca pictured the flamboyant Molly Mauler and her Burning-Man-Meets-Juggalette persona: striped tights, corsets, flouncy skirts, psychotic clown makeup. Then she tried to imagine Ruth lined up beside the notorious Painiac, in her cropped khaki pants, three-quarter-sleeve button-down shirt, and Toms.

"Aside from the fact that they're both dead," Becca replied dryly, "they have nothing in common."

"You really had no idea."

Can. Not. Hang. "My mom drove the carpool and organized bake sales to help homeless veterans." Becca narrowed her eyes. "She died in a head-on collision and you crashed her funeral."

"Veered off M-553," Stef said, nodding, "about a mile south of the old County Road and hit a tree, right?"

This chick knew *way* too much about her mom's accident.

"If that's true," Stef continued, "then why are there no signs of a crash on that stretch of road? Not a twig out of place or a skid mark on the asphalt."

Becca didn't give two shits about twigs or skid marks. "Let me get this straight, stalker," she began, barely able to contain her rage. "You shoot video of my family at, like, the worst moment in our lives, follow me to school, and then try to tell me that my mom was actually a serial killer and her death was a cover-up."

"Yep," Stef said solemnly, her faith in the narrative unwavering.

Becca clenched her jaw. If Rita or Rafa heard this insane conspiracy theory, it would be like reliving Ruth's death all over again. "I swear to God, if I catch you near my mom or brother with this bullshit, I *will* kill you."

Stef smiled slyly. "See? You're mommy's little girl after all."

Rita's words flew back into Becca's mind. *You're more like her than you realize.* No, this wasn't what she meant. Stef might be hot, but she was fucking delusional and Becca was officially done with the conversation. "I'm out."

She climbed back into the driver's seat, heart pounding, but as she reached out to pull the door closed, Stef wedged herself into the frame.

"I'm not crazy," she said, a hint of anger in her voice.

Becca was glad she managed to piss Stef off. "That's what a crazy person would say."

"I've got evidence."

"Blurry shots of Bigfoot in the forest? Alien spacecraft that looks oddly like a helicopter?"

Stef wrinkled her lips, seemingly irritated. "At my house. Come tomorrow after school and I'll convince you that Ruth Martinello was Molly Mauler."

"I'm sure the Fed-Xer crackpots on the Interwebz would *love* to see your 'evidence.' Me? Not so much."

"Afraid of the truth, huh?" Stef folded her arms across her chest.

"Kinda sad, considering you like to pretend you're not afraid of anything."

Becca set her jaw. What were they, best friends? "I'm not *afraid* of the truth."

"Then prove it."

Becca realized that Stef was playing her, pushing buttons until she got Becca to agree to come see her sad conspiracy-theory evidence, and she knew that she should tell the chick to fuck off, peel out of the parking lot, and never think about Stef Ybarra and her cute smile and funky hair ever again.

"Fine," Becca said, against her better judgment. Ugh, what the hell was wrong with her?

"Fourteen twenty-eight Stephenson, down in Escanaba," Stef said with a triumphant smile. "See you tomorrow." Then she swung around on her heel and jogged across the parking lot.

Becca yanked the SUV door closed so fiercely the whole car rocked back and forth on its ancient shocks, settling slowly as Becca gripped the steering wheel. She didn't know if she was more pissed at Stef for sharing her stupid theory, or at herself for being duped into driving an hour and a half down to the boonies to look at evidence she was sure would be suspect at best.

"My mom was *not* Molly Mauler."

She shouldn't have needed to speak those words out loud to cement their validity, but she did it anyway. It was ludicrous to even think that her smiling, doting, scrapbooking, Crock-Pot–obsessed mom had been moonlighting as a Painiac.

There were only a couple of straggler freshmen on their way to the bus stop to witness Becca race the aging Explorer out of the parking lot, tires screeching against the pavement as another thin layer of tread was sheared off. She hardly noticed the heads whipping around in her direction, or the acrid stench of burning rubber that filled the car. All Becca could think about was her mom.

She'd always wondered how Ruth had existed so cheerfully in the unchanging monotony of her domestic world. Not that Becca didn't appreciate the fact that Ruth did her laundry, kept the house clean, and showed up at every recital, soccer game, or school play, even when her wife was delayed by work. But Rita had the career. She did research and wrote articles and traveled around the country giving guest lectures. She had a driving passion that made Michigan's Upper Peninsula bearable. That's the life Becca wanted to have, not Ruth's small, quiet existence, no matter how happy it made her.

But what if? A teensy flutter of excitement erupted in Becca's stomach as she drove through the familiar streets of Marquette. What if her mom hadn't been as boring and vanilla as Becca had believed her to be? What if she'd been something more? Something exciting? Something dangerous?

You're talking crazy.

Just because there was a little part of Becca that almost kinda, sorta, maybe *wanted* Stef's theory to be true, didn't mean there was even an iota of probability that it actually was. And also, just because Becca wasn't 100 percent wholly grossed out by the idea didn't mean her mom and brother wouldn't be. One thing was very clear: she needed to make sure that Rita and Rafa never ever heard about this bullshit.

Becca's headache had blossomed into a full-blown migraine by the time she pulled into the driveway of her house. Rita was at work, Rafa at soccer practice, and as Becca dragged her backpack up to the front door, she just hoped she'd be able to shake both the headache and any thoughts of Stef Ybarra before they both got home.

The moment she walked through the front door and flipped on the lights, Becca knew that wasn't going to happen.

The house was completely trashed.

Becca stood on the threshold, door still wide open behind her, and stared at the chaos.

The small living room looked as if a tornado had blown through. All the books from the built-in shelves had been tossed onto the floor in piles, most of them open, faceup or facedown, as if someone had painstakingly flipped through each before casting them aside. Like the books, every DVD case had been opened, and the cushions had been pulled from the sectional sofa and sliced into, their foam innards peeking through long X-shaped incisions on their underbellies. Every drawer had been pulled from its frame—side tables, media stand, china cabinet—and had its contents dumped onto the floor. And that was just what Becca could see from the entryway.

For a moment, she couldn't quite process what had happened. Had her mom been looking for something? Had a freak, unprecedented earthquake hit Marquette? They were ludicrous ideas, but somehow, in the moment, they made more sense than the truth.

Someone had broken into their house.

And maybe they were still inside.

After shaking off the haze of shock, Becca turned away from the front door and pulled her phone out of her bag. As she began to dial 911, she felt a hand on her shoulder.

Becca tried to cry out, but before a sound left her lips, the hand shot from her shoulder to her mouth, clamping down to prevent her from making any noise. An arm gripped her from behind, right up against her throat. Not enough to cut off her airway, but the burly arm was strong, and as her assailant dragged her back into the living room, Becca realized that she was in deep shit.

A million thoughts raced through her mind, first and foremost being that she had to get the hell out of the house before this guy really hurt her. Her mom would be picking Rafa up from soccer practice and would then be home, but not soon enough. Could she overpower this guy? Try to kick him in the 'nads and make a run for the open door behind him?

As if he could read her mind, Becca heard the front door slam shut. Crap.

Maybe she could run from the kitchen to the laundry room, then through to the garage. She could hit the overhead doors and dash out to her car. That was the best option. Becca was just about to bite down on the fingers over her mouth when the assailant promptly spun her around and slammed her hard up against the wall.

Becca's head thudded against the stucco so fiercely she saw a flash of light across her eyes. While temporarily blinded, she felt the hot breath of the intruder against the side of her face. Panic welled up inside her. What was he going to do to her? Murder? Or something worse. She felt her airway constrict. The stench of his breath made her want to vomit.

Stay calm. She wasn't going to survive this if she panicked. She had to think. She had to be smart.

Becca squeezed her eyes shut, and when she opened them, her vision had cleared. The man who had her pinned to the wall was wearing a mask, a black knit thing with openings for the eyes, and he wore gray coveralls. Dressed just like the electrician they had out a couple of months ago to fix the overhead lights in the kitchen, which was smart because workmen like that were always coming and going in Becca's suburban neighborhood. No one would even look at him twice.

But now, Becca couldn't help but look at him. He pressed his elbow against her throat, forcing her neck back against the wall, and squeezed her cheeks together with his free hand. He smelled like sweat, fast food, and spicy cologne, and Becca tried to control her panic as she stared into his cold blue eyes—one of which drooped lazily at the corner from a disfiguring scar—and wondered what the hell he wanted.

He met her gaze for a moment, his eyes blank and expressionless, then slowly turned her face to the left. Becca squeezed her eyes shut again, afraid he was going to try to kiss her, but instead of a tongue against her cheek, her assailant yanked her head forward and slammed it against the wall again.

Becca's eyes shot open, but all she saw was a blaring white light as a sharp pain shot through the back of her skull. The light dissipated into tiny stars that zipped through her vision, and when she could focus again, she found that the intruder had angled her face toward the side table and the framed photo that sat there. It was a picture of Rafa and Ruth holding Rafa's MVP trophy from last year's soccer championship.

The intruder grunted, pulling his hand away from her face to point at the photo. He wanted her to see it.

"M-m-my brother," she stammered.

Satisfied, the man turned Becca's face back to meet his own, then slowly drew his finger across his throat.

The implication was clear: if she told anyone about him, he'd kill her brother.

There wasn't a whole lot in this world that she cared about, but Rafa was certainly on that list. At the top. She'd protect him at any cost.

The intruder grunted again, shaking Becca so her head slammed into the wall a third time.

"I understand," she said, realizing what he wanted. "I won't say anything."

His blue eyes narrowed, watching her intently; then, seemingly satisfied by what he saw, he released her and slipped out of the house.

SIX

BECCA WASN'T SURE HOW LONG SHE STOOD THERE IN THE entryway shaking like a late-winter leaf as it clung to a barren branch during a snowstorm. Five minutes? An hour? It was impossible to say. Time had ceased to exist.

Her thoughts returned to Stef. Not that she believed the Molly Mauler theory—it was still completely ridiculous—but what if Stef had shared her hypothesis with someone else? Posted it on the Internet? Becca had heard that the Fed-Xers had a secret Facebook group just like Postmanticism. What if Stef had "outed" Becca's family on one of them? Had the Fed-Xers come looking for "proof" that Ruth was Molly Mauler?

And more importantly, would they be back?

"Oh my God!" a familiar voice cried from the kitchen. Rita. "Oh my God! Becca, are you okay?"

She hadn't heard her mom pull into the driveway. Hadn't heard the garage door open and close.

The first thing Becca registered was that her mom was alone. "Where's Rafa?" The panic was instantaneous, and images of her lazy-eyed intruder pinning Rafa to a wall flooded her mind. "Where is he?"

"Dinner at the Yorks' after practice." Rita grabbed Becca's face between her hands and looked frantically into her eyes. "Are you okay?" she repeated. "What happened?"

Dinner at the Yorks' house. Rafa was safe. "I'm okay," Becca began. "I'm okay. I just got home . . . and . . ." Was she going to tell the truth and risk her brother's safety?

"And?"

"And the house was like this. I . . . I got here just before you did. I was about to call nine-one-one."

"Thank God you didn't walk in while it was happening."

"Yeah."

Rita stroked Becca's forehead, then broke away, her phone already out of her pocket. "I'm calling the police."

The police arrived just as Rita made arrangements for Rafa to spend the night at the Yorks', then Becca and her mom were asked to do a walk-through of their burglarized house. Which is when the whole situation got even more confusing. Because nothing was missing.

"Nothing?" the officer asked as they finished the inspection. "Are you sure?"

"Positive," Rita said, emerging from her bedroom with a look of relief on her face. The room was a total wreck—mattress overturned, drawers pulled from dressers. The only piece of furniture that wasn't dumped into a heap on the floor was the massive antique curio cabinet, and it had been thoroughly ransacked. "No jewelry, no electronics, no silver. There's nothing missing from this house."

The cop scribbled something on his notepad. "Well," he began, not looking up, "I'd say it was just kids being destructive, but the crime scene shows classic signs of a perp who was looking for something specific. Any idea what it could be?"

Rita quickly shook her head. "I'm sorry, but no. I'm a professor and my late wife was a stay-at-home mom. I can't imagine what anyone would want from our home."

Becca's heart raced as she remembered the masked figure in her house. What could he have been looking for?

The officer nodded, then shifted his attention to Becca. "And you?"

"Me?" Becca was caught off guard by the question. "I didn't see anything."

The cop stared at her. Could he tell she was lying? "I was going to ask if you were having any problems at school. Any trouble you might be in that would cause this."

Despite the disturbing events of that last hour, Becca had to stifle a laugh. She, Jackie, and Mateo were the three least likely kids in the entire school to get into trouble. "No, sir, Mr. Officer, sir. Nothing."

He eyed her for a moment, not entirely convinced she was telling the truth, then pulled a card from his chest pocket and handed it to Rita. "If you do notice that something has been taken, let me know. I'm so sorry, Dr. Martinello. I know it's been a hard couple of weeks for your family."

"Thank you." Rita forced a smile. "Do you think it's safe for my daughter and me to stay in the house tonight?"

"Oh, yeah," the officer said. "It's a rarity that the perp in a break-in will return to the scene of the crime, unless their search was somehow interrupted."

Great.

"So I think you'll be fine. But I'll have one of the guys do a drive-by every hour or so, to give you some peace of mind."

Rita closed the door behind him, then pressed her forehead against it, slowly breathing in and out. After a few seconds, she spun back around toward Becca, still smiling. "What do you say we order a pizza and clean up this mess?"

Half a meatball-and-olive pizza later, Becca and her mom began to put their house back in order. They started in the living room, where nothing—not even Ruth's bedazzled, embellished scrapbooks—had been left untouched. They'd been rummaged through and dumped on the floor, leaving little puddles of dislodged glitter on the carpet. It took an hour to get the room looking somewhat normal again. They worked in silence, for the most part, an occasional photo or favorite book from childhood eliciting a short conversation, and the whole time she straightened and restacked, Becca debated whether or not she should tell Rita the truth.

The description of the intruder was on the tip of her tongue half a dozen times, but each time, Becca kept quiet. She was afraid for her family's safety, afraid for Rafa, who was sleeping in Teddy York's upper bunk bed, blissfully unaware of the terror that had transpired at their house. How could she put him in danger? Nothing had been stolen, no one had been seriously hurt. She should just let it go.

After the living room was done, Rita took the kitchen while Becca started on her bedroom. It was a slow process, kind of like unpacking after a move but less orderly and more disturbing. It amazed Becca how much of the house had been violated. Nothing in her room had escaped inspection. The pile of books by her nightstand had been rifled through, the tiny plastic drawers in her childhood jewelry box had been yanked out and ditched on the rug, and even Becca's corkboard had been ripped from the wall, though the contents, thankfully, had been left intact. Concert stubs and movie tickets, Mateo's sketches and pictures of her family. Lazy Eye might have scanned them, but he hadn't touched a single item.

Except for one. Becca's eye was drawn to a blank spot in the upper corner of the board where something had been removed. A photo? Becca tried to remember what had been there. She cast her eyes around the wreck of her room, wondering if it had just fallen off in the violent ransacking, and after a brief search, Becca found what she was looking for.

It was a photo, from Rafa's fifth birthday party. He sat on Ruth's lap in the backyard screaming bloody murder while the clown who had been hired for the party tried to hand him a balloon crown. Rafa, terrified of clowns, was having none of it.

Becca had taken the photo herself because apparently even as a twelve-year-old she was an asshole. But that wasn't the reason she had the photo pinned to her corkboard. It was the look on Ruth's face, this perfect mix of patience, concern, and cheerfulness that pretty much embodied Ruth Martinello. Becca smiled. That was the way Becca would always remember her.

But her smile vanished as she recalled Stef's theory. She tried to picture her patient, perky mom dressed as the clown in the photo, her smile not one of kindness, but of bloodthirsty glee.

Becca sighed, shaking her head. Stef was out of her mind.

As she continued to gaze at Ruth and Rafa and the clown, Becca heard her mom rustling around in the master bedroom next door and a thought popped into her head. Maybe the memory might cheer her mom up. Photo in hand, Becca headed down the hall.

The door to her moms' bedroom was closed but not latched, and as

Becca pushed it silently open, the words "Hey, Mom, look at this!" poised on her lips, she stopped cold.

Rita stood at the far side of her room—still a tumultuous chaos of overturned furniture and smashed figurines—with her back to the door, staring at the wall. More specifically, she was staring at a part of the wall between the en suite bathroom and the walk-in closet, where the massive curio cabinet usually stood. It had been the only thing in the bedroom that hadn't ended up on the ground.

Only now it was pushed aside, blocking the bathroom door. And Rita was staring at the blank wall behind it.

After a few seconds, Becca realized what her mom was doing. She swung her arm outward, and Becca saw that she'd opened some kind of a door.

There was a safe in the wall.

As soon as the safe was open, Rita thrust her hands inside and then carefully, reverently, removed something. She turned to the side as she stroked the top of the object still cradled in her hands, and Becca could see that it was a wooden container, about the size of a shoebox but standing on its end. The rest of the safe appeared to be empty.

Becca's mom brought the box to her lips and kissed the lid. After a few moments, she let out a heavy sigh and replaced it in the safe.

The moment had been so personal, so intimate, that Becca was suddenly ashamed to have been spying in secret. She tiptoed back to her room, the photo from Rafa's birthday party all but forgotten, and sat down on the edge of her bed.

What the hell was going on? Not that it was a crime for her moms to have a safe in the house, but why hadn't Becca seen it before? And why were the only contents a wooden box?

Normally, the Mystery of the Hidden Safe wouldn't have bothered Becca. Whatever, her moms had a safe. Pretty normal, right? But the way her mom had checked it in secret, the way she held that box, practically with veneration . . . Had that been what the intruder was looking for?

Becca shook her head as she finished straightening up her room. She was being paranoid. Probably. Maybe.

Though she knew one thing for sure. She needed to see what was inside that box.

SEVEN

BECCA WAITED UNTIL RITA LEFT FOR WORK THE NEXT MORN-
ing before she made an attempt to open the safe.

She wasn't really thinking how she'd do it—a master safecracker she
was not—but she had to at least try. After watching from her bedroom
window while Rita's Subaru turned the corner at the end of their block,
Becca rushed to her moms' room.

The curio cabinet was heavy, a solid antique that had belonged to
someone's great-aunt, but not immovable, and with some careful wiggling
and a slow, steady pull, Becca was able to edge it away from the wall.

The safe was hidden perfectly by the large piece of furniture, and
though Becca had pictured an old dial lock like on her locker at school,
this safe had a modern keypad on its face. She'd just sort of assumed that
the safe had come with the house when her moms bought it fifteen years
ago, but the device Becca was staring at was shiny, new, and relatively
high-tech. Like her moms had it installed in the last few years. But why?
What could they possibly need to keep inside?

If she could only crack the code, maybe she could find out.

Easier said than done. Becca had no idea how many digits were
involved, and even if she did, the permutations would be seemingly

infinite. The odds of her randomly picking the correct code out of thin air were about as good as her getting elected prom queen.

Okay, but would her moms have wanted a random number? Probably not. If they were going to open the safe only rarely, it was better to have a code they'd know offhand. Birthdays. Anniversaries. Addresses. Social security numbers.

Becca spent the next half hour cycling through every permutation of every number even remotely important to the Martinello family. The month and day of Rafa's birthday. The month, day, *and* year. The month and day reversed like the Europeans do it. Then Becca's birthday. Rita's. Ruth's. Their wedding date. The day they first met. Becca even dug through the file cabinet in the garage to get all four of their social security numbers from last year's tax return. None of them worked.

She was about to give up when Becca had another thought. Ruth was a list maker. The kind of person who wrote everything down. There was even a file in the cabinet marked "Passwords" with everything from online bank logins to the Wi-Fi info. Could the code possibly be in there?

Becca raced back to the garage and pulled out the Passwords file. She had about ten minutes before she needed to leave for school, and the file was daunting. Passwords for old phones that no one used anymore, for out-of-date software programs and shopping rewards programs. Damn, her mom kept everything.

Everything except a note that said "Safe Password" of course.

"This is hopeless," Becca said out loud. She made it to the last item in the file, prepared to shove it back into the drawer and head to school unsatisfied, when she froze.

Behind the last piece of paper was a bright pink Post-it, stuck to the file folder itself. It had no label, no indication what it was for. Just a four-digit number written in black Sharpie.

2426.

Becca shrugged. It was worth a shot.

Her hand trembled as she pushed the code into the keypad. As soon as she pressed the 6, she heard the lock mechanism release.

The interior of the safe was empty except for the wooden box. It was a deep mahogany color with a simple metal latch at the front that kept the hinged lid in place, and on top, a darker wood had been inlaid to form the letter *M*.

Becca reached in to lift the box out. It was heavier than she'd expected, but when she shook it from side to side, there was no sound from within. The weight must have been from the wood construction, as the box itself appeared to be empty.

Why would her mom keep an empty box in a hidden safe in her bedroom? It made absolutely no sense at all. She was about to open the box, confirming its contents or lack thereof, when something else inside the safe caught her eye. Just a glint of light as she moved, reflecting the bright overhead fixture, and as Becca leaned in closer to the safe, she realized that the bottom was coated with a fine dusting of glitter.

Glitter? Seriously? Did her parents keep a pixie locked in the safe? Their house wasn't exactly a glitter, sequin, shiny bauble kind of a place. More like old wood and practical fabrics. Not even Becca's makeup was particularly shimmery. In fact, the only place in the whole house Becca had even seen glitter was . . .

Mom's scrapbooks.

Becca's eyes swept the interior of the safe. Glitter. And was that a stray sequin? A frayed bit of ribbon?

For Ruth, scrapbooking was as necessary as oxygen, water, and Lifetime original movies. At every momentous occasion in her family's lives, Ruth's eyes would dilate, her brows would lift, and a look of angelic euphoria would wash over her face. Whether it was one of Rafa's spectacular goalie saves or Becca's awkward first day of middle school, Ruth had been there with digital camera in hand to document the event from beginning to end. The scrapbooks were her pride and joy, proudly displayed in the living room, where Ruth would frequently take them out and subject the entire family—and whatever guests were unlucky enough to be visiting—to a walk down memory lane. They were meant to be shared and "enjoyed."

So why had at least one of them been shoved in this safe? And more importantly, where was it now?

It made even less sense than the empty box.

Becca stared at Mateo across the lunch table. He was waiting for her to respond, but her mind had wandered while he was talking, and now she had absolutely no idea what he'd said.

"Well?" he asked, sliding his phone across the table toward her. There was a photo of a girl on the screen: blond, blue-eyed, smiling coyly at the camera for three seconds of selfie video while posing like a vain duckling. "What do you think?"

Oh, right. Her friends were trying to find her a date to Winter Formal. "Not my type."

Jackie's turn. "How about her?" She flashed her screen toward Becca. "She's my cousin's best friend's sister."

Becca watched the Instagram story of some girl in the tiniest bikini known to human history, framed by palm trees, sipping Perrier through a straw while laid out on a beach towel in the sand with the text "#BestLife #SouthBeachGurl." She looked vapid and self-absorbed, and while Becca appreciated her friends' interest in her nonexistent love life, she was slightly concerned that they knew so little about her type. Funky. Edgy. An asymmetrical bob.

Stop it.

"Very cute," Becca said. "But she clearly lives in Florida."

"Right." Jackie sighed. "I'll keep looking."

Becca had absolutely no intention of going to Winter Formal—not only were school dances lame, but it was literally the last thing on her mind right now. She appreciated that her friends were trying to keep her distracted, but between Stef and the break-in and the safe in her moms' bedroom, Becca's brain was, like, 95 percent occupied. Should she tell her friends about the break-in? Should she ask her mom about the box? Or if a scrapbook had been in the safe? Should she even bother to go see Stef after school? And did any of these things tie together, or was it just shitty luck that it was all happening right now?

While Becca fumbled through the Winter Formal conversation, she found herself focusing on a tall, lithe figure walking across the cafeteria. Darlene Ahlberg wasn't one of Becca's favorite people in the world—her "I'm going to be very important someday" ego rubbed Becca the wrong way—but Darlene was going to Los Angeles to audition for *Who Wants to Be a Painiac?* in a couple of weeks. Hell, maybe her aunt, who had some kind of job in the entertainment industry, had a connection to the show. What if Darlene's aunt knew something about the original Alcatraz 2.0 killers? It was worth a shot.

"Hey, Darlene!" Becca called out, waving.

"What are you doing?" Jackie whispered, her eyes wide with horror. "I don't want to talk to her."

Darlene turned, head askew, clearly confused that Becca was talking to her. "Yeah?"

Not that Becca blamed her. She hadn't exactly spent the last three-plus years of high school hiding the fact that she thought Darlene Ahlberg was a pompous bullshitter.

"I heard you're going to LA over break," Becca started, trying to sound like she was sincerely interested in Darlene's travel plans.

Darlene raised a suspicious eyebrow. "Yeah."

"Is it true you're going to audition for *Who Wants to Be a Painiac?*"

"I still can't believe they're going to make a show about Alcatraz two-point-oh," Jackie said, before Darlene could answer. "They can't kill people on national television, can they?"

Darlene rolled her eyes. "It's not actual murder, Jacqueline. They're just casting actors to play pretend Painiacs who will commit fake murders for spikes. Just like on The Postman but without actual death."

"Sounds classy." Mateo smirked.

"It sounds," Becca said, trying to keep the conversation on track, "like The Postman is still involved maybe. Does your aunt know?"

Instead of a yes-or-no answer, Darlene just shrugged. "All I know is that the auditions are going to be nuts. They're just letting, like, anyone in off the street. No headshots. No reps. Total amateur hour."

Now it was Becca's turn to be confused. "So are you going or—"

"Why?" Darlene asked, pursing her lips. "Are you going to make some joke about how I'd look great in a DIYnona mask?"

"No!" Becca forced a laugh. "But that's a good one."

"Or ask if I'll be Oscar-eligible for that role?"

Jackie buried her head in Mateo's shoulder to keep from laughing out loud. After visiting her aunt two summers ago, Darlene had told everyone the independent film she'd supposedly auditioned for, landed a role in, and shot during her two weeks in LA would be out by Christmas so her role would be eligible for the Oscars. Turned out, she'd done a nonspeaking role in her cousin's short for his college film class. But, you know, samesies.

"Okay, but seriously," Becca said, unable to let that one go, "it was a student film, Darlene."

Darlene narrowed her already tiny eyes and jutted out her chin. "Well, you won't have anything to make fun of this time, Rebecca. My mom won't let me audition after the attack yesterday." She paused, lengthening her neck haughtily. "And my aunt would never work on a Merchant-Bronson production. They're notoriously cheap." Then she swung around and sauntered across the cafeteria.

"That went well," Mateo said.

"What did you expect?" Jackie asked. "Becca led a write-in campaign to get Darlene voted 'Most Likely to Pull a Muscle Trying to Kiss Her Own Ass' for the senior yearbook. Not exactly best friends."

It had been a long shot to think that Darlene's aunt actually had some connection to the upcoming reality show, but Becca had learned something almost as interesting. "What attack was she talking about?"

"Duh, in Georgia," Jackie said. "Can you believe they thought that guy was married to Hannah Ball? I mean, I know she wasn't exactly the hottest bod on Alcatraz two-point-oh, but she could certainly do better than . . ." Jackie paused for a millisecond to suck in a breath and noticed that Becca was staring at her, jaw slack. "Do you have any idea what I'm talking about?"

"Not a clue." Becca had spent the night searching the Internet for old Molly Mauler videos, with almost no success. The government was removing the bootlegged Alcatraz 2.0 videos almost as quickly as Postmantics were putting them up. There must have been a small army of techies scouring the Internet day and night. One video of Molly Mauler and a tank of piranhas even cut off while Becca was midstream.

Jackie planted both of her palms on the cafeteria table, a sign that she was about to tell an epic story with a considerable amount of relish. "Well, last night, a mob showed up at this dude's house in Georgia. Like, torches-and-pitchforks kind of shit."

"Why?"

Jackie leaned forward in excitement. "Some girl had it on good authority that Hannah was actually a restaurant owner and chef from Savannah, Georgia. Married, two stepkids. As soon as this hits, the Twitterverse goes apeshit, and by eight o'clock, a bunch of people had shown up at the house where this chef supposedly used to live."

"The news footage is pretty fucked up," Mateo added. "Throwing rocks and bottles. The dude who lived there came outside with his shotgun, and then someone launched a Molotov cocktail through his living room window. Cops showed up. All hell broke loose."

"The house was half burned down by the time the fire department put it out," Jackie said. "And the worst part? This dude's wife was home. With him. At the time. I'm pretty sure Hannah Ball didn't survive her swim in the boiling hot tub, which means they had the wrong person."

Becca's hands tingled, her feet had gone numb, and she felt as if someone had punched her in the stomach. The Fed-Xers and their Painiac witch hunts were getting out of hand. What if the guy who'd broken into her house had been one of them? What if he'd been looking for some kind of evidence that Ruth and Molly were one and the same?

Becca had half decided not to drive down to Escanaba after school, but now she *had* to go. If Stef had any evidence, even something shitty that might possibly link her family to Molly Mauler, Becca had to see it. And destroy it.

She wouldn't let her family be the next victims on the Fed-Xers' hit list.

EIGHT

AFTER MAKING EXCUSES TO JACKIE AND MATEO *AGAIN* FOR not hanging out after school, Becca trekked down to Escanaba, creaking the old SUV to a stop in front of a nondescript Craftsman house north of town. It felt like she was driving into the lion's den, and though she wished she were any other place on the planet at that moment, she knew she didn't have a choice. If there was even a minute chance that Stef's "evidence" could be construed as linking Ruth Martinello to Molly Mauler, Becca had to get rid of it. Her number-one goal was protecting her family from those crazed Fed-Xers.

It was what Ruth would have wanted.

With a steadying breath, Becca climbed out of her car and approached the house.

Stef was waiting for her at the front door, holding the screen open. She wore black leggings and a tank top despite the damp chill of the late-November afternoon, and the longer side of her bob was clipped back away from her face with a simple barrette. She looked really hot in a cool, easy-breezy kind of way, and Becca had to remind herself that Stef's hotness was not why she was there.

"Hey," Becca said lamely, her heart hammering in her chest with an unmistakable mix of excitement and apprehension.

Stef stood aside to let Becca enter. "Hey."

Becca turned sideways to slip through the door, her face inches from Stef, who smelled like peppermint toothpaste and baby powder. On paper, that sounded like a grandmotherly smell—something comforting, a little overpowering, and certainly not sexy—but Becca fought the urge to bury her face in Stef's neck and inhale deeply.

Ugh, *now* who was the creeper?

"Nice house," Becca said, trying to camouflage her awkwardness. It wasn't even a lie. The living room was tidy, tables dusted and clutter-free. Ruth would have been impressed.

"Not really," Stef said bluntly.

"Um, okay." How exactly was she supposed to respond to that?

Stef sighed in annoyance. "It's my grandparents' house."

"Oh." That didn't explain anything. "Doesn't mean it's not nice."

Stef crossed one hand over her body, gripping her opposite forearm, as she glanced up at the ceiling. "Nice enough if you enjoy peeling wallpaper, a leaky roof, and a basement that smells like mothballs."

That went well. "Let's get this over with."

Becca followed Stef out of the living room through a darkened hallway illuminated only by a thin strip of yellow light oozing out from beneath a closed door. Stef pulled it open, flooding the corridor with a warm glow, and without motioning for Becca to follow, trudged down a narrow flight of stairs.

Becca hesitated as all her stalkery, murdery fears from yesterday afternoon came flooding back. Following a stranger into a damp, dark basement was like horror-movie no-no numero uno. Had this all been an elaborate hoax on Stef's part to lure Becca into her kill room?

"I, uh, told my friends Jackie and Mateo where I was going," Becca said from the top of the stairs. Lame, but she had to think fast, give Stef reason to think twice about killing her and burying her dismembered body in the backyard. "Like, in case I had an accident on the way or something."

Stef glanced back up over her shoulder. "I'm not going to murder you down here."

Becca forced a laugh. "Right. No, of course not." *Just keep me prisoner for ten years . . .*

"Are you coming or not?" Stef sounded irritated, and once more, Becca found herself swayed by a desire not to appear weak in Stef's eyes.

"Yeah, duh."

Stef's grandparents' basement had been converted into a guest room, as evidenced by the queen-size bed against the far wall beneath the only window—a thin slit high up on the wall near the ceiling, the only part of the basement that wasn't completely underground. Instead of cushy carpet, the floor was lined with some kind of vinyl faux tile in an argyle pattern, and the walls were faced with dark wood paneling. The effect was cozy, though slightly depressing with a dilapidated 1970s vibe. Based on the rumpled bedsheets and the desk with two giant flat-screen monitors arranged in a V formation, Becca guessed this was Stef's bedroom.

Stef gestured to an overstuffed chair propped up on a stack of books due to a missing leg. "Sit here while I pull up some footage."

It was an order, not an offer. And Becca didn't take orders. Instead of sitting down, she stood behind the chair, leaning against the wall.

Stef shrugged with indifference, then yanked out the desk chair and sat with her back to Becca as she dragged a video labeled "mollymauler_january" to the center of one monitor.

"Footage from the beginning of the year," Stef said, her tone businesslike, her words economical.

"Where did you get that?" Becca asked. She knew from her own search the night before that Painiacs' kill videos weren't exactly readily available on YouTube.

But Stef ignored the question. "This is the Mauler's eighth kill."

Assuming that Stef had access to some kind of Fed-Xer video database and making a mental note to ask her about it later, Becca folded her arms across her chest as the video began to play.

A man lay on a tile floor wearing only his underwear, a dingy pair of tighty-whities, with his arms stretched out over his head and his light brown hair billowing around the sides of his face. The movement seemed strange and out of place, and as the camera zoomed out, Becca realized why. The man lay inside a pen that was filled with a few inches of water.

Aside from the Plexiglas walls of the enclosure, which were low enough for even a small child to step over, the man was totally unrestrained. Like he could have gotten up and walked out of there at any time. Yet he looked terrified. His eyes darted quickly back and forth as if expecting imminently approaching danger, and the deeply carved worry lines in the pale skin of his cheeks and forehead twitched with fear.

Becca recognized the video right away. It was one of Molly's more original kills, one that had earned her over a million spikes and a legion of new fans. Becca even remembered watching this video for the first time. She'd been home, at the dinner table with her moms and Rafa. Her phone was charging in her room, banned from family meals by Ruth's order, when she heard the double doorbell go off. Becca had held her breath, a forkful of penne primavera frozen halfway between her plate and her mouth, wondering if Ruth had heard the notification. Becca had been reprimanded before for watching The Postman, and she was pretty sure if her mom caught her again, she'd confiscate Becca's phone.

But Ruth had been telling a story about Rafa's teacher and didn't even pause to take a breath after The Postman notification went off. Becca continued her dinner, eating as normally as possible. As soon as she was finished and had helped her brother clean up the kitchen, she'd raced to her room, closed and locked the door, and indulged in some gruesome Molly Mauler goodness while her moms watched the news in the other room.

Becca gasped, as the realization of Ruth's innocence washed over her like a bucket of ice water after a Super Bowl win. "That can't be my mom! She was home with us the night this video went live."

Stef didn't even look at her. "Not all Painiac videos were aired live," she said. "And I know for a fact that this one wasn't."

Yeah, that was convenient. "How?"

Instead of answering, Stef pointed to the corner of the screen. "Here she comes."

The sound of footsteps echoed through the cavernous space, and a shadow came into view, distorted and elongated by a spotlight from behind. Then Molly appeared. She wore a red corset, laced tightly from behind, over a black-and-white polka-dot skirt with a mountain of red crinolines beneath and Molly's signature red-and-white-striped tights on her legs.

"Lawrence Fields," Molly cooed, giggling like a fiendish pixie after she said the prisoner's name. "Do you know who I am?"

The man's mouth quivered in fear, but he didn't respond.

"Oh, that's right," Molly said. She walked around behind him so she faced the camera. "I drugged you so you can't talk. Or move. Or escape. Sad face!" Molly looked at the camera and flashed an exaggerated frown, which appeared all the more maniacal with her overdrawn clown lips.

For the first time in her life, Becca paid close attention to Molly Mauler. She squinted as she scrutinized the Painiac's face, searching for any resemblance to her mom. The elaborate clown makeup and the shadows cast by the muted overhead lighting made it difficult to discern individual features, but based on the way Molly held her head and jutted her chin forward, Becca was pretty damn sure she wasn't looking at a video of her mom.

Next, she listened intently to Molly Mauler's high-pitched voice. Could she detect a trace of Ruth in the singsongy intonation? Not even a little.

"You have been convicted of the first-degree murder of your wife, Angela," Molly continued as she walked around to the side of the pen. "You bad, bad boy. And now it's time for you to meet my friend, Mr. Huggles."

As she said his name, Molly kicked a lever with her foot, and a section of the pen slid open, revealing a small chamber. Something was curled up inside. Something shiny and dark.

"I call him Mr. Huggles because he loves giving hugs!" Again, Molly dissolved into a fit of giggles, her voice so razor sharp it made Becca cringe.

The thing inside the chamber had begun to uncoil itself. Molly grew instantly serious.

"Mr. Huggles is a twenty-six-foot reticulated python," she said. "The largest in captivity. They've been known to eat deer, pigs, even the odd cow or alligator. Oh, and humans. Upon occasion." She clapped her hands in glee. "This is one of those occasions!"

Becca knew exactly what came next, but she still felt her pulse rate quicken in anticipation as Molly pulled a remote control from the folds of her skirt and pointed it at the ceiling. A red light illuminated the prisoner's body.

"That's a heat lamp," she explained directly to the camera. "To help this process along. You see, boys and girls, pythons are ambush hunters that lie in wait for prey to cross their paths. But Mr. Huggles is pretty hungry, and this heat lamp should draw him to the target. Are you ready for the fun?" A timer appeared on the screen, counting up from zero. "Bets are now open for time of squish!"

"Let's get to the important part," Stef said, and fast-forwarded the video.

The images on the screen raced ahead at quadruple speed. Mr. Huggles just lay there at first, but slowly, he moved into the pen, slithering through the shallow water. He rounded the prisoner a few times before he began to wind his way up the man's leg.

Becca hadn't been particularly squeamish about The Postman's executions, though she never quite understood the relish the Painiacs took in inflicting agony. But this was justice—punishment for a horrible, vicious crime. Molly's victim had killed his wife. What happened to him wasn't pleasant, but it was a direct consequence of his actions.

Still, the moment the pressure of the muscular reptile snapped the man's ribs, compressing his lungs and cutting off circulation until his heart stopped, Becca flinched. Even though she'd seen it before, in fast-forward, the effect was particularly brutal. His face, half-visible through the wound body of the snake, was purple, his eyes bulging, his mouth open in a silent scream. Then a jerk, and Becca could practically hear the crack of bones even though there was no sound coming through the speakers.

Once the snake had killed the man, he unwound from his victim and began the slow process of swallowing the corpse whole. The prisoner wasn't a large man, but Becca still marveled at the way the immense snake opened the free-floating cartilage of his jaw, pushing his V-shaped mouth over the man's head.

"I know how this one ends," Becca said impatiently. Watching this video with someone who believed the maniacal killer was her dead mom made her uncomfortable. "Can we skip to the important part?"

"No."

I hate you, too.

Finally, the man's bare feet disappeared, joining the rest of him. The python's body had stretched to accommodate his meal, the mound of a body visible beneath the shimmery green scales. Instead of slithering off, the snake just lay there, probably exhausted from ingesting his dinner.

That's when Stef cut the fast-forward, sending the video back into real time.

On the screen, Molly approached the docile snake, crouching beside his bloated body while she ran her fingers down the length of scales affectionately, proudly, like the caress of a lover. Which was super fucking gross.

"Did you wuv your dinner, Mr. Huggles?" Molly cooed. "Who's a big snakey face, huh? Who's a big snakey snake snake?"

Molly reached up to pat the snake's triangular head, and Stef quickly hit the space bar, pausing the video.

"Look at her hand," Stef instructed, pointing at the screen.

Becca sighed and approached the monitor, leaning over Stef's shoulder to get a closer view. What was she supposed to see, exactly?

"It looks like every other white person's hand," Becca said, her patience waning.

Stef shook her head and zoomed Molly's left hand into view. "Now look."

The image was fuzzy—not quite pixelated but certainly not crisp and hi-res—but as she gazed at it, something almost familiar began to take shape amid the light and shadows, the lines and curves. That darkish smudge might be a ring on Molly's hand, and the dot in the middle kinda, sorta looked . . .

"It's blue," Stef said, taking the words out of Becca's mouth. "Her ring is a sapphire. Just like the one your other mom wore around her neck at the funeral."

NINE

BECCA STARED AT THE SCREEN, UNBLINKING. WHILE SHE couldn't entirely dismiss the possibility that the fuzzy-colored blob was Ruth's sapphire-and-white-gold wedding ring, she also couldn't absolutely confirm it. In fact, the more she stared at it, the more she was convinced that the blue-hued pixel wasn't really blue at all, and that Stef was just seeing what she wanted to see.

"That could be anything."

Stef shook her head as she clicked through a cascade of file folders to open a photo. Becca's chest tightened. It was from the funeral. Between the heads and shoulders of the assembled mourners, Becca saw Rita's drawn face, her eyes puffy from crying, and Rafa, who, despite his great effort to appear stoic in public, had thick rivers of tears pouring down each cheek. Becca, on the other hand, looked absolutely poker-faced. She could have been watching an educational video at school, sitting through a church sermon, or burying her mom.

"Let's ignore for a moment," Stef began, "the fact that you're not crying."

"Hey!" Becca snapped. "That's none of your business."

Stef zoomed in on Rita's collarbone. The resolution was pretty good, even for as far away as Stef had been at the time, and you could clearly see the blue stone in its white-gold setting, hanging around Rita's neck. Stef then dragged the photo over to the video screen beside the freeze frame on Molly's blobby hand.

"I knew when I saw this video," Stef said, the inflection of her pitch rising, "that I was looking at a blue ring. But I didn't know for sure it belonged to your mom until I saw it at the funeral."

"You still don't know for sure," Becca said. "If this is the only evidence you have, I suggest you keep trying."

Stef gazed at her pityingly. "I can appreciate stubborn. But now you're just being stupid."

"Better stupid than delusional," Becca said. "You sound like one of those conspiracy websites the president is always re-tweeting."

"This isn't funny, you know," Stef said. This time, her voice shook. She was finally losing her cool.

"You sure about that?"

Stef took a deep breath, steadying herself. When she spoke again, her voice was razor sharp. "The world deserves to know who the Painiacs were."

"Who cares who they were?" Becca said, fighting the urge to scream in Stef's face. "They're all dead. Let it go."

"Do you ever take anything seriously?" Stef asked, eyes narrowing.

"Not if I can help it."

Disgust rippled across Stef's face, wrinkling her nose and stiffening every muscle from her forehead to her jawline. "I'm going to prove your mom was Molly Mauler."

"Over my dead body."

"Whatever you want," Stef replied. "But you're not going to stop me."

Stef's tone was unnerving. There was something lethal about it, and matched with the fanatical gleam in her eyes, it cemented the idea that Stef was a Fed-Xer fanatic who wanted to out the former Painiacs and their families. Well, Becca wasn't going to let her drag Rita and Rafa into this make-believe conspiracy, especially since there was no way in hell her dead mom had been that sadistic clown.

"How did you end up at my mom's funeral?"

Stef answered with silence.

"Let me guess: you just happened to see an obituary for someone whose death just *happened* to coincide with Molly Mauler's, and you made up this ridiculous theory to—"

"I didn't make it up!" Stef exploded, leaping to her feet. "I saw the rumors on—"

She caught herself in time, but Becca was already completing her sentence. "Online? On a Fed-Xer site?"

Stef was silent, but that was enough of an answer for Becca.

"Show me."

"It's none of your business."

Becca spun Stef's chair around to face her. "My mom, my business." Becca was simultaneously pissed off at Stef and intrigued by her, and as they stared at each other in a silent battle of wills, Becca wasn't sure if she wanted to slap Stef across the face or kiss her.

Stef was the first to break the spell. "Fine." She turned back to her computer, pulled up a Facebook page on her browser, and motioned for Becca to take a seat at the desk.

Becca pressed her lips together as she sank into a chair. Whatever she was about to see, it wasn't something she could delete or destroy, and she could only hope that the Fed-Xers' "evidence" in regard to Molly Mauler was nothing more than innuendo.

Otherwise, Becca and her family could be in a great deal of danger.

⋯

seen by 237,411
💀 by Judy Kline, Mark Xu **and 189,043 others**

Blake Flake is feeling self-righteous

ANNOUNCEMENT: the Fed-Xers' Painiacs Reward Offering (FxPRO) has grown to over $250,000 (as of November 26, updated daily)! The rules are simple: anyone who provides information that leads to the verifiable identification of a Painiac's secret identity is entitled to an equal share of the reward, to be determined by the Fed-Xer moderators. Tips and information CANNOT BE ANONYMOUS. Please see roundup posts below to submit your information.

    UPDATE (November 25): Due to the arson investigation in Savannah, Georgia, the Fed-Xers ask that members do not act upon tips until they have been fully vetted and verified by the moderators. Thank you.

NOVEMBER 13
....

RECENT ACTIVITY

Judy Kline Roundup post #4: Hannah Ball.
seen by 135,003
💀 by Tim Timmerson, Naydeen Doyle **and 97,220 others**

This is a roundup post for Hannah Ball. Any information about her true identity should be added here for vetting and investigation by the Fed-Xers. Please add information via comments!

NOVEMBER 21

Janeisha Barrett   I'm 100% sure on this one. So my uncle and his third wife live across the street from this couple in Savannah. She—the wife—hasn't been seen since the last day of Alcatraz 2.0 and he—the husband—is a chef at some local restaurant. It literally CANNOT be a coincidence. DM me for address details.

5d

Judy Kline   Noted. DMing you now...

5d

Judy Kline   IMPORTANT!!! After last night's events in Savannah, we must ask everyone not to act on the information they see here. Janeisha's tip WAS NOT VERIFIED.

20hr

Zenia Stanislavski   Hannah is the one I loathed the most. I mean, eating your victims? That is beyond disgusting.

5d

Marlon Unbrando   Do we really think it's true that The Postman had hired a whole new group of Painiacs to replace the OGs? And if it's true, shouldn't we be focusing on more than just the original lineup?

5d

Mark Xu This should probably be its own thread on the board.

5d

Marlon Unbrando Totally. Will do.

5d

Mitchell M. David Holy Hell, the Fed-Xers work fast. Saw the news today about the house in Savannah. Assuming that's the same one Janeisha mentioned a couple of days ago? Worried that this was not fully vetted by group . . .

1d

> **Judy Kline** Please see my comments above.
>
> 20 hrs

Judy Kline Roundup post #8: Molly Mauler.
seen by 74,519
💀 by Postman Opfive and 54,898 others

This is a roundup post for Molly Mauler. Any information about her true identity should be added here for vetting and investigation by the Fed-Xers. Please add information via comments!

NOVEMBER 21

> **Mr. Hef** Thanks, Judy. Nothing to add to the convo, but I'm just so damn happy to see these posts!!! I'll check on them every day.
>
> 5d

> **Tiny Striker** I wish I'd screenshotted the conversation about the Mauler from the old forum before they took it down. I remember there was an awesome one near the end. Something happened between Mara and #CinderellaSurvivor, I think, but only a handful of people saw it from the subscription feed. Anyone remember this or have a screen grab?
>
> 5d

> **Heather Oesterman** I totally remember that, Tiny! It was crazy because at the time everyone just thought Mara was some lame inmate and couldn't possibly have any real info on the Painiacs. Fuck! If only we'd been paying attention! But #CinderellaSurvivor had only been on the island for like 30 hours at that point. Who knew how this would all go down?
>
> 5d

Nikola Testicla Anyone involved in that on here?

5d

Madame Portland Nikola, your screen name makes my world.

4d

Conrad Verreros Tim Timmerson and Ishta Patel, you also had The Postman logins, right?

5d

Tim Timmerson I did, but I only vaguely remember this. I think someone had video but there was no audio because the ripping software sucked and everyone was trying to figure out what they were saying. They were in the kitchen or something.

5d

Ishta Patel Conrad—Not proud of it, but yes.

5d

Naydeen Dolye Okay, Mara aside, how could anyone be sure she was giving out accurate information? Girl seemed kind of whacked out. Besides, if she was anything like her father, she wouldn't voluntarily reveal the names of Painiacs!

4d

Conrad Verreros Unless she knew they were going to be replaced.

4d

Keahi Wong •raises hand• I was BabyEditrix on The Postman and I had recorded the feed without sound, but my fiancée's coworker could lip-read and translated it for us. Problem was that there were only like a few frames where you could actually see Mara's mouth, but the lip-reading expert was pretty sure that one of the words mentioned was "Michigan." And the one before it had two syllables, and started with an "M."

We did some research, since it seemed that Mara was telling #CinderellaSurvivor where Molly Mauler was supposedly from. That narrowed our choices down to the following: Macomb, Mansfield, Manton, Markey, Marlette, Marquette, Marshall, Martin, Mason, Matchwood, Maybee, Mayfield, Mayville, McBain, McBride, Mellen, Melrose, Melvin, Memphis, Mendon, Mentor, Merrill, Merritt, Mesick, Meyer, Midland, Milan, Milford, Millbrook, Millen, Milton, Minden, Mio, Mitchell, Moffat, Moline, Moltke, Monroe, Montrose, Moorland, Moran, Morley, Morrice, Morton, Moscow, Mottville, Mullett, Mundy, Munger, Munith, Munro, and Mussey.

Then someone else who had seen the live stream but didn't record it weighed in that Mara was definitely talking about a stay-at-home mom from the Upper Peninsula, which narrowed it down to Mansfield, Marquette, Matchwood, Mellen, Meyer, and Moran.

So there it is. If you believe that Mara was telling the truth and that she had access to the correct information in the first place, Molly Mauler was a stay-at-home mom from one of those places. Was she still living in Michigan at the time she died? Impossible to know. So the whole exercise wasn't exactly helpful. More like a mental challenge.

4d
....

TEN

BECCA FELT ALL THE WARMTH DRAIN OUT FROM HER BODY AS she stared at the monitor. Her hometown connected to a Painiac. This was how Stef wound up at Ruth's funeral. And she wasn't just some Fed-Xer lunatic: a piece of that $250,000 reward had been her motivation all along. It explained the video camera, the stalking. Stef had been looking for proof.

And the break-in? Was that associated with this theory, too? Maybe Stef wasn't the only one who had made the connection between Marquette and Ruth's funeral. He'd been searching for proof, just like Stef, and how long would it be before more showed up? How long would it be before proof was unnecessary and Becca woke up to a pitchfork mob surrounding her house?

It didn't even matter whether or not Ruth was *actually* Molly, only that the public might believe it. Becca tried to imagine her moms' friends and neighbors showing up at their house with rocks and bottles and, hell, maybe even a gun or two. Would they listen to reason? Would they calm down when they realized that Ruth had been home in Marquette during at least one of Molly's kills? Or would they be swayed by the same mob mentality that led to some poor couple's home burning to the ground in Savannah?

Becca's family was in danger, all because of a crazy theory and the coincidental fact that her stay-at-home mom happened to die around the same time as Molly Mauler, also a suspected stay-at-home mom. Now in addition to Ruth's death, her family was embroiled in a national conspiracy through no fault of its own.

"This is bullshit!" Becca exploded, pounding her fist against the desk. "A blurry photo and some hazy lipreading aren't facts."

"You just don't want it to be true."

"Yeah, duh," Becca said, throwing her hands up. "Did you see what happened in Savannah? There was ZERO creditable evidence that man was Hannah Ball's husband. Your precious Fed-Xers admitted as much. And yet innocent people almost got hurt."

Stef's face was stony. "Collateral damage."

"You're talking about my family!" Becca rocketed to her feet. "And let me tell you something, if this bullshit photo of my mom's ring ends up on the Internet, I swear to God—"

"You'll kill me," Stef said with a smile. "You already told me that."

Becca couldn't believe how callous Stef was acting. "You wouldn't feel the same way if it was your mom and brother they were talking about."

The color drained from Stef's face. She opened her mouth to say something, but the words stuck in her throat. Her eyes flitted to a spot on the wall as she shifted her legs uncomfortably in her chair, and suddenly, Becca wondered why, exactly, Stef lived with her grandparents.

"The Fed-Xers are being more careful now," she said after a pause. "Vetting the evidence. What happened in Savannah won't be repeated."

"Yeah, right." Becca wasn't willing to trust Stef's assertion, or the willpower of the Fed-Xers. And she sure as hell wasn't going to sit around and wait for the mob to show up on her doorstep. She needed to prove beyond a reasonable doubt that Ruth Martinello wasn't Molly Mauler.

"Who would know for sure?" Becca asked.

Stef arched an eyebrow. "Know the Painiacs' identities?"

"Yeah." *You know, what we've been talking about for an hour.*

"The Postman."

Becca sighed. "Someone we could actually talk to."

Stef turned away. "I—I don't know."

But the stutter combined with Stef's inability to look Becca in the eye while she said it signaled that she was lying. "What do you know?"

"Nothing."

It was like pulling teeth with this one. "What do you *suspect*?"

Stef sighed heavily, then crossed her arms over her chest. "It's nothing concrete."

"I haven't heard one piece of concrete evidence so far tonight," Becca snarked. "Why start now?"

"Do you want to hear or not?" Stef said, shooting Becca a dirty glance over her shoulder.

"Proceed."

Stef resumed her seat at the computer, talking while she typed. "Eight years ago, right before Merchant-Bronson had their first hit show, they had a mailing address listed as a production bungalow near the old Hollywood Center Studios on North Las Palmas. For like a hot minute. I found it on a directory listing cached from the company's website."

Those words literally meant nothing to Becca. "Okay."

"Yesterday, I was reading the latest *BeltBull* article about *Who Wants to Be a Painiac?*, which said that Postman Enterprises Inc. also had a mailing address at the same bungalow."

Becca perked up. "But I thought the show wasn't affiliated with PEI at all."

"I mean, that's what Merchant-Bronson is saying."

Right. PEI had like a bazillion lawsuits going against it, plus a criminal investigation. Of course Merchant-Bronson wouldn't want to claim that they were associated. Still, it seemed a stretch that Stef could somehow uncover information that the FBI didn't know about.

"If you found this," Becca said cautiously, "I'm sure the FBI has too. Wouldn't they shut down the production?"

Stef shrugged. "I don't know. I mean, they haven't."

Fair point. The auditions for *Who Wants to Be a Painiac?* were next month in Los Angeles. And if, by some off chance, the show was somehow connected to Alcatraz 2.0, the evidence that could exonerate her mom might, just *might*, be in Los Angeles as well.

A plan was forming in Becca's mind. She had a few hundred saved up between babysitting money and birthday gifts. What if . . .

"I'm going," Becca blurted out.

"Drive safely," Stef said, managing to look as if she didn't mean it at all.

"I mean to LA. I'm going to those auditions." It sounded completely nuts even as the words tumbled out of her mouth, but Becca realized that the only way she could protect her family was to prove, beyond a shadow of a doubt, that her mom was not Molly Mauler.

"By yourself?"

"If I have to."

"*Now* who's crazy?"

Becca sat back against the desk, close to Stef. "You should come with me."

Stef's eyebrows slowly climbed up her forehead. "Certifiable."

Keep your enemies closer. "I'm serious."

"Why would I want to go to LA with you? To help you try and prove me wrong?"

Becca smiled. She had one irresistible lure to get Stef to come with her. Money. "If you're so sure you're right, come with me and prove it. I promise if we find evidence that my mom was actually Molly Mauler, I'll make sure you collect that Fed-Xer reward."

She almost felt bad lying to Stef, since she had absolutely no intention of letting real evidence—if it even existed—fall into anyone's hands other than her own, but she needed Stef to come with her. She wasn't sure she could do this on her own, and besides, she didn't want to let Stef out of her sight. So far, she was probably the only one who had put the Molly Mauler–Ruth Martinello pieces together. And Becca wanted to keep it that way.

"All you have to do," Becca added, "is promise not to post about your theory until we have proof one way or another. Deal?"

Stef was silent as she mulled over Becca's offer. Becca wasn't sure if Stef would bite, but in the end, the money proved irresistible.

"We'll have to find a cheap hostel," Stef said. "I can't afford a hotel."

"Fine by me."

"You'll have your reasons for being there; I'll have mine."

Yeah, a Fed-Xer reward. "I know."

"So we're business partners, not friends. No chitchat on the plane, no getting-to-know-you conversations. And as soon as I have the evidence I need, I'm out of there, okay?"

"Message received." Whatever. Becca didn't need a friend.

"Okay." Stef stood up and extended her hand. "You have yourself a deal."

Becca took Stef's hand, giving it one hard shake. She had no clue how she was going to pull this off, and the whole idea was probably a horrible one, but for the first time in twenty-four hours, Becca felt as if she was in control of her destiny once more. LA might be scary, and leaving Rita and Rafa behind might be even scarier, but Becca had to take the risk. The only way to ensure her family's safety was to find out who Molly Mauler really was. And she was the only one who could do it.

CALLING ALL CELEBRITIES!

703,117 likes

tristan_mckee CALLING ALL #THEPOSTMAN CELEBRITIES! With our FundMyFun.com/whowantstobeapainiac goal easily exceeded, we are set to go with auditions for December 17 at Stu-Stu-Studio in Burbank! Wannabe Painiacs—show up in your best costumes and be ready to (fake) kill it!

Meanwhile, we'd love to get some real live #ThePostman celebrities involved in our pilot shoot! You hear me #DeathRowBreakfastClub? Or maybe someone else in the news recently? #GavinXanthropoulos, doesn't this sound like more fun than testifying in the impeachment trial? If so, head to the front of the line on December 17! We'll keep a spot open for you!

1 HOUR AGO

RECENT ACTIVITY

Nehir Asuman Do you seriously think #HottieGriselda would come out of hiding for your stupid game show? She's not an idiot.

Holly Hobbie @Nehir Asuman Agreed. Did you read the interview Sinclair gave Wired about how she hacked into The Postman's laptop? Def not an idiot but the way she used netsh to break the Wi-Fi encryption in less than ten minutes displays a criminal level of aptitude. She's not exactly an innocent little flower!

Tom Ecklestein @Holly Hobbie I'd like to innocent her flower.

Benny Nda Jetts Why not? Unlike Xanthropoulos, the #DeathRowBreakfastClub weren't included on the witness list for the impeachment trial. Not like they have anything else going on!

....

Holly Hobbie @Tom Ecklestein That's disgusting.

....

Former PM Fan Wait, who the hell is Gavin Xanthropoulos?

....

thegriff @Former PM Fan He's the star witness in the Presidential Impeachment Trial. #PIT I heard he's the key to the treason charge.

....

Former PM Fan @thegriff Doesn't treason mean, like, selling secrets to the Chinese or aiding a country that's at war with us? It doesn't sound like the president did either!

....

Dr. Mark X @Former PM Fan Article III of the Constitution defines treason against the United States as "levying war against them, or in adhering to their enemies, giving them aid and comfort." In the fallout of the Burr plot, the Supreme Court ruled that the "levying war" portion required an actual assembling of men, not just conspiring to do so. I believe Congress is attempting to prove that the president gave "aid and comfort" to a foreign power waging war against the United States. In this case, "war" might be construed as a continuation of the Cold War for the digital age.

....

Alfred E. Mnemonics @Dr. Mark X Ur smart

....

Dr. Mark X @Alfred E. Mnemonics Thanks?

....

thegriff $20 says Xanthropoulos doesn't live to testify. You think The Postman is the scariest thing involved in this trial? Think again.

....

ADD A COMMENT

ELEVEN

DECEMBER IN LOS ANGELES WAS NOTHING LIKE WHAT BECCA had seen on TV. She'd expected blaring sunshine, oppressive desert heat, people running around in short shorts and halter tops. Maybe it was like that in the summer, but December was kind of gloomy. Overcast skies blotted out the sun and threatened rain that never fell, but though it appeared gray and wintery, the temperatures were mild. So at least the weather didn't suck as she and Stef munched on vending-machine Danish while they walked from their Burbank hostel to Stu-Stu-Studio.

As promised, there had been no chitchat en route. In fact, Stef and Becca barely exchanged twenty words during the ten-hour journey from Sawyer Airport through Detroit, and finally to Los Angeles, which then required two different train rides and a mile-long walk to arrive at their hostel. They'd gone to sleep—Stef on the upper bunk, Becca below—in silence, and the next morning Stef had showered and dressed before Becca even managed to crawl out of her bunk, and spent the rest of the morning at her laptop, her knee-length winter coat buttoned up to her chin despite the warm weather, ignoring Becca completely.

Can. Not. Hang. As much as Becca pretended otherwise, the silence bugged her, like she was being punished. She glanced at Stef, trudging silently beside her in her long black coat, and smiled. Becca had taken a petty form of revenge, giving Stef's cell phone number to Jackie as an emergency contact. Her best friend had completely freaked out when Becca had asked her to cover for her while she went out of town, refusing to tell Jackie and Mateo where she was going. Jackie's anxiety was real, and the thought of Jackie calling Stef in a full-blown panic attack over Becca's whereabouts put a wicked smile on her face. Stef would hate that.

Becca was still smiling when they rounded a corner and found themselves surrounded by news vans and a swirl of cameramen and reporters scurrying around in the street.

"That's weird," Stef said, the first words she'd spoken all day.

"What is?" Becca kept it short, trying not to sound relieved by the return of conversation.

Stef checked her phone. "We're still blocks from Stu-Stu-Studio. Why isn't the media parked closer?"

As if in answer, a roar erupted from down the street.

"What the hell is that?" Becca asked.

A deep furrow appeared between Stef's eyebrows. "I heard there were going to be protesters."

"Do you think they'll keep us from auditioning?" Becca asked. Darlene Ahlberg had warned that this audition would be nuts. Would Merchant-Bronson shut down the open call over a few people with picket signs?

"We should motor," Stef said. And for the first time since they met, Becca agreed with her.

The streets around Stu-Stu-Studio were clogged with people. The seething mass before them—Fed-Xers, judging by the signs that sported slogans like MERCHANT-BRONSON IS SO AWFUL, EVEN INTROVERTS SHOWED UP! and THIS FED-XER SPECIAL DELIVERY IS A BOOT UP THE

POSTMAN'S ASS! paired with the unison chant of "Shut it down!"—filled the street and sidewalks, impeding their route.

"Can we get around?" Becca asked as Stef consulted the map on her phone.

Stef kept her voice low, barely audible over the crowd. "Looks like we can try to go down to Victory Boulevard," she said, pointing to her left. "And come up on it from the other side."

Becca nodded and followed Stef as they backtracked out of the Fed-Xer protest as quickly as they could weave through the bodies that were continuing to arrive, swelling the crowd with every passing moment. Becca felt her shoulders relax the instant they rounded the corner, putting the Fed-Xers out of view. What would they have done if they'd known that a suspected Molly Mauler relative had turned up right in the middle of their protest?

Becca shuddered. She didn't want to think about it.

At the next corner, Becca and Stef ran straight into a police barricade. Portable steel fences, chained together to form three-foot-high barriers, stretched across the entire street. Behind them four police cars were parked in the middle of the road, like a barricade in case some crazed protester tried to ram the fence with his car, and a dozen officers in full riot gear manned the perimeter.

"Can't get through here," the cop said as Becca approached, not even waiting for her to ask. He pointed back toward the Fed-Xer rally. "Back the way you came."

Um, no. "We're here for the audition."

The cop tilted his head, looking Becca up and down. "Yeah, right."

"I'm serious."

"Look, kid," the cop said. "There's zero tolerance for violence today.

You stay on your side of the protest and let them stay on theirs. No one gets hurt."

"We're really just here to audition," Stef said before Becca could unleash a torrent of snark on the riot officer. She unbuttoned her coat, peeling it off to reveal one of the weirder outfits Becca had ever seen.

Stef wore straight black pants and a matching old-fashioned jacket over a buttoned-up vest and a high-collared white blouse that tied around her neck in some kind of crazy scarf cravat thingy. She looked like a turn-of-the-century page boy, a far cry from the cozy leggings and tunic she'd worn since they left Marquette.

The cop stared at her. "What the hell are you supposed to be?"

Stef fished a British cabbie hat out of her coat pocket and pulled it over her head. "I'm Yentl. As portrayed on film by Barbra Streisand, the only woman to win a Golden Globe for best director."

Becca didn't even know where to start. First of all, Stef came in costume? When was she going to fill Becca in on that? And second of all, *THIS* was her costume? The cops were never going to buy it.

"Sure, why not?" the cop said, his gruff manner evaporated. Then he pointed in the opposite direction. "Go down another block. You'll see the line."

"You could have told me you were dressing up," Becca said between clenched teeth the moment they were out of earshot, not sure whether she was more annoyed that Stef had worn one, or that her crappy costume had actually gotten them past the riot police.

Stef draped her coat over her arm. "It's not my fault you didn't read the Instagram posts. Clearly said to come in costume as your Painiac persona."

Becca scowled and stared at the pavement. She was relatively sure Stef hadn't mentioned this before on purpose. Probably trying to sabotage Becca's chances of getting through the audition process. Now what was she going to do?

The sight that awaited them as they rounded the next corner momentarily banished Becca's worries.

A massive line of people stretched down the block, hugging the sidewalk on one side behind an endless row of police barricade fences. Becca would have approached someone in the line and asked "Are you here for the *Painiacs* audition?" but the question was totally and completely unnecessary.

The line snaking out of Stu-Stu-Studio looked like a Halloween casting call. Almost everyone was in costume: some outright homages to former Painiacs, others with an original persona of their own, and still others mixing the two. There were Robin's Hoods and Hannah Balls, Gassy Als and Barbaric Baristas, the details down perfectly. She also saw a fair number of Molly Maulers, complete with striped tights and clown makeup, which made her instantly sick to her stomach. She couldn't escape Molly.

Beside them, separated only by the barricade, the Postmantics had set up an encampment. Tents lined the street and sidewalk beside camper trailers and Airstreams that must have been parked there since before the police rolled in. One Winnebago had speakers mounted on the roof and was blasting some doo-wop 1950s song with the lyrics "Wait a minute, Mr. Postman," and street vendors were selling everything from bacon-wrapped hot dogs to bootleg The Postman T-shirts and Alcatraz 2.0 merchandise.

Becca took a spot at the back of the line, but Stef continued forward, pacing the auditioners. They seemed to stretch forever, an infinite file of dominatrices, nuns, mimes, lumberjacks, magicians, grown men dressed as babies, and even a dude in a green spandex unitard, leaning against the wall as he casually pulled his leg up behind him and wrapped his foot around his neck.

Now at least she understood why the cop hadn't initially believed that she was planning to audition. Compared to the costumes all around them, Becca looked sorely out of place.

She was going to need some kind of story to explain why her plaid skirt, tights, and denim jacket were, in fact, a costume. Catholic school-girl gone wrong? Griselda Sinclair had kind of lived that persona on Alcatraz 2.0. Maybe Becca could sell herself as an homage. Or maybe she was an android, dressed to look like the human she was replacing, Stepford Wives–style. Or a homicidal babysitter. There had to be a fake knife she could borrow from someone in this crowd. . . .

While Becca continued to brainstorm ideas, she noticed that Stef was slowly approaching her down the audition line. She held her hand low, coat draped over her arm, and it took a few seconds before Becca noticed that she was using her phone as a video camera, obscured beneath her thick jacket while she methodically filmed everyone in line.

"Stop it," Becca muttered out of the side of her mouth as Stef approached.

"What?"

"Filming."

"I'm just getting some B-roll for later, when we prove my theory is right."

"Cut it out!"

"Why?" Stef angled the camera up to Becca's face. "Worried someone might see you here?"

Becca narrowed her eyes. "Actually, yes. I'm supposed to be at Keyes Peak with my friends, remember?"

"Fine." Stef typed quickly into her phone, then slipped it back in her bag before joining Becca at the end of the longest line in the world. "But just remember why we're here. You want to find your evidence, and I want to find mine."

"Right," Becca said. *Unless I find it first.*

TWELVE

IT TOOK TWO AND A HALF HOURS FOR BECCA AND STEF TO reach the entrance of Stu-Stu-Studio, where an assistant wearing a too-tight Hawaiian shirt and khakis handed out clipboards.

"Please fill out this form completely," he said in a bored monotone with just a hint of an accent that Becca couldn't quite place. "Completely means everything."

My first chance to ask questions, Becca thought, flashing a friendly smile at the assistant. It was a long shot that this guy would know anything—he wouldn't exactly be manning the door if he was some high-ranking producer—but she wasn't going to leave any stone unturned.

"So, like, I can just fill out some of the questions and leave the rest blank?" Becca said as she took her clipboard. A joke, to lighten the mood and open casual conversation. But her attempt at humor was totally lost on him.

"Please fill out this form completely," he repeated, his dead-fish eyes giving her a cursory once-over. "And sign the release before you reach the desk. No form, no release, no audition. Move forward. You're holding up the line."

"Right," she said, edging ahead. "Sorry." Well, that was a depressing start.

"Really?" Stef whispered in her ear. "That's your plan?"

Becca shot her a look. "Like you have a better one."

"Maybe next time you should just straight out ask if he knows who Molly Mauler was?"

"Maybe I will," Becca hissed back. She noticed that Stef had ignored her challenge about a plan. Was Yentl going to somehow charm the producers into giving her the info she wanted? Based on Becca's experiences with Stef so far, she highly doubted her "charm" would work.

Stef snorted. "I'm sure that'll go down well."

Stef did have a point: short of asking straight out who Molly Mauler really was, she didn't have much of a plan for how to prove her mom wasn't the notorious serial killer. Maybe her inquiries needed to be that direct? Or should she be coy about it? Snoop around and see if she could stumble upon some kind of evidence?

Ugh. A superspy she was not.

Turning her back to Stef, Becca pulled the cheap ballpoint pen from the top of the clipboard and began to read through the paperwork as they wound through stanchions toward the front of the lobby. The first set of questions were pretty basic: name, address, contact information. She hesitated, remembering the retaliations and the rabid swarm of Fed-Xers protesting just down the street, then wrote "Becca Martinello" in overly large print anyway. She had to take the chance that if anyone working on this show actually knew who Ruth Martinello was, they'd recognize her name. That was like worst-case scenario in Becca's mind, but then at least she'd know for sure.

Are you over the age of eighteen?

She was two months away and figured that was close enough. *Yes.*

Are you a citizen of the United States?

Pretty standard. *Yes.*

Do you have a next of kin?

Huh. That was weird. Why the hell would the producers need to know that? Should she leave it blank?

By this point, they'd looped back around in the winding line to where the dead-eyed assistant was still repeating his mantra as if he could read Becca's thoughts. "Please fill out the form completely. Completely means everything."

Maybe *next of kin* was just a tongue-in-cheek, *Who Wants to Be a Painiac?* way of saying "emergency contact." Becca wasn't about to argue semantics. She needed to stick around this audition long enough to find proof that exonerated her family from any Molly Mauler association. With a shrug of resignation, she marked a huge X beside *Yes*, then wrote Rita's name as next of kin. Just in case.

She flipped the page and skimmed through a long paragraph of legalese that must have been the release form. She pretty much had no idea what it said, but they were almost at the front of the line, so she quickly signed it, then clutched the clipboard to her chest and waited for her turn.

Another assistant sat at a folding table at one end of the lobby, collecting the clipboards. He was older, with salt-and-pepper hair and a face like a cheese grater, dressed simply in jeans and a sensible flannel button-down. Unlike Dead Eyes at the door, this guy wore a headset.

"Next!"

Stef stepped up to the desk and handed over her clipboard. Becca stood back, listening, but couldn't pick up any of the brief conversation over the dull roar of the dueling protests going on outside. After less than a minute, Headset Guy pointed to his left toward the soundstage. Stef didn't even look at Becca as she turned and headed down the hallway.

Wow. Stef did it. She made it past the gatekeeper. That didn't seem too hard.

"Next!"

Headset Guy held out his hand as Becca approached. "Paperwork?" Once again, Becca thought she detected a twinge of an accent in his voice.

"Here you go."

He scanned the pages, noting the signature. "Becca Martinello," he said slowly. Slowly like he was trying to pronounce it correctly, or slowly like the name sounded familiar? Becca wasn't sure.

"That's me!"

"Right." He scribbled a few notes. "No costume." It wasn't a question.

"So I know it looks like I don't have a costume," Becca said, jabbering nervously. She needed to sell herself, convince this dude that she should be on the show. "But really, this *is* my costume."

"Sure." Scribble, scribble, scribble.

Really, Becca? What the hell are you doing? "I'm, um, like Two-Face. From Batman. Regular girl in the front, deformed maniac in the back." That literally made no sense.

Headset Guy flipped through Becca's paperwork. "Hm-mm."

"Think of how cool that could be," Becca said. OMG, why was she still talking? "I'd be like—"

The dude cleared his throat, not even listening. "Thank you for coming down today, Miss Martinello." He pointed to his right as he dropped her clipboard onto a pile on the floor. "If you would please exit this way, we will—"

Becca felt a wave of panic well up from the depths of her being, realizing that she was about to be dismissed, her mission a failure before it even began. She had to get through to the next round, had to gain access to the producers, who might have had some connection to The Postman. She was about to open her mouth and beg for a second chance, when Headset Guy froze midsentence. Becca heard a beep. Headset Guy put his hand to his ear, listening intently. "Copy," he said after a few seconds, then lifted Becca's clipboard from the pile. "Miss Martinello, if you would kindly go down the hall, you'll find the door to the soundstage."

"Th-thank you."

Whoa, what just happened? Becca glanced around the lobby as she followed Stef down the hall. Were they being watched? And if so, what was it about Becca that had earned a reprieve? Her looks? Her youth? Her lack of a costume?

Or was it my name?

💀 ◯ ◁

seen by 166,980
💀 Capuchin Ghost, Tonya Bologna **and 118,204 others**

Darkness Falls   is feeling naughty

This is a secret group for all the displaced "fans" of The Postman. It is absolutely private. Posts will not show up on your wall, and none of your friends will know you are a member unless they are also a member. Potential members must have verified login IDs from The Postman, and must be submitted to the moderators for approval. Screen grabs of the contents of this group are prohibited and will result in your immediate removal from the group and the eternal wrath of the Postmantics.
Like   Comment

NOVEMBER 15
....

RECENT ACTIVITY

seen by 1,561
     by Postman OpFive **and 452 others**

Capuchin Ghost How many of us are here at Stu-Stu-Studio right now? Auditioning? Just chilling? I've got the lawn chairs out and a cooler of PBR. Camped out next to the guy with the red-and-white sign that reads "Neither snow nor rain nor heat nor gloom of impeachment." COME SAY HI.

DECEMBER 17 AT 10:02AM
....

Froolia Freud So jealous right now.

45M   Like   Reply

Phoebe Temptressta I'm in line to audition! Wearing my *cough* professional outfit. Just look for the six-foot-tall blond dominatrix in black latex. (Yes, I'm available for hire.)

45M   Like   Reply

Jazzy Jayson I'm in line too! Near the back. White tux and top hat. Where you at Temptressta? Sounds like our black and white would look pretty rad side-by-side.

43M   Like   Reply

Dr. Eliseo Mendez Still en route. LAPD has the streets cordoned off. I believe they're attempting to keep the Fed-Xers from rioting. They're corralled about two blocks from Stu-Stu-Studio right now, as far as I can tell. Trying to make our way around to you guys. Save a Pabst for me!

43M   Like   Reply

Phoebe Temptressta Sorry, Jazzy. I work alone. (Trust me, you'd prefer it that way.)

41M   Like   Reply

Postman OpFive   created a poll.

For those of you watching live or via the nine billion feeds on YouTube and Facebook Live, what is your favorite costume so far?

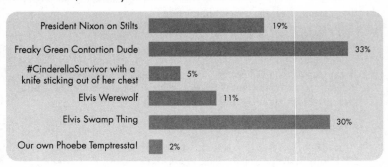

DECEMBER 17 AT 10:25AM

Jazzy Jayson I feel so unseen. HAHAHAHAHA

15M   Like   Reply

Onyekachi Eze Can we add the guy riding a fake mechanical bull? #genius

15M   Like   Reply

Count Burgundy I mean, those Elvi are pretty epic.

13M   Like   Reply

Froolia Freud Temptressta representing!

12M   Like   Reply

Phoebe Temptressta You guys are SO SWEET.

6M   Like   Reply

Chol K'Golmad

Any word on the Fed-Xers? I was going to try and harass them but traffic getting into Burbank this morning was insane. I heard they were going to try and storm the studio to shut down auditions. Are the police keeping them away? Seemed like a pretty robust po-po presence from what I saw.

DECEMBER 17 AT 10:45AM

....

Regina Showalter Totally OT, but is your name in KLINGON???

5M   Like   Reply

....

Dr. Eliseo Mendez They've got a huge turnout but the PD does too. Full riot gear. I think they'll keep those terrorists in their place. Freedom of speech but not freedom of disruption.

5M   Like   Reply

....

Chol K'Golmad *grins* Yes. Yes, it is.

3M   Like   Reply

....

Regina Showalter MARRY ME.

1M   Like   Reply

....

THIRTEEN

WHEN BECCA STEPPED THROUGH THE DOUBLE DOORS ONTO the soundstage, she'd expected to enter a world of half-built sets, bustling executives, and an army of gaffers and grips scurrying around, hard at work hauling two-by-fours and lights and a rainbow array of cabling in a cacophony of entertainment production. Instead, the soundstage at Stu-Stu-Studio was a bare, empty shell.

The floors were concrete and meticulously clean, which seemed incongruous with the warehouse-like interior. It should have been dusty, scuffed with boot rubber and littered with splinters of wood and wads of discarded electrical tape instead of power-blasted to a gleaming shine. This squeaky cleanness was highlighted by the sunlight streaming in from an open cargo door at the far end, which reflected off the concrete and illuminated the two-story walls with the efficiency of a mirror.

The walls themselves were lined with catwalks and dotted throughout by open metal staircases that climbed into the flies, a latticework of steel that ran the entire length of the building, suspended from the roof like a loft. It reminded Becca of the theater at her high school, where the massive stage lights and set pieces would be prepped. But there were no follow spots installed for today's audition. Other than the natural light streaming through the open door, the soundstage was only lit by relatively dim orange bulbs embedded in the ceiling. There was no furniture except for a single long table next to the door she'd entered through, displaying small bottles of water, bags of chips, fruit, cookies, and a variety of granola bars.

The auditioners who had made it past the initial cut were spread out in clusters. Everyone was in costume, and the effect of twenty outlandishly clad performers made Becca think of the footage she'd seen from Comic-Con. Bright costumes, feathers, prosthetics, enormous props, fake blood, all with a creepy, horror-movie slant that made Becca not want to touch anything.

Some of the potential castmates were leaning against the walls, faces buried in their cell phones, which, especially in the case of what appeared to be an Elizabethan judge, presented a strange anachronism. Others remained in character, like the Godzilla monster and Japanese schoolgirl duo who cycled through a pattern of scare and scream moves that was either a rehearsal of their act, or foreplay. Hard to say.

Becca spotted Stef by the food table, riffling through a pile of granola bars. Her shoulders were relaxed, her face neutral. If she was at all anxious about Becca's fate, she certainly didn't show it.

"Hey," Becca said, approaching the table.

Stef didn't look up at her. "You made it."

Becca wasn't entirely sure if Stef was excited by the prospect, or just stating the facts.

"Yeah."

"This is weird," Stef said, gazing around.

Becca's eyes drifted to a huge guy dressed as a sumo wrestler, who had rolled out a yoga mat and was upward-dogging it on the floor. "Certainly not something you see every day."

"Not that." Stef flicked her head toward the food. "This is the saddest craft services display I've ever seen."

"I've heard that Merchant-Bronson is notoriously cheap," Becca replied, repeating what she'd heard from Darlene Ahlberg, who certainly wasn't the most reliable source of information on the planet, but Stef didn't contradict.

"There's no one here checking us in, telling us where to go." Stef paused, glancing toward the door. "Going to make it kind of hard for me to slip away."

So that was Stef's plan. She was looking for a chance to snoop around the studio. Becca had to admit it was ballsy in a Woodward-and-Bernstein kind of way, and she admired the fact that Stef had showed up in LA with a plan, unlike Becca, who probably should have put more thought into the whole trip.

Whatever. She'd made it this far. If she had to piggyback on Stef's plans in order to get the information she needed, so be it.

"You mean for *us* to sneak away."

Stef's eyes narrowed. "We are *not* partners, remember?"

Becca was about to answer, when a guy stepped up behind them. He was youngish-looking with sandy-brown hair and vapid blue eyes, wearing a billowy white shirt that laced at the neck, cropped black pants, a red bandanna around his head, and an eye patch, currently flipped up onto his forehead.

"Papa, can you hear me?" Pirate Dude said. He smiled sheepishly, exposing a tooth that had been blacked out with stage makeup.

"Um, what?" Becca said, eyeing him up and down.

He cleared his throat, and this time he sang in a croaking voice, *"Papa, can you see me?"*

Becca grabbed Stef's arm. "Time to leave this crazy train."

But instead of following, Stef just laughed, then totally out of character, she broke into song. *"Papa, can you find me in the night?"*

"Okay," Becca said, holding up both of her hands. "What the fuck is going on?"

"It's from *Yentl*," Stef explained. "My costume, remember?"

"Oh."

Pirate Dude laughed, light and airy. "My mom was a huge Barbra Streisand fan. I must have seen that movie a dozen times before I could walk."

"My mom was too!" Stef met his smile, and something deep inside of Becca tightened. They had a connection, Stef and this stranger, and as Becca gazed back and forth between them, she was suddenly, irrationally annoyed.

"It's like I've landed in musical-theater hell."

Pirate Dude paused for a second, unsure whether she was joking or serious, then his smile returned and he laughed again. "Good one!" He pointed at Becca while he spoke to Stef. "I like her. She's wicked."

Stef arched a brow. "You have no idea."

"I'm Cooper, by the way," he continued. "Friends call me Coop."

"Nice to meet you—" Becca paused before intentionally using his full name, "Cooper."

"Yes!" he cried as if she'd made the greatest joke in the world. "Wicked *and* quick. I love it."

As irritated as Becca was by Coop and Stef's instant connection, she realized that this guy, having been there longer, might actually know what was going on, so she tamped down her jealousy and forced a friendly grin. "So what's the deal with this audition? Have they told you anything? Like what we're supposed to be doing?"

"Not really, Wicked," Coop replied, cementing her nickname. "But I think we're on the short list."

"Becca," she replied, pretty sure she didn't want "Wicked" to stick. "And this is Stef."

"Becca," he repeated, then shook his head. "I think I like Wicked better."

"Me too," Stef murmured.

Becca pursed her lips. Years of snark were coming back to haunt her, and these were practically strangers. They hadn't even witnessed the full brunt of her assault.

"I heard someone say that the producers would be in soon to explain things," Coop said. "Until then, we just wait, I guess."

"Look," Stef said, her voice low as she nodded toward a small group of people on the far side of the room. Chatting with a guy and a girl in purple jumpsuits and bowl-cut wigs and a becloaked vampire with a stuffed bat taped to his shoulder was a Molly Mauler clone.

"I'm surprised she made it this far," Stef continued. "There aren't any other Painiac rip-offs in here."

"Hey!" Molly Mauler marched across the room toward them. "Did you just call me a rip-off, bitch?"

"Uh-oh," Coop muttered. "Arise. The queen approaches."

But Becca merely smiled as Fake Molly planted her hands on her hips before them. She loved a good fight.

"Which one of you said it?" Fake Molly demanded. "So I know whose ass to kick."

"I did," Becca lied, tilting her head to the side and regarding Fake Molly's costume with an air of extreme pity. Something about bullies brought out the best in her. "And I have to say, seeing you up close is even sadder. You have the most unoriginal costume in the room."

Fake Molly clearly wasn't expecting that response. She paused a moment, rattled, then gathered herself. "I have a personal connection to the Mauler."

Becca perked up. Five minutes past the gatekeepers and someone was laying the information she sought right at her front door? This seemed too good to be true. "Really?"

"My aunt's best friend's hairdresser was the real Molly Mauler, and I personally met her on three different occasions while staying with my aunt. I've earned the right to wear the Mauler."

"That literally makes no sense," Stef said.

Yeah, because it contradicts you. Despite her dislike of Fake Molly, maybe this was a chance to punch holes in Stef's theory? "But how do you know your aunt's best friend's . . . um . . ."

"Hairdresser," Fake Molly said with total confidence.

"Right." This was feeling less like a lead the further she dove in. "How do you know she actually was the Mauler?"

Fake Molly rolled her eyes. "Duh. Because her name was Molly. And she died like a month ago."

Becca snorted. "You think the Mauler used her real name?" Even Becca, who wanted to believe her, found that to be a stretch.

Fake Molly's clown-makeup'ed eyes narrowed. "You calling me a liar?"

"I'm calling you an idiot."

"You're just jealous."

If only. "Why haven't you gone to the FBI with this information? Or the Fed-Xers. I hear they're offering a huge reward."

"How would you know?" Fake Molly sneered. "Are you a spy or something?"

The idea that Becca was somehow secretly a member of a group that, should they even get wind of Stef's theory, would probably hunt her family down like a pack of rabid dogs, was so ludicrous that Becca literally burst out laughing.

"What's so funny?" Fake Molly snapped.

"Sorry," Becca said, wiping pretend tears from her eyes. "I didn't realize you were just doing your stand-up routine. Your delivery still needs work."

Fake Molly pressed her lips together, the effect made more noticeable by the heavy red and black makeup she wore. "You're on my list." Then she turned and stomped back to her group.

"Nicely played," a voice said, seemingly from nowhere, as Fake Molly rejoined her friends. Becca looked around, but the closest people to them were at least ten feet away and she was pretty sure the voice had come from . . .

"Down here."

Becca, Stef, and Coop dropped their eyes to the floor to find the green-clad Gumby guy curled up beneath the craft services table. Like literally curled up. Gumby Man rested on his chest, his face smiling up at them, while his body was curled back over his head so that his feet, facing forward, were planted firmly on either side of his cheeks, his hands lightly grasping his ankles. His hair was bleached blond, his eyes thin and smiling, and as Becca stared at him, trying to process exactly what she was seeing, he used the big toe on his left foot to scratch the end of his nose.

"What are you doing down there?" Coop asked.

"Really?" Becca said. "*That's* your first question?"

"I find it's best if I stay out of the way when I'm practicing chest stands," he said, grinning broadly. "Or people tend to trip over me."

Coop nodded. "Makes sense."

"Excuse me." Gumby waved his hands to indicate that he wanted them to back up. Becca, Stef, and Coop obliged, then watched dumbstruck as Gumby pushed himself up on his hands, walked out from beneath the table, then unravelled his knees and legs until he was fully upright in a handstand. With the same amount of control, he lowered his legs one at a time until they were flat on the ground again, then rolled his body up. He was short, maybe an inch taller than Becca's five feet and four inches, and incredibly slight of build, so thin that Becca was pretty sure her forearms were thicker than his thighs.

"Lars Togtokhbayar," he said, sticking his hand out in greeting. "I'm a contortionist."

Becca snorted. "You think?"

Coop grabbed Lars's hand and pumped it up and down. "You have got to teach me how to do that."

"Ooo," Lars cooed. "I do love a challenge." He stepped closer and put his hand on Coop's abs. "First things first, I should inspect—"

Before Lars could inspect anything, a huge roar erupted from somewhere outside, filtering into the soundstage through the open cargo door. It sounded as if thousands of people all screamed at once, and the first thought that ripped through Becca's mind was that the Fed-Xers had somehow broken through the police barricade and were about to storm Stu-Stu-Studio.

Apparently, she wasn't the only who had that thought. The room fell instantly silent, all chattering and movement ceasing as everyone turned toward the cargo door as if expecting an angry mob to rush through it at any moment.

The roar of the crowd waned, replaced by the wailing of sirens. A dozen or more. And while Becca was eyeing the walls of the soundstage, looking for additional exits in case they needed to make their escape, suddenly all the chaos outside went silent.

Then, as if on cue, a small group of men strode through the cargo bay door, silhouetted by the muted sunshine.

"Okay, everyone!" one of them said, clapping his hands sharply. "Can I have your attention?"

FOURTEEN

BECCA'S HEART RATE QUICKENED AS SHE WATCHED THE GROUP march across the soundstage. Seven, maybe eight of them. All men. She recognized the guy from the casting table and the dead-eyed clipboard drone from the door. The rest were dressed similarly—jeans and casual shirts.

All except one.

He walked in the center of the posse wearing a crisply tailored suit, dress shirt open at the collar, and though he was shorter than the rest of the dudes who surrounded him, he strutted with the kind of bravado that signified Alpha Male. There was something about the way he led with his hips that Becca respected. A cocky confidence of leadership and a swagger that suggested he not only enjoyed the attention, but he needed it in order to live, as necessary to his body as oxygen and water.

His suit was navy with a slight sheen, which he paired with burgundy shoes polished to within an inch of their lives, and his butter-yellow shirt enhanced the blond streaks in his slicked-back hair. A small smile hung about his lips, while his bright blue eyes scanned the room, not lingering on any one individual for longer than a nanosecond but seeming to take in everything all at once.

This has to be the guy in charge. Becca made a mental note as he stopped in the center of the room: Target Number One.

"First of all," he said in a voice both deeper and more commanding than Becca had expected, "I want to thank you all for coming out today. *Who Wants to Be a Painiac?* is a grassroots, fan-funded endeavor, and our ridiculously successful FundMyFun campaign plus the massive turnout for today's audition is proof that television audiences are craving this kind of entertainment."

A round of "absolutely" and "totally" rippled through the auditioners. Shiny Suit flashed them a winning smile of perfect, bleached teeth, and Becca wondered if he was willfully ignoring the massive Fed-Xer protest outside, or blissfully unaware of it.

"My name is Victor Merchant," he continued, then paused to let the effect of his name sink it.

Becca had been right. Victor Merchant, one half of Merchant-Bronson. The guy in charge and the one person who might actually know something about the original Painiacs. If there was anyone on the planet who could exonerate her mom from Stef's accusations, it was him, and immediately, Becca began formulating a plan on how to get him alone. Maybe she could corner him in the parking lot after the audition today? Or maybe he had an office in the building? If they had a lunch break, she could pull him aside and ask for a meeting.

Victor Merchant was the reason she was here. For the first time since she landed in Los Angeles, Becca felt like she just might be able to accomplish her goal.

Victor picked up after his dramatic pause. "You *may* have heard my name. I'm one of the executive producers of *Who Wants to Be a Painiac?,* conceptualized as a nonlethal game-show version of the events that transpired on Alcatraz two-point-oh. Thanks to the generous contributions of thousands of fans across the country, we are here today to pay homage to The Postman." He lifted his hands and began a slow golf clap. "Can we give ourselves a round of applause? It was you, the fans, who funded our campaign and made this possible."

Awkwardly, everyone began to applaud. Everyone but Stef.

"So here's how this will work," Victor said, cutting them off. "We're going to whittle this group down to between ten and twelve of you before we shoot the pilot. We'll have a few days of rehearsals here, but I want to get your costumes and personas locked down by tomorrow when we take a field trip over to the set, so we're going to do a little rejiggering of those now. When you leave here today, I want you to think about the original Painiacs, okay? What made them great. What made them addictive. We want to re-create that feeling . . ." He paused and pointed at Fake Molly. ". . . without copying it."

It was hard to tell with her thick layer of white clown makeup, but Becca was pretty sure that Fake Molly's face flushed.

The guy in the giant lizard costume opened the jaws of his mask wide, revealing his face. "Question!"

Victor turned to him. "Yes, lizard man."

"King Colossus," he said, patting his chest with a costumed claw hand, "and my partner, Prissy." Prissy curtsied, then giggled like a sugared-up tween, perfectly matching her schoolgirl costume.

Victor didn't look as if he particularly cared what their names were. "Your question?"

"Yeah," King Colossus said, gesturing to his partner. "So we're, like, trained in improv, mime, Meisner, kinetic movement, and practical aesthetics. Will we be, like, acting and stuff? Or is this gonna be more like *Survivor*?"

"Excellent question," Victor said. "I was just getting to that."

"Cool, dude."

Becca wasn't positive, but she thought she caught a whiff of weed drifting out of Colossus's costume. Was he hotboxing in there?

"So while this show is an homage to The Postman and Alcatraz two-point-oh," Victor began, "obviously there won't be any actual murder. Think of this more like *American Ninja Warrior* meets *American Idol*."

King Colossus laughed out loud. *"American Ninja Idol!"*

Victor shot him a glance. "Each week," he said while King Colossus practically disappeared into his costume beneath Victor's withering gaze, "you'll perform a series of fake kills, based on your Painiac persona. Fans will vote online for the favorites, giving spikes just like on The Postman. The Painiac with the least spikes is eliminated each week until we have a winner."

"And the winner gets?" Prissy asked, her voice as high and squeaky as her giggling suggested.

Victor flashed a huge, forced grin. "The winner gets a cash prize, plus the chance to come back next season. Those details are still being worked out and—"

"But it doesn't sound like we'll be acting," Prissy whined, then elbowed King Colossus in the ribs. "You promised me a real acting gig."

Victor sighed. "If you two will see me after today's rehearsal, we can discuss this privately, okay?"

King Colossus saluted, his tiny lizard arm only reaching as far as his chin. "Aye, aye, Captain."

"Now," Victor continued, "it's important that we keep everything that happens here top secret. The media will be desperate for inside information, which is why we had you sign a nondisclosure agreement with your audition paperwork. You cannot tell *anyone* about this show."

A beefy shirtless dude raised his hand. He wore a grotesque demon mask with spiked shoulder pads and wristlets, paired with what appeared to be billowy red pirate pants and a fake peg leg.

"Yes?" Victor pointed to him, sighing wearily. He hadn't opened up the room to questions, but King Colossus and Prissy seemed to have done it for him. "Space-pirate demon guy."

"I'm Mr. GWARnacle," he said, his voice muffled by the mask. "Like half pirate, half lead singer of GWAR."

Victor tilted his head to the side. "Is that a band?"

Mr. GWARnacle struck an air guitar chord. "Fuck yeah, it is."

Victor stared at him for a moment, eyes blinking slowly like he was trying to placate a tiger. "You have a question?"

"Hell yeah!" If nothing else, Mr. GWARnacle was enthusiastic. "Can I tell my girlfriend I have, like, a gig on a TV show?"

"That dude has a girlfriend?" Becca muttered. Stef elbowed her in the ribs.

"Sorry, no," Victor said.

"Like, I can't lie to her. I mean, our relationship is built on trust." On the word "trust," Mr. GWARnacle pounded his fist into the palm of his opposite hand, as if to emphasize the cornerstone of his relationship.

"As I was saying, the constraints of the nondisclosure agreement you signed prohibit acknowledgment of this show in any way. No social media. No mentioning to friends. No nothing."

"But—"

"Come talk to me after rehearsal, and we'll discuss."

Mr. GWARnacle shot Victor a thumbs-up. "Sweet."

A flash went off, accompanied by the fake shutter sound from a cell phone, as if someone had just taken a picture.

The posse of producers all tensed up, as Victor swung around toward the sound. "Who did that?"

A thin, gangly-limbed guy in a three-piece suit that appeared to be made entirely of newspaper, plastic garbage bags, and butcher's wrap held a cell phone in his trembling hands. "I . . ." he stammered. "I d-d-did."

"Who are you?"

He swallowed. "Recyclone."

"What?"

"Recyclone." Then without waiting to be asked, Recyclone pulled something from his shoulder that had been camouflaged by his patterned outfit. They were two round white balls, each attached to a rope, and with a flick, Recyclone turned on a blue strobing light within each ball. Then he spun them around in front of him, creating swirling cyclones of blue light.

"Get it?" Recyclone said. "I'm a recycling cyclone. Here to bring awareness to the world for the need to reduce our carbon footprint on the global—"

"Stop!" Victor roared.

Recyclone froze, arms to his side. The spinning balls of light smacked him in the head and stomach as they lost momentum.

"Thank you," Victor said, back to his composed self after the uncharacteristic outburst. "Will you see me after rehearsal as well?"

"Um, sure," Recyclone said, glancing around nervously. "I'm sorry. I didn't know we weren't supposed to take photos."

"No photos," Victor repeated, spinning around to face each of the other auditioners in turn. "The nondisclosure you signed also prohibits video from rehearsals. Understand?"

Dracula with a stuffed bat mounted on his shoulder raised his hand,

speaking simultaneously. "So who will the victims be? For our 'fake'"—
he used air quotes—"kills."

"We're still working that out as well," Victor said. "We'll discuss the
fine points tomorrow when we visit the set." He paused, his eyes zeroed in
on Becca. "When everyone needs to be in costume."

"Costume," Becca said, feeling her face burn as every single person in
the room turned to her and stared. "Right. Totally."

Fake Molly snickered with her friends. Whatever. Becca didn't give a
shit what these people thought. But maybe advice on her costume would
be a good excuse to have a conversation with Victor?

"And anyone who doesn't like the setup is welcome to walk away at
any time. Just come talk to me and we'll release you. Sound good?"

Victor scanned the crowd, expecting a response. A few people nodded,
and Becca heard one or two "yeahs," but that wasn't what Victor was
after. "I said, sound good?"

This time a big unison "Yeah!" exploded from all the potential
contestants.

"Great! Now let's get a look at these costumes."

Victor seemed mostly impressed with the costumes. He liked the sexiness
Mistress Distress, the dominatrix, brought to the show; could see the
spectacle of Sumo Sutra, the yoga-posing sumo wrestler; and appreciated
the British judge Lord Cancellor's use of a comically oversize mallet prop.
Victor had King Colossus and Prissy do their entire prerehearsed routine,
where King Colossus would terrorize the poor schoolgirl until she finally
jumped on his back and retaliated by beating his head in with her fists
until he lay motionless on the floor. Victor seemed to be mulling something over in his mind during their routine but said nothing afterward.

But Jax-in-the-Box, an ax-wielding dude wearing a brightly painted box with a pop-up lid that hung from shoulder straps proved to be somewhat problematic.

"What's your movement like in that thing?" Victor asked.

"Pretty good." Jax danced around in a circle, hopping from foot to foot while he waved his arms up and down through long slits in the sides of the box.

"Could you climb a rope ladder?"

Jax shrugged, pursing his clown-red lips. "I don't know. Maybe."

"A rope ladder?" Becca asked Stef. "What the hell is this show?"

"Does every thought you have need to come out of your mouth?" Stef asked.

Becca smiled. "Just the funny ones."

"Hm," Victor said. "Let me think on it." Then he turned to Coop. "But this . . . What are you?"

Coop's winning smile beamed with confidence. "I'm Captain Eyepatch, the Pirate."

Becca cringed at the name. Captain Eyepatch? It sounded like the host of a PBS Kids show.

"This looks like something a child would wear to school, and then the other kids would laugh at him until he cried." Victor shook his head, pitying the imaginary child. "Besides, we've got too many pirates. Kill it and bring me something different tomorrow."

Coop's face fell. "Oh, okay. Sure."

Becca had to agree with Victor. Coop's outfit was only slightly more impressive than something you'd buy in a bag at a seasonal Halloween store. She could even see the fold marks in his pants. She was pretty sure she'd seen other pirate riffs in the audition line—better, scarier, more original. So why was Coop the one who made it through? Becca scanned the room, looking at all the costumes. For the most part, they were a weird, uneven group, but there had been hundreds of costumed people in line this morning, most looking like they were trying out as extras on *The Walking Dead*. Surely those personas—chain-saw-wielding madmen, zombie cheerleaders, werebeasts of every shape and breed—would have been better options?

"This I love," Victor said, throwing his hands wide before Lars, who stood perfectly balanced on one leg while the other was wrapped around his head. "Human Gumby! Now tell me, how could you potentially kill someone?"

"I can wrap my legs around your neck and pop your head off with a single squeeze," Lars replied. Somehow, that surprised Becca not at all.

"Beautiful. Perfect. Sold." Victor applauded. "Also, you scare the crap out of me."

Lars unwound himself, smiling slowly. "Duly noted."

Next, Victor pointed to a set of twins. "Who are you?"

"The Wonder Twins!" they said in creepy twin unison.

"Yes, I know that," Victor said with a sigh. "Anyone with eyes and ten cents' worth of superhero knowledge can recognize Zan and Jayna. What are your names?"

The unison continued. "Kylie and Kayden."

Somehow, those names seemed to totally make sense, as the perfectly tanned twins looked like the offspring of a *Real Housewives* star.

"If you're going to do a superhero riff," Victor said, addressing the group, "give us something new. Something unexpected. What can Zan and Jayna do that no one would see coming?"

Kylie and Kayden looked at each other, bewildered.

"Kung fu?" Kylie suggested.

"Make out?" Kayden added.

"Um, ew?" This time Becca's voice wasn't so low.

"I agree with the girl who didn't bother to dress up," Victor said. "Ew. Ditch those costumes by tomorrow and come up with something fresh. But keep the twins theme. And remember, people: Your costumes need to have a potentially lethal element. If the killing was real, how would you do it?"

That was a thought exercise Becca didn't need to experience.

Lastly, Victor turned to Stef. "This nineteenth-century page-boy androgyny thing has got to go," he said, looking her up and down.

"I'm Barbra Streisand in *Yentl*," Stef volunteered. "The only woman to win—"

"Too long, didn't read," Victor interrupted. "Something new by tomorrow." His gaze shifted to Becca. "Do something with bigmouth here. A duo like the Hardy Girls."

Stef's jaw dropped. "What? No way. I—"

"Nine o'clock tomorrow morning," Victor said, breaking eye contact and intentionally cutting off Stef's protest. "Don't be late!" Then he marched toward the double doors that led back into the Stu-Stu-Studio lobby. "Demon pirate, giant lizard and friend, box guy, and recycling dude. Can I see you all upstairs in my office?"

FIFTEEN

DEE WATCHED THE VIDEO IN SILENCE, HER HAND CLASPED IN Nyles's beneath the kitchen table. It was footage of a long line of people, mostly dressed in outlandish costumes, stretching down the block and around the corner in a warehouse district somewhere in Los Angeles, judging by the palm trees.

In the background, the sound of muted chants mixed with blaring rock music and the cheers of a crowd. It could have been a familiar scene at a comic book convention or at Halloween, only this was neither.

Dee recognized many of the costumes, which sent shivers down her spine as her nightmares came to life. Gucci Hangman devoured by flames. Hannah Ball's blistered face. D.I.Ynona encased in hot wax. Molly Mauler's clownish costume and demonic makeup being ripped to gory shreds by a pack of ravenous wolves. Hell, there was even a woman in a baby-blue Cinderella ball gown, a long fake knife embedded in her chest as she re-created Dee's intended fate on Alcatraz 2.0.

The images would never, ever leave her mind. Nor would the shrieks. They woke her up at night, the excruciating wails of the dying, sometimes so realistic that Dee could swear she was still in Prince Slycer's maze being hunted down by a pack of psychopaths. The only decent nights' sleep she'd gotten since she left the island prison were the ones where she was heavily medicated, and even then the faces of dead Painiacs haunted her and she'd wake up panting, her fear palpable.

Dee knew that the dreams weren't real just like she knew the cosplay Painiacs on the video weren't the real things reincarnated. They were merely a line of TV-star wannabes waiting outside a studio in Burbank. But that didn't make the visuals any less disturbing.

"They're dead, you know," Nyles said softly, squeezing her hand. "The real ones. They aren't coming back."

"Aren't they, though? Coming back?"

Nyles's eyes drifted back to the video, where a Prince Slycer lookalike was brandishing a twelve-inch-long plastic carving knife, practicing his moves. "I sincerely hope not."

The video continued for what felt like an eternity, the line stretching on and on. It finally zoomed in on one girl—young, with light brown hair and weirdly out of costume in a plaid skirt, black tights, and a denim jacket. The camera held on her for a moment, her freckles coming in and out of focus on the screen, and then the girl rolled her eyes and said something to the cameraperson. The film stopped.

Dee let out a slow breath. "We should call Gris."

Griselda picked up her FaceTime call before the second ring.

"Can you fucking believe this bullshit?" she said, without even saying hi. Good old Griselda. Straight to the point.

"Unconscionable," Nyles said.

"And I only sent you one." Griselda raised her eyebrows. "There are at least forty of these floating around the Internet. With hundreds of thousands of views already."

Dee groaned, leaning her head on Nyles's shoulder. Between *Who Wants to Be a Painiac?* and the bounty the Postmantics had placed on their heads, Dee, Nyles, and Griselda would never see this nightmare end.

Griselda smiled, small but genuine. "You guys finally took my advice and got a room, huh?"

"If by that you mean a two-bedroom flat with Dee's dad and a small army of bodyguards down the hall," Nyles began, "then yes, Gris. We got a room."

"Sounds romantic."

"How are you?" Dee asked. She hadn't seen her friend since her first surgery, and though she and Griselda hadn't always gotten along, Dee owed her life in part to Griselda's bravery, hacking skills, and quick thinking.

"The usual," Griselda said with her characteristic nonchalance. "Half the world wants to kill me; the other half wants to fuck me. And New Jersey smells like the inside of a dumpster."

She smiled again as she said it, but even over the halting Wi-Fi connection, Dee could see that this one was strained.

"How is Ethan's great-grandma?"

Griselda shrugged. "She keeps referring to me as her granddaughter, and I can't tell if that's wishful thinking or dementia."

"A little of both, I would presume," Nyles suggested.

"There are photos of him everywhere." Griselda's eyes glinted, and she swallowed, forcing back emotion. She'd been hiding out with a cousin in Virginia, but insisted on going to visit Ethan's family alone, to tell them in person how he died and how he'd saved her life. And though Griselda had spent all her time on Alcatraz 2.0 rebuffing Ethan's attempts to play the boyfriend role, when he died, Griselda's grief had been genuine. Dee recalled how close she'd been to losing Nyles. She could only imagine what Griselda was going through.

"Anyway," Griselda said after a pause, snapping back into her old self. "This audition crap. What do we think?"

"I have to say, it was rather disturbing to see the Painiac fandom gathered in one place," Nyles said. "They do realize that those people were psychotic killers, yes?"

"Please." Griselda shook her head. "They're dressed like that *because* the Painiacs were psychotic killers."

Nyles pressed his lips together. "You'd think I could get a royalty on that term or something."

"The question is," Dee said, steering them back on topic, "is any of this illegal?"

"I'm a bit hazy on your legal system," Nyles said. "But I'd guess that there's nothing here to legislate."

"Just bad taste," Griselda said.

"What about the lawsuits?" Dee vaguely remembered some story about a retired football star who might have killed his ex-wife and had been acquitted of murder, but the family of his victim sued and made sure that he'd never capitalize on the crime. Wouldn't that same principle apply here in regard to all the wrongful death lawsuits that had been filed against The Postman's old company? "If PEI is profiting from this show, maybe a judge could shut it down?"

"According to the press release," Griselda said, "Merchant-Bronson is a third-party production company. Not affiliated with PEI."

"Does anyone really believe that?" Nyles asked.

Griselda shrugged. "The FBI seems to. There's some old cached info on the web linking The Postman's mailing address to one Merchant-Bronson had years ago, but that address is used by thousands of production companies as a mail forwarder. Not enough for a case."

"Merchant-Bronson." Ever since she'd first heard it on the ad, the name had sounded familiar, but Dee couldn't quite remember why.

"Yeah," Griselda said. "They're like a B-rate reality-TV prodco. Had a hit a few years ago with *Lend Me Your Ear*, but they haven't done anything since."

Dee stiffened. *Lend Me Your Ear.* Now she knew why the production company had sounded familiar. Her dad had worked on that show.

"Any chance you came across their name on Kimmi's laptop?" Nyles asked.

Griselda shook her head. "Sorry. Besides, the FBI has combed through that thing. If Merchant-Bronson came up anywhere, they'd know."

Dee sighed, uneasiness gripping at her stomach. "The Postman, or what's left of his organization, is behind this somehow. I feel it."

"You sure about what you saw that night?" Griselda asked. It wasn't the first time she'd asked, which was fair, since Dee hadn't been a terribly reliable narrator at the time, considering what she'd just endured, but she knew what she saw. And she knew what it meant.

"Positive," she said, without hesitation. "While we were waiting at the rocks to be rescued, Nyles kissed me. And right at the same moment, one of the crow cameras moved. Pointed right at us."

Later, after they'd been rescued, Dee had told first the police, then the FBI about this incident. She needed them to understand what that camera movement meant. Because it shouldn't have happened. Whatever the tabloids chose to believe, The Postman really was dead. Which meant there shouldn't be anyone else who could possibly have sent the command to rotate that camera.

The FBI had blown her off, blaming her supposed memory on pain and hormones, or the crow camera's movement to residual programming. But Griselda and Nyles had taken the news much more seriously. Only The Postman—or someone who had access to his system—could have overridden Griselda's computer control of the island, and both he and his daughter were dead. So who the hell had sent that camera command?

Griselda sighed. "I just . . . hoped."

"We have to face facts," Dee said, hoping her voice sounded strong even as her insides were twisted up in a Gordian knot of anxiety. "PEI didn't die that day on the island."

"That may be true," Nyles said, "but perhaps we should leave this to the authorities. After all we've been through . . ." His voice trailed off. "This isn't our fight anymore."

Dee wanted to agree with Nyles, knew it was the smart move, but she just couldn't. "Isn't it?"

"Dee, I—"

Dee shifted to face him. "Yes, all that we've been through. All that Ethan and Blair went through, too. Only, they weren't as lucky. We can't just sit here and let that happen to somebody else, Nyles. *I* can't let that happen."

Nyles winced. "Then we should tell the FBI. Let them handle it."

On the other end of the FaceTime call, Griselda snorted. "Good luck with that."

"If someone's out there," Dee said, "intent on resurrecting The Postman's work, we can't do nothing. Even if we're just being one hundred percent selfish. The Postmantics have a price on our heads, and the host of that game show shared an open invitation for us to show up at auditions. This isn't going to go away. Sooner or later, they're going to come for the Death Row Breakfast Club."

Just like they came for Monica. Could Dee live with more deaths on her head? Could she really do nothing if it meant people's lives were at stake?

Nyles would want her to. He was desperate to protect her. She had to get him on board.

"Besides, we're not really *doing* anything," she continued. "Just researching. That's harmless, right?"

Nyles's eyes pleaded silently with her for half a heartbeat before his shoulders sagged in defeat. "Where do we start?"

Dee clenched her jaw, dreading what came next. There were two options, actually. One was safe, and one made her stomach do backflips. She decided, for now, to go with the safe choice. "I think I know."

Nyles's head snapped around, his eyes wide. "What?"

Dee cast her mind back to a day long ago in the white room where Kimmi had held her captive for almost six days. During one of Kimmi's long interrogations, she'd asked Dee to come up with a list of things they'd do together as sisters. Dee—exhausted, starving, and no longer sure what the emotionally unhinged Kimmi wanted to hear—had suggested video games.

Kimmi's response had been quick and vicious: *I can do that with my brother.*

"Kimmi had a brother, remember?"

"That's right." Griselda sank her face into her hands. "Do you really think we're dealing with The Postman Jr.?"

The Postman had been a bloodlusting killer. His daughter had one-upped him by adding "sociopath" to the list of family attributes. What kind of monster would his son be?

"He's got to be the one behind this," Dee said. "The Postman didn't trust anyone but family. Kimmi had the passwords to Alcatraz two-point-oh command. It's safe to assume her brother does as well."

Nyles nodded slowly. "That would explain what you saw. But it doesn't help us figure out who he might be."

Nyles was right. If the federal government hadn't been able to ferret out The Postman's real identity, how could they?

"If we just had something to go on," Griselda said.

That was a stumbling block. What Dee and her friends *didn't* know about their former tormentor and his band of psycho killers dramatically outweighed what they did. The only one who'd had any insight was the one person she didn't want to ask.

Dee's body went rigid. No, wait. There *was* someone else. Kimmi, when she was posing as Mara, had shared information about one of the Painiacs as a way to gain Dee's trust. She said she'd figured out Molly Mauler's real identity. Could that have been true? Was Kimmi sharing real information? Dee couldn't remember the name Mara had mentioned, but she remembered the city and state. They both started with the letter *M*, just like Molly Mauler. Somewhere in Michigan . . .

"Marquette, Michigan."

"What?" Nyles asked.

"Molly Mauler was from Marquette, Michigan. At least that's what Kimmi told me."

"It's not much, but it's a start." Griselda's fingers flew over the keyboard. "I'll check in tomorrow. Hopefully I'll find something that will lead us back to The Postman."

"Gris?" Dee said, using her nickname for the first time. "Be careful, okay?"

Griselda glanced up at the camera and smiled. "You too, Princess. You too."

SIXTEEN

BECCA STARED AFTER VICTOR, SURROUNDED BY HIS TEAM OF assistants and the auditioners he'd asked to meet with, and realized that her chances of interrogating him today had just vanished. Which meant she needed to come back tomorrow.

Which means I need a costume.

"We need to find something to wear," Becca said, turning to Stef. "Like now."

"Like *how*?" Stef countered. Then dropped her voice. "And with what money?"

She had a point. They'd budgeted for three nights at the hostel, plus food, and a return ticket to Michigan. Costumes weren't exactly a luxury they could afford. "We'll figure it out."

"Mr. Merchant was right," Lars said, appraising Becca and Stef together as he stretched his right arm behind his head, pulling down on his elbow until the entire limb seemed to disappear into his skull. "You two should definitely be a couple."

"We're not a couple," Stef said quickly. Too quickly. Stef avoided Becca's eyes as she grabbed a handful of granola bars from the craft services table and shoved them in her backpack.

"I mean as an act," Lars said, clicking his tongue. "Those Wonder Twins can't be the only duo on the show."

The idea of doing a couples costume with Stef gave Becca a little flutter of excitement in her stomach, which she instantly suppressed. "We don't have a clue where to go shopping."

Lars raised a carefully manicured eyebrow. "Not from around here?"

"Not even close."

"You're in luck," Lars said, shepherding them toward the lobby. "I happen to know all the best costume shops in the Valley. If you don't mind schlepping with me on the bus."

"Thanks," Stef said, "but we don't—"

"Sounds good!" Becca certainly wasn't going to let Stef's suspicious nature turn down help from a local.

"Or," Coop said, scurrying to Lars's side, "I can drive. In exchange for help with my costume, of course."

Stef's jaw shifted as if she were chewing on a piece of gum; then she relaxed, letting her guard down. Once again, Becca felt an unwelcome pang of jealousy as she watched Coop's offer sway her slow-to-trust partner. "Okay," Stef said. "Sounds good."

Coop smiled broadly. "Sweet!"

"I love it when a squad comes together," Lars cooed, looping his arm through Coop's as the pirate led them out into the street.

Though the warring crowds of Fed-Xers and Postmantics seemed to have been on the edge of a riot just an hour ago, Becca would hardly have known it by the almost-deserted streets. The protests had dissipated, and as Coop led them down the block that had once held a carnival atmosphere and a never-ending line of auditioners, it felt as if they'd been transported to another world completely. The music was gone, as were the angry shouts and bullhorn crowd control. There were a few stragglers, of course. A camper was still parked across the street, lawn chairs and beer cooler packed back up inside while its owner probably slept off his buzz. At the far end of the street, the police were busy dismantling the barriers that had kept the two warring parties at bay, and beyond, Becca could see the last of the Fed-Xers, protest signs resting on their shoulders, as they trekked back to their cars. Discarded water bottles and food wrappers littered the streets, and the occasional trash can overflowed onto the sidewalk. It was as if a huge parade had marched through town, and the moment it ended, the crowds had vanished.

"This way," Coop said, gesturing around the corner, his voluminous pirate sleeve billowing in the breeze. The block was deserted except for one car, a massive black SUV with tinted windows and shiny chrome rims that glinted in the muted afternoon light. Coop pulled a key fob from his pocket, and the SUV beeped as he unlocked the doors.

When they'd arrived at Stu-Stu-Studio that morning, surrounded by protests and thousands of auditioners, Becca had thought her task might end up being herculean, but just hours later, she'd made it through to the second stage of auditions; had two new allies, one of whom had a freaking car; and had identified the person who might be able to give her the information she needed. All that, and she'd only made one mortal enemy in Fake Molly.

Not bad for a Wednesday.

Of course, she was about to get into a car with a total stranger in an unfamiliar city, and no one other than her sullen travel companion knew where she was. It was like points three through six on Ruth Martinello's Top Ten List of Things Never to Do.

What could possibly go wrong?

/\\

"This place is fantastic," Lars said as Coop pulled the monstrous SUV into a mini mall parking lot thirty minutes later. Lars slid out of the front seat, still wearing his green unitard, hood pushed back, and matching ballet flats. "It's all secondhand outfits from TV and film shoots. All kinds of crazy stuff, and pretty cheap."

"I like cheap," Becca and Stef said in near unison.

Lars draped a hand over each of their shoulders, guiding them toward the entrance. "Do you have any clue as to who or what you want to be?"

"Supergirl," Becca said, half joking.

Coop grinned as he held open the glass door. "Sexy Supergirl?"

"Eleanor Roosevelt," Stef countered, equally as tongue-in-cheek.

"Sexy Eleanor Roosevelt?"

Becca fake gagged. "I'll never get that image out of my head."

Lars frowned. "Superheroes are so passé, and Eleanor, bless her heart, had the fashion sense of a cloistered nun. You need something interesting and original. Fan out, grab whatever strikes your fancy, and do not, under any circumstances, listen to Coop."

Despite Lars's optimism, Becca and Stef weren't faring particularly well in their costume search. After an hour of poring over racks of clothing, the best they'd come up with was the nonsensical combination of prison jumpsuits and silver sneakers with a button on the back that released two retractable pairs of roller-skate wheels. They looked like off-balance carrots, which was a far cry from the Painiac-inspired personas Victor Merchant was expecting.

"I guess you could be like roller-derby ex-cons?" Coop suggested, eyeing the oversize boxy orange onesie skeptically as Becca tried to keep her balance on the skates.

"I like the roller-derby part," Stef said, steadying herself against a pillar. "Girl power, feminism."

Lars curled his upper lip. "But those orange onesies look like ass."

"Wait!" Coop shot to his feet. He was wearing a sequined white flared jumpsuit à la late-stage Elvis. "I've got it." Then he dashed deeper into the shop, reappearing moments later with colorful sequins draped over one arm and two blond wigs tucked under the other.

"Are those . . ." Becca squinted at one of the outfits. ". . . ice-skating costumes?"

"Close." Coop smiled broadly, displaying shining white teeth that were all perfectly straight and aligned. "They're from the *Dancing with the Stars* collection."

"And the wigs?"

Coop had Becca hold a lavender sequined dress in front of her, then pulled one of the wigs over her head. "Okay, go with me. Disco Derby Dolly Parton."

Lars leaped to his feet, throwing his arms wide to Coop. "Marry me?"

"No way I'm wearing that," Stef said, backing up.

"But you'd look amazing!" Coop cried.

"No means no."

Coop frowned. "If she's Wicked, then you're Buzzkill."

Lars picked up a pink minidress and twirled around. "I'm completely on board with this."

"Then you wear them," Becca said.

"I wish!" Lars shook his head. "Alas, no walk-throughs in one of these."

"You could be Wicked and Buzzkill," Coop said, refusing to give up. "The Disco Dollies."

"Yes!" Lars hissed. "It's got sex and sociopathic tendencies. I bet Victor Merchant would totally go for this."

That was the one thing that might get Becca to wear these horrible outfits. "You think?"

"I *know*." Lars beamed. Then his face dropped. "Wear them or we can't be friends."

Meanwhile, Coop had gathered up the pile of clothes, wigs, and accessories, and headed to the register. "Meet me at the front."

Stef watched him go, the space above her nose wrinkling up in worry. "Are you sure this is going to work? What if Victor hates it?"

Lars sighed. "Just trust Uncle Lars, okay? I spent six years in a Russian circus. I know what sells."

Becca slipped her phone out of her pocket and checked her bank balance while they slowly walked to the front of the store. She'd just be able to cover the costume, but that would only leave enough for two more nights at the hostel and no meals. Stef was right: What the hell were they going to do then?

"Coop," Becca said, hurrying toward the counter, where the checker was ringing up Coop's purchases. Maybe they could get by without the wigs. "We'd better look through that before—"

"Hey!" the clerk said, looking up at Becca from the register. She was probably Coop's age, with a thick fringe of hot-pink hair and a tattoo that said "Can't Touch This" scrawled across her collarbone. "Did you just come from the Painiacs audition?"

Becca glanced around to make sure the clerk was talking to her. There was no one else nearby. "Um . . ." Yes? No? Maybe? What was the correct answer?

"I saw you," the clerk continued. "On YouTube."

Becca went rigid. "What?"

"Yeah. Some undercover Fed-Xer filmed the audition line." She raised a ring-pierced eyebrow. "You were the last shot. Kinda looked like you were in on it with the camera person."

Holy shit. "Excuse me," Becca said, spinning around. Stef was still talking to Lars by the dressing room, and the look on Becca's face as she stormed up to them must have been epically ragey because the contortionist threw his hands up in front of his face, shielding himself from her temper.

"I didn't do it!" he said, cowering.

"Not you." Becca grabbed Stef's arm and dragged her back into the vacant dressing room.

"What the fuck?" Stef said, shaking Becca off.

"That's my line." Becca was breathing heavy, barely containing her anger. "I thought we had a deal."

Stef dropped her voice. "What are you talking about?"

"I promised to share whatever info I might find on the original Painiacs," Becca said, feeling only a passing twinge of guilt as she recalled that she had absolutely no intention of following through, "and you promised not to share your theory about my mom with anyone else."

"I haven't."

"But you did post that video from this morning."

Stef hesitated for a moment, her bravado faltering, then shrugged. "That's not a violation of our agreement."

"The clerk recognized me!" Becca hissed, trying to keep her voice down. "What if someone else does? What if your Fed-Xers put two and two together—"

"They won't."

"You don't know that!"

"Okay, fine!" Stef cried, her self-control abandoned. "Fine. I'll take the video down."

"And no more of that bullshit," Becca said, narrowing her eyes. "Or our deal is off."

Stef met her gaze steadily. "As long as you keep up your end of the bargain," she said, as if she knew that Becca was lying, "I'll keep up mine."

"Yeah," Becca said as she followed Stef out of the dressing room. "We'll see about that."

"Here." Coop shoved a bag into Becca's hands as she returned to the counter. He'd changed out of the Elvis getup and had a second shopping bag tucked under his arm.

"What's this?"

"Your shit." Coop was smiling like a crazy person, all wide and loony.

Stef was instantly flustered. "Oh, thanks, but, um, we need to pay for these."

Coop's grin only widened as he held up a long receipt. "Taken care of."

"Seriously?" Becca felt as if a weight had been lifted.

"Seriously."

The panic of being stranded in LA without enough money ebbed, and though Becca didn't love the idea of owing a favor to an almost-perfect stranger—especially one that had been flirting with Stef—letting Coop pay for their costumes seemed like less of a bad idea than going hungry. "Thank you!"

Stef, on the other hand, clearly wasn't seeing it the same way. "We . . ." she began. "I mean, I can't."

He turned his back on her, heading toward the door. "I'm not taking your money."

"But—"

"Ladies," Lars said, escorting them to the car. "Just let the boy pay for them, okay? I promise I won't let him take advantage of you."

Coop gave Lars a quick salute. "Thank you, sir."

Lars snuggled against Coop's arm as they strode back to the car. "However, I can't promise that *I* won't take advantage of *you*."

"Aw." Coop smiled. "That's the sweetest thing anyone's ever said to me."

THE CAST HAS BEEN CHOSEN

1,645,982 likes

tristan_mckee THE CAST HAS BEEN CHOSEN! Today's auditions were epic, a massive turnout of Postmantics, and the cast has been whittled down, to be revealed on our big live show December 20th! But YOU CAN GET EARLY ACCESS TO THE FUN! How? Go to FundMyFun.com/whowantstobeapainiac and register for a special sneak preview. You don't want to miss this!
#painiacs #whowantstobeapainiac #auditions #realitytv #merchantbronson #realitynetwork #thepostman #postmantics

4 MINUTES AGO

RECENT ACTIVITY

genesisjen OMG I can't wait!

jiwoo_s Registering now. NOW.

wicked_josh PICS OR IT DIDN'T HAPPEN

snowqueenwinter AAAAA!!!!! So jealous of all the new cast members. Can I be your new best friend? All of you?

melissa_ngo Any hints? I'm hoping that Godzilla/schoolgirl pair made it. They looked amazing.

dominojoe So fast? No callbacks or anything? There had to be 2000 people in line today. You cut it down like that?

oregonmadame Can't wait to see how this is gonna work. Like America's Got Talent but with murder?

....

skye_v @oregonmadame No real murder, remember?

....

thegriff Like there was ever "real" murder. #DontTrustTheFeed #WideAwakeEyesOpen #FakeNews #ThePostmanAlive

....

darkness_falls @thegriff Do you ever shut up?

....

ADD A COMMENT

SEVENTEEN

THE STRAINED SILENCE WAS STARTING TO WEAR ON BECCA.

It was actually kind of depressing to share a room, share a costume, share this whole insane experience with someone and not talk to them. Their argument in the dressing room had been the last words they exchanged in over sixteen hours—total silence since Coop had dropped them off at the hostel—and even though Becca was still pissed off about the video Stef had posted, when Stef buttoned her jacket up to her neck and shivered against the slight chill as they walked to Stu-Stu-Studio the next morning, Becca seized the opportunity to break the tension.

"Come on," she teased. "This is like a warm spring day in Escanaba."

She'd expected Stef to ignore her, but perhaps the silence was stressing her out too. Instead of a rebuff, Stef half smiled. "I didn't grow up there. Last winter was my first."

Finally! A glimpse at Stef's past! "Where were you before that?"

Stef paused, and Becca knew she was debating whether or not to let Becca into her tightly guarded world. Whether Becca had earned her trust or she was just tired of maintaining her fortress walls, Stef finally loosened up. "Austin."

"Texas?"

"Yep." She paused again, then added, "I really miss good Mexican food."

Becca laughed. "What, the Taco Bell in Escanaba not doing it for you?"

"Barf," Stef said. Another pause, like she had to gear herself up each time she shared a piece of her past. "My mom used to make the best arroz con pollo."

Becca wasn't sure what that was—although she did recognize the word for chicken—but Stef's Spanish was perfect, just like Mateo's mom's. "Sounds yummy."

"Yeah. I . . . I miss it."

"I'm sorry." *I miss her* was how Becca translated Stef's words. She hadn't missed the fact that Stef had spoken about her mom twice in the past tense. Maybe a dead mom was something they shared? Becca was about to ask a follow-up question, when she felt her cell phone vibrating in her jacket pocket. Becca pulled it out and saw the word "Mom" plastered across the screen.

"Shit," she said.

"Who is it?"

By way of answering, Becca swiped the call and held her phone up to her ear. "Hey, Mom."

"Hi, sweetie. Are you having fun?"

"Oh yeah," she said, trying to sound perky as she lied through her teeth. "The base is perfect. Wet and powdery all at the same time. Did, like, a dozen runs yesterday." God, she hated lying to her mom. It felt so dirty after all they'd been through recently.

"I'm so glad. Honey, something's come up."

Becca swallowed. If her mom needed her to come home right away, this whole charade would implode. "What's wrong?"

"It's Tabitha. Her cancer's taken a turn for the worse and she has no one to help her."

"Oh no," Becca said, not sure where her mom was going with this. Was she going to have to fly out to Arizona? "That's awful."

"Your mom would have gone to her in a heartbeat," Rita said. "And I feel like I need to be there in her place."

"Of course."

"I'm taking Rafa with me. But we're not flying home until the twenty-fourth. Do you think you can stay with Jackie until then? I don't want you at the house alone after the break-in."

Becca let out a slow, silent breath. In case she got delayed in Los Angeles, this gave her a few extra days before she had to be home. She couldn't have planned it better if she tried. "Yeah, of course. It'll be fine."

"Are you sure?"

"Absolutely."

"Okay." She could hear her mom exhaling on the other end. "I'm sorry we won't be together as a family until Christmas Eve."

"It's okay."

"I love you, Becks."

"Love you too, Mom."

When Becca shoved her phone back into her pocket, she expected Stef to ask what the call was about, but instead she was staring at the ground. Her mood had shifted—tentatively chatty Stef had regressed to the sullen reticence Becca had gotten to know so well.

"My mom has to go to Arizona," Becca said, hoping she could recapture the lightness that had existed between them before the interruption. "That's just like a state away, and she doesn't even know I'm here. Crazy, right?"

No response. Becca had no idea how it had happened, but Stef's protective walls had slammed back down into place.

"What's going on with you?" Becca asked, unwilling to return to their status quo.

"Nothing," Stef replied quickly. Which of course meant *something*.

"Bullshit."

Stef pressed her lips into a thin line, a mix of annoyance and contemplation. "Why are you here?"

Not the response Becca was expecting. "You answered my question with a question."

"Are you going to answer it?"

Becca sighed. The battle of wills was exhausting. "You know why I'm here."

Stef stared straight ahead. "You said you wanted to prove me wrong." She paused, the furrow between her brows deepening. "But what if you find evidence that I'm right? What are you going to do then?"

Now it was Becca's turn to go quiet. The real answer was *I'll destroy it*, but she wasn't about to tell Stef that, especially since she'd promised that Stef would get her reward. "Then you'll have your proof," she said, anger seeping into her words. "And you can claim that Fed-Xer reward. Isn't that why *you're* here?"

As usual, Stef ignored Becca's question. "But what about your family? If you handed me proof and I claim that reward, you know someone's going to come after all of you."

Duh. "No biggie," Becca lied. "We'll move. Change our names. At least we'll know it's coming."

Stef's eyes flashed toward Becca's face. They held suspicion, confusion. Stef didn't believe a word out of Becca's mouth, which meant if there *was* evidence, Becca had to find it first.

Suddenly, her quest to exonerate her mom and protect her family had become a race.

Becca had expected the streets around Stu-Stu-Studio to be quiet when they arrived that morning, but the raucous shouts of diehard protesters met them as soon as she and Stef rounded the corner. There were significantly fewer of them today—two dozen max, cordoned off behind police barriers at the far end of the block and supervised by four cops who looked bored, at best, by their assignment—but what the Fed-Xers lacked in numbers they made up for in enthusiasm, chanting and jeering as Becca approached the main door. One protester even attempted to spit at her, and despite the fact that he was too far away to hit his target, the look of abject hatred on his face as he hocked that loogie made Becca pause with her hand on the door. That guy wanted to kill her. She could see it in his eyes.

Before she could recover from the shock, the door to Stu-Stu-Studio was pushed open from the inside by a young guy with a clipboard and a thick, curly mop of black hair.

"Name?" he asked unceremoniously, perusing his clipboard.

Becca pushed aside her encounter with the irate Fed-Exer. She had a job to do. "Becca Martinello," she said, watching to see if he gave any hint that the name meant something to him. He didn't.

"And Stef Ybarra."

"Check and check." He pointed them down the hall that led to the soundstage. "Take the stairs at the end to the second-floor dressing rooms. Vic wants everyone in costume by nine thirty. And remember, no cell phones downstairs. Leave them in your room."

"No cell phones," Becca repeated, wondering how Victor Merchant would feel about this dude referring to him as Vic. "Got it."

A door at the end of the hallway opened to a set of concrete stairs. Unlike the soundstage, which had been power-blasted to a sheen, the stairwell was dusty, the scent of mold and damp heavy in the air, as if it hadn't been used in years. The large windows had been papered over and the masking tape that seamed the yellowing butcher's wrap together was brittle and peeling with age. But what it lacked in ambiance, the upper floors of Stu-Stu-Studio apparently made up for in structural integrity. The Fed-Xers must have been just outside that end of the building, yet from inside, Becca couldn't hear their protest at all.

The stairs continued to a third story above, and Becca immediately spotted the casting guy from yesterday, hanging out on the upper landing. Which probably meant that Victor Merchant was inside.

That must be his office.

"This way," Stef said, tugging at her arm as they reached the second floor. Becca had unconsciously moved toward the next flight.

"Right," Becca said, forcing a smile. She didn't want Stef to know what she was planning: how to get an audience with Victor Merchant.

The hallway didn't look particularly Hollywoodesque, more like a generic office building with hard fluorescent overheads running its length, and four doors on the left, facing the street. As she passed the first room, Becca saw that it had been furnished with portable makeup vanities—high square wooden tables and an attached mirror rimmed with large lightbulbs.

Three cast members were already prepping themselves inside. Even out of their Wonder Twins costumes, Becca recognized Kylie and Kayden, with their almost-identical builds and height and matching pixie cuts—shaggier on him, sleeker on her—of their dark blond hair. The third station was occupied by an African American girl about Becca's age, applying moisturizer to her face. Her sleek hair was pinned into two donut-shaped buns on each side of her head, and though Becca was pretty sure she didn't recognize this girl's face, there was something familiar about her that Becca couldn't quite put her finger on.

"Let's try the next one," Stef said, nodding down the hall. "We'll need two diva stands."

"Diva stands?" Becca asked. "Is that what they're called?"

As she spoke, the girl with the buns craned her head toward them. Her eyes widened in recognition, then narrowed.

"Look who's back," she said. "I put money on you not making it past the Fed-Xers downstairs."

Her face may have been hidden behind a mask of clown makeup yesterday, but Becca knew the voice instantly. Fake Molly.

Kylie leaned forward to see through the doorway. "You owe me twenty bucks, Fiona."

Becca felt Stef's hand on her arm. "I think I hear Lars." Like yesterday, she was keen to avoid a confrontation.

Becca? Not so much. Though intellectually she knew that picking a fight with a cast member wasn't a good idea, her basic programming didn't allow Becca to let shit go. "You mean you *hoped* we wouldn't," she said, shoulders square. "The only way you and the Wonder Twins here are going to get cast is if the rest of us bail."

"It's too bad this isn't actually Alcatraz two-point-oh," Fiona replied. "Or I'd show you exactly how much I belong here."

"As predator or prey?" Becca asked.

"Do I need to remind you who I'm connected to?"

Becca laughed. "Your aunt's boyfriend's cousin's dry cleaner's florist's neighbor? That's a total fucking joke."

Fiona's nostrils flared. "Look who's talking about being a joke. Did you manage to come in costume today?"

"Come *on*." Stef tugged Becca firmly, backing her into the hall. "We don't have time for this."

"See you downstairs, Fake Molly." Becca waved sweetly as she retreated, hoping that nickname would stick.

"It took you exactly one day to pick up an enemy," Stef said under her breath as they poked their heads into the next room, where Sumo Sutra was lacing Mistress Distress into her corset.

"More like one hour," Becca said, correcting her.

"Is that normal for you? Or did Fiona's Molly Mauler story get under your skin?"

"Not even close." Becca wasn't sure that was entirely true, but she certainly wasn't going to let Stef think her theory had any sway.

"Darlings!" cried a familiar voice as they arrived at the last door on the floor between the ladies' room and an emergency exit. Lars was doing a handstand against the wall, his legs fanning from vertical to horizontal and back again. "You made it."

Aside from the four diva stations and the garment rack, there wasn't much to their dressing room. The windows were papered over like the ones in the stairwell, allowing in a glow of natural light. The room had probably been an office at one point in time. There were phone jacks and networking outlets on each wall, meant to accommodate at least three different desks, and wedged into the corners on the dirty tile floors were remnants of the room's past: paper clips, misshapen staples, a pushpin from a corkboard.

Coop poked his head out from behind one of the diva stands. "You'd better hurry. They want us downstairs in thirty minutes."

"We saved these spots for you." Lars pointed to the two empty makeup stands with his foot. "Had to fight off the dominatrix and that judge dude. But I might have enjoyed that."

"Thanks, guys." Becca dumped her bag on the floor beside one of the diva stands. Then she grinned at Stef. "See? I don't piss off everyone I meet."

Stef rolled her eyes. "Just seventy-five percent of us."

Lars kicked his feet off the wall and curled down into a standing position. "I brought you some makeup. If you're going to be Dolly, you need to *be* Dolly." He pulled a plastic bag from beneath his makeup stand and handed it to Stef. "Just some extras I had at home."

"Eye glitter," Stef said, riffling through. "Body glitter, lip glitter, lipstick, lip gloss, lip stain, and liquid liner in three different shades."

Becca arched an eyebrow. "That's just your extras?"

Lars grinned. "Jealous?"

Stef poured the contents out on her table. "I don't think I know how to use any of this."

Lars sucked in a quick breath and looked as if he was about to cry. "I'll help you. Let me help you? Please, please, pretty please?"

Stef's eyes grew wide in genuine terror. "I don't think—"

But Lars wasn't taking no for an answer. He steered Stef toward the nearest diva station and plopped her down in her director's chair. "Just relax and let it happen. Time to Dolly-fy!"

EIGHTEEN

"HEY," GRISELDA SAID, THE MOMENT DEE ANSWERED HER FaceTime call. "Nyles there?"

Dee shook her head. "He's meeting with his attorney about his parents' estate."

"Don't you mean his solicitor?" Griselda said with a fake British accent. Then she cracked up.

After all they'd been through, Dee truly appreciated how Griselda managed to keep things light. "So did you find anything?"

In answer, an alert popped up on her iMessage.

"That is the obituary of one Ruth Martinello," Griselda said. "In the *Mining Journal* of Marquette, Michigan."

Dee tried to stay calm as she opened the file. There was no photo, just a short entry stating that Ruth Martinello, forty-three, of Marquette, Michigan, died after she lost control of her car on the highway and crashed into a tree. But it was the date that caught her eye. "November thirteenth?"

"Yep."

Just three days after Molly Mauler's death on Alcatraz 2.0. But there were probably hundreds of deaths around that time, even in Michigan. "That doesn't necessarily mean it's her."

"Keep reading."

Dee's eyes raced down the column. Ruth Martinello didn't have much going on, apparently. Other than her death, the obituary merely noted that she was a stay-at-home mom and was survived by her wife, Rita, and children, Rebecca and Rafael. "What am I looking for?"

"Rebecca Martinello," Griselda explained, "who goes by Becca, is a senior in high school."

Just like I'm supposed to be. It was hard not to be bitter when she thought that Molly had tried to murder a girl who was the same age as her daughter.

"And Becca has an Instagram feed," Griselda continued.

Another ding on her iMessage delivered a web link that opened to the Instagram page of Becca Martinello.

It was mostly photos of other people—soccer games of a boy, younger than they were, who might have been the brother mentioned in the obituary. Two friends popped up frequently, tagged as Jackie Orachevsky and Mateo Jimenez, and there were pictures of other cities—New York, San Francisco, Seattle—that looked too professional, as if they'd been downloaded from a travel website. Finally, there was an untagged photo of a girl.

She was white, her skin pale with a stripe of freckles across her nose and cheeks. Her hair was light brown, cut shoulder length, which she wore parted down the middle and tucked behind each ear, and her eyes were bluish gray, pale like her skin, and with a tug of sadness at the corners.

"You've seen her before," Griselda said.

"I have?"

"Yep."

Dee furiously tried to remember. The hair, the freckles, the pissy look on her face. Yeah, they were kind of familiar. Where had she seen them?

It must have been recently. But she sure as hell hadn't been in Marquette, Michigan, and unless Becca had been in Los Angeles . . . "Oh shit."

"You remember?"

Dee quickly pulled up an Internet browser and began to type. "That video you sent yesterday. The one from the TV auditions."

"Exactly," Griselda said. She smiled as a clacking from the other end signaled that Griselda was hard at work. "Don't bother looking for it. The user took it down, but not before I downloaded it."

Another message popped up with a link, and Dee muted her player as the video rolled, keeping her thumb poised over the trackpad as the camera panned down the street at all the costumed auditioners.

"One minute and thirty-three seconds," Griselda said.

Dee scrolled ahead. Near the end of the video, the camera zoomed in on a girl not in costume. She immediately paused the playback. "Holy shit."

"Yep," Griselda said. "Ruth Martinello's daughter auditioned for *Who Wants to Be a Painiac?*"

"I knew something was dirty about that show." Dee clenched her jaw as she compared the Instagram selfie to the face on the video.

"If she really is Molly's daughter," Griselda said slowly, "that means the show has got to be connected to The Postman. Somehow."

"We should tell the FBI." It was the smart thing to do, putting this information in the hands of the authorities and letting them deal with it. But so far, the FBI had seemed less than interested in Dee's input, and she seriously doubted this would be any different.

Griselda nodded. "On it."

Dee leaned back against the wall of pillows that separated her from the headboard. The morning she and Nyles and Griselda had been airlifted off Alcatraz 2.0, she'd truly believed that the nightmare was over, and that Kimmi and her family would never again inflict pain and suffering upon her and those she cared about. That had been six weeks ago. Six weeks, and the horror was back, lurking around her in the darkness, waiting to pounce.

Only this time, Dee wasn't going to be the victim. She wouldn't be taken unawares. She wouldn't stumble upon her sister's dead body. She wouldn't be blindsided or railroaded through a sham trial. This time, she was going on the offense.

"Gris," she said, almost dreading the words that were about to come out of her mouth. "We need to be prepared for them not to believe us."

"Then what do we do?"

There was one more option, one more lead that Dee had been avoiding. She thought of her dad, who was making breakfast in the kitchen. Several months after Kimmi had been convicted of kidnapping a ten-year-old Dee—then known by her real name of Dolores—Dee's dad had picked her up from school and announced that they were leaving their home in Manhattan Beach, changing their names, and starting new lives. Dee wasn't allowed to talk to her old friends, to use her old name, or to tell anyone who she had been.

The reason behind the drastic life change had always confused Dee. The trial was over. Kimmi was locked up. Why did they need to move? Her dad would never say, and eventually, Dee had given up trying to figure it out.

Until six weeks ago on Alcatraz 2.0, when Kimmi had made it all very clear. *Daddy went to talk to your dad a few months after my trial ended. . . .*

That would have been the exact time that Dee's dad uprooted their lives. Kimmi's father—The Postman—had offered Dee's dad money to buy the rights to the story of her kidnapping. Which meant her dad had direct contact with The Postman.

Was that how it had all happened in the first place? Had Dee's dad been working for The Postman on one of his shows? Had he been one-half of Merchant-Bronson?

Only one way to know.

"There's one person who might know The Postman's real identity," she said slowly.

Griselda stared hard at the camera, then seemed to understand. "Do you think he'll tell you?"

I doubt it. "I don't know, but he's the best shot we have."

Dee crutched down the narrow hallway of the condo, pausing at the end, where it opened up to the main living space. Javier sat at the dining room table, sorting through a pile of mail that must have been forwarded from their Burbank house, while her dad stood in front of the six-burner stove, humming atonally to himself.

He had three different pans going, and though Dee couldn't see their contents, she knew exactly what each contained: one large frying pan for the crumbled sausage, a smaller one for sautéing vegetables, and a third, probably still empty, for the omelet. Her dad scurried around the kitchen, giving a few moments of attention to each pan, then returned to a large bowl of eggs that he whisked with reckless abandon.

"Hey, Javier." Dee smiled as she leaned forward on her crutches.

"Good morning, Miss Guerrera," he said formally. "How are you feeling?"

"Better," Dee said. Her usual answer. Then she dropped her voice. "Do you think you could give me a minute with my dad?"

Without hesitating, Javier nodded his head, whisked the unsorted portion of the mail back into a large bag, and disappeared through the front door into the condominium's exterior hallway.

"Did Javier go out?" her dad called from the kitchen. "I'll have his omelet ready in a sec."

Dee sighed as she hobbled to the kitchen. She'd done everything she could to avoid this moment. But it was her only option, and it couldn't wait.

She forced her lips to move. "Can we talk?"

"Sure." He didn't face her, keeping his focus on the onions and peppers sizzling on the stove top. "What's up?"

There was no simple way to ask, but instead of leading with *Tell me who The Postman was*, Dee decided to ease into the topic.

"Remember back when we lived in Manhattan Beach?" she started, trying to sound more like a nostalgic teen and less like an FBI interrogator.

"Of course."

"You worked on a show. . . ."

He snorted. "I worked on a lot of shows, DeeDee."

"Right, but you worked on a game show where contestants had to guess a popular song in as few notes as possible." Was it her imagination, or did her dad's entire body just tense up?

"I worked on a lot of shows," he repeated, his voice not quite as light and airy as before. "I don't really remember—"

"Wasn't it called, like, *Lend Me Your Ear* or something?"

He shrugged, focusing intently on the sausage pan.

"It was a Merchant-Bronson production," Dee said, pronouncing the name very carefully. "Wasn't it?"

He didn't answer, just continued to move the sizzling meat around in the pan absently, like a person whose mind was far away.

If Dee needed confirmation that Merchant-Bronson was somehow tied to The Postman, this was it. "Dad . . ." She paused, taking a deep breath. "Who was The Postman?"

She watched him closely, his back and half profile. He'd switched to the pan of vegetables, dabbing at the onions and peppers gently as if Dee had simply asked what day of the week it was or when breakfast would be ready. But Dee knew her father well; she recognized the tension in his stiffened back and the hard line that had appeared around the corner of his jaw. Her dad was desperately trying to remain calm, but inside, he was wrestling with a response.

"He was a madman," he began at last, "who conned a nation and made a fortune off his own bloodlust. And now he's dead."

He said the last line with finality, as if that would end the conversation. Normally, Dee would have taken the cue and let it go, but she couldn't. Not this time.

"What was his name?"

"Do you want cheese *in* your omelet?" he asked.

"Dad . . ."

"Or on top with chile?"

"Dad!"

Dee's voice was sharp, angry, and her dad spun around. The pinched look on his face betrayed the casualness of his tone, and Dee realized she wasn't the only person in the room who was upset.

"Let it go, Dolores." He hadn't used her real name in years. "I mean it."

Anger wasn't going to help, but she needed her dad to understand how serious the situation was. "Dad, I know you're trying to protect me. That you've been trying to do so since the day I escaped from the white room. I know you blame yourself for what happened."

She'd never spoken those words before because she knew the impact they'd have. Her dad flinched, whipping his face to the side as if he'd been slapped.

"I know you've seen the stuff about this game show on the news. *Who*

Wants to Be a Painiac?" Her upper lip curled as she said it, her face unable to hide her revulsion at the name.

"That has nothing to do with you," he said quietly.

"But it does," she pleaded. "Don't you see? It's a Merchant-Bronson production."

Her dad's sadness turned to frustration. "You've been talking to Griselda again, haven't you?"

"Yes." No point in denying it. "We saw a video from the auditions, and, Dad, I know you want me to stay out of this, but something's going on. Something dangerous."

"Great." He clapped his hands and walked over to the ancient wireless phone mounted on the wall of the kitchen. "We'll just call up the FBI and fill them in so they can deal with it."

"Dad—"

"The FBI, Dee. That's their job. Not yours. Your job is to go to high school, then college." His eyes teared up, his jaw trembling as his voice caught in his throat. "To grow up and live a long time and never, ever put your father in the position of having to lose his . . . his only child. I already buried your mom and your stepsister. I won't bury you, too."

A sob racked Dee's body. Since her arrest, her dad had been hiding his emotions, burying them deep so he could stay strong for his daughter. After the trial, Dee had doubted that her dad believed in her innocence, but her lack of faith was unfounded. Her dad had *always* believed in her, tried to help her even after her conviction, and never given up on proving that Dee had been framed. He'd sacrificed so much for her, and now Dee realized that the idea of giving this—this piece of information she so desperately needed—was too much. His emotional strength had abandoned him, and as her dad rounded the table, kneeling at her feet, the tears she'd never seen came pouring down both cheeks.

"He's dead," she said, repressing a sob. "I killed him."

"I know."

"I'm not afraid. He can't hurt me now." She felt like a hypocrite saying it, since the nightmares of Kimmi and The Postman that plagued her sleep proved her fear was as real as it had ever been, but she needed her dad to believe her. To trust her. "What he started . . . This show. People might be in real danger, and I can't let—"

"I won't do it, DeeDee," he said, cutting her off.

"But—"

"I can't lose you."

"I'm still here," Dee pleaded. "I'm still alive."

His eyes flitted to her leg, bound and stapled together from multiple surgeries.

"Enough!" He slammed his hand down on the tile floor then rose to his feet. "I will do everything in my power to keep you safe, DeeDee. And that includes taking that man's name to the grave." Then he turned toward the stove. "Now, do you want chile and cheese on this, or what?"

BELTWAY BULLETIN

POLITICS—US Edition
December 19, 9:01 am ET

Xanthropoulost

by Adrienne Quiñones

It's day two of the presidential impeachment trial and in a total shock to all present, Gavin Xanthropoulos—star witness against the president—was scratched at the last minute from the witness list due to the fact that he appears to be missing.

While the House managers asked for a recess—granted until tomorrow by the chief justice—the president's legal team left the Senate chamber with a bounce in their step and smiles on their lips. A bullet had just been dodged.

At this hour, there is no news as to the reason for Xanthropoulos's absence, whether due to cold feet, a change of heart, or something more dire. The FBI director was not available for comment, but judging by the massive mobilization of law enforcement inside the Beltway, it appears as if Xanthropoulos is officially Xanthropoulost.

It's an early Christmas present for the president.

Rumors have been flying as to the star witness's whereabouts, including reports that he was seen leaving the Russian embassy just last week. Could this be another case of Mother Russia tinkering with our justice system?

More details as they arise. Check this space.

Please send feedback to the author @TheRealaquinonesBB.

NINETEEN

"NINE THIRTY-FIVE, PEOPLE. I GAVE YOU FIVE EXTRA MINUTES. That won't happen again." Victor Merchant strode into the soundstage through the double doors that led to the lobby. The assistant who'd been manning the front door scurried behind him with a pastry in one hand and his clipboard in the other.

"We would have been early," Fiona said, patting her hair, "if we hadn't been searched coming down here." She pursed her lips, looking even pissier than usual. Which was a feat.

Victor grinned broadly. "Sorry about that. After our friend Recyclone's little photo shoot yesterday, we can't be too careful. Don't want any temptation to violate that NDA you signed, right? Right." Without giving Fiona a chance to respond, Victor snapped his fingers. "Eddie. Cast list. Stat."

The assistant crammed the rest of the Danish into his mouth and rushed to Victor's side, cheeks puffy with sugar-glazed dough and fruit jelly, holding the clipboard out before him. Becca had kind of expected an iPad, digital camera, or some other kind of technology, but like yesterday at the auditions, this production was super low-tech.

"Here, Mr. Merchant." Bits of flaky pastry sputtered out between Eddie's lips.

Victor snatched the clipboard out of his hand, giving his head a minuscule shake. "If your mother wasn't my cousin, I swear to God I'd fire you on the spot."

Eddie hung his head, swallowing down the huge gob of food. "Sorry."

Becca stood in line with the other auditioners, arms crossed over her chest, feeling utterly ridiculous in her costume. The one-shoulder pink sequined minidress with matching leotard crotch thingy was bad enough, but paired with glitter eye makeup, enormous fake eyelashes, and the silver sneakers with the retractable roller-skate wheels, she kinda wanted to die. Weirdly, she found the voluminous blond wig comforting. It was the most disguising part of her costume, even more so than the makeup. Blond tendrils that she could disappear into while the glitter lips, contoured cheekbones, and shimmery highlighter transformed her face. She wasn't Becca Martinello anymore, she was Wicked, the Dolly Parton disco derby girl.

"I think I'm going to throw up," she said.

"Not on the dress," Lars warned.

"Just suck it up," Stef said, without an ounce of sympathy. She looked equally as uncomfortable in her lavender sequin halter dress, her hair tucked up into her Dolly wig, and her face practically lacquered with silver glitter.

"You both look amazing," Lars said, smiling. "He'll love it. I promise."

"People, all right," Victor said at last, looking up from the clipboard. "We've got eleven of you back today, which is perfect. Exactly what we were aiming for. So, congratulations, you guys! You're the new cast of *Who Wants to Be a Painiac?!*"

"Wait, what?" Becca blurted out. She gazed around, suddenly realizing that several of their fellow auditioners had not returned for day two.

King Colossus and Prissy were gone, despite their amazing costumes, as well as Mr. GWARnacle, Recyclone, and Jax-in-the-Box.

"Ah," Victor said, his attention drawn to Becca. "I see you two took my advice and came up with matching costumes." He eyed Becca and Stef from head to toe. "What are they, exactly?"

"We're the Disco Dollies," Stef said, then kicked the back of one shoe against the toe of the other, releasing the double track of wheels concealed in the soles. With a graceful push, Stef glided across the concrete floor.

"Not sure what the killer hook might be," Victor mused, rubbing his chin as he watched Stef execute a graceful arc and skate back to him. "But if you're supposed to be Dolly Partons, you're going to need bigger boobs."

"Are you kidding me?" Becca said, not even attempting to hide her disgust. Her plan to win Victor's favor was not going so well.

"You don't have to get implants," he said soothingly. As if that had been on the table. "Maybe water balloons." He pointed at Eddie. "We'll need those ASAP."

"Water-balloon boobs," Eddie said dutifully. "Check."

"That's demeaning," Stef said, but Victor wasn't listening. He scanned down the line to the next new costume, stopping at Fiona. "What are you supposed to be?"

Fiona threw her shoulders back with the same display of cockiness she'd displayed yesterday in her Molly Mauler outfit. As she stepped forward, Becca got her first good look at Fiona's costume other than the massive buns on the sides of her head. She wore a white gown, splattered in red to look like blood, and she pulled a massive ax, also crusted in fake gore, from its folds.

"I'm Princess Slaya," she said, heaving the ax onto her shoulder.

"I love it!" Victor cried. "This is exactly what I'm talking about. Pop culture with a lethal spin. That's what made the original Painiacs so great."

That and the graphic murder.

Fiona preened as she returned to the lineup. Stroking that girl's ego was like holding a match to a barrel full of lighter fluid.

"We're a three-legged race," Kylie and Kayden said in unison as they stepped forward, emboldened by their friend's success. They'd ditched their Wonder Twins outfit for matching yellow jumpsuits with one giant shared leg between them, so that Kayden's right leg and Kylie's left fit into the shaft together.

Victor rubbed his chin. "Horrible name," he mused, "but the visual of you two moving around like that could be epic." He snapped for Eddie again. "Let's call them the Conjoined Twins, okay?"

"Um, I guess?" Kayden said.

Victor patted his arm. "So glad you agree." Then he stepped down the end of the line, pausing in front of Coop.

He wore brown cargo pants and a formfitting green T-shirt with the name "John" stitched across the breast pocket in white lettering. Around his waist was slung a tool belt—laden with hammer, screwdriver, wrench, pliers, and little snap pouches for smaller items—that connected to a harness that clasped over his chest, and down his back for stability. Instead of an over-the-top Painiac persona, Coop looked like he was about to do some weekend warrior contracting work around the house.

"What do you think?" Coop said, his face bright with excitement.

"Who's John?" Victor said.

Coop squared his shoulders. "I'm John Carpenter, *Actual* Carpenter!"

Lars and Becca exchanged a glance. Becca was pretty sure this was a joke they didn't understand.

"I don't get it," Victor said.

Coop's face fell. "John Carpenter. The horror director. But see . . ." Coop jangled the tools hanging from his belt. "I'm an actual carpenter."

"Oh." Victor sighed and turned back to Eddie. "It'll have to do," he mumbled. Then he cleared his throat and addressed the whole cast. "Okay, everyone. Are we ready for our field trip to—?"

Before he could finish, muffled voices drifted into the soundstage from the lobby. Becca couldn't understand any of the words, but the inflection sounded angry. An argument.

"Who's in charge here?" a woman shouted. "I want to talk to him, or I swear I will call the police."

The word "police" spurred Victor into action. He snapped at Eddie, who scurried across the soundstage floor, reaching the double doors just as two of Victor's production assistants escorted a woman through. She was professionally dressed in a business suit and heels, her black hair twisted into an elaborate bun at the nape of her neck.

"And who are you?" Victor asked coldly.

The woman sighed. "As I told your assistants, my name is Janet Yamashiri. I'm Madoka's aunt. She and her boyfriend, Sean, have been staying with me, but they didn't come home last night from your auditions."

"Who?"

Ms. Yamashiri clicked her tongue impatiently. "Sean and Madoka. They dressed up like a giant lizard and a schoolgirl."

Victor's attitude changed on a dime, shifting from combative to sympathetic so quickly it felt like an act. "I'm so sorry, Ms. Yamashiri." He gestured up the stairs. "If you could just step upstairs to my office," he said, guiding her back through the double doors, "we can discuss your situation."

"I just want to know—" Ms. Yamashiri pressed, but Victor quickly cut her off.

"Of course you do. Sergey?"

The casting guy from auditions put his hand on Ms. Yamashiri's arm, escorting her back into the hallway. She looked as if she was about to put up an argument, then sighed.

"Fine. But I don't have much time."

"Absolutely," Victor said, leading her upstairs. "This won't take but a moment."

Then the double doors quickly shut behind them.

The rest of the cast broke into small groups, leaning against a wall or sitting on the floor, casually waiting for Victor to return—Fiona holding court with the twins, Sumo Sutra and Mistress Distress deep in conversation while Lord Cancellor looked on silently. Bram, the vampire, headed out of the soundstage, probably to the men's room. And Lars jabbered loudly about Coop's new costume. But instead of joining in, Stef grabbed Becca's arm and hauled her to the corner of the soundstage.

"What are you doing?" Becca asked.

Stef took a deep breath, then spoke in a low voice. "Did you notice who's missing today?"

Becca shrugged. "A few people."

"*Specifically* who," Stef pressed. "Mr. GWARnacle, who told Victor that he couldn't lie to his girlfriend about where he was. Jax, whose costume seemed to cause Victor some concern for whatever reason. King Colossus, who was clearly stoned out of his mind, and Prissy, who complained about the acting she wanted to do. Plus our nervous photographer, Recyclone."

Becca snorted. "You think Victor fired him because he took a photo yesterday? Half the line outside was posting photos online." She raised her eyebrows. "Or posting videos."

"Becca." Stef grabbed her by the shoulders. "They searched us to make sure we didn't have our phones on us when we came down today."

Becca shrugged. "So?"

"There's something else going on here. I don't like it."

Stef was one step away from wearing a tinfoil hat so Victor Merchant couldn't read her thoughts.

"Okay, let's say for the sake of argument that you're right. Firing people from a reality show isn't exactly a crime."

"What if they weren't fired?" She looked up toward the third floor, where Victor had his office. "Sean and Madoka never got home last night. What if . . ."

"Shit, you think Victor kidnapped them?" Becca backed away. "That's insane."

"I'm not saying that." Stef shook her head. She seemed confused by her own arguments. "But have you been following the news?"

Becca blinked. "About the show?"

"About the impeachment trial. *BeltBull* has some great articles."

"Wow. Non sequitur much?"

Stef scowled. "One of the key witnesses went missing this morning. The FBI isn't sure if he's dead or alive. Doesn't this sound like the same thing?"

So now Stef was drawing a connection between the presidential impeachment trial and a crappy cable network game show. Yeah, Becca was out.

"Okay," she said, straightening her wig. "Time to end this thing once and for all."

"What are you doing?" Stef followed Becca as she marched across the soundstage.

"Enough dancing around. I'm going upstairs to ask Victor Merchant what he knows."

"Becca!" Stef spun her around by her shoulders. "You can't."

"Why not?"

"Because . . ." Stef dropped her eyes. "It might be dangerous."

"Seriously?"

"I don't want anything to happen to you."

Oh, *now* Stef cared? *Can. Not. Hang.* She was just trying to prevent Becca from getting to Victor before she did, manipulating Becca's feelings in the process. Well, Becca wasn't that gullible, no matter how hot Stef looked in that lavender halter dress.

"Nice try," Becca said. "But I'm getting the information I need and then I'm getting the hell out of here. Have a good life."

TWENTY

BECCA CLIMBED THE STAIRS, HALF EXPECTING TO HEAR STEF racing up behind her. But the staircase was deserted. She didn't see Ms. Yamashiri being escorted out or any of Victor's assistants manning the door to his office. The stairwell and the third-floor landing felt eerily dead.

At the top of the stairs, Becca found the door half-open. She poked her head inside, her heart thundering in her chest at the prospect of finally getting some answers. "Mr. Merchant?"

No answer.

Not to be deterred, Becca slipped through the door into what appeared to be a lobby, stretching about a third the width of Stu-Stu-Studio. The room had the same industrial beige tile as the floor below, but most of the lobby was covered in a plush carpet, pristinely white, that stretched from window to wall. Two rows of white plastic chairs faced each other—four against the windows, four against the wall—which seemed to drag the eye forward toward a single door at the opposite end.

The door was wooden, a light polished oak, and it was flanked by two oversize potted ferns, their vibrant green branches draping over raised metal stands, lending the room a weird Zach Galifianakis vibe.

Most importantly, the lobby was empty. Time to try the door.

She crept across the floor, instinctively not wanting to interrupt the silence of the room with her heavy footsteps. As she approached the closed door, she thought she heard noises from within—muffled voices followed by the sound of something being dragged across the room. Victor must have still been inside with Ms. Yamashiri, and suddenly, a new idea struck Becca. Victor had seemed unwilling to get stuck in a conversation with Madoka's aunt and had now been in the office with her for at least ten minutes. What if Becca interrupted him? Gave him an excuse to cut the interview short? Maybe Victor would be grateful. Maybe he'd be inclined to answer her questions. . . .

KNOCK KNOCK KNOCK.

There was a pause, and Becca waited patiently, expecting Victor to swing the door open at any moment, the look of vexation on his face melting into relief. But after several seconds, all Becca could hear from inside was more silence.

At first, she was disappointed at once again missing the opportunity to interview Victor, but then a new idea dawned on her. Maybe this was the perfect opportunity to look for information on her own. Files or photos or something. She wasn't exactly sure what. But *something*.

It was worth a shot. Becca turned the knob and slowly pushed open the door.

A stark desk sat in the middle of the office, a generic black piece made of particleboard and plastic joints, which looked like it had been purchased at IKEA, with a mesh, high-back office chair tucked in behind it. The office itself was relatively bare for such an enormous space—desk, chair, sofa, lamp—and there were two doors behind the desk on the back wall. One was closed but the other door was ajar, and the interior lights illuminated a large metal file cabinet.

Jackpot.

Becca crossed the office in a flash and slipped into the filing room. Well, it was more of a walk-in closet than an actual storage room, holding one four-drawer file cabinet and a pile of junk on the floor beside it. There was no overhead light, but a glow from the fluorescents in Victor's office streamed through the open door, giving Becca just enough light to see.

She half expected the file cabinet to be locked, but as she pressed the latch to release the bottom drawer, it slid open easily.

Becca smiled. This was neither a safe that needed cracking nor a computer that required a hack, and Becca mentally thanked whatever weird personality quirk that made Victor eschew technology. She'd never seen him with a cell phone in hand, and all the checklists and paperwork Eddie handed him were hard copies on a clipboard, just like the forms they filled out on audition day. So it made perfect sense that the documentation he might have would exist in physical form. In a file drawer.

The bottom drawer was empty. The next up held a bunch of stacked clipboards. The third, which was at chest level, held a hanging file folder stuffed with stapled packets of paper. Becca recognized them immediately. The forms from audition day.

She slid the first from the folder and held it to the light. It was Bram's form, filled out in a rushed, messy handwriting. Becca was about to put it back in the drawer, when she noticed a red circle, bleeding through the top page from the one below. She flipped open the stapled packet and saw that someone had drawn a circle around Bram's next-of-kin answer in a thick red marker. "None."

She let his paperwork drop back into the file and pulled the next one, belonging to someone named Elizabeth Martinez, who must have been their resident dominatrix. Becca caught sight of the red ink before she even turned to the second page to find Elizabeth's "N/A" answer to the next-of-kin answer had been circled.

Fiona's was the same. And Kylie and Kayden's. Stef, weirdly, hadn't listed her grandparents, though that might have been because they didn't know where she was, and even Sean and Madoka hadn't listed Ms. Yamashiri. In fact, every single one of the auditionees who'd made it through the casting round had answered the same way: no family, no next of kin.

Except for one person.

Becca had put Rita's name down. Just in case.

But Becca's paperwork wasn't in the drawer. She searched back through, pulling out each stapled packet and rippling through it to make sure hers hadn't ended up stuck to someone else's. Nothing. She searched the bottom of the drawer, in case it had slipped through the hanging folders and was lying on the base. Also nothing. She dug through the clipboards, then the top drawer, which was too high for her to see into, but she patted around with her hand, feeling nothing but the cold metal base of the drawer.

Becca paused, thinking. Why was she the only one who had listed family on her audition form? And the only one whose paperwork was missing?

The sound of voices startled her. Shit, someone was coming and she was hiding in Victor's storage room, perving through the boss's stuff. That wasn't a good look. She didn't even have time to close the closet door and just barely ducked behind the file cabinet, hoping her giant blond wig and sequined dress didn't catch too much light and draw attention to her presence.

"Sit, sit." It was Victor's voice, casual and friendly. From her vantage point, she saw the back of his head as he wheeled the chair back up to his desk, then gestured to one of the leather visitor chairs. The casting guy from audition day took up a position at the front door of the office, followed by someone else.

Becca could see him clearly, the vampire makeup and cheap plastic costume. It was Bram, his face calm and smiling.

He didn't sit in the chair as Victor had offered, standing off to the side of the desk instead, arms folded across his chest, and though his smile was easygoing, Becca noticed that he kept shifting his eyes back and forth between the executive producer and the assistant who stood by the door like a guard. Suddenly, this friendly conversation felt chillier than it appeared. What was going on?

"What's up, Mr. Merchant?" Bram began.

"Well, I was just wondering what you were doing downstairs," Victor replied coolly. "Poking around in closed rooms."

Bram shrugged. "Just looking for the john."

"I see."

"Please tell me you're not cutting me at the very last moment," Bram said. "I've already told my family about the pilot this week. Everyone's so excited."

Friends and family? Becca pictured his audition form: no next of kin, no one to contact in case of an emergency.

"Family?" Victor asked. He sounded amused. "I was under the impression that you didn't have any."

"Oh yeah," Bram said. "Big family. They all know I'm here for rehearsal today."

It sounded as if Bram was making a big deal out of letting Victor know that he'd told people where he was. Why? If he was worried about getting cut, violating the NDA would surely do it.

"Interesting, interesting." Victor gestured toward the chair again. "Are you sure you won't sit?"

Bram didn't move. "I'm good."

"I'd much prefer it if you'd take a seat."

Instead of complying, Bram pressed his initial question. "What do you want?"

Victor sighed, a disappointed child, and nodded to his assistant. Faster than Becca thought he could move, the assistant lurched toward Bram, grabbing him by the arm. But what was more surprising was how deftly Bram deflected the attack. He whipped the guy around and then used the momentum of his body to send him careening into the wall. The room shook from the force of his impact.

Bram had gone from a chuckleheaded weirdo to a superhero in the blink of an eye. Who was this guy?

As if in answer to her unvoiced question, Bram reached to his shoulder, up underneath the large stuffed bat, and pulled out a gun from its hollowed-out interior, pointing it at Victor.

"Everybody stay calm," Bram said, his voice smooth yet commanding. "Let's not do anything foolish."

Becca could see Bram clearly, his focus and his gun shifting back and forth between Victor and the guard, his eyes steely and sharp.

"Bram," Victor said with the hint of a laugh. "What's this all about?" He leaned forward, arm reaching toward something under his desk.

"Don't move!" Bram barked. "Hands where I can see them, Victor. You too, Sergey. Up."

The casting guy had risen to his feet and slowly stretched his hands in the air, palms facing Bram, like a villain in an Old West movie.

"Good," Bram said. "Now hands behind your heads. Both of you."

Victor and Sergey exchanged a glance, and after an almost imperceptible nod from Victor, Sergey obeyed.

"Are you going to do me the courtesy of telling me who you are?" Victor asked coolly. "Or shall I guess. NSA? FBI?"

Bram didn't respond. Instead, he pulled two long plastic straps from his pocket and tossed them onto Victor's desk. "Around your wrists. Tighten it with your teeth."

"Hmm," Victor said. Becca couldn't see his face, but his voice sounded disappointed. "Local PD, then? I thought we ranked at least an FBI investigation." He busied himself with the zip tie.

FBI? LAPD? Why would Victor expect an investigation from either? What the hell was going on? Becca's stomach clenched. What if this had something to do with The Postman? What if Merchant-Bronson really was connected to Alcatraz 2.0?

Bram removed an ID from his pocket. "Special Agent Callum. Federal Bureau of Investigation. Victor Merchant, you are under arrest for—"

Before he could finish his sentence, two puffs of air shot through the room. Bram froze, midsentence, his body suspended in time, as two bright red spots appeared on his white shirt. Then his body crumpled to the ground.

Becca's mouth dropped open. Her gut reaction was to scream in terror, but her brain took control, recognizing the danger she was in. She clamped her hand over her mouth as she stared into the office, too afraid to breathe, much less move.

But even more disturbing than seeing Bram murdered before her eyes was the realization of who had pulled the trigger. Standing in the doorway, gun still raised, was a man in a black suit. She hadn't seen him around the studio, but she'd definitely seen him before—his scarred, lazy eye burned into her memory for all eternity.

It was the man who had broken into her house.

TWENTY-ONE

BRAM'S BODY HAD FALLEN TO THE FLOOR BESIDE VICTOR'S desk, his head turned toward Becca with eyes open. Becca stared at him, her body trembling from shock.

As Bram lay there, somewhere between life and death, the shooter stood above him, jostling the body with his shoe. The killer's eyes were etched into Becca's brain. She could still picture his arm at her throat, pushing her against the wall as he threatened the lives of her mom and brother. It had scared her enough to keep her mouth shut, but now her fear of this man had doubled. Quadrupled. Millionupled. Becca felt her skin go clammy as she watched him prod Bram's body, which wiggled like a rag doll, then rolled away from her, facing the ceiling. The shooter aimed the gun at his forehead and added a third bullet hole right between Bram's eyes.

Becca's breaths came in ragged heaves, and she could feel the panic welling up inside her. Stef was right. Something sinister was going on. Bram was dead. He'd been an undercover FBI agent, and they'd murdered him. Would Becca be next? Or her friends?

Victor pushed his chair away from the desk with his foot and stood up, thrusting his bound hands out before him. "Alexei, cut these fucking things off me, will you?"

The gunman tucked his weapon back into a holster beneath his jacket, then pulled a knife from the same place while he crossed to Victor. The other man, whom Bram had called Sergey, crouched beside the FBI agent's body.

"About time," Victor muttered. He wandered into Becca's view, rubbing his wrists, then he turned to Alexei. "And what the fuck took you so long?"

"We dispose of woman with others," he said in a thick accent that Becca couldn't quite identify, her heart beating so rapidly that the scene in Victor's office was beginning to disappear into her tunnel vision. Ms. Yamashiri. *Others*. Holy shit. Was Stef right about that too? Had everyone who had been cut from the show ended up dead?

Sergey stood up, handing Bram's ID to Victor, who glanced at it, then stared down at the floor. "That's going to stain the rug."

"I think we have more to worry about than your office decor," Sergey sneered, curling his lip at Victor in disgust.

"Yes, yes. I know, Sergey. I haven't forgotten. Not that you'll let me." He paced around the desk, rubbing his chin. "This pilot will show your boss what I can deliver. He'll get what he paid for."

"He had better," Sergey said. "For your sake."

Victor waved him off. "We need to get everyone out of here stat. Agent What's-His-Name here will have friends, and when he doesn't check in, they'll come looking for him."

Sergey arched a brow. "Will everything be ready?"

"Of course, Sergey. What kind of a show do you think I'm running here? We'll just be a few hours early. We'll keep everyone under wraps until then. These morons don't suspect a thing."

Suspect a thing? What were they supposed to suspect? This situation was getting shittier by the moment. Thoughts of her mom and Molly Mauler vanished. Suddenly, Becca had more immediate worries. *She* was one of the morons Victor referred to—she and her friends. What was he going to do with them? And how, stuck in a storage closet in Victor's office with an armed murderer just feet away, would she be able to warn her friends?

Maybe she wouldn't have to. There were four uniformed police officers just outside on the street. They would have heard the gunshots, right? They might be at the front door of the studio at that very moment.

If you can't hear them, they can't hear you.

Right. Becca couldn't even discern an echo of the loud chants coming from the street below. Which meant the police had no idea what was going on inside.

"Put him with the others," Victor said. "But keep it quiet."

Sean and Madoka and her aunt. Recyclone. Mr. GWARnacle and Jax-in-the-Box. Their bodies must be in the building somewhere, stacked like lumber in a closet. Like the one she was in. Becca's stomach convulsed, the bile gurgling up the back of her throat, and it took every ounce of self-control not to barf up her bagel-and-coffee breakfast.

Meanwhile, Alexei grabbed Bram by the arms and dragged him toward the far corner of the office. Becca's eyes trailed after them; her stomach clenched as she saw Bram's limp body, head lolled backward, and imagined a trail of blood smeared across the floor.

"Load everyone on the bus," Victor said, walking with Sergey out of the office. "No phones, no bathroom breaks, understand? I want the whole cast under lock and key before anyone gets suspicious."

"*Da.*"

"Do the head count yourself. I don't trust Eddie."

"And if anyone refuses to go?" Sergey asked. They were out of sight now, but in her mind, Becca could see the wicked smile curling up the right side of Sergey's grizzled face.

Victor didn't even hesitate. "Shoot them."

Becca wasn't exactly sure what prompted her to move. She should have stayed rooted to the ground, tucked away in her hiding place. Maybe they wouldn't find her. Maybe they'd all leave and she'd be able to get down to the police, let them know that Stu-Stu-Studio was full of assassins and dead federal agents, and have them track this bus Victor was talking about to wherever it was going. But eventually, someone was going to find her. They'd do a head count, realize she was missing, and scour the building until they found her crouching behind a cabinet in Victor Merchant's closet.

No, staying there wasn't an option. She wasn't about to die in this horrible place, and she had to protect her friends.

And that meant getting to her phone.

Without thinking that Victor might turn around at any moment and see her, without considering that Alexei and his gun might still be lurking nearby, Becca slipped out of the file room. Victor and Sergey had gone out the main door, but Alexei had dragged Bram toward the second door at the back of the office. Was it another way out?

Becca sprinted across the back of Victor's office to the second door. As she had guessed, it opened onto another stairwell. Becca could hear Alexei's grunts as he carried Bram's body somewhere below her. She pressed her back against the wall, trying to keep entirely in shadow so Victor wouldn't see her if he returned to his desk. But she couldn't stay there. Didn't have much time. Sergey would be back downstairs, rounding people up. As silently as her clunky skate shoes would allow, Becca tiptoed down the stairs.

She spotted Alexei, moving slowly ahead of her, Bram's body heaved over his shoulder. But he'd passed by the door that led to the second floor and was still descending. As quickly and silently as she could, Becca padded down the next flight and reached for the door, praying it was unlocked. Her cell phone was sitting in her dressing room, just feet away. Holding her breath, she twisted the handle and pushed. But the door wouldn't budge. It was locked.

With a sinking sensation in her stomach, Becca realized she couldn't possibly get to her phone. Then, from below, she heard the sound of a door swinging open. Alexei, taking Bram's body to the ground floor.

She couldn't get to her phone, but maybe she could make it outside the building? The police were there, literally feet away from the front door. They'd find Bram's body, call for backup, stop the bus from leaving. If she could just get to them.

She had to try.

At the bottom of the stairs, she found the door unlocked. She inched it open, eyeing the corridor for Alexei, but by some miracle, the coast was completely clear. Time to make a break for it.

Becca whipped the door open and dashed into the hallway. The double doors to the soundstage were closed, the lobby empty. She was going to make it.

Becca was halfway to the front door, when she realized that her plan had hit a snag. The front doors had been chained shut with thick coils of metal, secured with a massive padlock. Victor was taking no chances.

"You've got to be kidding me!" she said out loud.

"Hey!" a male voice cried out from behind her. "Where are you going? What are you doing out here?"

Coming at her from the opposite end of the lobby was Alexei. He reached into his jacket as he approached, and Becca froze, realizing he was reaching for his gun.

"What are you doing out here?" he repeated, his hand frozen at his chest. Becca could practically see the tendons in his hand flex as he wrapped his fingers around the weapon.

"Bathroom," Becca said lamely. "I had to go."

Alexei didn't look as if he believed her, but he relaxed his grip on the gun and let his hand fall back to his side. "Back to stage," he said, shooing her away from the front doors. "Victor needs everyone on bus."

Becca cast one furtive glace at the sidewalk outside, the sunlight glinting off the concrete, teasing her with freedom, then turned, and trudged back into the soundstage feeling very much like a dead girl walking.

♥ ○ ◁

872,245 likes

tristan_mckee THIS IS AN EMERGENCY ANNOUNCEMENT! Reality Network has canceled Saturday's live airing of Who Wants to Be a Painiac? citing pressure from victims' advocacy groups and unwanted attention from law enforcement. Therefore, we're going rogue! Who Wants to Be a Painiac? will air TONIGHT at 7PM PST live from a secure Internet link. Did you get your all-access pass? Good! You can use that to log into whowantstobeapainiac.ru. Don't have one yet? Hit that link and you'll be able to sign up! Don't let a wussy cable network ruin your chance to see the hottest thing to hit television since satellite!
#whowantstobeapainiac #wewontbestopped #funded #willofthepeople

6 MINUTES AGO
....

RECENT ACTIVITY

mcdonnelson CENSORSHIP! This screams conspiracy. Reality Network bending to the will of a few lunatic terrorists calling themselves Fed-Xers. Why isn't the FBI investigating them?
....

thegriff Yeah, now you come around to the conspiracy. You're a bit late to the party!
....

judy_kline THE PEOPLE HAVE SPOKEN! The protests at auditions have clearly influenced this decision, along with the barrage of e-mails and a signed petition threatening to boycott Reality Network's advertisers if the show continues as planned. That's democracy and Freedom of Speech at work, people! The Fed-Xers made magic.

....

wicked_josh Canceling my cable. This is some serious BS.

....

nikolatesticla This has absolutely made my day! But what about this website? They aren't really going to continue this show online, are they? And is that a Russian site?
#wtf

....

carternoirtv Hold up. I work for Reality Network. No one here canceled your show. We got an e-mail from Victor Merchant saying they were pulling out for a digital platform. Don't blame this on us!

....

ADD A COMMENT

TWENTY-TWO

THE VEHICLE PARKED BEHIND THE SOUNDSTAGE WAS LESS THE prison transport Becca had pictured and more like one of those minibuses she'd seen scurrying around LAX shuttling travelers to their rental cars. It was black, with tinted windows so dark Becca wondered if the passengers would be able to see out any more than passersby would be able to see in.

The rest of her castmates had already been loaded onto the bus when Alexei escorted Becca outside, the yellow-jumpsuited twins awkwardly ascending the short set of steps into the heavily tinted interior, and as Becca approached the outward-swinging doors, she paused, glancing around the parking lot, searching for any means of escape.

But if the bus didn't live up to Becca's prison-like expectations, the Stu-Stu-Studio parking lot certainly did. A twelve-foot-high chain-link fence, topped by a spiral of razor wire, ringed the small, rectangular patch of asphalt. A security door opened onto a back alley, but it was closed tight, and floating up from the distance, Becca could hear the tantalizing chants of the Fed-Xers, still protesting at the corner. She could cry out for help, but there was no way they'd hear her, and she'd only reveal to Victor and his thugs that she was onto them. Which wasn't a good idea. Becca was so close to safety, and yet so far, and the panic that she'd been tamping down since she watched Alexei put a bullet in an FBI agent began to rise once more.

She felt a hand on her shoulder and shuddered as Alexei guided her up the steps onto the bus. It was the second time she'd felt his strong fingers dig into her flesh, and now, as then, Becca had reason to fear for her life.

Despite her fear, when Becca climbed onto the bus, her jaw dropped. If the exterior was all business-executive, the interior looked like a mobile strip club.

Two rows of black leather benches lined either side of the bus, facing each other across an aisle that had not one but two stripper poles affixed to the floor and ceiling. A fully stocked bar and mini fridge sat tucked behind the driver's seat, glasses tinkling and chiming with the rumbling of the idle vehicle, and the shiny black floor and heavily reflective windows glowed brilliant shades of purple and pink from the thin strips of LED lights embedded in the ceiling.

Her friends sat near the back, and when Coop saw Becca, he immediately scooted over on his bench seat to make room for her.

"I know, right?" Coop said, misinterpreting the shock that must have been reflected on Becca's face as she sat beside him. He leaned forward and patted one of the stripper poles. "I was like, 'Are we going to a studio, or a bachelor party?'"

She wanted to say something, to warn her friends that they were in grave danger, to tell them that under no circumstance should they willingly be on this bus, but she was too afraid to open her mouth. Two of the guards stood at the back of the vehicle, just feet away. They'd definitely overhear. Plus, what could they do? There were six guards on the bus, including the driver and a visibly nervous Eddie doing a head count from the front, all of whom were probably armed like Alexei, who was positioned at the front door like a bouncer. Though the guards were outnumbered, the eleven cast members didn't stand a chance against those guns.

Meanwhile, Stef sat beside Becca, body rigid, and though her face reflected concern, she made no attempt to ask Becca what had happened upstairs. But when Stef dropped her hands to her sides, Becca felt the pressure of Stef's fingers against her leg. The message was clear: *I know something's wrong.*

Even Lars, who was rarely quiet for more than thirty seconds at a time, took Stef's cue and remained silent. Which must have been torture for him—Becca could only imagine the commentary running through his head about the bus, the stripper poles, and whether or not Victor Merchant owned this monstrosity or just kept a rental on speed dial.

Thankfully, nobody needed to talk because Fiona was doing enough for all of them.

"A stripper bus?" she sneered from her seat across from Coop. "Are you kidding me? How is this safe? There aren't even seat belts. Like, could nobody find a minibus with regular seats?"

Becca's eyes involuntarily flashed to Alexei, who watched Fiona closely. She hoped he wasn't completely fed up with Fiona's bitching and had decided to silence her once and for all. He was expressionless, however, hearing Fiona's complaints with unemotional stoicism. Which Becca would have found admirable if he hadn't just killed an FBI agent right in front of her.

"Wait, where's Bram?" Fiona stood up, eyes sweeping the minibus for the definitely not undead vampire.

Eddie nervously glanced at Sergey, doing his own head count from the door. "Bram's been, uh . . . cut."

"What, just now?"

"Yeah."

Fiona planted her hands on her hips. "Why?"

"No more questions," Sergey said.

Much to no one's surprise, Fiona ignored him. "Is he still here?" She moved forward as if she was going to exit the bus. "Because he borrowed my best black eyeliner, and I'm not just going to let that—"

"Sit!" Sergey barked. And for the first time since Becca had met her, Fiona did exactly as she was told. Her butt hit the cushioned bench at record speed, and though Fiona looked as if she wanted to unleash a tirade on the tyrannical guard, she bit her tongue and stayed quiet.

Sergey turned to the driver and said something in a language Becca didn't understand; then the motor turned over, the doors closed, and the minibus pulled out of the parking lot. As Becca watched Stu-Stu-Studio disappear around the corner, she wondered with a visible shudder whether or not she and her friends were about to end up like Bram, Ms. Yamashiri, and "the others."

The drive seemed to take forever. An hour? Two? Honestly, she had no freaking idea. No cell phones, no watches, and windows too dark to see out of. It was like she was in purgatory—a place where time had no meaning and where their very existences had been forgotten.

Forgotten. Becca thought of her mom and brother in Arizona. They thought she was back in Marquette, safe and sound, enjoying the slopes with Jackie and Mateo, who also had no idea where she was. She pictured her mom's face when she found out that Becca was missing, imagined Jackie's panic and guilt, and Rafa's sorrow. First his mom, then his big sister. It was more loss than a ten-year-old should have to endure.

Becca shook off the despair threatening to overcome her. She couldn't give up now. She had to stay sharp, look for a chance to escape. They'd have to load them off the bus at some point, and maybe then she could make a break for it.

She had to hope.

When the bus finally came to a halt, Sergey jumped off the moment the doors opened. Without a word, the guards followed him, as if there'd been some prearranged plan of what was to happen upon arrival. Except for Alexei. He muttered something in that same foreign language to the driver, then took up a position at the front of the bus, blocking the door.

Lars leaned across Coop. "No one leaves," he whispered. "That's what he told the driver."

"How do you know?" Becca asked.

"Nikto ne ukhodit," Lars said in what sounded like a perfect accent. "I was with a Russian circus, remember?"

"Russian?" Stef said, her body tensing up.

Lars nodded. "Any idea why Victor Merchant would have a bunch of Russian production assistants?"

Production assistants my ass. More like Russian assassins. Stef's conspiracy theory seemed less and less insane by the moment.

"I have to pee," Kylie whined. She raised her hand, like a schoolchild. "Mr. Assistant Person, sir? Can I get off the bus to use the ladies' room?"

Alexei turned his stony face toward her and blinked. "No."

"Oh." Kylie snatched down her hand as if she'd been burned.

"I don't like this," Stef said to no one in particular. Unfortunately, she said it loud enough for Fiona to overhear.

"Not too late for you to leave," she said, smiling sweetly.

Actually, it is. That's what Becca wanted to say, but for once in her life, she kept her mouth shut. Standing up to Fiona wasn't important right now. Keeping herself and her friends alive was the only thing that mattered.

"Okay, everyone!" Victor said, with a clap of his hands as he climbed on board. "Sorry for the delay. Just had to make sure everything was ready."

"Mr. Merchant!" Fiona said, shooting to her feet. "I've had enough of this. If you don't tell us right now—"

"Princess Slaya," Victor said, walking forward. He had an amazing knack for interrupting Fiona's rants. "All your questions will be answered inside." He beckoned her forward as he exited the bus. "Come on. Time is money."

"Can I pee yet?" Kylie whined.

"What's going on?" Kayden asked.

"Whatever happens next," Lars said, sauntering past them, "at least we're getting off this bus."

TWENTY-THREE

BECCA WAS THE LAST TO EXIT, FOLLOWING STEF CLOSELY. SHE kept her eyes open, casting them furtively from side to side like a criminal, searching for a means of escape, but the Russian guards surrounded Becca and the rest of her castmates as they were escorted through a small side door at the corner of a massive concrete building. It loomed above them, windowless and menacing, and as they passed out of the Southern California sunshine into the darkened interior, Becca felt cut off from the world in this prison of a building.

They were shepherded underground, down a steep flight of stairs, then through a dark, narrow corridor lit only by stark light fixtures every ten feet. At the end, the corridor opened up into some kind of dressing room—mirrored on three walls with built-in makeup stations but noticeably windowless. Other than the door they entered through, there was only one in the dressing room, which opened into a single-stall bathroom. One way in, one way out, and as the guards withdrew, Becca noticed that Alexei locked the door behind them.

Kylie unzipped herself from her brother, stepping out of the shared jumpsuit in just a white tank top and boy shorts, and sprinted for the bathroom the instant Alexei closed the door, while the rest of the cast spread out, claiming little corners of the dressing room. All except

Fiona, who stood with her hands on her hips, surveying the new space.

"*This* will be our dressing room?" she said, her upper lip curling in disgust. "Where are the amenities? The craft services? I expected more from a Merchant-Bronson production even for a field trip."

"Please," Lars said, rolling his eyes. "Did you see *Lend Me Your Ear*? Cheapest production ever."

The door to the bathroom opened, and Kylie emerged. "*So* much better," she said, as if anyone cared. But at least that meant the bathroom was free. It offered privacy, which Becca needed in order to fill her friends in on what the hell had just happened.

Silently, Becca nudged Stef and nodded toward the bathroom. Lars and Coop caught her hint, and one by one, they filed inside.

"What are you doing?" Fiona said loudly. So loudly, in fact, that any guard standing outside would easily have overheard. Ugh, was Fiona *always* going to be a problem?

"I'll explain it later," Becca said, closing the door in Princess Slaya's face. Though she loathed the former Fake Molly, she didn't want to see Fiona or any of her other castmates end up like Bram, but she also wasn't sure she could trust them with this information yet. She'd start with her friends and then figure out what to do next.

As she clicked the lock, she heard Fiona growl with anger. Tough titties. Becca had bigger things to worry about than Fiona's FOMO.

"What's going on?" Stef said as soon as Becca turned around.

She'd had the entire bus ride to think about how she'd break the news to her friends about what had happened in Victor's office, but now that she had arrived at the moment, subtlety eluded her.

"Bram's dead," she whispered. "Alexei, one of Victor's guards, shot him."

Stef's eyes grew wide as the color drained from her face, leaving her skin a sickly shade of yellowish brown. "What?"

Lars was more skeptical. "Are you sure?"

"I watched it happen." Becca swallowed, the image of the red gunshot wounds spilling blood from his body made her stomach flip-flop. She quickly outlined how she'd been hiding in the file room when Victor, Sergey, and Bram arrived. "Bram was an FBI agent. They caught him poking around the studio."

"Holy shit." Coop ran his fingers through his hair, gripping the long-ish strands at the back. "I mean, holy *shit*."

"FBI?" Lars shook his head. "Why would they care about some stupid reality show? And what the hell were you doing in Victor's office?"

That was such a loaded question. Becca looked at Stef. "It's a long story."

Lars crossed his arms over his chest. "I'm not going anywhere."

Becca wasn't even sure where to start. Thankfully, Stef had no such issues. "She was trying to find out if Victor had any information on the original Painiacs."

Lars arched a brow. "Why?"

"Because I believe that Becca's dead mom was Molly Mauler," Stef said. It sounded so easy, so matter-of-fact coming out of her mouth, that Becca almost laughed out loud. "And Becca's trying to prove me wrong."

"Molly Mauler?" Coop said, scratching the side of his face. "Seriously?"

Becca wanted to say, *No, not seriously!* She'd never believed Stef's theory, had always been confident she'd be able to prove Stef wrong. Though now, she wasn't sure. Why would a Russian assassin ransack her house? Was it to find out if Ruth Martinello really was Molly Mauler? Or was it *because* she was Molly Mauler?

"I . . ." Becca began, struggling for an answer. "I don't even care anymore. The only thing that matters is finding a way out of here."

"I wish *my* mom had been Molly Mauler," Lars mused while he absentmindedly stretched his leg up behind him. "She had great style."

Coop tilted his head to the side. "I thought you'd be more of a Gucci Hangman kinda dude."

"Why?" Lars let his leg flop back into place. "Because he was gay?"

"Nah," Coop said, gesturing to Lars's bedazzled onesie. "Because you both love sequins."

"Touché."

"Guys," Becca said, staring at her friends in disbelief. Had they not heard a word she'd said? "Bram is dead."

"Yeah, yeah," Lars said, waving his hand dismissively. "So a Russian mobster murdered an FBI agent. That's not exactly news."

"Man, what world do you live in?" Coop asked.

"I was raised in a Russian orphanage," Lars said, his voice deadpan. "We call that 'Tuesday.'"

"It's not just Bram," Becca said, then paused to swallow, her throat parched and raw. "I think Sean and Madoka were killed, too. And her aunt that showed up today. And *everyone* who's been cut from the show."

"Everyone?" Coop asked.

Becca remembered Victor's words. *Put him with the others.* "Yeah."

"That means . . ." Coop let his body fall back against the wall with a thud. "Guys, I think we're in real danger here."

Lars arched an eyebrow. "You think?"

A pounding on the door made Becca jump as Fiona's muffled voice cut through the silence. "What are you doing in there? You're not the only ones who need the bathroom!"

"What did you find in Victor's office?" Stef asked, ignoring her.

"There's nothing up there on the original Painiacs," Becca said, "but I did find all of our paperwork from yesterday."

"And?"

"The people they chose for callbacks listed no next of kin."

"All of us?" Lars asked sharply.

More pounding on the door. "You can't ignore me!" Fiona grumbled. "I know you're in there."

Becca wasn't sure she could say the words, since they confirmed that there was another reason—something all too close and personal—that had gotten her into the callback pool for *Who Wants to Be a Painiac?*, but now was not the time to play her cards close to the chest. They needed to know the truth.

"No," she said, shaking her head. "All but me."

TWENTY-FOUR

STEF SAT DOWN ON THE EDGE OF THE TOILET BOWL, LEANED forward, and sunk her face into her hands. "I knew there was something weird going on."

"If you *are* the daughter of the Mauler," Lars began, "it would be excellent publicity."

"But then why all the secrecy?" Becca asked. "Why wouldn't Victor just say, 'Hey! Molly Junior, can we use you to promote the show?'"

Lars stretched one leg up behind him. "Good point."

Coop was rubbing his face again, obsessively this time. "Why do you think your name means anything to Victor Merchant one way or another?"

"Merchant-Bronson used to share a mailing address with PEI," Stef replied. "Back in the day. It was the closest connection to The Postman we've been able to find."

"We?" Lars asked.

"She's a Fed-Xer," Becca replied, feeling a sharp pang of anger as she said it. It was Stef's fault she was caught up in this mess in the first place. She and the Fed-Xers and their stupid reward for information.

Lars nodded approvingly, alternately flexing and pointing his foot behind his head. "Sounds like the FBI figured the same thing."

"This isn't good," Stef said, standing up. "We need to call nine-one-one."

"How?" Lars asked. "Psychic dialing? Our phones are all on the other side of town."

But instead of answering, a slow smile spread across Stef's face. She pulled the Dolly Parton wig away from her right ear, then reached up beneath it and fished out her cell phone.

"Oh my God!" Becca cried. "I could kiss you."

"Couple . . ." Lars murmured through partially closed lips.

Becca ignored him. For once, she wasn't annoyed by Stef's paranoia. But her excitement vanished almost as quickly as it was ignited. As Stef held up her phone, Becca could clearly see the *X* where a network connection was supposed to be displayed. In the bowels of the concrete megastructure, Stef's cell had no reception.

"Fuck." Stef moved around the tiny room, waving her phone slowly as she tried to find a signal. "This can't be happening."

Coop laid his palm against the wall. "The concrete in this soundstage is probably ten inches thick with a slab ceiling to block sounds from outside."

"Great," Becca said. This place really was a prison.

"There's got to be a landline somewhere," Stef said.

"Probably," Lars said. "But how are we going to get past Alexei the Assassin out there?"

Becca shuddered at the recollection of Bram's murder. She took a deep breath, trying to suppress the growing panic that she and her friends were next. *Stay calm. Be rational.* "They didn't bring us here just to let us sit in a dressing room all day. At some point, they'll move us. We have to look for a chance to break away. Find a phone, or some crew person. Tell them to call the police."

The handle on the bathroom door jiggled. "Okay, seriously," Fiona said. "I'm going to get one of those guards in here to open this fucking door if you don't come out."

"She is the worst," Becca muttered, then lifted her voice so Fiona could hear her. "Okay, okay. We're almost done."

Stef gave up searching for a signal, her face worn and weary, despite the glittery stage makeup. "We're going to die in here."

"No, we're not," Becca said, not entirely sure she believed it. "We just have to stay calm."

Coop pushed himself off the wall, suddenly animated. "And stick together. Don't let them separate us."

"Good," Lars said. "I like squad goals."

Becca turned to Stef. "Don't panic, okay?" It felt disingenuous, since she was having difficulty suppressing the growing anxiety that threatened to swamp her. "And whatever you do, don't lose that phone."

Stef nodded and immediately shoved it back up into her wig before she unlocked the bathroom door.

Lars smiled wryly. "Dolly, don't fail us now."

"What were you doing in there?" Fiona asked, the instant the door opened. "Planning a secret strategy? I don't think the rules of this show include collusion."

"Uh, I don't think there are any rules," Becca said. Not entirely a lie.

"You think you're going to impress Victor, huh? By banding together. Making some kind of deal. Well, I'm not going to let you."

"Fiona," Coop said, forcing a laugh. "We weren't doing anything."

"Yeah, right." Fiona shoved a finger in Becca's face. "I'm watching you guys."

Becca sighed. Great. So now they'd have Fiona glued to their every move. If someone tried to slip away to find a phone, would Fiona draw the guards' attention and ruin the whole thing? But the other option was to let Fiona in on what was happening, and Becca wasn't sure she could be trusted.

"Fiona, we're not in competition with each other."

Fiona folded her arms across her chest. "You've had it out for me since day one."

"You're the one who picked a fight."

"You were making fun of my costume." Fiona's body language was still rigid, but her eyes looked wounded. "I heard you and your girlfriend."

"She's not my girlfriend," Stef and Becca said together. It was like they were doing a comedy routine at this point.

"Look," Becca said, trying to sound as genuine as she was capable of doing. "I'm sorry if I mocked you. I honestly didn't mean to. I thought your costume was fantastic."

"Oh." Fiona let her arms fall to her side. That was the olive branch. The truce. "Thanks."

Becca wasn't sure it would be enough to keep Fiona from ruining their plans, but at least she was less salted. She turned away from Princess Slaya and saw that Stef was smiling at her.

"What?" she asked under her breath.

Stef shrugged. "I didn't think I'd ever see you apologize."

Becca felt a blush creep up from her chest and desperately hoped the glitter makeup obscured it from Stef's view. "Yeah, well, I'm not always an asshole."

"I know."

They sat down side by side on the floor, backs to the wall, eyes forward, facing the only exit. The silence in the room felt oppressive, the kind of uncomfortable stillness that Becca had basically spent her entire life trying to fill. Not today, though. She sat close to Stef, knees hugged to her chest, and all the words she wanted to say were dammed up inside.

She wanted to thank Lars and Coop for being so awesome. She wanted to tell Stef that she was beautiful. She wanted her mom and Rafa to know she was sorry for being such a pain in the ass all the time. But mostly, for the first time in months, she wanted to cry.

Becca had spent the last few days pretending that she was an adult—someone cool and worldly who had flown to Los Angeles and auditioned for a TV show and made friends with strangers. So grown-up! She didn't need parents or friends who worried about every little thing she did like she was a wobbly-legged foal not yet ready for the real world. Now all she wanted was to be home with her family, eating pizza around the dinner table while Rafa explained every play of his last soccer game in minute detail, Rita pretended to be totally engrossed and not at all confused, and Becca texted with Jackie and Mateo underneath the table.

The tears were just forming in Becca's eyes, when the door to the dressing room flew open.

"O-okay, everyone." Eddie walked into the room, clipboard in hand with a plastic shopping bag hanging from one arm. "We're just about ready."

"Ready for what?" Becca asked, instantly on alert. Any piece of information they had right now would be helpful.

Instead of answering, Eddie handed the bag to her with a quivering hand. "Th-these are for you two."

Becca glanced inside. "Water balloons?"

"Victor, um, wants you to wear them."

Becca wanted to launch those water balloons at Eddie's pale face, but Stef placed her hand on Becca's, calming her anger.

"Sure," she said, sounding less than enthusiastic. "Whatever Victor wants."

"G-great." Eddie forced a smile. "If you'll, um, follow me." His face looked paler and more distraught than usual. Which seemed like a bad sign.

"Where are we going?" Becca pressed as Stef lifted two D-cup-size water balloons out of the bag.

Eddie turned away, unable to meet her eyes. "Upstairs." Then he hurried down the corridor as the guards stepped in to escort them.

TWENTY-FIVE

"NOT TOO LATE, OKAY?" DEE'S DAD LEANED INTO THE passenger-side window of the black TrailBlazer, smiling but serious as he gave instructions to Javier. Then he shifted his focus to Dee and Nyles in the backseat. "I know you need a change of scenery, but you're not fully recovered yet."

"Dad . . ." Dee said, trying not to look annoyed. That was the expected reaction when your dad was being overprotective.

"And keep the windows up," he continued. "I don't want anyone recognizing you."

"I'll make sure no one does, Mr. Guerrera," Javier said, his gravelly voice oozing authority.

Dee's dad sighed. He looked miserable, like he was sending his daughter back to Alcatraz 2.0 instead of an innocent drive around LA on a sunny afternoon.

Dee smiled. "We'll be fine."

Her dad frowned, still uncomfortable with the situation. "What if someone sees you? The press—"

"These windows have a seventy percent VLT," Javier said. "No one's seeing inside this vehicle."

Dee's dad sighed again. "I just worry."

"Mr. Guerrera," Nyles said, "I promise I will take excellent care of your daughter."

"I know you will, son," he said absently. "I know you will." Then he backed away and waved as Javier rolled up the passenger window. "Seat belts, remember!"

"Bye, Dad!" Dee said, waving happily. She kept the big, fake smile on her face even though her dad couldn't see through the heavily tinted glass, maintaining the facade until Javier pulled the SUV out of the underground parking lot and onto Wilshire Boulevard. Then her face fell, her body tightened, and when she spoke again, she was all business.

"Javier? The airport, please."

"Do we have a deal, Miss Guerrera?" Javier asked, eyeing them in the rearview mirror.

"Yes." Dee nodded. "I promise, we won't get out of the car."

Javier didn't look convinced, but he made a U-turn at the next light and headed back toward the 405 freeway. "LAX it is."

Dee let out a long breath, then turned to Nyles. "What time does her flight land?"

"Thirty minutes."

"Good." Dee pulled out her phone. "That will give me time to come up with a plan."

Nyles was relatively quiet on the drive to LAX, and Javier, per usual, didn't speak a word. Which was fine with Dee. She was busy laying out a search grid for Manhattan Beach housing developments, and Nyles wouldn't know how to help. Besides, what kind of conversation were you supposed to make when you were taking your girlfriend to find the house where she'd been held captive as a child?

Certainly not first-date material. Except that's exactly what they were doing. The drive, escorted by her bodyguard, was the closest thing they'd ever been to alone.

Sure, they'd been on Alcatraz 2.0 together, sometimes even isolated from their friends. But the cameras were always on, so you were alone except for the hundred thousand sicko fans following your every move and waiting for you to be graphically murdered. Though her dad tried to give Dee and Nyles some privacy at the condo, it wasn't the same as being *alone* alone, and Dee recognized the suckiness that on their first ever alone date-like thing, they were lying to her dad, picking up a friend with a price on her head, and engaging in a potentially dangerous activity.

Or maybe that was exactly how their relationship was supposed to go? Dee shook her head. Nothing about their romance had been normal so far. Why start now?

LAX was surprisingly calm in the middle of the afternoon, which still meant it was freaking packed with cars and rental-car buses and cabs whizzing around. Javier inched the TrailBlazer around the terminal, while Dee and Nyles kept a close eye out for their friend.

Nyles's phone buzzed as they approached. "'Look for a redhead in a baseball cap and a dumpy gray tracksuit,'" Nyles said, reading from his phone. "Must be her disguise."

Literally the least likely clothes fans of "Hottie Griselda" would expect to see her in, and Dee spotted her right away. The red wig was pulled back into a ponytail, sticking out from the back of a Houston Astros baseball cap, with a thick fringe of bangs in front. She wore large white sunglasses, a charcoal velour tracksuit that reminded Dee of something old ladies might wear around a retirement home, and she had a messenger bag slung over her shoulder. If Dee hadn't known exactly what to look for, she'd never have guessed that was her friend. The disguise was perfect.

Griselda stood by the curb, typing into her phone with one hand and ignoring everything else around her. She looked pissed off, her resting bitch face a perfect mask of *Don't talk to me*, but when she saw Javier pull the tinted-windowed SUV up beside her, a grin crept across Griselda's face.

"This ride is perfect if you're a mobster," she said, yanking open the front passenger door and slipping inside.

"Thank you?" Javier said, unsure whether or not it was a compliment.

Griselda slid her sunglasses off her nose and eyed the driver. "Does he come with the car?"

Nyles leaned forward, smiling. "I see you haven't lost any of your Alcatraz charm."

"Never."

"Griselda, this is Javier. Javier, Gris."

The bodyguard nodded curtly, then eased the SUV away from the curb while Griselda continued to check him out, her eyes lingering briefly on the muscly arms that were barely contained by his black suit jacket. Then she turned to Dee, beaming. "This Brit taking care of you, Princess?" She nodded toward Nyles.

As much as Dee hated to admit that she needed anyone to take care of her, she couldn't help but smile as she thought of how tender and patient Nyles had been during her recovery. "Like Florence Nightingale."

"But with better legs," Griselda added.

"Thank you," Nyles said curtly. "I think. Any trouble getting here?"

Griselda shook her head. "Fake ID worked like a charm. I should do this for a living."

Nyles arched an eyebrow. "Don't you?"

In answer, she blew Nyles a kiss, then sat back in her seat. "So where do we start, kids?"

It felt so good to have all three of them together again, Dee almost didn't want to get down to business. She'd only known Nyles and

Griselda for a couple of months, and yet somehow, with all that they'd been through, it was as if they'd been friends all their lives.

"Based on the building info you found—" Dee began.

"Stole," Nyles corrected.

"I'm sorry," Griselda said. "But I prefer the term 'appropriated.'"

Dee started again. "Based on the building info Griselda *appropriated*, there are six contenders. All tract-home developments built in the Manhattan Beach area in the last twenty years."

"Okay," Griselda said. "That shouldn't be too hard." She slipped her laptop out of her bag and fired it up. "Seventy-four blocks. Seven hundred and fifty-two houses. If we find the right one, I should be able to figure out who owned it back then."

"Where to?" Javier asked.

Dee gave him the first address, which the driver keyed into the GPS.

"Do you really think you'll be able to recognize it?" Griselda asked. She glanced out the window as they emerged from the airport overhang. "It'll be dark in a few hours."

Dee clenched her jaw. "I'll recognize it." That house had been in her nightmares since she was eleven: the white room, the stairs to the kitchen, the foyer, even the marble steps out front. She'd sat huddled in the mail van for twenty minutes after her rescue while the police arrived, arrested Kimmi, and questioned people at the scene. She'd stared at the front of that house the entire time, its outline and features burned into her brain.

Oh, she'd recognize the house all right.

But would anyone in the house recognize her?

TWENTY-SIX

EDDIE'S SKITTISHNESS WAS THE FIRST CLUE THAT THEY WERE screwed.

He led the way through a winding maze of identical corridors to a cargo elevator, flanked by two Russian guards with a third bringing up the rear. Eddie kept looking back over his shoulder, tentatively and scared like he was lost in a dark alley at night, and every time he made eye contact with one of the guards, his face would alternately flush pink or drain of all color, swelling and ebbing like some kind of human lava lamp.

Becca, Stef, Coop, and Lars made sure that they were the last ones to leave the dressing room, hoping that being at the back of the line would give one of them an opportunity to slip away down a side hallway, or into an office, or through an emergency door. Anything that would allow a call for help. Unfortunately, Alexei followed directly behind Becca and her friends with his eagle eye and lethal weapon: either Victor had an inkling that the cast was getting anxious, or else he was leaving nothing to chance.

While pretending to rearrange the giant water balloons tucked precariously into her bra, Becca scoped out the corridors. She hadn't spotted a single opportunity to escape or reach a phone, and as they marched deeper and higher into the concrete building, it was as if she could feel one of Gucci Hangman's seasonal scarves tightening around her neck.

The elevator was deep and wide—the kind used to carry heavy machinery or, in this case, large set pieces—and Becca closely eyed their progress on the light-up panel as they slowly crept up to level "G," which she assumed meant the ground floor. *That's a good thing.* Ground floors meant easy exits, maybe even a cell signal. Or maybe the elevator would stop at a loading dock, or a soundstage like the one at Stu-Stu-Studio with an enormous roll-up door that would be wide open, allowing the December sunshine to stream through. She had to be ready to kick out her roller-skate wheels and speed to safety as soon as the elevator stopped.

But instead of an open cargo bay, the elevator revealed another hallway—shorter this time, with a set of double doors at the far end flanked by two more Russians (because the first three weren't enough), and it wasn't until after Alexei and his countrymen herded the cast out of the elevator that Becca noticed Eddie had remained inside.

"You're not coming?" she asked sharply as he frantically pushed the "door closed" button.

Eddie had gone deathly pale. "N-no." The doors began to close. "Sorry."

"Sorry?" The elevator snapped shut, and Becca felt her heart thundering beneath her sequined spandex dress.

We are so fucked.

Alexei stepped in front of her, two of his goons on either side, blocking her access to the elevator. "That way," Alexei said, nodding down the corridor.

As if she had a choice.

The rest of the cast, though not privy to Becca's experiences earlier in the day, seemed to have absorbed some of her tension. Lord Cancellor kept looking around, as if trying to get his bearings, while Sumo Sutra stood protectively close to Mistress Distress. Even Fiona looked concerned, her ever-present scowl replaced by knitted brows and a worried grimace.

The defensive line of Russian thugs marched them forward toward the doors. Becca had no idea what was on the other side, but she had a feeling it might be the last thing she'd ever see.

"Guys," she whispered, gripping Stef's arm as they reached the closed doors. "We need to get out of here. Now."

Stef sucked in a sharp breath through her teeth. "How?"

Ten people against five armed guards? They probably had no chance even if they worked together, but they couldn't just give up. "We could—"

Too late. The doors opened, swinging noiselessly outward by remote control, revealing the craziest, most overwhelming scene Becca had yet experienced in her seventeen years, and she was momentarily stunned by the sensory overload of what she saw before her.

The interior of the soundstage was built to look like an enormous arena, reminiscent of an indoor Roman Colosseum. Three rows of balcony seats rimmed the entire space, overhanging the main floor twenty feet above their heads. The entire studio was lit by a variety of swirling strobes and spotlights, whose intensity and speed had been turned up to eleven. Industrial house music blasted through the speakers, the thump of the beat immediately intertwining with the roar of blood in Becca's ears, and dancing lasers raced around the arena, highlighted by billowing fog emitted through several pipes scattered around the perimeter.

But more than the lights or the music or the musty mildew stink of the smoke machine, Becca's eyes were drawn to a massive two-story jungle-gym thing looming above.

Part pirate fort, part military training obstacle course, it was a towering steel-and-Plexiglas construction. Becca could see through the walls, the distorted images from within suggesting an almost fun-house-like interior, and there were exposed sections that hinted at the trials it held. Some were familiar playground obstacles: ropes, monkey rings, balance platforms. Others were not. Flames shot toward the roof, round platforms suspended from the ceiling promised terror from above, and on either side of the structure were wide-open areas potted with holes like a putting green gone wild.

Coop gazed up through the swirling lights. "I was not expecting this."

"Remember when Victor asked Jax about a rope ladder?" Becca said. "Now we know what he meant."

"This is not just a visit to the set." Stef nodded toward the walls. "Look."

Becca followed her eyes. Despite the lights and the smoke, she noticed a red dot that seemed to be coming out of the wall. Then she spotted wires strung across the structure from the ceiling, suspending several free-moving cameras. Her eyes attuned to what she should look for, she suddenly discerned dozens more red lights—on the ceiling, on the turrets of the structure, and fuzzy through the Plexiglas walls. Becca had watched enough of The Postman app back in the day to know exactly what that meant.

She swallowed. "They're filming us."

"What do you mean?" Lars asked.

But before Becca could answer, a voice boomed through overhead speakers. "Welcome, everyone, to the first episode of *Who Wants to Be a Painiac?* I'm your host, Tristan McKee, and I'm so excited to have you all here today, logged in and watching from around the world."

"First episode?" Becca said.

"Around the world?" Stef said. "Reality Network doesn't broadcast internationally."

"Logged in," Coop said, repeating Tristan's words. "I think they're streaming this."

If this show wasn't on cable, that meant all bets were off. No restrictions, no FCC laws to break. Had this been the plan the entire time? Had the auditions and the deal with Reality Network all been a ruse to get people to audition for something that would be more lethal than a "fake" Alcatraz 2.0 game show?

She sure as hell hoped not.

Stef's hand found Becca's, and she threaded their fingers together. Despite the chill of fear that had descended upon her, Becca felt the pleasant warmth of Stef's hand, and she squeezed it tightly, never wanting to let go.

"We've got an amazing lineup for you today," Tristan continued. "Full of surprises and celebrity guests."

"I love celebrities!" Kylie said, clapping her hands.

Kayden was less excited. "But I thought this was just a rehearsal or something?"

A spotlight blazed to life, focused on a platform jutting out from the lowest level of the balcony. On it, Tristan McKee stood with a handheld microphone, his overly tanned skin glistening with sweat. "Let's not waste any time! Welcome to *Who Wants to Be a Painiac?*!"

On cue, a video projected onto the wall—the name of the show in bright neon letters, along with its logo, accompanied by a raucous theme song. The opening title credits. As soon as it began, Becca felt a guard's hand on her shoulder, pushing her toward the entrance. She stumbled forward, hanging on to Stef's hand with a death grip as they entered the arena. The smoke machines had stopped and the layer of thin fog began to dissipate, but the swirling lights were disorienting, and though the thundering music had been turned down for Tristan's announcement, it still rumbled in the background ominously.

Another set of spots blinded Becca, erupting from the far wall of the arena, and she turned her head to avoid the searing pain as her pupils raced to constrict. Behind her, the guards had backed out of the room. A creepy sensation rippled down Becca's neck as her eyes met Alexei's disfigured baby blues. Slowly his cracked lips broke into a smile—a twisted, macabre interpretation of joy, but a curved-lip, crinkled-eye, yellowed-teeth full-blown smile nonetheless.

"Bye-bye," Alexei said, waving like a toddler, just before the door slammed shut behind him.

Becca pulled her hand from Stef's grip and raced to the door. There was no handle, though she could see the small screw holes where one had once been connected. Without a handle, there was no way to pull the door open, if it was even unlocked, which she doubted.

The music ended, and the arena became eerily quiet as Tristan took up his microphone. "And now it's time . . ." He paused dramatically. "To meet . . ." Another pause, his eyebrows high with anticipation. "Our contestants!"

Becca was pretty sure the word "victims" was a more accurate description of their intended role.

"Victor!" Fiona screamed, not waiting for an answer. She spun around, scanning the balcony for signs of the executive producer. He was nowhere to be found, so she spun to face the announcer instead. "What is going on? This was supposed to be a field trip."

Instead of answering, Tristan continued with his speech. "Hailing from six different states, our contestants all came here for one reason. They all wanted to be Painiacs! Isn't that hilarious?" He paused as if waiting for applause. But though the cameras continued to film, the stands were empty.

"So let's meet . . . Mistress Distress! Sumo Sutra! The Conjoined Twins!" Stoplights raced around the stage, illuminating each of them in turn.

"We're a three-legged race!" Kylie protested. "Like, at the fair." Not that Tristan was listening.

"Human Gumby! Lord Cancellor!"

Lord Cancellor played along, taking a step forward when he heard his name and swinging his rubber mallet like a baseball player aiming for the bleachers.

"Princess Slaya and John Carpenter, Actual Carpenter." Tristan laughed, as if getting the joke for the first time. "Oh, clever that."

"At least someone got it," Coop grumbled.

"And last but not least, the Disco Dollies!"

Fake thunderous applause erupted from the speakers, then the spotlights cut out completely, leaving them in darkness. At the same moment, the lights in the arena went out, all but a few purple LEDs from within the giant structure in front of them, which gave it a surreal twilight glow.

"Shit," Becca said out loud. It felt as if something big was coming. The anticipation was palpable.

"And now," Tristan's voice boomed, the echo effect turned on, "the moment you've all been waiting for. Picked out by The Postman himself. Brought here today to face our contestants in the arena known as the Juggernaut. I present to you: the New Painiacs!"

TWENTY-SEVEN

FIONA GRABBED COOP'S ARM. "WHAT THE FUCK IS GOING ON?" For the first time since Becca had met her, Fiona's confidence seemed shaken.

Lars answered for him. "I'm pretty sure we're in some deep shit."

The New Painiacs. Picked out by The Postman. There had been rumors on the Internet that he'd been planning to replace his lineup and was using #CinderellaSurvivor as a device to get rid of the old ones, but Becca hadn't realized that those replacement serial killers had already been vetted, selected, and hired. No wonder the chosen few auditioners at Stu-Stu-Studio had been so crappy—it didn't matter what their costumes were because they'd be thrown to the lions. Victor merely needed people with no next of kin to come looking for them.

"We're not here to be the predators," Stef said, reading Becca's mind. "We're the prey."

"What's happening?" Kylie clung to her brother, confused. "I don't like this."

"Do you have a signal yet?" Becca asked, her voice just barely loud enough to carry over the booming music.

Stef nodded, then crouched down, hiding herself behind the bulk of Becca's enormous wig while she slipped the cell phone from her own.

Cupping it in her hands to try to shield it from Tristan and the cameras, she squinted at the screen.

"Nothing."

Becca felt her stomach drop. That was their one shot at freedom.

"These buildings are designed to dampen interference," Coop said, sidling up to them as Stef shoved the phone back into its hiding place. "Probably won't get reception until we get outside."

"Easier said than done," Becca muttered.

"First up," Tristan boomed, "he's a fast-talking dummy with a penchant for mob movies, and *he's* an actual dummy! Meet Talky Montana and Little Friend!"

From the nearest turret, a man emerged. He was dressed in a white wide-collar suit and blue silk shirt, sporting an oversize white fedora that covered the top half of his face with eyeholes that had been cut just above the brim. On his arm, a ventriloquist's dummy, dressed in a matching outfit. The dummy took a bow, while the ventriloquist scowled at him.

"From merry old England," Tristan continued, "she's a British nanny *and* a nitrate-loving thrill seeker, meet Nanny McEvil!"

Rising up from the floor thirty feet away, umbrella aloft as if the skies might open up at any moment, Nanny McEvil wore a black period overcoat, matching lace-up boots, and a hat with some wicked black feathers pluming from its brim. As her platform stabilized at ground level, she closed the umbrella and reached into her pocket, removing a small yellow bottle, which she quickly twisted open and held to her nose, inhaling deeply.

"Nanny McEvil," Coop said, shaking his head. "More like Nanny McPoppers."

"How about Nanny McGoing-To-Kill-Us if we don't get the hell out of here." Becca dragged Coop toward the handleless double doors behind them. "We need a screwdriver or something."

Coop staggered beside her, his props flapping around his tool belt like a grass skirt on a hula dancer. "On it." He pulled out a flat-head screwdriver and attempted to pry open a gap between the two doors, but it was too thick to fit between. Next, he tried the claw on the back of his hammer, but the curved angle and the length of the handle meant he couldn't get it wedged in.

Meanwhile, Sumo Sutra was inching his way along the wall of the soundstage, patting the smooth surface with his meaty hands as if searching for a hidden door. Mistress Distress took his cue and started down the other side, while Lord Cancellor, seemingly shell-shocked, plastered himself against the door beside Coop, clutching his rubber mallet to his chest.

"From the hot alkaline lake bed outside Reno, Nevada," Tristan cried, "I give you: the Burning Man."

Becca spun around in time to see two massive spouts of flame projected into the air from the other side of the Juggernaut. A tall African American guy, dressed in an orange sequined jumpsuit like a sun-devil Elvis, waved around handheld flamethrowers attached to a tank of fuel on his back. The Burning Man laughed, his voice joining Tristan's through the speakers.

"They're miked up," Stef said. "I bet they've been rehearsing a lot longer than we have."

"Or, you know, at all," Becca said as she dropped to the floor, attempting to wedge the screwdriver underneath the lip of the door and force it open that way. It wouldn't budge.

"One plays guitar, and the other, a wicked tambourine. Put your hands together for the folk music sounds of Psychoman and Gorefunkel!"

"Okay," Lars said, snickering. "That's actually funny."

From another turret, a short guy and a taller one with a tightly curled strawberry-blond perm stepped into the light. They both wore turtlenecks rolled up over their mouths and noses, and true to Tristan's description, one had a guitar, the other a tambourine. Becca was pretty sure neither of them made music.

"And dropping in from the skies, it's Bungee Boyd!"

Becca craned her head toward the ceiling, where a woman in a pink flight suit and visor helmet had climbed out onto one of the platforms three stories up. She fanned her arms above her head, then dove off the platform, executing a perfect 180-degree turn before touching down on the ground beside the Burning Man. But her toes had barely hit the Astroturf when the elastic cord attached to her back recoiled, pulling her gracefully back up toward the ceiling.

They'd be coming out of the floor, out of the sky, and out of the Juggernaut? This was going to get real bloody, real fast.

Becca gave one last heave on the screwdriver as she attempted to open the door even a fraction, but no luck.

"I think it's locked," she panted, climbing to her feet while Coop was searching his belt for anything else they could use.

"There must be another way out," Stef said from over her shoulder.

Lars pointed to Tristan's perch on the balcony. "Yeah, where did that asshole come from?"

Becca caught her breath. Of course. There had to be some exit from the balcony. If they could just get to it.

"We need to find a way up there," she said. "Everybody start looking."

Moving as a group, Becca and her castmates stepped tentatively away from the wall to get a better view of the balcony, the Juggernaut, and the general layout of the arena. The balcony itself was shrouded in shadow—the area near Tristan was lit with a sharp circle of yellowish-blue light from the spotlight that projected his animated shadow across the empty rows of seats behind him. As Becca turned around, taking in the whole room, she noticed a faint green glow in each of the four corners of the balcony. She squinted at the nearest one, trying to figure out what they might be, and realized that several shadowy figures were moving beneath the lights. Like people coming in through a door.

"The emergency exits!" Becca cried, pointing excitedly. Someone had tried to cover them up, but their signature green lights bled through into the darkness.

"Yes!" Stef cried. Her eyes darted to each of the corners. "I bet they all lead directly outside."

Tristan McKee droned on with his overly dramatic echo effect, but Becca was only half listening as he introduced Vladerina, the vampire ballerina, who toddled out onto a rampart on pointe, blood dripping from her fake fangs as she executed a perfect arabesque; FitzKill'em Darcy, dressed in an early nineteenth-century cravat, waistcoat, and breeches ensemble reminiscent of Jane Austen's most famous heartthrob; and King Gut, an obese guy culturally appropriating an Egyptian pharaoh, though Becca wasn't sure if the "gut" was in reference to his massive bare belly or the fact that he supposedly enjoyed mummifying people alive.

"There," Coop said, pointing to the highest turret of the Juggernaut. From the platform where FitzKill'em Darcy stood, straightening his cravat, it was a six- or seven-foot jump to the platform built out from the balcony where Tristan stood. The nearest emergency exit was right at the top of the aisle. If they could get up there, they might catch Victor's thugs off guard, giving them a slim chance of getting out of the building alive.

Of course, getting there was the problem. It meant entering the Juggernaut. And whatever lay within.

"And last but very much not least," Tristan cried. "The Sikh with the sickest ride in town, Mandeep Steamroller!"

From the back of the arena, an entire wall opened, rolling up like an overhead garage door. Smoke poured through the opening, obscuring what lay in the darkened room beyond, but even with the thumping beat of the music, Becca could hear an industrial engine roar to life. A train whistle hooted—two blasts, one short and one long—and then something began to emerge from the smoke. It was a massive piece of machinery, an actual road steamroller like Becca had seen many times repaving sections of US-41 between Marquette and Negaunee after winter had potholed it to oblivion. It had an immense metal wheel in the front, as wide as the tractor cab it was attached to, and another in the back. Sitting at the steering controls, wearing a white turban that extended down over the top half of his face, was Mandeep Steamroller.

"There you have them—the New Painiacs!" Tristan applauded, slapping the side of his arm with his free hand, then dramatically raised the microphone to his mouth and looked directly at the camera. "Let's get this *killer* party started!"

TWENTY-EIGHT

"I DON'T LIKE HIS IDEA OF A PARTY," LARS SAID. UNLIKE BECCA, who was almost paralyzed by fear at the sight of the giant steamroller attempting to maneuver through the open door on the other side of the room, Lars looked absolutely calm and composed. Becca needed to be more like that if they were going to figure a way out. . . .

"The door!" she cried, realizing that the steamroller hadn't yet cleared the opening. The door was still open. And that meant an exit. "Come on."

"Where are we going?" Kylie cried. Tears streamed down her face, streaking her makeup. "I don't understand what's happening." She and Kayden stumbled, still not particularly good at using their bound third leg, but Coop caught her, looping an arm beneath hers. "Just keep moving."

They started across the floor, which was littered with small round holes, picking their way as carefully and quickly as they could. Becca wondered what the holes were for, but quickly decided that she didn't really want to know. The important thing was getting to that door before it closed. Sumo Sutra and Mistress Distress had already come up with the same idea. The enormous wrestler showed amazing agility as he practically danced through the golf-cup-size obstacles, soaring over some with balletic ease. He was almost to the door, clearing another of the small potholes, when something shot up from the ground beneath him. Long, moving fast, and with a sharpened end.

Sumo Sutra let out a scream as the spear impaled his upper thigh. He fell, the ground shaking from impact, but still tried to claw his way across the floor toward the open door. Becca and her friends froze, eyes on the floor beneath them as they realized that the spear had come from one of the holes that dotted the floor. Becca scurried to keep her body clear of the deadly booby traps, then watched in horror as four more spears shot up from the ground beneath Sumo, burrowing straight through his forearm, abdomen, and throat. As he lay there, immobile, pinned to the floor by the spears, the screen behind Tristan shifted to a close-up shot of the impaled wrestler while a tally below showed the worldwide views. Two million. Two and a half. Three.

The tally raced ahead toward four million viewers just as Mandeep Steamroller finally cleared the door and accelerated his machine into the arena.

"Get up," Becca said under her breath. She'd never exchanged two words with Sumo Sutra, didn't even know his real name, but she desperately wanted him to get up, to make it to the rapidly closing door, to survive. As his impaled body twitched, Mandeep steered his steamroller in Sumo's direction, gathering speed with every inch of ground he covered. "Get up!" Becca screamed.

The wheel of the steamroller had reached Sumo's head when Becca forced herself to look away, bile rocketing up the back of her throat. She avoided the visual spectacle of her castmate popping like a smushed grape beneath the immense steel drum, but not the sound. The squicky, liquidy sucking sound of Sumo's death would haunt her forever.

"Oooh, that had to hurt," Tristan said, feigning concern. "Had to hurt . . . the *steamroller*. Am I right?"

Becca opened her eyes. The steamroller covered Sumo's body, and Mistress Distress, who had been near Sumo when the spears got him, was now splattered in red. Sumo's blood. It had spackled her black latex and silky skin like a macabre Jackson Pollock, dripping from her arms and face. She stood frozen for an instant as Mandeep maneuvered his machine toward her. He shifted into reverse to make a three-point turn, and a series of beeps emanated from the vehicle.

The back-up beeper woke Mistress Distress from her stupor. She shook her head, her long braid whipping back and forth across her shoulders, then sprinted toward the closing garage door. She reached it just as the door clicked shut.

Meanwhile, the Burning Man had made his way around the back side of the Juggernaut and was advancing on Mistress Distress. Spotlights illuminated both of them, tracking their progress while the video on the wall showed them in split screen. Mistress Distress must have sensed his approach—with a quick flip of her wrist, she unlatched her whip from the patent belt around her waist, and as the Burning Man aimed his double flamethrowers at her, she let the whip fly and managed to wrap it around one of his weapons.

The assault caught the Painiac off guard, handing Distress a momentary advantage. She yanked on the whip, ripping the flamethrower from his hand.

The Burning Man stared at his weapon as it sailed across the room, clattering against the wall, and the other still attached to his hand blew out like a candle. He looked like a child deprived of a cherished toy, but his disappointment turned to rage in an instant. He refired his remaining flamethrower, clicking at the tank on his back with his now-free hand.

They had to get those flames put out or Mistress Distress would be toast. Literally. If only they had an extinguisher.

Or water.

"Stef!" Becca cried, pointing to her chest. "Our boobs."

Stef looked at Becca like she had lost her freaking mind before remembering that her boobs were, in fact, water balloons. Simultaneously, they reached into their dresses, hauling out their falsies. Without a moment to spare, Becca reared back her arm and heaved a water-filled D-cup at the Burning Man.

It hit him square in the chest instead of the arm, bursting on contact and showering him with its contents. His flamethrower sputtered but didn't go out. She tried again, this time missing her target entirely. Thankfully, Stef had better aim. The third and fourth water balloons were direct hits. The flames were extinguished.

The Burning Man looked stunned, and Mistress Distress took advantage of it. She ran straight at him, an impressive feat across a pockmarked floor in five-inch stilettos, and rammed her shoulder into his chest.

He staggered backward, and she might have been able to finish him off, if it hadn't been for Bungee Boyd. She divebombed Distress headfirst from the ceiling, grabbing the dominatrix beneath her arms and hauling her up to the rafters with the recoil on her cord. At maximum height, three stories up, Boyd let go.

Becca couldn't look away as Distress's flailing body plummeted to the floor, landing with disturbing silence, the sound drowned out by the house music. The scene was surreal, distant, as if Becca was watching it on TV. The Burning Man approached the unmoving body of Mistress Distress, his impotent flamethrower dark and unmenacing, and Becca wondered what he was planning to do. As if in answer, he hauled the fuel tank off his back and dumped its contents onto Mistress Distress.

It was too much to hope that he didn't have a lighter.

"Nice try, my dears," Tristan said, shaking his head from his balcony platform. "But this lady is about to get flambéed. Hannah Ball, eat your heart out. No wait, she might enjoy that."

Becca could feel the heat on her skin even from a hundred yards away as the Burning Man set fire to Mistress Distress. Becca's vision was blurred, and she felt her body trembling from Dolly Parton wig to roller skates. *Is this what a panic attack feels like?* She knew she had to move, to get out of that spear-filled minefield, but she felt frozen in place, the fear washing over her in erratic, ice-cold waves. Behind her, Coop had managed to half drag the twins back to the relative safety of the entrance. Fiona clung to his free arm as Lars was elegantly hopping his way behind them.

But Stef was still by her side, and when their eyes met, Becca felt a strange moment of calm. Stef was afraid—she'd be an idiot not to be— but there was something else. Concern. For Becca.

"Come on," Stef said, nodding toward their friends. "We gotta move."

Becca felt like she'd been injected with liquid bravery. She shook off her stupor, dropped her eyes to the floor, and began to weave her way around the holes.

"What a great opener, folks, wasn't it? Drama, surprise, intrigue."

Becca didn't look up at the announcer, but Tristan's voice made her sick to her stomach. He was describing two horrific deaths, not a scoring drive in an NFL game.

"With that taste of what's to come," he continued, "let me direct your attention to our celebrity judges for this evening."

"Judges?" Becca said as she reached the entrance. "What the fuck are they judging?"

"They're actually trying to kill us!" Lord Cancellor screamed. He paced back and forth in front of the locked doors they'd come in through, his judge's wig flapping around his ears like wings. "Sumo's dead. Actually dead." Then he flung himself at the double doors, flattening his body against them. "Let me out! I don't want to die!"

Lars rolled his eyes. "Like the rest of us *do*?"

Meanwhile, Tristan spoke directly to the suspended camera, which was slowly following him across the balcony as he moved up the aisle. "The Painiac awarded the most points for his or her kills tonight will gain a bonus they can put toward new weapons." He pointed to the wall where the projection now showed a point tally for each of the Painiacs, with Mandeep Steamroller leading the way. "Those of you watching at home can get in on the fun as well. At the end of each show, vote for your favorite Painiac and they'll earn something special for next episode."

"*Next* episode?" Stef clenched her jaw.

Becca's mouth had gone dry. She had no idea how Victor was planning to get away with it, but the words she overheard in his office took on a sinister new meaning. *This pilot will show your boss what I can deliver.* "Your boss." Did that mean Russia?

Becca turned to Stef. "This isn't a pilot for a TV network—it's an audition. For the Russian government."

"What?"

"Victor said something to Sergey about giving his boss what he paid for. That's why the Russians are here. Victor crowdsourced the funds to start this up, but all the while, his target was Russia. Their own version of The Postman."

"We can't let that happen, Becca." Stef grabbed her arm, the grip tight and desperate. "We have to stop them."

"Right, of course." At the moment, Becca wasn't even sure they could stop themselves from getting killed, much less put an end to whatever nightmarish plan Victor Merchant had in store.

"Awarding the points this evening, we have three celebrity judges." Tristan walked down a row to where three people sat in shadow. "Representing the first ever Painiac to die in the line of duty, it is my great pleasure to introduce the Caped Capuchin's brother!"

One of the shadowy people from the balcony stood up, waving to the cameras as the spotlight moved to encompass him. He wore the brown robe of a friar, fastened at the waist with a white rope, the hood pulled low over his head to shroud his face.

"In honor of everyone's favorite asphyxiator, the woman who gave birth to all nine pounds of poison-gas goodness, it's Gassy Al's mom!"

Tristan reached forward and helped an elderly woman to her feet. She was taller than the announcer, though shaky and frail in her movements, and Becca could see the flowing white hair spooling out from beneath the black mask and droopy cap that covered her head. She gave a curt nod to the cameras, businesslike and dismissive, before easing back into her seat.

The announcer stepped to the last judge with a theatrical flourish of his arm. "And her love of animals might be gone, but her legacy remains. Stepping into the shoes of the late, great Molly Mauler, we have her wife!"

Becca felt all the warmth drain from her body as the final judge stood up. She wore one of Molly's outfits—black corset with a flouncy skirt buoyed by a mass of tulle petticoats paired with the ever-present striped tights—and though her face was painted with the clown makeup, Becca recognized her immediately.

It was her mom.

TWENTY-NINE

THE LIGHTS, THE NOISE, THE SOUNDS OF KYLIE'S SOBBING AND Lord Cancellor's screams faded into the background. The Juggernaut vanished. The New Painiacs didn't exist. The desperate need to escape receded from Becca's mind. All she saw in that moment was Rita.

My mom was Molly Mauler.

It was almost impossible to believe, even with the evidence staring her in the face. Literally. Rita gazed down at Becca and her friends with a detached curiosity, not an ounce of recognition detectable in her cold, scientific eyes. Becca could have believed that Rita had been a Painiac—she possessed the ability to separate work from emotion, science from feeling. But Ruth? Her doting, smiling, always-there-with-a-hug-when-you-needed-it mom? No way.

Except *yes* way. Ruth, who had adamantly opposed Becca's obsession with The Postman. *Of course she had.* She'd been worried that Becca might recognize her own mom beneath Molly Mauler's flouncy dresses and clown makeup. Stef had been right—about the prerecorded kills and the blue-sapphire wedding ring and the cover-up of Ruth's "accident"—and all the evidence suddenly crashed down upon Becca like a tsunami wave as she stared up at Rita.

Rita, who had known all along.

Did that make Rita a cold-blooded killer like Ruth? Becca wasn't sure. But even if Rita was, she couldn't possibly stand by and watch her own daughter murdered. If Becca could just make her mom recognize her, maybe Rita could help Becca and her friends escape?

Becca was about to cry out, to tell her mom who it was down there in the Dolly Parton wig and sequined disco dress, when someone appeared on the top of the wall, over the entrance to the Juggernaut. It was Talky Montana with his *Scarface*-themed ventriloquist's dummy, who held, in his tiny dummy's hands, a miniature machine gun.

"Say hello to my little friend's little friend!" Montana yelled.

"Get down!" Coop pushed the twins to the floor, then pancaked himself on the ground beside them.

Becca, Lars, Fiona, and Stef followed his lead just in time as Montana's puppet-size machine gun proved to be just as lethal as the real thing. A hail of bullets sprayed the area, striking the double doors behind them with a series of dull pops. Lord Cancellor, intent on somehow hammering his way through the door with his rubber mallet and bare fists, was caught in the fire, and Becca watched as his body shuddered erratically from a dozen gunshot wounds, twitching and flailing like a marionette, before the gunfire stopped and his body crumpled to the ground.

Talky Montana reloaded, the puppet momentarily discarded. With Mandeep Steamroller circling back around from one side and Bungee Boyd prancing around on an overhead platform above, Becca realized they had to move. Immediately.

And there was only one way to go.

"Inside the Juggernaut!" she cried, hauling Stef to her feet. "We've got to get out of here."

"Is that a good idea?" Stef said. "That's exactly where they want us to go."

Becca glanced at the other two options: the massive steamroller filled the narrow space beside the building, leaving no room to maneuver around it, and she definitely didn't want to get caught by the bungee queen or the floor spears. "I don't think we have a choice."

"I agree." Coop still supported Kylie, whose sobs of terror had made her practically immobile. "Can't be worse, right?"

Lars walked over to the bullet-riddled body of Lord Cancellor, picked up his mallet, and swung it onto his shoulder. "Follow me!" he said with an impressive amount of manufactured bravado as he marched inside.

Just as Talky Montana finished reloading, Becca and her friends fled into the Juggernaut.

She half expected to find Montana still above them, but the walkway he was on only faced the outside of the structure. Inside, he was blocked by a wall, which bought them a little time. Unfortunately, instead of the psychotic ventriloquist, Becca spotted a black dome perched in the corner of the Juggernaut's roof. She recognized it right away—she'd seen plenty of The Postman's security cameras on Alcatraz 2.0—and the red dot sent a shiver down her spine. Duh, of course they were being filmed the entire time. That was the point. This was a reality show, filmed for an audience.

Was their image being projected onto the big screen outside the Juggernaut? Becca could only hope. She turned to a camera and pulled off her wig. "Mom!" she cried, waving her arms. "Mom, it's me. It's Becca."

"Who the hell are you talking to?" Fiona asked. "Do you think your mom is watching online?"

Becca ignored her. "MOM!"

Immediately, the light on the camera went out.

"Dammit." Becca tossed her wig aside in frustration.

"I doubt they can hear us anyway," Stef said quietly. There was no gloating in her voice, no *I told you so* on her face. She looked genuinely concerned. "If we can get to the top, maybe she'll recognize you."

Becca sighed. "Right." Glancing around, she saw that the Juggernaut presented two options.

Straight ahead, a web of knotted rope netting had been strung at an angle from the ground to a floor above, stretching over some kind of walled-off room. It looked like something you'd see at a playground or an obstacle course, and once again, Becca was reminded of Victor's critique of Jax-in-the-Box's costume: *Could you climb a rope ladder?*

The other path, which looked like a long metal corridor jutting off to their right, seemed the safer, easier option. "The turret is this way, right?" Becca asked, pointing down the hall.

Coop nodded. "Think so. Far-right corner of this building, a flight up."

"Okay." Becca took a few steps toward the hall. It looked too easy. "This way, I gue—"

She never got the word out of her mouth. Without warning, the two sides of the metal hallway slammed together with such force, the expelled air blew Becca backward. The walls remained mashed together for a few seconds, then slowly drew apart. If she'd been an inch or two closer, she might have been crushed to a bloody pulp.

Stef's arm slipped around her waist. "You okay?"

"Yeah." The walls smashed together again with a thunderous crash. "Rope ladder it is, then."

"I don't think Kylie can make it," Kayden said, looping his sister's arm over his shoulder. She'd practically given up, panic and fear overwhelming her fight to survive.

Coop supported her on the other side. "Can we get you guys out of this costume? That might be easier."

Kayden pointed to his back. "Yeah, just unzip us."

Like helping a sleeping child get ready for bed, Fiona unzipped the Conjoined Twins costume while Coop supported them. Kylie's body was limp, the only sound she made was a faint whimpering, and when Coop tried to stand her up, her knees buckled.

"I'll carry her up," Kayden said, stripping down to shorts and a T-shirt as he disentangled himself from his half of the jumpsuit. He grabbed his sister's arms and pulled them over his shoulders, hitching her up like a human backpack, then tilted his body forward and began to pull them both up the netting. Coop started to follow, but his weight shifted the rope ladder so drastically that Kylie began to slide off her brother's back.

Lars pushed her back up. "You get to the top," he said. "Then we'll follow."

It was slow going as Kayden grunted his way up the unstable ladder. Kylie was able to hook her arm around his chest, which made the pair more stable, but it didn't help them climb any faster, and Becca was beginning to worry. Tristan had introduced ten serial killers, and even though Bungee Boyd and Mandeep Steamroller couldn't reach them inside, that still left eight others on the loose. One or more of them should have shown up by now. What were they waiting for?

"There's some kind of room down here," Kayden said, straining for every word. He was halfway up the twisted rope, past the low wall that apparently cordoned off the space beneath.

"Can you see anything?" Becca asked. Secret spaces seemed like a really bad thing inside the Juggernaut.

"Nuh-uh," Kayden said. "Too dark."

The instant he said it, a light flooded the room. The walls, which had seemed like solid, opaque plastic, were actually Plexiglas, and as the lights came on, Becca could see through to the interior. It was cluttered with gold-colored statuettes and crude pottery, with several hand-painted sarcophagi leaning against the far wall. In the middle, the potbellied King Gut stood beside a table with an array of knives and tools laid out upon it.

Kayden saw the danger lurking just below him, so close he could have reached down and touched the top of King Gut's fake gold headpiece, and tried to climb faster. But it was no use. King Gut took his time, painstakingly selecting an implement from his table of death. It was long and metallic, gleaming in the orange light of the room, and with a satisfied smile at the camera perched on the wall, King Gut arced his arm through the air and sliced through both Kayden and the rope.

Blood spurted against the clear walls as Kayden and Kylie both crashed to the ground inside the room. Kylie screamed as she rolled off her brother and shook him, desperately trying to wake him. Kayden's head flapped back and forth from a deep wound in his neck that had almost completely decapitated him. He looked like a grisly Pez dispenser, except when his head rolled back it offered a geyser of blood instead of a hard sugar treat. Kylie's panic intensified, and she shook her brother harder, either unable or unwilling to believe that he was actually dead. The force of her movement finally dislodged Kayden's head from the thin bit of flesh still holding it to his body, and it broke loose, rolling across the room like a bowling ball before it smacked into the wall, eyes wide, facing Becca.

King Gut wasn't paying attention to the spectacle he'd created. Instead, he busied himself at his table, first wiping Kayden's gore from the long knife, then switching it out for something even more disturbing—eight inches of twisted metal that looked like a jumbo-size corkscrew.

Becca and Fiona recognized Kylie's danger at the same time. They hurled themselves at the wall, pounding on it with their fists.

"Kylie!" Fiona screamed. "Get out of there! Kylie!"

Becca pointed at the remnants of the rope ladder, which hung limply into the room. "Use the rope!" Kylie could easily have scrambled up to safety.

But terror had completely immobilized the surviving twin. She scooted backward across the floor from the advancing King Gut, shaking her head in abject fear.

"No!" she cried. King Gut loomed over her. "No, no, no, no, no!"

Suddenly, the lights went out inside the room. Kylie let out a blood-curdling scream. And then fell silent.

THIRTY

"HOW DID YOU LIKE THAT LAST KILL IN NIGHT VISION? LIVE mummification looks amazing in green and black." Tristan chuckled from the safety of his perch somewhere above them. "Five down, five to go. And now we're at over fifteen million subscribers. I hope you're enjoying the show!"

"We're all going to die," Fiona said, still staring at the spot they'd last seen Kylie.

Coop spun her around to face him, holding her by both shoulders. "We're not giving up, okay? We can't."

"But the only way out," she said, pointing at the metal masher, "is through there."

Becca sighed as she turned to face the lethal corridor. Fiona had a point. They could either stay where they were and wait for someone else to arrive and kill them, or figure out some way through Mr. Smashy Smash. Unless . . .

"Maybe we should go back out?" Becca suggested. "Take our chances against that steamroller. It doesn't exactly move at Mach one."

Stef shrugged. "That's not a bad idea. If we could get into the cab, we could use it as a battering ram."

"Oooh!" Lars cooed. "I bet that thing would punch a hole through a wall faster than—"

As he said the words, the wall behind them rattled. Turning to face the entrance, Becca saw that Mandeep had driven his steamroller right up to the front of the Juggernaut. The whistle hooted, and then Becca heard the engine cut out. He wasn't going to take the Juggernaut down, but the massive steel wheel, still stained with Sumo's blood, effectively blocked the door. They were cut off.

"Okay," Becca sighed. "I should have seen that one coming."

Fiona buried her head in Coop's shoulder. "This is hopeless."

Becca couldn't disagree. Between the smasher and the serial killers, they were literally in between a rock and a hard place.

"Wait." Stef approached the smashing walls, currently pulling apart from each other. She stared at it, silent and watchful as the walls hesitated for a moment, then snapped together again.

"There's no way we can run that fast," Becca said, her voice low. "That wall is, like, twenty feet long and—"

"Sh!" Stef held up her hand while her lips moved silently. She began counting as soon as the walls parted. "One Mississippi, two Mississippi, three Mississippi . . ."

"It's not enough time," Becca protested, realizing what Stef was thinking. "An Olympic sprinter couldn't make that run."

"Seven Mississippi, eight." She pointed to the hallway as she said the last number, and like a conductor directing an orchestra, the walls slammed together once more.

"Seven seconds," Becca repeated. "We'd never make it."

But Stef only smiled, and kicking the heel of one foot to the toe of the other, she released her roller-skate wheels. "Not on foot, we won't."

"Do you think you can?" Coop asked quickly.

Stef eyed the square space between the steamroller and the room where Kylie died. "With a rolling start, yeah, I think so."

"Then what?" Fiona asked. "You two can get out, but what about us?"

Stef pointed down the interior side of the wall as they clamped together. There was a gap of a few inches through which Becca could see the steel bars and large pronged wheel that was powering the mechanism. It was at the other end of the corridor cranking away like the inner workings of a grandfather clock. "If we can get over there," Becca said, understanding Stef's plan, "maybe we can stop this thing."

"Or jam it long enough for everyone else to get through," Lars said. He hoisted Lord Cancellor's mallet off his shoulder. "Here. This might work."

Stef smiled as she took the mallet from Lars and tucked it down the back of her dress, keeping her arms free. "Good idea."

"Looks as if our survivors are coming up with a new plan," Tristan cooed. "What do you think, judges? Will they succeed?"

But Becca didn't like it. Victor was watching. Would he be able to alter the timing on the smasher once Stef skated between the walls? "I should go first."

Stef only laughed. "I'm a better skater."

Becca knew Stef was right, but her heart ached at the idea of Stef timing it wrong and getting pulverized. "I can't—"

Stef pressed her index finger against Becca's lips, silencing whatever feeble protest she was about to make. "You know I'm right."

Fear twisted at Becca's innards, worse somehow than ever before because it wasn't fear for her own life, but for someone that she cared about.

Stef pulled off her Dolly wig, catching her phone as it slipped from her head. Freed from its prison, the long side of her asymmetrical bob fell across her face. "You keep this," she said, pushing the phone into Becca's hands. Still no signal, but it was only a matter of time before they'd find one. "Just in case."

"You can't die, okay?" She reached out and tucked the long side of Stef's hair behind her ear, Becca's fingers lingering against the side of Stef's cheek. *"Okay?"*

As an answer, Stef just smiled. "You wanna give me some room?"

Becca, Lars, Coop, and Fiona flattened themselves against the walls to give Stef as much space as they could. She started circling the small area, gaining speed, while keeping her eyes on the smasher. Becca could see her counting, estimating her speed and position. Finally, she cut the last turn short as the walls smashed together and pumped her legs as she headed directly for the corridor.

Like a magic trick, the walls began to spread apart the instant Stef reached them. She barreled full speed down the corridor, pumping her legs and arms for maximum acceleration. In her head, Becca counted along. *Four Mississippi, five.* It was difficult to estimate where Stef was in relation to the end, and though Becca was attempting to count accurate seconds in her head, she felt that they must have calculated wrong. Stef was taking too long. She wasn't going to make it. She was going to—

The walls slammed together.

"Stef!" Becca cried, rushing toward the closed-off corridor. *She didn't make it. I know she didn't make it.*

As the walls pulled apart, Becca held her breath, expecting to find the grizzly remains of her I-know-you're-not-but-I-wish-you-were-my-girlfriend. But instead of blood and gore and sequins, she saw Stef waving from the other end.

"She made it!" Becca burst into laughter, a strange reaction considering where they were and what was happening to them, but she couldn't help herself. The relief was overwhelming.

"She made it!" Tristan echoed. "I didn't see that coming."

Stef waved lightheartedly, but Becca knew the danger hadn't passed. She still had to wedge the mallet into the mechanism and pray that it would stop the masher long enough for everyone to get through. Becca watched in silence as Stef waited one, then two cycles. On the third, she jammed the mallet through the gap.

The motor screamed in protest. The doors quivered, opening just enough for them to be able to shimmy through sideways. It looked like a long shot at best—odds of getting smooshed flat like a crepe, maybe 85 percent? But it was their only chance.

"YOLO!" Lars cried, and slipped in between the walls. He was almost slight enough that he could have walked normally, but side-skipping his way down the sleek passageway, he was halfway to Stef in a matter of seconds.

"You next," Coop said, pointing Becca toward the passageway. She nodded, shoved Stef's phone into her bra, and kicked out her wheels. She turned her feet into an awkwardly balletic second position, then slid her way into the passage. Using her hands against the wall, she was able to glide quickly down, practically overtaking Lars at the end. They popped out one after the other, much to Stef's visible relief.

"Halfway there," Stef said.

But on the other end, there was a problem. Coop was trying to get Fiona into the passageway, but she wouldn't budge.

The motor screamed louder, and the walls shuddered. "Hurry up!" Becca cried. "What the hell is wrong with Fiona?"

"She's petrified," Lars said, shaking his head sadly. "I've seen it before with aerialists. One moment they're fine, the next, totally paralyzed."

"She'd better snap out of it," Becca said, "or she's going to end up a permanent resident."

After what felt like forever, Coop finally squeezed into the passageway. He'd taken off his tool belt to fit, dangling it from his lead hand as he slowly inched his way toward them. He was a tighter fit, his progress slow, and though Becca couldn't see beyond his tall figure, she prayed that Fiona was with him.

"I couldn't get her to come," Coop panted as he popped out of the passageway. "I tried everything. She shook me off and wouldn't move."

Becca stared down the narrow gap. Fiona stood, her hands by her side, staring at them with an absolutely blank expression. Her buns were sagging, the hair frizzing out from their tight coils, and with her blood-splattered white costume, she looked more like an apparition than a human.

Suddenly, something moved. As if rising right out of the floor, Becca saw the enormous umbrella of Nanny McEvil emerge behind Fiona.

"Fiona!" Becca screamed, trying to knock her from her stupor. "Behind you!"

"Looks like Nanny McEvil has a truant child to punish," Tristan said. "You should have followed your friends, Princess Slaya."

Fiona didn't even turn around, not that Becca blamed her. Everything that had happened so far was horrific enough that you might not want to see it coming.

Becca certainly didn't. Sumo, Distress, Cancellor, Kylie and Kayden. So much gore and bloodshed. She looked away, eyes to the ground. She couldn't watch.

You're more like her than you realize.

Rita's words flashed into Becca's mind. Was she? At the time, she thought her mom was comparing Becca to the cheerful, soccer-mom version of Ruth that Becca knew. But what if this is what she meant? What if she thought Becca was just as callous and coldhearted as her mom?

NO! That wasn't who Becca was. Killing came easily to these Painiacs, her dead mom included, but Becca wasn't like Ruth. Would never be like her. And she wasn't going to stand by and let Nanny McEvil claim her first victim.

Before she could change her mind, Becca squared her feet into second position again and heaved herself back into the passageway.

"Becca!" Stef cried. "What are you doing?"

"What does it look like I'm doing?"

"This thing isn't going to hold much longer," Coop called out after her. "Hurry up."

"Right," Becca panted to herself, "because this is so easy."

She made it to Fiona even more quickly than her first trip through Mr. Smashy Smash. Fiona still stood there, eyes blinking but unseeing, and for a moment, Becca thought that Nanny McEvil had drugged her or something. But the nanny held another bottle of nitrate to her nose, inhaling deeply. She was gearing up for her big scene.

"Fiona," Becca said, sliding out of the gap. "You're coming with me. Now."

Fiona shook her head, more of a shudder than a nonverbal response, and didn't move.

No time for niceties. McEvil had ditched her bottle and was closing her umbrella. Becca was going to have to take extreme measures. She reared back her hand and slapped Fiona as hard as she could across her cheek.

"Hey!" Fiona roared. "What the fuck?"

"Jump-starting your motor." Becca grabbed her hand. "Time to move."

Fiona was confused, but one look behind her and whatever reticence might have remained was extinguished. Nanny McEvil held her umbrella like a bazooka on her shoulder, aimed directly at them.

Fiona jumped into action, pushing Becca down the passageway just as McEvil let out a barrage of projectiles. They were shot with so much force they were able to pierce the metal wall above Becca's head, long needlelike things with little nubs on the end. Fiona cried out in pain but kept moving. They were almost to safety, and Becca could feel the walls trembling beneath her touch as the motor fought against Lord Cancellor's mallet. Then the wall opened wider, just an inch or two. The mallet was failing.

They were so close to the end, yet so far, as she pulled Fiona along behind her, and Becca realized they weren't going to make it.

The walls clicked, and the motor transitioned from a scream to a roar, and just as Becca was sure she was about to be mashed to an atomic paste, she felt hands on her free arm. Someone pulled her with so much force she had to crunch Fiona's hand to keep from losing her grip; then she tumbled free of the passage, collapsing onto Lars, with Fiona falling on top of them both, just as a sickening crack of the mallet splintering brought the metal walls careening together once more.

THIRTY-ONE

"LOOKS LIKE THIS SMALL GROUP OF SURVIVORS HAS DECIDED to work together." Becca couldn't see Tristan from inside the Juggernaut, but she could picture the smarmy grin on his overly tanned face. "An interesting turn of events! Let's look at the board and see how it affects our scoring."

Becca was relatively sure that if she ever got her hands on Tristan McKee, she was going to make him eat that microphone.

"You saved my life," Fiona said as Coop helped her up. "But you hate me."

Becca rolled off Lars onto her side. "Not enough to watch you die," she said with a smile. "Besides, I did slap you."

"About that . . ." Lars said, sitting up. "We need to work on your technique."

Stef cradled Becca's arm as she guided her to her feet. "I can't believe you did that."

Then she leaned in, lashes low on her half-closed eyes, and kissed Becca.

It wasn't the first time Becca had been kissed—by a girl or a guy—but it *was* the first time she'd been kissed by someone she was really, really into. The near-death experiences, the current danger, the fact that her mom was up there watching her almost die, and her other mom had been a sociopathic serial killer—Becca forgot about all of it for one glorious moment. The kiss was quick, little more than a brushing of lips against each other, but the fluttering in Becca's stomach, the way her breath caught in her throat as if she was being strangled . . .

Becca was pretty sure she'd never been in love, but this felt an awful lot like it.

Stef broke the kiss, turning to Coop, who was examining Fiona's wounded arm. Lars stood stretching beside them, but he was grinning at Becca like the Cheshire cat. *Couple,* he mouthed.

"This is going to hurt," Coop said to Fiona.

Fiona closed her eyes and turned her head away. "Just get them out."

"On three," Coop said. "One . . ." But before he even got to two, he yanked something out of Fiona's arm. She winced, sucking in a sharp breath, but didn't cry out. Coop dropped the item to the ground, then pulled another and another. When he was done, Fiona hugged her arm to her chest and Becca saw five red spots bleeding into the white fabric of her dress.

"What the hell *are* those things?" Fiona asked.

Becca crouched down and gingerly picked up one of the discarded projectiles. It was four inches long with an opalescent nub at one end and a needlelike point at the other. "It looks like an old-fashioned hat pin."

Lars chortled. "That's a new one."

Becca dropped the pin and turned to Fiona. "You gonna be okay?"

"Just until we meet the next serial killer."

"Speaking of," Coop said as he rebuckled his tool belt, "we'd better keep moving."

The hallway on the other side of the masher offered only one route, which twisted at a ninety-degree angle deeper into the Juggernaut. The group moved cautiously along the corridor, edging around the turn as if they expected someone to jump out at them at any moment. But the hall just stretched farther before turning again, and when they'd made the second ninety-degree bend, they found that the hallway abruptly ended.

"A dead end?" Becca said, pushing at the walls as if she expected them to move.

"Don't use that phrase," Lars said. "It might give someone ideas."

"Too late."

The voice came from behind them, and when Becca spun around, she found the two folk singers had appeared in the corridor.

The shorter one held an acoustic guitar; the taller one, a tambourine, which jangled with each movement.

Becca wasn't sure if it was rescuing Fiona or Stef's kiss that had bolstered her confidence, but she was completely fed up with these dickwad Painiacs.

"Aha," she said, smiling tightly at the hipster musicians as she tried to recall the names on Tristan's Painiac leaderboard. "Psychoman and Gorefunkel?"

Psychoman counted off under his breath before strumming a chord. "And a one, two, three, four . . ." Then, together, the duo sang in tight, folksy harmony, *"Old friends. Old friends. Stood in the Juggernaut like bookends."*

"Wow." Becca clapped slowly, nodding in pity. "The Postman really scraped the bottom of the barrel with you two. Was D-league roller derby not an option?"

Psychoman and Gorefunkel stared at her blankly. Combativeness clearly wasn't the reaction they were expecting. Good. Becca wasn't about to let them see her fear.

"What are you doing?" Stef whispered.

"Just trying to find a way out of here."

"You realize you're picking a fight with serial killers, right?"

Another strummed chord from Psychoman. *"You realize we can hear you, right?"* they sang, again in perfect harmony.

"Look," Becca said, stepping forward, "we're running a little short on time, so if you could just get to the part where you try and kill us, that would be great."

Gorefunkel, the taller one with curly blond hair, slumped to the side, jutting out his hip like a child who was about to throw a temper tantrum. "But we rehearsed a whole song!"

"Shut up, man," Psychoman said through his teeth. "You're making us look bad."

Gorefunkel's hand flew to his chest. *"I'm* making us look bad? You were so flat during that first couplet I thought you were singing in a different key."

The duo continued to argue, and Becca brought her team in for a huddle. "Um, what the fuck is going on?"

Coop shrugged. "I can't tell if this is part of the act or not."

"Either way," Stef said, "we need to find a way out of this maze."

Behind them, Psychoman was now shouting at his partner, "I'm the one people like, okay? *I* write the songs. *I* play guitar. I'm cuter and I'm the one that'll have a solo career one day."

"Solo career," Gorefunkel sneered. "As what, a jockey?"

Psychoman looked wounded. "Really? A short joke?"

"Sorry." Gorefunkel slouched in contrition. "I'm just . . . This turtle-neck is so itchy."

"Shall we just finish them off and go home?"

Gorefunkel bowed. "Absolutely."

"Okay, guys," Becca said, breaking up the confab, "stay alert."

Psychoman reached into his pocket and pulled out the end of a long black cord. Becca hadn't noticed it before, snaking down to the floor and disappearing into the wall behind them, and as Psychoman plugged it into his guitar, she heard an audible pop, followed by some low feedback. Then he counted off again, but without strumming a chord first.

"*We'd like to kill a little bit about you for our files,*" they sang. "*We'd like to help you learn to kill yourself.*"

"That is *not* how that song goes," Lars said.

"*And when darkness comes,*" they crooned, "*and pain is all around.*"

"That's a different song!" Lars threw up his hands. "What the hell is wrong with you two?"

Meanwhile, the feedback had grown louder and louder, emanating from the guitar. Like it was powering up.

"Cover your ears!" Becca cried just as Psychoman lowered the neck of his instrument. He pointed it directly at Stef and pulled back his hands to strike a chord.

Nanoseconds before his fingers strummed the strings, Becca threw her body to the right, tackling Stef to the ground. They slid across the floor as Psychoman's guitar let out a thundering acoustical clusterfuck of a noise. It wasn't loud, per se, and so low in the range that Becca wasn't even sure she could hear it as she pressed her hands to her ears. But she could definitely feel the resonance wave passing over her, the sensation so intense that she began to shake with its violence. It seemed to last forever; then, suddenly, Becca heard a crash, like rocks collapsing, just before the sound abruptly ceased.

Becca rolled on her side to find Psychoman and Gorefunkel high-fiving. The rumbling sound from the guitar had gone silent after the resonance wave it shot out, and behind her, a three-foot hole had been blasted into the concrete wall of the Juggernaut.

"Holy shit," she said, climbing to her feet.

Psychoman strummed a normal, melodic chord. *"Jubilation!"* they sang.

So, that thing took a while to power up, huh? Time for a speedy exit.

Thankfully, Psychoman and Gorefunkel's missed shot provided their means for immediate escape. As the dust cleared from the wall collapse, Becca could see a set of stairs on the other side. Leading up. Hopefully toward safety.

Stef was already on her feet and had seen the escape path as well. "This way!" Stef cried, then grabbed Becca's hand.

While Psychoman and Gorefunkel fiddled with their guitar, trying to amp it up for another blast, Becca and her friends climbed through the hole in the wall and up the staircase, where they popped out of the Juggernaut's interior and onto a walkway in the relatively open air of the arena.

Tristan McKee was close enough that Becca could see the lights glinting off his impossibly white teeth. Just a few feet separated Tristan's perch from the turret that rose up from the end of the walkway. The gap appeared to be easily jumpable. There was only one problem—or two, to be exact. Flanking them on each side were Vladerina and FitzKill'em Darcy.

THIRTY-TWO

"WHOA!" TRISTAN CRIED, SOUNDING AUTHENTICALLY impressed. "Our little band of misfit toys has made it to the top of the Juggernaut." He paused, examining Becca and her friends. "Relatively unscathed. I'd say that's better than we anticipated, right, judges?"

The judges sat in the stands, a few rows up from the edge of the balcony where Tristan stood on his perch. They were partially in shadow, but Becca could see the Caped Capuchin's brother and Gassy Al's mom nod their consent. Rita didn't move. She was staring directly at Becca.

With the wig gone, Becca wondered if her mom recognized her now that she was so close. The costume and the drag makeup aside, didn't she still look like herself? Or was it too huge of a stretch to connect the dots? Becca was supposed to be on a ski trip in Michigan with Jackie and Mateo. Would Rita be able to draw that line?

And did Becca even want her to? A sickening thought crossed Becca's mind—would Rita save her if she could? Or was she as committed to murder as her late wife? An accomplice. An enabler. A Painiac.

"But let's see how our contestants do," Tristan continued, "against the combined efforts of Vladerina and FitzKill'em Darcy!"

Vladerina pirouetted on pointe and sunk into a deep curtsy as Tristan introduced her while FitzKill'em bowed at the waist. When he stood up, he advanced toward Coop and Fiona, his closest targets, one hand clasped to his breast.

"In vain I have struggled," FitzKill'em Darcy said. "It will not do. My feelings will not be repressed. You must allow me to tell you how ardently I want to kill you."

"Oh, come on!" Coop cried, throwing up his hands. "You're ruining *Pride and Prejudice*."

Becca cocked her head, surprised. "You read Jane Austen?"

"Um, yeah." Coop sounded like Becca had just asked him whether or not he breathed air. "She's, like, the greatest relationship author ever."

"I really didn't see that coming," Becca said, shaking her head.

Lars elbowed her. "I did."

"So what's it going to be, huh?" Coop said, guiding Fiona behind him as he stood his guard against Darcy. "Death by fencing? Strangulation by cravat? This is completely fucking stupid."

Vladerina, fangs still dripping with fake blood as if they had some kind of reserve tank, hauled herself back up on pointe, then quickstepped toward Becca, Stef, and Lars, her stiff tutu flopping jauntily with her stuttering movements. Becca wasn't sure what lethal twist to expect from the vampire ballerina, but as she approached, Becca got a better look—in her hands, Vladerina held long, pointy stakes, Buffy-style.

"Wait, aren't those supposed to kill vampires?" Becca asked.

"Probably not a time to talk details," Stef answered. Vladerina's tutu wiggled more violently as her teeny toe steps grew faster, and though she probably only weighed about ninety pounds, Becca didn't want to risk taking one of those stakes in her chest. She backed toward the stairs, searching around to see if there was another way to reach the turret near Tristan's platform.

Suddenly, from behind, Becca heard a rumbling. Glancing over her shoulder down the stairs, she saw Psychoman and Gorefunkel, who had managed to reach the base of the stairs.

"Just pull it," Psychoman complained, pointing to the amp cord, which was stretched taut behind him.

"I did," Gorefunkel replied. "This is as far as it goes."

Psychoman sighed heavily. "That's the last time I ask you to buy equipment."

So their extension cord only stretched so far. Still, they were close enough to get off a resonance blast that could take out Becca and her friends. Meanwhile, a high-pitched cackling from the ceiling made Becca arch her head back. Prancing around from the rafters, Bungee Boyd had positioned herself directly above. They were literally surrounded on all sides.

Before Becca could even figure out a plan of attack, she saw someone moving in the balcony, descending the aisle to the row where the judges sat. It was a small man, judging by the stature and the outline, and before he even slid into the seat beside Rita, Becca knew it was Victor Merchant.

There was enough light for her to tell that Victor was smiling as he straightened the cuffs of his dress shirt that stuck out from beneath his jacket sleeves. Becca couldn't hear them, but judging by the way Rita turned toward him, she realized he must have been talking to her.

Suddenly, Victor pointed directly at Becca. Rita's head jerked back toward the Juggernaut. Now there was no doubt that she was looking directly at her daughter. She slowly rose to her feet, hands clasped before her. Had Victor just told Rita that her daughter was one of the victims in the arena?

Whatever he'd said, it seemed to have the effect Victor was looking for. He stood up, patted Rita on the shoulder, and retreated up the aisle.

"Mom," Becca said, her words drowned out by the noise and music. But Rita nodded gently. She knew.

"Becca, look out!" Lars cried.

Snapping back into the present danger, Becca caught sight of Vladerina's arm swinging toward her. She ducked, barely missing a stake to the back, then stumbled forward as Vladerina brought her other arm down, striking the top of the walkway just inches from Becca's thigh.

Stef let out a strangled cry and launched herself at Vladerina, leaping onto her back from behind. The ballerina flipped her stakes around and attempted to stab Stef through the eyes, but Becca kicked at her toe shoes, spinning her around on the edge of the parapet.

Meanwhile, Coop and FitzKill'em were doing some kind of Gorn–Kirk man dance, arms locked together in a death grip while each tried to throw the other off-balance. The roar from the bottom of the stairs intensified, and Becca realized that Psychoman was about to generate another destructive sound wave.

"Duck!" she screamed, tearing Stef from Vladerina's back, just as the entire wall of the Juggernaut shook violently.

Below, the stairs crumbled from the impact of the feedback while the side of the building swayed precariously. Vladerina, still on pointe, lost her balance and pitched forward, screaming as she careened headfirst onto Gorefunkel below. On the other side, Fiona had managed to get behind FitzKill'em and was punching him in the kidneys. Despite his height, the blows knocked him backward, and with a final heave, Coop tossed him sideways off the parapet.

For the first time since they'd met the Juggernaut, Becca felt a spark of hope.

"Come on," she cried, pushing herself to her feet. The coast was clear. They just had to get to the turret.

Becca, Stef, and Lars raced down the parapet toward Coop and Fiona, who had already ducked into the base of the turret. A ladder led to the top. Coop scrambled up, then reached an arm down for Fiona, helping her. Stef scurried after her, followed by Becca.

"What the ever-loving hell!" Tristan exclaimed as Becca popped up beside her friends. He was a few feet away, staring at them like he'd just seen a ghost. "How did you—"

But Coop wasn't about to let him get another word into that microphone. With a short running start, he planted his foot on the edge of the turret and flung himself like a long jumper across the gap to the platform, landing easily beside the announcer, who looked utterly stupefied.

"Victor, I think—" But before Tristan could call for help, Coop was able to get a hand on the mike, wrenching it from Tristan's hand.

Becca had assumed Tristan McKee, the egomaniacal television announcer who was well-paid to do this job and lacking enough of a moral compass to feel any guilt or compunction about what was happening in the Juggernaut, would cut and run the moment there was any kind of trouble. But instead of sprinting up the aisle toward the exit, Tristan lowered his chin. His perma-smile had vanished, replaced by a curled lip and a sinister flash in his eyes. That was a look Becca recognized, one she'd seen on Molly Mauler's face when she was about to kill a prisoner. Tristan was ready to murder Coop, and his bloodlust was as real as any Painiac's.

She couldn't let that happen. Becca was about to throw herself across the gap when someone appeared on the other side of Tristan. Now it was Becca's turn to see a ghost in the form of Molly Mauler, only this version lacked the same gleam, the same ferocious glee as the original. But Rita was ready to kill, just like her dead wife. And with one explosive shove, she sent Tristan toppling over the balcony to the floor below.

As he fell, the video screen above him went dark. Someone had cut the feed.

"Come on!" Rita said, gesturing to Becca. "Jump!"

"Go!" Becca shoved Stef forward. She needed to get her friends out first. Stef nodded and, just like Coop, ran up to the turret and catapulted herself into Rita's arms. Fiona was next. She had to hike her gown up to her waist to attempt the jump, and she barely made it, hauled into the stands by Rita and Coop.

"Your turn," Lars said, standing behind her. "I'll go last."

"Okay." Becca turned toward her mom and Stef, standing side by side in the balcony, and prepared to fling herself toward them.

But before she could make the jump, someone grabbed her from above, yanking her feet off the floor. The arena whizzed past Becca in a blur as Bungee Boyd hoisted her into the rafters.

Becca had only a moment to think. Boyd had her under the arms, just like she'd grabbed Mistress Distress before dropping the dominatrix to her death. She had to grab on to something. Flailing around with her hands as they reached the top of the bungee's recoil, Becca managed to wrap her arms around Boyd's helmet a split second before Boyd released her grip.

Becca hung suspended from Boyd's head, mouthing a silent prayer for the structural integrity of the chin strap holding the helmet in place, as they plummeted downward toward the Juggernaut, pulled by gravity. Boyd batted at Becca's hands, trying to dislodge them, but Becca held on for dear life. She looked down, hoping she'd land close to where Boyd had snapped her up, or, even better, in the balcony, where her friends would catch her, but as both rapidly approached, Becca realized they were going to fall between the two, in the gap that separated the turret from the balcony. If she fell, there would be no way she'd ever make it back to the top of the Juggernaut.

As she hurtled past her friends, Rita, Stef, Coop, and Fiona all reached out to try to catch hold of her, but they weren't close enough, and Becca couldn't release her grip on Boyd's helmet to give them her hand. The bungee cord hit its maximum and began to recoil, and Becca felt her hands slipping. She was going to fall.

Just as Becca's strength was about to give way, something slammed into her from the side at the exact moment she was racing up past the turret again. She saw a flash of green and instinctively let go of Boyd's helmet as Lars grabbed her around the waist.

For a moment, the world moved in slow motion. Becca and Lars tumbled through the air, arcing toward the balcony platform from the force of Lars's running start off the top of the turret. Becca was over Lars, then under him, then over again as they descended. She couldn't see anything but Lars's face smiling at her; then someone grabbed her arm and yanked her away as Lars continued to fall into the gap.

"No!" Becca screamed. She reached out for Lars at the same time as Coop, Stef, and Fiona did. But they couldn't reach him.

Lars was gone.

TECHNICAL DIFFICULTIES

☠ ○ ◁

872 likes

tristan_mckee THIS BROADCAST IS EXPERIENCING TECHNICAL DIFFICULTIES. PLEASE STAND BY.

2 MINUTES AGO

RECENT ACTIVITY

ajay_vaulted Technical difficulties? Are you kidding me? We just watched a bunch of people die. You said this was supposed to be a non-lethal version of Alcatraz 2.0!

dominojoe I can't believe what I've been watching. I mean, who are these poor people?

eltonjohn4evzz You mean "were."

jiwoo_s I'm in LA and I'm calling the police.

splendour420 Good idea. If that was even shot in LA. I mean, we were viewing it through a Russian website. What if the cast was transported out of the country?

tommy_ecks Or into international waters.

....

melissa_ngo Dude, how could that giant three-story set be at sea?

....

tommy_ecks Cruise ship? I mean, some of those are monsters.

....

theokojak Call me jaded, or maybe I've spent too much time reading thegriff's blog, but I thought the whole thing was probably faked. There's no way Merchant-Bronson would be mixed up in actual murder, especially of innocent people. Special effects and CGI. We don't even know if any of that is live!

....

thegriff You're welcome.

....

genesisjen Whoa, everyone turn on CNN. There's been a discovery up at Stu-Stu-Studio . . .

....

ADD A COMMENT

THIRTY-THREE

BECCA STOOD ON THE PLATFORM, A STRONG ARM HOLDING her upright as she watched Lars crash headfirst onto the concrete floor. She stood frozen, waiting for him to get up. But he didn't move.

"FUCK!" Becca screamed, her voice raw. "Fuck you! Fuck you! Fuck you!" She was crying, a mix of rage and sadness, while someone cradled her from behind.

"I'm so sorry, baby girl," Rita said. "I'm so sorry."

Becca spun around, pushing her mom away. Lars had sacrificed himself to save her, and it was all Rita's fault.

It was as if Rita could read Becca's mind. "I can explain," she said, her face pinched with pain. "I know how this looks."

You're more like your mom than you realize.

All the Martinellos had blood on their hands.

"Becca, look!" Stef grabbed her hand and pointed to the corner of the balcony where a massive digital camera had been mounted. All of its lights were off. The cameras had stopped recording. "Nobody's watching. We have to go."

Stef was right. They probably had seconds before Victor and his thugs burst into the balcony from wherever they'd been watching the camera feeds, but Becca needed to say something to her mom. Not that anything was going to make it better—no shouts or screams or curses would repair this rift. Her mom—*both* of her moms—felt like complete and total strangers.

A door burst open at the opposite end of the balcony, and Victor strode through, pointing his finger at Becca and her friends. "Stop them!"

Stef pulled Becca's arm. "We have to go *now*."

Reluctantly, Becca broke eye contact and turned to follow Stef.

"Wait!" Rita cried.

Becca spun back just as Rita lifted the chain around her neck, pulling it over her head. She stared at the ring, kissed it, then pulled back her arm and threw it across the balcony to her daughter.

The ring, chain and all, flailed through the air, losing momentum as it went. But Becca thrust her arm forward just in time to catch the looped chain with her outstretched fingers. Hanging from it was Ruth's sapphire wedding ring.

When Becca looked up, Rita was already gone, racing up the steps toward Victor and his thugs. They were armed; she was not. It was suicide.

"No!" Becca screamed as Rita launched herself at Victor's guards.

"There's nothing you can do." Stef dragged her through the exit door. As she raced down the steps, hardly aware of her surroundings, Becca was relatively sure she heard gunshots.

From above, a door slammed open, ricocheting against the wall of the stairwell from the force of impact, as Alexei, Sergey, and the rest of Victor's thugs raced after them. Becca had to force the confused jumble of feels out of her mind. Everything they'd done, Lars's sacrifice, Rita's too—it would all be in vain if they couldn't escape.

Three flights down, Coop reached the exit first, throwing his body against the release bar as if he thought he'd have to break it down. But the door gave easily, unlocked and unblocked, and he went floundering into the twilight of early evening. Fiona and Stef followed, then Becca stumbled out behind them. How long had they been in there?

"Let's move," Coop said, turning to face them. "Those guys were right behind us."

They broke into a run, following Coop down the length of the building, and as they reached a cross street, he slowed down, trying to get his bearings.

A horn beeped, loud but high-pitched like from a child's toy. A golf cart pulled around the corner, skidding to a halt as Coop braced himself against the hood.

"Watch where you're going!" the driver yelled. He wore a guard's uniform.

"You need to call nine-one-one!" Becca cried, racing up to him. "There are a bunch of guys with guns chasing us, and at least six people are dead inside that soundstage." *Six or seven.*

"Ha-ha," the guard said. "Very funny."

"We're serious!" Stef pleaded.

The guard pointed at Fiona's blood-splattered dress. "Right. Next thing you're going to tell me is that stuff is real. Please, kids. I've been on this lot for fourteen years, and I can tell fake blood when I—"

The door to the soundstage burst open, Alexei in the lead, spotting Becca, her friends, and the security guard. He raised his arm, not even bothering to hide the weapon in his hand, and fired.

"Holy shit!" the driver said. Then he fumbled with his walkie-talkie while Becca and her friends took shelter behind the cart. Alexei continued to fire, advancing slowly, as his men fanned out beside him.

"Clyde!" the guard shouted into his walkie. "Clyde this is Mathers.

I've got these kids here a-a-and there's gunfire . . ." He paused, flustered. Not the best-trained guard in Hollywood, clearly. "Shots fired. I repeat, shots—"

One of Alexei's bullets caught him straight in the forehead, and Mathers slumped over the wheel, dead.

"Move!" Coop cried. He grabbed Fiona's hand and, crouching low, made a break for the shelter of the building across the street. Stef and Becca raced after him, not daring to look back at the golf cart or Alexei or the barrage of bullets whizzing around them. They ducked into the alley behind the next soundstage, temporarily shielded from the Russian bullets, and sprinted down its length. At the end of the building, they paused.

"What do we do?" Fiona panted, her hand still firmly grasped in Coop's.

"That gunfire should get the police here pretty fast," he said.

"Not fast enough." Becca didn't want to sit around and wait for Alexei to find them. He'd already killed a federal agent and a security guard. She doubted he'd drawn the line there, even if the police arrived. "We need to get out of here."

"How?" Stef said. She nodded toward the twenty-foot-high fence around the lot. "No way we can climb that."

"If Alexei is half as smart as I think he is," Coop said, "they'll be watching the main entrance for us."

"We could just find a good hiding place," Fiona suggested, "and wait for the police."

An idea popped into Becca's head. "Or we can drive out of here and go *to* the police."

"In what?" Stef asked. "The golf cart? I'm pretty sure we can run faster than that thing can drive." She looked exasperated. Exhausted. She'd been so strong through all of this, but now it was Becca's turn to carry the weight.

And she knew just how. "How about a giant stripper bus?"

Becca was pretty sure Alexei wouldn't suspect that they'd doubled back to the main soundstage, certainly not that they'd be bold enough to try to steal Victor's bus, so it seemed like a decent plan. Sneaking between the buildings proved easy enough. They skirted the perimeter of the lot to keep from being seen in the open and came upon the bus on the far side of the building they'd just escaped from.

The good news was that they hadn't been caught. The bad news was that it had been at least ten minutes since Mathers had been killed, and no sirens could be heard in the distance. Which was a really bad sign. Had Alexei gotten to Clyde too? Had anyone left on the lot thought that the gunshots were just props and sound effects in the same way that Mathers had thought they were just actors?

The stripper bus was exactly where they'd left it. More importantly, there was no one inside. The guard must have been called in for the search.

"Anybody know how to hot-wire a bus?" Becca asked, climbing on board behind Coop.

"Nope," he said, then turned to her with a wide grin. "But I know how to use the keys." He dropped into the driver's seat, jangling a pair of old-fashioned car keys still shoved into the ignition as he brushed past.

Stef sighed, resting her head on Becca's shoulder. "That's the most beautiful thing I've ever seen."

"Can you drive it?" Fiona asked, less awed by the miraculous appearance of the keys than she was concerned about the practicality of driving an actual bus.

Coop just shrugged. "No time to learn like the present."

The bus engine roared to life, louder than normal because the door was still wide open. Coop hit a few buttons, trying to close it, and only managed to turn on some swirling disco lights and a thumping house sound track.

"What the hell?" Becca cried. She leaned forward to try to turn off the media and strobes, when out of the corner of her eye, she saw someone running toward them.

"Coop," she said, watching the figure grow larger as he approached. "I think we better move."

"But the door . . ."

"Screw the door!" The figure reached into his jacket pocket, a move Becca recognized all too well as he reached for his gun. "Go!"

Coop threw the bus into reverse and stepped on the pedal. The tires screeched from the force of acceleration, and Becca was thrown forward against the dash.

"Hang on!" Coop cried, then cranked the wheel to the left. The bus turned sharply, and this time, the momentum tossed Becca toward the wide-open door. She managed to grab hold of the hand railing and clutched at it frantically as Coop slammed on the brakes and shifted into drive.

Stef and Fiona scrambled forward, grabbing Becca by each arm and hauling her back into the bus as several pops sounded from outside. A crack appeared on the driver's-side window, but the glass didn't shatter.

"Heh," Coop laughed. "Victor had bulletproof glass installed. How cool is that?"

"Great," Becca panted, climbing back to the bench seats.

"Becca," Stef said, her hand on Becca's arm. "What about your mom? Should we go back and . . . and see?"

Becca's stomach clenched, the sickening reality of Rita's death washing over her. Becca had heard the gunshots as they fled the soundstage, and she knew, in that moment, that Rita had sacrificed herself for them, to help them escape. Just like Lars. The only thing they could do now was honor their deaths and survive.

"She's gone," Becca said, feeling herself choke on the words. "We can't save her."

"I'm so sorry."

Becca clenched her jaw, fighting back the tears. "Coop, can you get us out of here?"

"Yes, ma'am."

Coop floored the accelerator and bounced the bus out of the parking lot onto one of the internal streets that crisscrossed the lot. Becca gripped a stripper pole with both hands as he careened around a corner toward the main gate, hardly slowing down. The bus tipped precariously and she thought for one horrific moment it might topple onto its side, ending their escape before it had barely begun, but as the centrifugal force of the turn ebbed, the bus righted itself and Coop gained more speed as he raced toward the entrance.

"Where are the police?" Fiona asked, a note of panic in her voice. "They should have been here by now."

"They're not coming." Stef sounded incredibly calm, and Becca appreciated that she wasn't freaking out. At least not on the outside.

Fiona's panic escalated. "What do you mean? That guard is dead. He told his partner to—"

"Alexei and his goons must have gotten to them," Becca said, hoping she matched Stef's coolness. "Which means no one's called. . . ." She gasped, reaching into the bodice of her dress. "The phone!"

"Oh my God, I forgot!" Stef grabbed the phone from Becca's outstretched hand. Her face lit up as she stared at the screen. "There's a signal!"

"Guys," Coop said from the front of the bus. "We have a problem."

Becca groped her way to the front and leaned down to see out of the windshield. The guard tower was approaching fast, the gates on both the entrance and exit sides still down, and standing in their way with guns raised were Alexei and three of his goons.

"What do I do?" Coop asked. Becca felt him ease up on the accelerator.

Murder and violence had not been a part of the life that Becca had known. Her parents rarely fought, there were no murders in her town, and the closest Becca had ever come to killing a living thing was the occasional spider she washed down the drain when it somehow made its way into the bathtub. But as she watched Alexei and his men begin to fire, bullets striking the windshield and leaving round shock-absorption pools in their wake, she knew that it was either her or them, her friends or a bunch of hitmen.

"Floor it," she said, gripping the back of Coop's seat. "And don't slow down." Then she turned back to Fiona and Stef. "Hold on, you guys."

Fiona braced herself against one pole while Stef shoved the phone into her dress and grabbed the other pole with both hands. The engine revved, and Becca anchored her shoulder against Coop's seat. Alexei's men scattered first, the wash of fear on their faces identifiable as they realized Coop wasn't going to slow down. But Alexei held his ground. It looked as if he was going to die firing his gun at that bus—they were so close Becca could even see the crooked scar on his left eye. Then, at the last moment, he dove out of the way.

"Impact!" Becca cried.

The bus crashed through the barrier, ripping the gate from the mechanism, then bounced over a speed bump so fiercely Becca was momentarily airborne. The force of the bump must have released the bus door, which slammed shut as Coop peeled down the driveway and onto the street.

And just like that, they were free.

THIRTY-FOUR

BECCA COULDN'T STOP SHAKING.

Bram's death had been a shock, but somehow watching an undercover FBI agent shot by a Russian hitman made more sense to her than what had happened in the Juggernaut. That was pure madness.

Kylie's scream. The squishy sound that Sumo Sutra's body made when the steamroller hit it. Kayden's decapitated head. The smell of Mistress Distress's burning flesh.

Then there was Lars.

Did Becca deserve his sacrifice? Had she deserved his friendship? She pictured the smile on his face as he flung her toward the balcony before falling to his death. It was the most horrific thing she'd ever seen.

Hypocrite.

Becca thought of the Molly Mauler video Stef had shown her, a video where her own mother fed a man to a giant snake. Someone had cared about that man. His family. And they'd watched him die a cruel, painful death while people like Becca watched from the comfort of their own homes, confident nothing like that would ever happen to them. Because *she* was a good person. *Her* family were good people. *Those* people were criminals. They'd deserved what they'd gotten. And so everyone could watch their gory deaths and root for the Painiacs, guilt-free.

Of course, with all the revelations during the last days of Alcatraz 2.0, could she really be sure that anyone who died on the prison island was actually guilty of a crime? And either way, considering what Becca had just experienced in the belly of the Juggernaut, she was pretty sure that no one, no matter what their crime, deserved to die like that.

Not even her mom.

Heavy tears spilled from Becca's eyes at the memory of Molly Mauler's death. She'd tried to climb up the side of the cage to get to Dee Guerrera. The Cinderella Survivor had used Molly's remote control to open the gate, releasing a pack of ravenous wolves on her mom, her body torn apart in a matter of minutes.

My mother's body torn apart. My other mom dead back on that soundstage.

Maybe her moms deserved it, after all the deaths that had come by their hands—Ruth's literally, Rita's by association. But Becca couldn't hate them for it. Now they were both dead, and Becca would never be able to tell her moms how much she loved them. And how she forgave them for the horrible things they'd done. All Becca had left now was Rafa. Where was he? There was no way Rita had brought him to LA— was there?

Wherever he was, she'd find him, and she'd never let him learn the truth, that was for damn sure. She'd spend the rest of her life protecting Rafa from the knowledge of what their parents had been. He was her only priority now.

The bus rocked as Coop took a corner. "Sorry," he said, his voice weary. "I'll get the hang of this eventually."

"Doing great," Becca replied, trying to hide the fact that she was crying. She wasn't the only one. Fiona whimpered softly from the backseat, wiping her nose with the hem of her dress. The purple overhead lights glistened off the tears that streamed down her cheeks.

"Y-yes." Stef's voice was jagged as she spoke into the phone. "I'd like to report a murder."

The cell phone! Duh. Becca crept her way back to Stef's side. The hand that held the phone to her ear trembled.

"Yes," Stef continued. "There are multiple victims." She paused, and Becca heard the muted sound of the 911 operator on the other end. "This isn't a hoax!" Stef cried. Her voice cracked. "There are at least seven people dead at . . . at . . ." She covered the microphone with her hand. "Does anyone know where the hell we were?"

"Culver Studios," Coop said without hesitating. "Soundstage number three."

"Culver Studios," Stef repeated as Becca wondered how Coop knew so specifically where they'd been. "Soundstage number three. There are Russian mobsters or something with—"

The operator interrupted her, and Stef paused, her eyebrows drawn together in confusion. "Yes, I said Culver Studios." Another pause. The furrow between Stef's eyes deepened. "N-no, I'm not there now."

Becca didn't like the way this conversation was going. "Put it on speaker," she whispered.

Stef held the phone in front of her and hit speakerphone.

". . . your current location. Ma'am, are you there?"

"Why do you need to know my current location?" Becca asked, her suspicions rising.

"Ma'am, are you in a vehicle?" Becca heard clacking on the other end as if the operator was typing furiously. "Can you describe the vehicle?"

"Black sedan," Becca lied.

What? Stef mouthed.

But Becca held up her hand, begging Stef to be patient.

"Black sedan," the operator repeated. "And you're calling from a cellular device? Do you know your current location?"

Cellular device. Which could be traced. Holy shit, they were being treated as suspects. With a flick of her finger, Becca swiped the call and hung up on the 911 operator.

"What the hell?" Stef cried. "We need the cops, like, ASAP."

Becca shook her head. "She was trying to find out where we were."

"So?"

"Don't you see? Victor must have gotten to the police already. *We're* the suspects!"

Fiona pulled herself to her feet. "They won't believe that, will they? They can't think we killed all those people."

Becca had to admit that it seemed ludicrous, but was it worth risking?

"Even if the cops did listen," Coop said, deftly navigating the stolen bus through the darkened Southern California streets like he had some kind of destination in mind, "if Victor finds us, he will kill us. No one was meant to escape that studio." Becca marveled at how calm he sounded, but his anxiety manifested in his constant fidgeting—checking the rearview mirror, the side mirrors, looking out the windows to the left and right. He was worried they were being followed.

"I don't know," Stef said, maintaining a firm grip on the phone. She wasn't willing to give up the one thread that connected them to safety.

But Becca had an idea. She climbed back up to the front of the bus. "Does this thing have a radio?"

Coop pushed a few buttons on the steering wheel. The club music came on first, then an FM rock radio station. A few more clicks and the stations cycled through until Coop landed on a local news network.

"It's coming up on six o'clock here in the Los Angeles basin, and here's your traffic and weather on the eights. . . ."

The announcer then ran through a list of city and neighborhood names, most of which meant nothing to Becca, merely a litany of numbers, all designating a different freeway, and all of which seemed to be in some stage of gridlock. After he was done, a female voice took over.

"And now for our top stories on the hour. The body of Gavin Xanthropoulos was discovered this afternoon in a dumpster behind a Dunkin' Donuts in Bethesda, Maryland. The thirty-two-year-old former White House adviser was set to testify in the president's impeachment hearing this morning, and his disappearance set off a nationwide manhunt that ended less than a mile from Xanthropoulos's suburban Maryland home. Authorities have not yet released a cause of death, but eye witnesses on the scene describe the body as having been shot twice in the chest and once in the head."

"That can't be good," Coop said.

"The Dow Jones closed today at its lowest point since last January. Analysts blame the recent market free fall on uncertainty sown by the current state of politics, and continued evidence of foreign meddling in the last election.

"But now we go to Burbank with breaking news from a small sound-stage called Stu-Stu-Studio, where an on-set accident has taken the lives of seven people."

Becca caught her breath. What, now?

"Thanks, Anita. I'm here at the nineteen-hundred block of Glenoaks Boulevard, where a fire has completely destroyed a soundstage. The fast-moving blaze seems to have erupted from the lower floor but spread so quickly that one LA firefighter thought the use of an accelerant must have been the cause. The studio, purchased by the Merchant-Bronson company in early 2015, had not been used in several years but was recently reopened to facilitate auditions for the Merchant-Bronson reality show *Who Wants to Be a Painiac?*, which was abruptly canceled by Reality Network this morning, just days before the pilot was set to air."

"Canceled my ass," Fiona said.

Becca held up her hand for silence. She wanted to hear about the bodies.

"Authorities say the remains of at least seven bodies were found clustered together in what might have been a storage room on the ground floor of the structure. It is too early to determine cause of death. Reporting for KNZX News Radio, I'm Stasia Cordero."

Anita, the first announcer, then picked up the story. "Victor Merchant and Luke Bronson, owners of Merchant-Bronson Productions, were not available for comment. Bronson has been isolated on his private island since 2017. Victor Merchant is the son of the late television producer Karl Merchant, who passed away last month."

Becca leaned against the pole, swaying with the motion of the bus. The news reporter had moved on to another story, but Becca wasn't listening. Her brain was chewing on a problem, the solution just within grasp.

"Seven bodies," Stef said. "That's everyone who's missing."

"Bodies?" Fiona asked sharply. "What are you talking about?"

Becca really didn't want to explain, but since Fiona was in the middle of this horror show now, she deserved to know as much as the rest of them.

"Alexei killed Bram," Becca said.

Fiona paused, thinking. "The guy that was shooting at us?"

"Yep."

Another pause. Becca had expected her to freak out a little bit more, but instead, Fiona appeared to be calmly processing the information. "How?"

Becca took a steadying breath. "Shot him in the chest, then the head."

"Just like the guy in the Dunkin' Donuts dumpster," Coop said absently. "I can't believe that was just this morning."

Becca wasn't thinking about the relative passage of time; she was thinking about what Coop had just said. The similarity between Bram's death and that politics guy who was supposed to testify against the president. Could they be related?

"That Xanthropoulos guy," she said, still puzzling out this problem. "Why was he so important?"

"He was supposed to be able to connect the president directly to the Alcatraz two-point-oh corruption," Stef said. "I think he's the only one who could."

"And that would be bad for the president, right?" Becca was almost embarrassed to ask the question, but she never paid attention to politics.

"It would cement the impeachment case against him," Coop replied, "and possibly lead to criminal charges."

Becca chewed on the inside of her lip. "That's definitely something to kill for."

"The Russians." Stef's voice was breathless, as if she'd just realized something groundbreaking. "They've supposedly been involved since before the election."

Becca caught her breath. The pieces were coming together. "They're trying to protect themselves. I mean, if someone could prove that both the president *and* the Russian government were behind Alcatraz two-point-oh . . ."

"That would be a major international incident," Stef said, finishing Becca's thought. "Like, the kind that starts wars."

"But how does that connect to Victor Merchant?" Fiona asked.

Victor Merchant was the son of a famous producer, who had died last month. About the same time The Postman was killed. "Aren't the FBI looking for The Postman's son?" She was pretty sure she'd read that on the Postmanticism page.

Coop's head snapped around from the driver's seat. "What?"

"Yes!" Stef cried. "Supposedly, he has a son, but no one knows who The Postman was."

"Why do you think The Postman's son is involved?" Coop asked. He sounded utterly confused.

"Don't you see?" Becca said, excited. "That's the only way it makes sense. Victor's dad died in November? That's exactly when The Postman supposedly died on Alcatraz two-point-oh. And they were both reality TV producers. This show, so much like what The Postman did. Access to investors. Support from the Russians."

"The FBI has been turning themselves inside out trying to figure out who The Postman really was," Stef added. "And judging by how the impeachment trial is going, without that link to the president, he may stay in office."

"We have to tell someone," Fiona said. "The police. The news media." She glanced down at her blood-soaked dress. "I want to change before they interview me."

A chime sounded on the radio. "Hold up," Coop said, and cranked the volume.

The news report spoke quickly, her voice solemn. "Breaking news from Culver City, where a group of terrorists shot their way out of the Culver Studios lot this evening."

Becca's head whipped around toward the radio dial, as if the reporter was right there talking to her. "Wait, what?"

"We're hearing that one of the historic Culver Studios soundstages is on fire, a deliberate act of arson, with multiple people trapped inside.

Two guards were killed when the armed terrorists escaped the lot in a black minibus. Anyone who has seen this vehicle in the vicinity should call nine-one-one immediately, as police are investigating a connection between this event and the fire earlier today at Stu-Stu-Studio, where seven people's bodies were discovered. The suspects are thought to be armed and incredibly dangerous. LAPD's Air Support Division is on the scene."

"They *are* blaming us," Stef said, as if not quite believing what she was hearing.

"They can't do that," Fiona said, her voice raising in pitch with each word. "The police won't believe them, right? I mean, we're just regular people."

"Regular people who auditioned to be serial killers," Becca said.

Fiona sank down onto a bench. "Oh my God. We'll go to jail. I can't handle jail. I couldn't even handle detention."

"There's got to be enough DNA evidence to prove we didn't do it," Stef continued. "We'll just drive to a station, turn ourselves in—"

"We are *not* going to the police," Coop said as he continued to drive. His fingers gripped the wheel so fiercely Becca could see his knuckles turning white. "Victor won't let us survive long enough to be proven innocent."

Becca had to admit he had a point. "So what do we do?"

Coop glanced back at her just before he made a sharp right-hand turn off the main road. "I've got an idea."

THIRTY-FIVE

"WHERE THE HELL ARE WE?" BECCA ASKED, NOTICING THEIR surroundings for the first time. Coop had driven them to a neighborhood full of mansions.

"My house." Coop pulled the bus over to the curb at the end of a quiet cul-de-sac. The house in front of them looked like a palace compared to her midcentury Craftsman in Marquette. The Spanish-tiled roof and bright yellow paint seemed quaint and traditional, but the oversize four-car garage, domed entranceway, and twin garden terraces were anything but. An army of floodlights lit the exterior where a grand staircase curved up to the double front door beneath a pillared overhang, and the rounded two-story foyer was packed with windows, which must have flooded the interior with natural light during the day.

Becca continued to gaze at the mansion as Coop shifted the bus into park and pushed open the doors. He bounded up to a security pad beside one of the driveways. After keying in some kind of access code, two of the garage doors rolled up in unison.

"*This* is your house?" Becca asked as Coop climbed back on board and eased the bus into the garage beside a white SUV that was like the photographic negative of Coop's other car.

"Yep."

"Are your parents going to freak out when we show up like this?"

Coop shook his head. "My parents are dead. It's just me."

Becca blinked. How the hell could Coop, hardly older than Becca, afford a house like this by himself?

The bus neatly tucked away inside the cavernous garage, Coop cut the engine. As they all bundled out of the bus, legs wobbly as if they'd spent the last hour at sea instead of in LA traffic, Coop triggered the garage doors, which noiselessly slid shut; then he keyed in more numbers on a pad by an interior door, which swung open noiselessly.

"Come on," he said, beckoning them inside. "I need some food and a beer, and then I have something I need to tell you."

"In that order?" Becca asked, stepping inside behind him.

"That's what I love about you, Wicked. You never miss a beat." Coop winked at her. "Hope you guys like cold pizza."

Coop led his friends into a massive kitchen, crossing the slate-tiled floor to the refrigerator with laser focus. Meanwhile, Becca ogled the room. Granite countertops, stainless steel appliances that looked as if they'd never been used, and a massive island that was as big as Becca's full-size bed, this kitchen alone could house a family of four, and it was as pristinely clean and well-appointed as the "after" shot from an HGTV makeover show.

"Damn," Becca said, afraid to touch anything. "You actually live here?"

"Sometimes." Coop's face was hidden by the open fridge door. "There's a bathroom down the hall if you guys want to clean up."

Fiona stayed in the kitchen with Coop while Stef and Becca trudged down the hallway to the bathroom. Like the kitchen, it was pristinely clean, meticulously outfitted, and spartanly decorated. Coop's house seemed both impressive and sad at the same time—like a girl who got jilted on prom night. All dressed up but no one showed.

But as weird as the house felt, at that moment it was the homiest, most welcome place in the world. Coop's house felt safe, and it gave Becca a chance to process everything she'd been through over the last few hours.

All of which showed on her face. Becca took one look in the mirror and almost yelped at her reflection. It didn't even look like her. The glitter eye makeup was streaked and smudged, and the heavy mascara had left black paths down her cheeks, deposited by her steady stream of tears. Her hair, long free of its wig, was matted and dirty, sticking out from her head at weird angles, and her arms and legs were splattered with dried bits of dirt and gore. Saddest of all, she couldn't even remember whose blood she was splattered with. Sumo's? No, she hadn't been close enough to him. Lord Cancellor's? That poor guard's? The memories made her shudder.

Becca twisted on the faucet and splashed some refreshingly cold water on her face. It didn't solve her problems, but as she toweled off, smearing the white bath towels with a thick coating of black mascara and silver glitter, at least she felt more alive.

As she hung the towel back on the rack, she felt Stef's hand on her arm. "You okay?"

Becca wasn't even sure how to answer that question. "My mom was about to judge my execution, and then our friend died helping us escape." Her hands shook as she covered her face. "Just another day."

"Sarcasm isn't going to help you heal," Stef said.

Becca tensed. Who the hell was Stef to tell her how she was supposed to be dealing with this news? Especially when it was Stef's fault Becca even discovered the truth in the first place. "You were right. My mom was Molly Mauler," Becca said, her voice cold. "You can collect your Fed-Xer award now."

Stef reared her head back as if she'd been slapped. "You think that's what I want?"

"Why else did you come with me?" Becca said. "Travel halfway across the country and spend almost every dime you had? I promised you'd see your money, and now you will. Congratulations. You won."

"I don't care about the money." Stef's nostrils flared, and she scowled at Becca's reflection. "I came to find out the truth."

"Why does it matter to you who Molly Mauler was?"

"It just does," Stef snapped, then turned on the faucet again so fiercely that a gush of water exploded from the spout.

"Fine," Becca said, eyeing Stef as she washed her face. "I'm sorry." But she made sure she didn't sound like she meant it.

"Not as sorry as I am."

"Sorry that you were right?" Becca asked.

"Yes."

Becca's sorrow over Lars and Rita turned to anger in a flash. Stef was sorry? She'd started this whole thing. Stalking Becca. Feeding her the conspiracy theory. Displaying the evidence. It was as if she had some kind of vested interest in knowing the Mauler's real identity, and now she was sorry she knew?

"Gee, this must be *so* upsetting for you," Becca said, her voice pointed, her words dripping with sarcasm. "Maybe if you hadn't suggested it to me in the first place, we could have been spared this fucked-up day."

Stef, who was always so cool and composed, finally lost it. She whirled on Becca, shoving her hard against the shower door. "I didn't want to know that your mom was a psychotic killer. That your other mom aided and abetted her murders."

"Murders? You're acting like they were serial killers or something." *Um, wasn't that just the argument you were having with yourself, Becks?* Clearly, Becca wasn't ready to accept that her mom killed all those people for no reason. Ruth must have believed in the justice of what she was doing. The prisoners on Alcatraz 2.0 were convicted killers, the worst humanity had to offer. They deserved their fates. "My mom executed prisoners."

Stef's face was red, her cheeks still wet, and anger spilled from every pore as she shoved her finger in Becca's face. "Your mom was a criminal. Just ask Cinderella Survivor."

"Who was a convicted killer."

The redness drained from Stef's face, her features rigid with pain as if she'd just been punched in the gut. "You're the same as they are."

"I'm their daughter!"

Stef stumbled backward out of the bathroom. "I thought you were different."

Becca turned her back on Stef, squeezing her eyes shut. *You're more like your mom than you realize.* Becca had experienced what it was like to be the victim of a Painiac. She'd watched people die—colleagues, friends. She wasn't like that. She wasn't one of them. And yet there she was, defending her mom's actions. Maybe Stef was right?

She glanced into the hallway, looking for Stef, but she had already returned to the kitchen. Becca wanted to go to her. To say she was sorry. But what was she sorry for? The words that she'd said? What she really wanted to apologize for was who she was.

And that wouldn't do either of them any good.

THIRTY-SIX

DEE'S LEG ACHED. SHE'D BEEN TRYING TO KEEP THE PAIN under wraps, worried that Nyles would call off the search and have Javier take them home at her first sign of discomfort, but for the last half hour, she'd been unable to hide the grimace on her face, and she'd caught Nyles glancing at her several times.

"Are you okay?" he asked at last.

Dee nodded, not trusting her voice.

"She's in pain," Griselda said, her fingers still clacking away on her laptop keys from the front seat. "Has been for at least the last hour."

Thanks, Gris.

"That's it," Nyles said, leaning forward from the backseat. "Javier, I think we should take Dee—"

"No!" The pain in her leg was temporary. She'd get home, elevate and ice it, and be fine. She was going to push through this search. She had to. "How many developments are left?"

"Two," Griselda answered. "The entrance to the next one is a block away."

Nyles dropped his voice. "We can do this tomorrow. It doesn't have to be tonight."

"Yes," Dee said, her eyes meeting his. "It does." They were running out of time, and without firm evidence to go on, they were never going to convince the authorities that Victor Merchant and the whole *Who Wants to Be a Painiac?* setup was nothing more than a charade. "People might die."

"If they haven't already." Griselda turned toward them, rotating her laptop to face them. "Look at this shit. The cops are searching for a mini-bus that shot its way off a lot in Culver City. Plus those bodies they found earlier today."

"See?" Dee said, already feeling like those deaths were on her head. "We can't wait."

"Miss Guerrera," Javier said, catching her eye in the rearview mirror. "Perhaps Mr. Harding is right. Your father wouldn't like this."

"No, he wouldn't," Nyles muttered. "And he's probably going to kill me when he finds out."

Time for a compromise. "One more," Dee said. "Then we'll go home. Okay?"

Reflected in the mirror, Javier's eyes shifted to Nyles; then with a curt nod, he turned to Griselda. "Which way?"

How many homes had they driven past that day? Hundreds. At some point, the Spanish style and tile roofs all began to look alike. It had been years; the day had been traumatic. Could her memory even be trusted? Dee was beginning to worry that they'd already passed the house and she hadn't even recognized it. And if that were true, there was a chance that no one would ever figure out The Postman's true identity. Her memory represented their last hope.

Dee gazed out the window as the lineup of enormous houses marched by. It was dark, and the way the streetlamps illuminated the McMansions made them all kind of look the same. Of course, it was a housing development, so that was the point. But it certainly didn't help.

The throbbing in her leg had become a throbbing in her head, and Dee felt the full weight of what she was trying to do. Maybe her dad was right? She should stay out of this. Government agents and lawyers and trained freaking adults who did this sort of thing for a living were on the case. How could two teenagers and a twenty-year-old hacker accomplish what the entire United States government could not? She and her friends had done the impossible: they'd survived Alcatraz 2.0. It was enough. They'd been through hell, watched people they care about die in the most violent and horrific ways, and were left with scars both physical and psychological that would never fully heal. It was someone else's turn to fight this fight. Cinderella Survivor's role in all this should be officially—

Dee gasped. She'd been only half paying attention as Javier drove, lost in her own thoughts and fears, when suddenly it was no longer night, she was no longer seventeen, and she was no longer safe.

The house stared at her as if alive. Taunting. Laughing. The lights from the foyer streamed through the front door, illuminating the stairs like a set of buckteeth amid a perpetual grin. The last time she'd seen this house, it had been in the bright daylight, when she had been sitting in the back of a US Postal Service van, while police swarmed the area. The current situation couldn't have been more different, but it didn't matter. The sweeping staircase, the twin palm trees.

She was stopped in front of The Postman's house.

Javier hit the brakes the instant Dee made a sound. "Is this it?"

"I think we've found it," Griselda said, answering for her.

"My God," Nyles breathed.

Griselda's fingers flew over the keys of her laptop. "I'll start on the property records."

Dee felt Nyles's hand on her shoulder. "Are you okay?"

"Yes," Dee lied. *Kimmi's dead. The Postman's dead.* Dee reminded herself of these facts at least three times a day, but sitting in front of this house, it was hard to believe that either of them were actually gone. *But they are.* And whoever owned the house now probably had no knowledge of what had happened there so long ago. She had no rational reason to be afraid of it now, but suddenly, Dee felt the need to prove that to herself. She opened the door, pushing it wide with her good leg. "Gris, can you hand me my crutches?"

"Dee, what are you doing?" Nyles sounded alarmed. Like she was about to do something crazy.

I am.

Javier was out of the car in a heartbeat. He raced around to the passenger side just as Griselda helped Dee out of the backseat. "Miss Guerrera, you promised."

"I just need to ring the doorbell," she said. It sounded much stupider when she said it out loud.

"Why?" Nyles asked.

Ugh. Why was he being difficult? "I just need to."

"Here." Griselda reached past Nyles and pulled Dee's crutches from the backseat. "I'll come with you."

"Gris!" Nyles cried.

"What? Girl needs to ring the doorbell."

"Miss Guerrera!" Javier said. He stood at the end of the walkway, blocking their path to the house. "I refuse to let you put yourself in danger."

Nyles looked as if he agreed with the bodyguard, but Griselda was smiling. "How about this: You let us go up the stairs and I'll let you ring the doorbell?"

"Please," Dee added. "Javier, people are dying. Don't you want to help?"

Javier looked unconvinced.

"Look," Griselda pressed. "I'm sure you're packing, so we're not going to be in any real danger. And I promise to throw myself in front of Princess here if shit goes sideways. Deal?"

Javier's eyes shifted from Griselda to Dee; then without a word, he stepped aside and escorted them up to the front door.

Dee grinned at Griselda as they started up the tiled steps. It was nice to have another girl around who understood her in a way that Nyles never could. She'd had that kind of relationship with Monica, and as Griselda helped her up the last few steps, Dee realized how much she'd missed girl friendship.

"Just for the record," Nyles said, climbing the stairs behind them, "I don't approve."

"Duly noted," Griselda said over her shoulder. "I'll be sure to tell Mr. Guerrera that you filed an official protest. I'm sure that will give you . . ." She paused, glancing sideways at Dee. ". . . diplomatic immunity."

Nyles paused midstep. "I hate you."

Dee laughed. She couldn't help herself. And suddenly, confronting the house that had taken so much from her didn't feel nearly as terrifying. She wasn't alone anymore. She had friends who would stand by her no matter what.

Javier reached out and rang the doorbell. "Stay behind me, Miss Guerrera."

"There's probably no one home," Nyles said nervously as they waited.

Griselda corrected him. "You mean you hope there's no one home."

Footsteps across the foyer proved otherwise.

The guy who opened the door wasn't exactly what Dee was expecting. A five-million-dollar home within spitting distance of the beach? This was the territory of the middle-aged film executive. But this guy looked only a few years older than Dee and her friends, young and tall and eating a slice of pizza. Someone's adult son who had failed to launch, probably.

"Can I help you?" he asked.

Dee opened her mouth, unsure what to say. *Did you know your house was the site of a kidnapping?* probably wasn't a good opener. But as she stood there, trying to formulate words, someone behind the pizza guy pulled the door open, swinging it wide.

And then Dee felt her face go cold.

"You," Dee said, staring at a face she'd only seen on the Internet.

"You," the girl said back to her. Then her face hardened. "You killed my mom."

Becca wanted to throw herself on Cinderella Survivor, to claw at her face and pound her head into the tiled doorstep of Coop's house. This girl had killed her mom. *Her mom.* Who had been literally ripped apart by ravenous wolves because of this bitch.

"I'm going to kill you," Becca said. Then she froze, her hands trembling. *You're more like your mom than you realize.* Holy crap, was she?

Chaos broke out around her. The blond guy who had arrived with Cinderella Survivor had thrown himself in front of her as Stef pulled Becca away from the door.

"No!" Stef cried. "That's not who you are."

Becca whirled on her. "Isn't it? Isn't that what you told me thirty seconds ago? That I'm just like my mom."

"I was wrong." She reached out and touched Becca's cheek. "You don't have to take revenge for something that had nothing to do with you." She sounded so wise, as if she knew exactly what she was talking about. And for the second time that night, Becca felt her chest heave as a wave of sobbing overtook her.

Fiona rounded the corner from the kitchen. "What the hell . . ." Her voice trailed off as she stared wide-eyed at the newcomers. "Cinderella Survivor," she said, her tone reverential. Then she pointed at the other two in turn. "And you're Nyles. And you're Griselda."

"Guilty," Griselda said. She was smiling, much more confident than anyone else in the room, and as she stepped aside, Becca could see why. Emerging from the darkness behind her was an enormous, bull-chested man with arms so thick and muscly they made Dwayne Johnson look like the scrawny kid at the beach. And in one hand, he held a gun. Pointed right at Coop. "Now very calmly, you're going to tell us what the fuck you're doing in this house."

Wait, what? Why was she focusing on Coop? Becca was the reason the Death Row Breakfast Club and their bodybuilding sidekick were there, right? Just like Stef, they'd figured out that Molly Mauler was her mom and they'd come for . . . No. That didn't make any sense.

"How did you find us?" Becca asked.

"Oh my God!" Fiona gripped Coop's arm, her eyes locked on Dee. "You're going to turn us in. We didn't do anything, okay? They were trying to kill us!"

"Who?" Dee asked. It was only the second word she'd spoken. Her face was pinched, like she was in pain, and then Becca noticed the crutches, the bandaged leg, and she remembered the injuries Dee had sustained that last night on Alcatraz 2.0.

The night Mom died.

"Victor and the Russians!" Fiona was crying again, the tears streaming down her face in well-worn tracks. "They said it was just a game show and then Sumo . . . and . . . and Kylie. Kayden."

Dee turned to Nyles, the look of pain on her face deepening. It wasn't just about her leg anymore. "We're too late."

Griselda wasn't distracted, though. Her eyes were trained on Coop, as was Javier's handgun. "You haven't answered my question."

"It's not what you think," Coop replied. He looked miserable. Not afraid, not angry, just utterly and completely miserable.

"Do they know?" Griselda asked.

Coop shook his head, hair wagging in front of his eyes.

"Do you want to tell them, or should I?"

Coop took a deep breath, blowing it out through pursed lips. "You know how when we got here," he started, turning sheepishly to Becca and Stef, "I said that after we ate I needed to tell you something?"

Becca felt a twinge of panic in her stomach. Coop looked so serious, so distraught. On a day that had gone from weird to bad to totally fucked up in the course of just a few hours, Becca felt like they were about to get one last sucker punch. "Yeah."

"Here's the thing." His gaze shifted from Becca to Fiona, lingered there for a moment, then back to Becca. "Victor Merchant isn't The Postman's son."

"That's your big news?" Fiona asked. She laughed nervously, still gripping his arm. "I thought you were going to tell us that you were one of those Russians or something."

Only Becca saw that Coop wasn't laughing along. His face, if anything, had become more troubled. "How do you know he's not The Postman's son?" Becca asked slowly.

Coop's eyes dropped to the floor. "Because I am."

THIRTY-SEVEN

COOP WAS THE POSTMAN'S SON? HAD HE BEEN IN ON IT WITH Victor the whole time?

Can.

Not.

Hang.

No, it was impossible. There was no way Coop could have been protected inside the Juggernaut. There was too much chaos, too many ways to die. And no one in their right mind would have voluntarily entered that arena if they'd known what they would find. Besides, Becca had seen the horror on Coop's face as people began to die around them. That wasn't an act.

"I don't believe it," she said.

Griselda smirked. "Believe it."

"If you're The Postman Jr.," Stef said slowly, still piecing things together, "then how is Victor Merchant connected to The Postman?"

"I am *not* The Postman Jr." Coop spat the words out.

"I hate to point out a technicality," the Brit said, "but if The Postman was your father, then you are, at least in some technical sense of the word, Junior."

Coop ran his fingers through his hair, eyes cast to the ceiling. "There's so much of this you don't understand."

"Ya think?" Becca asked.

Coop laughed. Easy, affable Coop. "Touché, Wicked. Look, I can explain everything. But I think you guys should come inside."

The Rock raised his gun, reminding everyone it was there, as Griselda smiled at him approvingly. "Into the house with the creepy white room of torture?" she said. "Yeah, no thanks."

"That room was dismantled years ago," Coop said. His eyes drifted to Dee. "I'm so sorry about what happened to you. I didn't know about it until years later."

Nyles arched a brow. "You expect us to believe that?"

"I really *can* explain." Coop poked his head through scanning up and down the street. "But apparently the cops are looking for us in conjunction with, like, a dozen dead bodies."

"More like fifteen," Becca mumbled.

Stef glared at her. "Not helping."

"Right, fifteen," Coop said. "And I'm worried that a couple of runaway teens in sequined dresses, a bloodstained gown, and Cinderella Survivor herself hanging out on my front steps is going to draw some unwanted attention from the neighborhood watch."

"I think we should call the authorities," Nyles said. "The whole bloody country is looking for you."

"Technically," Coop said, correcting him, "they're looking for The Postman Jr. And like I said, that's not me. I may have been Abe Bronson's son, but I am not the heir to his business."

"Abe Bronson . . ." Becca's eyes grew wide. That was Victor's connection. He wasn't the son of The Postman; he was his business partner.

Nyles rolled his eyes, slipping his cell phone from his pocket. "Either way, the police should be informed."

"Don't!" Becca cried, stepping forward.

The bodyguard's gun swung to face her. "Why not?" he growled.

Becca felt her words catch in her throat. Weirdly, it wasn't the first time she'd had a gun pointed at her—not even the first time that day—but the muzzle was so close she could practically see down it, and the bodyguard's eyes were cold and calculating where Talky Montoya's had been crazed and wild. This man didn't enjoy killing, but he clearly had no qualms about doing so.

She swallowed, feeling the weight of her words. She didn't trust Cinderella Survivor, her friends, or this bulked-up dude with a handgun, but at that moment, she needed *them* to trust *her*. "Because we won't stay alive long enough to tell the truth about what happened on *Who Wants to Be a Painiac?* tonight. A lot of people died in there. People we cared about. And someone needs to pay for that." Her eyes shifted from the bodyguard to Dee. "If the police find us, I don't think Victor Merchant will let us live long enough to see justice served."

As the words came out of her mouth, Becca realized two things. The first was that her rage toward Dee Guerrera had vanished. Just like that. Dee was no more to blame for her mother's death than she was—it was The Postman who had put Ruth in that position. Now someone new was carrying on his legacy, and like Stef had said on the floor of the Juggernaut a few hours ago, they had to stop it.

The second thing she realized was that she was talking to perhaps the only three people on the planet who had any idea of what Becca and her friends had just been through. They'd all watched people they cared about die, and they all wanted to find some kind of justice. And they were going to have to work together to find it.

"I think you know exactly what I'm talking about," Becca said quietly.

Dee crutched forward, standing beside her bodyguard's raised arm. "I don't want to speak for everyone, but I'm willing to listen to what they have to say."

"Are you sure?" Nyles asked.

Dee nodded, then her eyes drifted to Becca. "I think we all want the same thing."

Griselda nodded at The Rock, who somewhat reluctantly lowered his gun. "Fine," he said. "But I'm keeping this thing close."

Coop gestured for them to come in, holding the door wide for Dee to get through with her crutches, then closing and locking it behind them. "You guys want some pizza?"

They sat around the dining room table—all except the bodyguard, Javier, who stood in the arched doorway, ever vigilant—staring at Coop. He'd just finished his monologue, explaining his connection to Dee, the house, and *Who Wants to Be a Painiac?* Which wasn't much.

Coop had apparently been in the dark most of his life about his dad's and sister's homicidal tendencies. He'd been sent off to boarding school when he was ten, soon after his mother died. "I knew my dad and Kimber had a special bond," he explained. "I just didn't know how special."

"Kimber." Dee said the name slowly. "So that's her real name."

"That's what most people called her," Coop said. "But when she would talk to Dad, she'd use this little-girl voice and refer to herself as Kimmi. Like she turned into someone else. It was weird."

"Yes," Dee said quietly. "It was."

"I've been at college in New York the last few years," Coop continued. "To be honest, I hadn't been home since before I started high school. Since my mom died, I never really felt comfortable here. Kimber and my dad—it was like I was intruding. A lot of kids at Choate stay for summer and winter breaks, and Dad was always willing to pay for the extra room and board. So I stayed away through high school. Then college.

"I didn't even know my dad was dead until I got an e-mail from the Merchant-Bronson lawyer last month. Something about the company facing bankruptcy and how they were keeping my dad's death a secret from the press by claiming he had moved to his private island in the South Pacific, but they needed me to sign my shares over to Victor. I was all like, 'My shares?'" Coop shrugged, the lack of emotion apparent. "That's how I found out my dad had died."

Becca traced circles with her index finger on the shiny surface of the dining table. "Do you think Victor knew your dad controlled Postman Enterprises, Inc.?"

"If he didn't before, he found out last month for sure," Coop said. "I signed the shares over because, like I said, I wanted nothing to do with my dad or my sister, especially after I figured out what they had done. I've been using my mom's maiden name since college. No one knew who I was, and I was going to keep it that way. But then when I saw the *Who Wants to Be a Painiac?* audition notice, I got curious about what Victor was up to. A crowdfunded game show? There wasn't enough potential profit in that for Victor Merchant. So I came out to LA. Found the house the way dad had left it before he relocated to San Fran, and moved in." He paused, chuckling to himself. "You know my room hadn't been touched since the last time I was here? Eight years ago. Dad just closed it up and left it, Miss Havisham–style."

Nyles nodded his approval. "Nice reference."

"Did Victor know who you were when you auditioned?" Stef asked. She sat beside Becca, arms tightly wrapped around her sequined dress.

Coop laughed for real this time. "Hell no. I never met the guy. Dad formed the partnership after I was out of the house, and I doubt the name Abe Cooper meant anything to him."

"Abe's your real name?" Becca asked. Somehow, it didn't fit. He would always just be Coop to her.

Coop cringed, his face pinched. "Abraham Bronson Jr."

"So you *are* Junior!" Nyles cried. "I knew it."

"Technically, I guess," Coop said with a weary sigh. "But there's a reason I use my mom's name."

Griselda rotated her finger in a circle whoop-de-do-style, signaling her impatience. "Yeah, yeah. We all have daddy issues. Get to the part where you justify Javier not shooting you." She had a set on her. Becca had to admire it.

"Well, I started poking around the house, but I didn't find much. Financial records, mostly. Best I can tell, PEI had some investors other than my dad. But the company names don't mean anything to me."

Griselda perked up, a sly smile spreading across her face. "You got those names handy?"

"In my dad's office."

"Get them." Griselda signaled to Javier as Coop stood up; then the bodyguard followed him out of the dining room toward the back of the house while Griselda slipped out the front door.

Becca looked at Nyles. "What's happening?"

"Gris is a bit of a computer professional," he said. "Her laptop is in the car."

Stef smiled. "He means hacker. What she pulled off that last night on Alcatraz two-point-oh was impressive." She sounded genuinely intrigued by the gorgeous and sassy Griselda, and even though Becca was still angry with Stef, that admiration irritated her to no end.

Griselda and Coop returned to the dining room—one with a laptop, the other with a stuffed file folder—and huddled together. Fiona watched them carefully, and Becca detected the same hint of jealousy toward Griselda that she'd felt seconds earlier while Stef was lavishing praise upon the Alcatraz 2.0 survivor.

"Do you need my Wi-Fi password?" Coop asked.

Griselda snorted. "Do you want the FBI showing up here in thirty minutes?"

Coop clearly wasn't sure what the answer was supposed to be. "Um, no?"

"I've got an encrypted satellite link," Griselda said, flipping through the file folder. "I'm good."

"Those are the three investment companies," Coop said, pointing to one of the pages. "They all had revenue share based on their level of funding."

Dee leaned over, eyeing the files. "Forty percent? I can't believe The Postman would give that much control to anyone."

"He didn't," Griselda said, her fingers flying over the keyboard at breakneck speed. "That company is a shell for Merchant-Bronson."

Coop's jaw dropped. "How did you find that out? I spent, like, a week researching it."

Griselda smiled. "I had access to Daddy's laptop, remember? I managed to send myself a few files before the FBI confiscated it."

"Nice," Coop and Stef said in unison.

"This next one is also Merchant-Bronson related," Griselda continued. "Shit, that company had a lot of capital invested in Alcatraz two-point-oh."

"No wonder Victor crowdsourced this whole thing," Coop said, reading over Griselda's shoulder. "Merchant-Bronson is completely broke."

"With so much tied up in Alcatraz two-point-oh," Griselda explained, "once the government froze all PEI assets, Victor Merchant was totally fucked."

Becca rested her head in her hand, propped up on the table with her elbow. "But what about the Russians?" she asked no one in particular.

"This is interesting." Griselda typed rapidly. "TP, LLC was the majority shareholder in PEI."

"Mean anything to you?" Becca asked Coop.

He shook his head. "And nothing came up when I googled it."

Griselda laughed to herself, eyes darting back and forth across the screen. Everyone waited quietly, the tension in the room thick and meaty. Would this be the piece that they'd been looking for? After a few moments, Griselda sat back, staring at the screen. "Well, now you have your answer, Disco Queen. Proof the Russians are involved."

"Seriously?" Becca asked.

"I had to trace TP, LLC through eight different shell companies, but finally landed on United Conglomerates." Griselda turned the screen around so they could all see. "Which is a state-owned enterprise of Russia."

THIRTY-EIGHT

BECCA STARED AT THE SCREEN. IT WAS AN ARTICLE FROM THE Washington, DC–based news website *Beltway Bulletin* tracing potential connections between the president of the United States and a Russian-based hospitality company called United Conglomerates. The contact between the two dated back to before the president was elected, when he was just a businessman and reality television star with enough ego to want to be president. Ego, but apparently no cash on hand, according to the article, which interviewed an anonymous source linking campaign funding to the Russian government–backed United Conglomerates.

"If that's true," Coop said, sliding into a chair beside Becca, "that means the Kremlin was funding Alcatraz two-point-oh."

"And if your president facilitated it," Nyles added, "it would constitute treason."

Griselda swung her laptop back around to face her. "Unfortunately, treason requires two witnesses to the treasonous act. *BeltBull* claims their anonymous source has disappeared. Congress thought they had the connection through Gavin Xanthropoulos, until he turned up dead."

"I wouldn't be surprised if Xanthropoulos was the source," Dee said, shaking her head. "And now impeachment is in jeopardy."

"What do you mean?" Becca asked.

"Without a direct link between the president, Alcatraz two-point-oh, and Russian involvement, he probably retains his office."

Stef tapped Coop's hand across the table. "And there's nothing here in the house linking your dad to the president?"

Coop shook his head. "I've turned this place upside down. Even the, um, storage room downstairs." His eyes assiduously avoided Dee. "If it existed, I have no idea where it is."

"And we're just supposed to take your word on that, I suppose?" Nyles said, leaning back in his chair.

"Yes," Becca snapped. "You are." Maybe it was all that they'd been through in the last couple of days, or maybe it was the fact that they both had psychopathic killers for parents, but she felt protective of Coop, who had been totally up-front with the Death Row Breakfast Club and their gun-toting bodyguard, and she didn't like the insinuation that he was somehow withholding information.

"You've known him for, what, three days," Griselda countered. "And you're just going to trust him completely?"

Dee smiled. "I'd known you for three days when I trusted you with my life."

Griselda pursed her lips. "Fine."

"I wonder . . ." Stef's voice drifted off. She was staring out the dining room window into the darkness of the evening, her brows furrowed up in that now-familiar way that meant she was grappling with a problem. "If there was evidence in existence, something that linked the president and the Russians and Alcatraz two-point-oh, that would be important, right?"

"Um, yeah," Griselda said.

Becca caught her breath.

"What?" Stef said quickly. "What is it?"

The house burglarized but nothing taken. The way Victor spoke to Rita in the Juggernaut . . .

"He was threatening her." The realization dawned on Becca, the truth flashing into her brain like a bolt of lightning. "That's why I made it through auditions."

"Slow down," Griselda said. "You've lost the rest of us who didn't want to be on a creepy reality show."

Becca ignored the snark. "They were going to cut me," she explained, looking around the room. "The day of auditions. Then someone called the casting dude and, suddenly, I was in."

"He was watching," Stef said. "He recognized your name."

"I must have seemed like a gift." Becca couldn't believe she'd been so stupid. "They thought my mom had something that linked the Russians and the president to The Postman. A few days after my mom's funeral, someone ransacked our house."

Stef's face dropped. "You never told me that."

Becca wanted to remind Stef that she'd been initially banned from conversation that wasn't entirely business-related, but decided now was not the time.

"Do you know what they were looking for?" Dee asked, pushing herself up in her chair. She looked eager, determined.

"I think so," she said slowly. The safe in the bedroom. The remnants of glitter and sequin. "My mom's scrapbooks."

"Scrapbooks?" Griselda snorted, then burst into laughter. "With, like, glitter and stickers and shit?"

"Gris . . ." Dee said quietly.

"Sorry." Griselda tried to suppress her laughter. It took her several tries. "I just wasn't expecting that."

Normally, Becca would have joined in Griselda's derision of her mom's scrapbooks. She thought it was a useless, ridiculous hobby, one that had always embarrassed her. But her mom was dead, and those silly scrapbooks might just hold the key to finding justice and closure.

"My mom took photos of literally every single thing that happened in our lives. Makes sense that she would include her interactions with The Postman and Alcatraz two-point-oh."

"I'm surprised The Postman allowed that," Nyles said.

Coop cleared his throat. "Well, my dad did have a healthy amount of narcissism. I can totally see him enjoying the fan-girling."

"But if they stole the scrapbooks from your house," Stef said, "why bother keeping you on the show?"

"I don't think they found the scrapbooks."

"Did your mom destroy them?" Dee asked.

"No way." She doubted Rita could have brought herself to destroy the last connection she had to her wife. But she'd definitely moved them out of the house before the break-in. "She hid them."

"Any chance you know where?" Griselda asked.

Rita's office would have been Becca's first guess, but that was probably the second place the Russians looked too. Maybe she buried them in the woods? Or stashed them on campus? She reached into the bodice of her dress and pulled out the ring that hung around her neck. Her mom's wedding ring. Rita had tossed it to her in the arena. Was it just her way of saying good-bye? Or did it mean something more?

A sharp vibration broke the silence of the dining room as Stef's phone vibrated from the counter. She stood up, confused. "No one should be texting me."

Becca realized with some sadness what she meant: no one, not even her grandparents, cared where she was.

"'Not sure who this is,'" Stef read slowly from her screen. "'Is Becks with you?'"

Becca groaned. "Jackie." It had been a couple of days since Becca checked in, and a freaking-out Jackie had texted the emergency number Becca had given her.

She took the phone from Stef's outstretched hand, ready to type a response, then paused. "What do I say?"

"Ask if she knows where your mom's scrapbooks are," Griselda said absently, her attention focused back on her laptop screen.

"Funny," Becca said. Her best friends who had always been there for her. She couldn't even imagine getting Jackie and Mateo any more involved in this than they already were. "I'm glad you think this is—"

Her best friends who were always there for her. Like at Ruth's funeral.

Becca lifted the chain over her head and held the ring up before her. The sapphires had been Ruth's favorite gemstone, and she'd never taken that ring off. Not washing the dishes, not taking a shower, not even, apparently, while killing people on Alcatraz 2.0. But Rita hadn't buried her with the ring on her finger.

Becca's mind raced back to the scene she'd witnessed when Rita opened the safe in her bedroom. The box inscribed with the letter *M* that Rita had kissed so reverently.

It wasn't an empty box. It was an urn.

And if Ruth had been cremated, her ashes stored in a safe in Rita's bedroom, then what had been buried in her coffin?

Becca bolted to her feet. "I know where the scrapbooks are."

"What?" Stef said. "Where?"

They were going to need shovels. And the spare key to Becca's house Jackie's mom kept in the kitchen drawer. Jackie wasn't going to understand, but at least she'd be happy that Becca was coming home. She picked up Stef's phone and typed quickly.

"Becca," Stef said, laying a hand on her arm. "What the hell is going on?"

"Road trip," she said as she hit *send* on the text. Then she turned to Coop. "We're going to need to borrow your car."

THIRTY-NINE

THIRTY-NINE HOURS IN AN SUV IS THIRTY-EIGHT HOURS TOO long.

That was Becca's takeaway from the drive from Manhattan Beach to Marquette. Not that they had a choice. While photos of them hadn't been released to the public, there was a manhunt under way for "four young persons, aged seventeen to twenty-two," in connection with the incident in Culver City, which had claimed eight lives.

It was the number eight that stuck in Becca's head throughout most of the drive. She counted out the victims over and over again: Sumo Sutra, Mistress Distress, Lord Cancellor, Kayden and Kylie, Lars, the guard in the golf cart. That was seven. So who was number eight?

Initially, she thought it had to be Rita. Becca had heard the gunshot after all. But then she remembered Alexei standing in the guard station. Was the eighth victim another guard? The one named Clyde who was supposed to call the police?

Becca wouldn't allow herself to hope that she was right, but she also couldn't face the idea that she wasn't. There was nothing she could do about it anyway. She had to think about herself, and Rafa.

Becca called Rafa's cell from Coop's house before they left. It was a struggle to keep from bursting into tears the second he answered the phone. "Hey, buddy," she said, desperately trying to keep her voice from cracking. "How are you?"

"Bored," he said. "Aunt Tabitha doesn't have any video games."

Rafa's ten-year-old priorities were refreshing. He clearly had no idea what was going on.

"You okay, though?"

"BORED," he repeated, as if she hadn't heard him.

Becca took a silent breath to steady herself before her next question. "Can I talk to Mom?"

"Mom had to fly to LA for work or something. Didn't she tell you?"

Tears spilled from Becca's eyes and down her cheeks. "Right. Yeah, of course. I forgot."

"She was supposed to be back by now. I wish I was at Keyes Peak with you. At least there's something to *do* up there."

Becca wanted to stop in Arizona and hug her brother, but bringing him into this would be dangerous. And right now, she had to keep him safe at all costs. "You be nice to Aunt Tabitha, okay?"

"Yeah."

"And hey, I lost my phone, so you can call me on this number if you need me."

"Okay." Rafa paused. "I miss you, Becks."

"I miss you too, buddy. But I will see you soon. Everything is going to be okay."

The instant Becca ended the call, she sobbed uncontrollably as she leaned against Coop's kitchen counter. Everything is going to be okay? No, everything was not okay. Would never be okay again. And what would happen to Rafa if she didn't survive this? Would Tabitha take care of him? Or would he end up in a foster home? Or worse? Whatever "worse" was.

Becca felt an arm around her, pulling her into someone's body. "He's okay," Stef said. "He's going to be okay."

Becca looked up, Stef's face inches from hers. The anger she'd felt after their argument in the bathroom had vanished. "But what—"

"Don't." Stef wiped a stream of tears from Becca's cheek with her thumb. "We have to believe it'll be okay." Then she pulled Becca close and rested her head on Becca's shoulder.

They stood there, clinging to each other, until Coop cleared his throat from the doorway and told them it was time to get on the road. Stef and Becca had left so much unsaid, but in that moment, it didn't matter. They'd gone from enemies to business partners to friends. And now to something deeper.

Dee, Nyles, Griselda, and their bodyguard wished them luck before piling back into their SUV. Dee had wanted to accompany them to Michigan, but Nyles and the bodyguard had strictly forbidden it. The only people more sought than Becca and her friends at that moment were the Death Row Breakfast Club. They'd be more of a hindrance than a help, and so Dee had offered Becca a silent smile of concern through the open SUV window as the bodyguard escorted them back to LA.

They drove in shifts, starting with Coop and Fiona while Becca and Stef slept on the two bench seats in the back. A description of Coop's ride hadn't appeared in any of the reports about them, and with Griselda planting a false lead with the police, placing the group somewhere north of Los Angeles, they hoped that they'd be able to reach Marquette unrecognized.

Even still, they were hardly unnoticeable. Their faces might not have been all over the news like Dee's, Nyles's, and Griselda's, but their descriptions were. *One male, Caucasian, six feet to six feet one, dressed in cargo pants and T-shirt embroidered with the name "John." One female,*

Caucasian, medium build and height, last seen wearing a sequined mini-dress. One female, Latina, five feet six to five feet seven, also last seen in sequined minidress. One female, African American, slight build, five feet five, wearing white dress stained with red dye.

The costumes had been ditched at least, and Becca was pretty sure she'd live happily ever after if she never had to wear sequins again. She, Stef, and Fiona had gone through Coop's sister's closet, looking for something that fit while trying to ignore the fact that they were wearing the clothes of a dead sociopath. Stef and Fiona had no problem finding leggings, shirts, and sweaters—they must have been almost perfect matches for Kimber's height and size—but Becca had more difficulty. Her boobs would not fit into most of Kimber's tops, and her hips were too wide for any of her pants, so she had to settle for a heinous midi peasant dress and button-up cardigan that made her look like she'd pulled clothes blindly from her grandma's closet. She just kept reminding herself that it was only temporary, and she'd be able to wear her own stuff in just a couple of days.

Even with a change of wardrobe, as a precaution, only two of them ever sat up in the car at any given time, because four young people in a white SUV was probably going to cause a double take. They'd stopped at two or three different gas stations cycling through bathroom breaks, just to make sure no one put the four of them together and called the authorities.

They drove straight through, with night turning to day and then night again. Ears popped through the Rocky Mountains, and snow from Cedar Rapids through Wisconsin slowed them down, but as they climbed north out of Green Bay, Becca felt a coldness come over her. She was driving home to dig up her mom's coffin, unsure whether or not she and her brother were currently orphans, and the only bright point in all of this was that Rafa was safely two thousand miles away in Arizona.

"It feels weird to be back in Michigan," Stef said from the backseat. The sun was up as they crossed the border into Becca's home state. Coop and Fiona were chatting in the front seat as they'd done constantly through their driving shifts, while Becca and Stef napped in the back.

"I can't believe we've only been gone five days."

Stef's head popped up over the seat back. "Really?"

Becca grinned. "We left on the sixteenth, remember?"

"Damn."

"Ladies!" Coop called from the front. "I can see you."

Stef rolled her eyes, then heaved herself over the back of her seat and sat on the floor in front of Becca, knees hugged to her chin. Becca remembered their kiss in the Juggernaut, and their fight at Coop's house. Which version of Stef would she get now?

"I know I've been kind of a bitch," Stef started.

"Not a bitch," Becca said quickly, which was true. Difficult? Yes. But not horrible.

"There's just a lot going on," she said, resting her cheek against her knee.

"You don't say."

"I will," Stef said, ignoring Becca's snark. "Someday." She glanced up, smiling at Becca, then went back over to her bench seat.

Two hours later, they pulled into Becca's driveway.

"BECCA!!!" Jackie ran down the front walkway as soon as the back door opened, and threw her arms around Becca, hugging her close. "I'm so glad you're not dead."

She laughed dryly. "Me too."

Mateo followed close behind his girlfriend. "When we didn't hear from you . . ."

"I kinda freaked out," Jackie said. Then she squeezed Becca again. "Your mom would have killed me if anything happened to you."

At the mention of Rita, Becca's stomach sank and her voice caught in her throat. Neither of which Mateo missed.

"What's wrong?"

Becca shook her head, forcing down the emotion. It wouldn't do her any good right now. "Nothing. Um, you guys should meet my friends. This is Coop, Fiona . . ." She paused, feeling her face grow warm. "And Stef."

She wasn't exactly sure what kind of reception Jackie would give this group of strangers from Los Angeles, but she tackled Stef in a bear hug.

"Thank you for keeping Becca safe," Jackie said, practically in tears.

"Calm down, Meryl Streep," Becca said. "Your drama is showing."

Jackie grinned sheepishly as she released Stef, who, far from looking discomfited, was smiling.

Becca shivered. "We should get inside."

They bundled into the house, which Jackie and Mateo had prepped for their arrival. The heat was on, fighting off the chill of late afternoon, and there were cartons of Chinese food on the counter, with sodas in the fridge. "Bless you guys," Becca said, heaving a sigh of relief. Despite the reason for her return, it felt good to be home. "Did you get the other stuff too?"

Mateo nodded. "I borrowed three shovels from my dad. Plus there's one in your garage.

"Awesome."

"You going to tell us why you need them?"

Becca's eyes faltered under his gaze. As much as she hated keeping secrets from her friends, it was for their own safety that they not know what was going on. Information kept getting people killed, so the less Jackie and Mateo knew, the safer they'd be.

"Look," Becca said, taking each of them by the hand. "I hope I can tell you all about this when it's over. But you have to trust me when I say you don't want to know."

"Becks," Jackie began, "we want to help."

Becca smiled. "I'm worried that something bad might happen to you."

"But—"

"Jackie!" Becca never got sharp with her friend, and the inflection shut down Jackie's protest immediately. "Please. Promise me you'll go home, watch a movie, and forget about all of this until tomorrow."

Jackie's face fell. "Now?"

Becca nodded. "Please." She didn't know if there was a proper facial expression for *I don't want you to die*, but she hoped the combination of desperation and sincerity she was feeling was close enough.

"Fine," Jackie said after a suitably dramatic pause. "But you'll text me in the morning, right? When you're done with whatever it is?"

"As soon as I can," Becca said. *Whenever that is.*

Becca waited on the front porch until Mateo's car disappeared around the corner before she went back inside. Coop and Fiona had already dug into the Chinese food, but Stef waited for her in the living room, perched on the edge of the sofa.

"We go tonight?" she said as Becca closed the door.

"After nine," Becca said. "This town will be half-asleep by then."

Stef's eyes strayed to Coop and Fiona, who were laughing in the kitchen. "So we have a couple of hours."

Something deep inside Becca shifted. She'd felt it before, several times, but always when she was alone. This time her breath shortened as

Stef slowly approached, eyes locked onto hers. Stef took her hand, stroking the back of it with her thumb. Before Becca could even think about what she was doing, she slipped her hand around Stef's back, pulled their bodies together, and kissed her.

It was a hard kiss, not soft or gentle like the girl-on-girl kisses Becca had seen on the Internet. Nor was it tentative like their kiss had been in the Juggernaut. Becca had no more experience at kissing now than she had then, but it didn't matter. Any worries she might have had about Stef being more experienced were banished from her mind the moment she felt Stef's hands on the sides of her face as they pressed their lips together.

If Coop and Fiona saw anything, they remained discreetly quiet, but again, the thought had hardly flitted across Becca's mind before it was gone. Stef broke away from the kiss, her hands still cradling Becca's face, eyes searching. Becca wasn't sure what Stef was searching for, had never been sure exactly what she'd wanted, either from Becca or from the trip to Los Angeles, but in that moment, Becca knew that she wanted Stef. And she was pretty sure Stef felt the same way.

"Your room . . ." Stef began breathlessly.

"End of the hall."

They stood unmoving, frozen in the living room until Stef's right hand strayed from Becca's face, trailing down the side of her neck to her chest, then down to the waistband of the ugly peasant skirt. Becca's body quivered. The timing was horrible, the weight of their situation heavy upon them, but Becca didn't care. She took Stef's hand, turned toward the hallway, and led Stef to her room.

FORTY

IT FELT GOOD TO PULL HER OWN CLOTHES OUT OF HER OWN closet, even if Becca wasn't entirely sure what to put on.

"What's the appropriate outfit to wear to your mom's disinterment?"

"Considering how cold it is outside," Stef replied, pulling her shirt on over her head, "I'd say a coat."

Becca winked at her. "That's why I like you. Always thinking."

It was a surreal moment, the nightmare of the last few days juxtaposed upon the utter bliss she felt in Stef's arms, and though she'd wanted them to snuggle under the covers together until the sun came up, Becca realized that wasn't an option. They were being hunted, the danger of their situation was ever present, and until they got their hands on the evidence they could use as leverage, the nightmare would never be over.

So Becca fought off the desire to put on a cute skater skirt and a booby top for her new girlfriend, and went with the more practical option of jeans, thermal shirt, sweater, boots, and a thick woolen hat. It definitely wasn't the flirty choice, but it would stave off hypothermia.

Coop was watching the news in the living room, the volume muted, while Fiona slept beside him, her head resting on his leg. He toggled back and forth between all three of the major news networks, which ran a continuous feed of talking heads discussing the latest developments at the impeachment trial, while chyrons at the bottom updated the events in Los Angeles.

"Anything new?" Becca asked, her voice low so as not to wake Fiona.

"Still nothing about Victor Merchant or the Russians," Coop said, flipping the channel again. "I don't know how he's managed to keep that under wraps."

"Money," Stef said. "Power. The usual suspects."

Becca opened the hall closet and pulled out a variety of winter coats. "What about us?"

"Thanks to Griselda, they still think we're in California," Coop said. He switched off the TV and edged aside, easing Fiona's head onto a cushion.

Fiona started. "Is it happening?" She pushed herself into a sitting position. "Are we going?"

"You know," Becca said, busying herself with a tangle of gloves, scarves, and hats, "you don't have to come with us."

"Huh?"

"You and Stef." Becca wouldn't look at either of them. "You can get out now. In case there's trouble."

Stef folded her arms across her chest. "What the fuck are you talking about?"

She wasn't entirely sure, but suddenly, all Becca wanted to do was keep Stef safe, and staying home while Becca and Coop went to dig up a coffin seemed like a logical step toward that goal. "My mom was Molly Mauler. Coop's dad was The Postman. We're the only two that are stuck in this mess. You two get out now and we'll . . . we'll tell the cops or the press or whatever that it was just the two of us all along."

Fiona laughed. "Yeah, well, the cops already know we're involved."

"Not really," Coop added. "Not if we tell them—"

"Save it," Fiona said. She marched across to the chair where Becca had laid the coats and picked out the thickest, fluffiest one. "My aunt's best friend's hairdresser's neighbor might not be Molly Mauler, but I'm still a part of this bullshit whether you like it or not."

"Me too," Stef said.

Fiona pulled on the coat, then wound a scarf around her neck. "The way I see it, we won't be safe until we get what's in that coffin. And Stef and I can't trust the two of you not to fuck that up."

Now it was Stef's turn to laugh. "Truth."

"So let's get some goddamn shovels and start digging." Fiona planted her hands on her hips. "That grave isn't going to open itself."

Disinterring a body was a hell of a lot harder than it looked.

In the movies, it was the scene you cut to when the hole in the ground was already four feet deep, piles of fluffy brown dirt amassed on one side, while two people stood inside, heaving out shovelfuls. The reality was that in late December, the ground in northern Michigan was half-frozen at ten o'clock, even on a relatively warm thirty-five-degree night, and getting through the first foot of dirt at Ruth's grave site took almost an hour.

The good news was that they had seven more hours until sunrise. The bad news was that the temperature was dropping by the minute, and though the dirt deeper down wasn't as hard as the stuff near the surface, the colder it got, the harder their bodies had to work for each inch, and two hours in, they were dirty, sweat-drenched, and exhausted.

Like with the cross-country drive, they worked in shifts, one pair resting while the other dug. Unlike the cross-country drive, they worked in total silence. Becca wasn't sure if it was the ambiance of the cemetery, the fear of getting caught, or the personal demons they each wrestled with that contributed most to the unspoken agreement to stay quiet, but if everyone else's brain was working like hers, it was mostly the latter. The deeper they dug, the closer she was to finality: the reality that her moms were both dead, her life forever altered, and the gripping, chronic fear that they'd fail. What would happen then? A president who should be in jail would probably not only avoid a prison sentence, but retain his office. Russian government agents and their collaborator would never be brought to justice for their killings. And yet another band of Painiacs would not only feel justified in their acts but, if Victor got his way, would continue the Painiac legacy of terror and death in Russia, as the newest state-sponsored program of capital punishment.

Just the fate of democracy and the moral future of the Western world on their shoulders. No pressure.

So she dug. Her coat and hat discarded, her sweater and jeans caked with dirt, Becca drove the spade into the ground with her foot, then crouched to heave its contents out of the deepening hole. Again. And again. And again.

Until eventually, just as the sky was beginning to lighten, her shovel hit something solid.

Becca leaned against it, panting heavily. "That's it."

"We did it," Stef gasped beside her, totally wiped from the latest pull.

Fiona grabbed one of the LED lanterns Becca had brought and held it over the edge. "Can you get the lid open?"

It took another half hour to clear away enough dirt from the coffin to be able to get the upper door free. Becca wiggled her fingers down the side of the lid and felt for the edge.

"Do you want me to do it?" Coop asked, his face illuminated by the rapidly rising sun.

Becca shook her head. "I'm good." She wasn't entirely sure that was true, but this was her mom's coffin, and even though she was pretty sure there was no body inside, it felt disrespectful to ask someone else to do the dirty work. Becca squeezed her eyes shut. *One. Two. Three.*

It was heavier than she expected, still encumbered by earth at its corners, but after raising it a few inches, she was able to get her arm underneath and, pushing up with her legs, finally threw the lid open.

The lack of a putrid stench was the first indication that no body had been buried in that coffin. The interior smelled musty and damp, like the onset of mildew, but it wasn't the same smell as the time a rat had died in the walls of her moms' bedroom when she was six and the whole house smelled like rotting garbage. The second, of course, was the lack of a mangled corpse staring up at her. Thank goodness for small favors.

What Becca did find were three blue-covered photo albums. The kind Ruth used for her scrapbooking.

With shaky hands, she lifted the books up one by one, passing them off to her friends, then Coop and Stef hauled her out of the hole. She lay on the ground, panting to catch her breath, eyes fixed on the scrapbooks that had been the cause of so much death.

They looked exactly like the ones at home—embossed leather covers, ribbon ties to keep them closed, and puffy stickers on the front denoting the year—only these were just from the last two years. The two years that Molly Mauler had existed.

Stef, Fiona, and Coop didn't touch the books, waiting for Becca to do the honors. There was a part of her that didn't want to know what was in them—she'd had enough horrific revelations in the last few days to last a lifetime—but she knew she had to. If there was anything inside that would establish the link between Coop's dad, Russia, and the president, they needed to know.

She passed one book to Coop and Fiona, one to Stef; then holding her breath, Becca reached out to the remaining volume and flipped open the cover.

This was definitely late-stage Molly Mauler, judging by the first photo. It was Ruth smiling beside an attractive African American man with a smooth bald head, posing in full selfie mode on what appeared to be a dock, judging by the water on either side, with the sunlit skyline of San Francisco framed behind them. She wasn't wearing makeup, and he wasn't wearing a mask, but Becca realized immediately that her mom was posing with Gucci Hangman on Alcatraz 2.0. The photo was labeled from January of that year with a stickered title that read "Two Ships Passing in the Night." Maybe one of them had just come from an execution while the other was arriving. It churned Becca's stomach to think that one of the smiling people in this photo had just killed a terrified inmate. Even worse that one of these smiling people was her mom.

She flipped the page and this time, her mom was in some kind of dressing room, getting ready. Her hair was pulled back in a clip, and just her white base had been applied. She posed with duck lips with the caption "Ghostly White," while a succession of photos below it showed every step of her makeup process until the familiar evil clown face of Molly Mauler appeared in the final frame.

The saddest part to Becca was how happy her mom looked.

"Dude!" Coop cried. "That's Gavin Xanthropoulos."

"The guy who died?" Fiona asked.

"Yep." He held up the album so Becca and Stef could see. "Now we know why." The photo was of Molly Mauler, full costume, posing beside a skinny dude with adult acne and a smarmy grin.

"There's one piece of the puzzle," Stef said.

"Keep searching," Becca said as she flipped the page. A man lying immobile in his underwear in the middle of a shallow tank of water. It was the video Stef had showed her.

There were several snapshots of this kill, some taken from above, as if Ruth had been up in a balcony at the time, others from closer to the action, including an incredibly disturbing one of the victim's face close-up after the snake had strangled him—face purple, eyes frozen wide in terror and pain, lips parted in a now-silent scream.

Then the last photo of the snake, bloated after consuming its meal. The victim's body was just a mound inside the reptile, and Ruth posed beside it, her face half in the frame, with a thumbs-up. The caption beneath the photo had been written in purple glitter pen.

"'Bye-bye, Lawrence,'" Becca read silently. "'The murder of your wife, Angela Ybarra, has been avenged!'"

FORTY-ONE

BECCA STARED AT THE NAME.

Ybarra.

The same as Stef.

Whose mom was dead and who lived with her grandparents.

Because her dad is dead too.

The trees and headstones around her began to swim, a dizzying, swirling mass of muted light and shadow at the periphery of her vision, while her eyes hyper focused on the name of Angela Ybarra. The name of Stef's mom.

This was why Stef had been obsessed with discovering the true identity of Molly Mauler. Why she'd gone to audition for *Who Wants to Be a Painiac?* Becca had assumed it was for the Fed-Xer reward. But this reason . . . this explained the hot and cold behavior, the open Stef and the closed Stef.

My mom killed her dad.

Becca looked up at Stef, who was slowly flipping through her book, oblivious to what Becca had uncovered. What had Becca been to her? A source of information? A means of revenge? Could she really believe anything that had happened between them?

"Holy shit," Coop said, staring at the third scrapbook. "Is that—"

"Yep." Fiona turned the book around for Becca and Stef to see. "That's Molly Mauler with the president."

Stef leaned in to get a better look. "Oh my God."

"There are a few from this series. Some kind of party." Coop grabbed Stef's cell phone and began taking pictures of the scrapbook pages, the flash lighting up the early-morning sky. "How much do you want to bet there's a Russian ambassador in here somewhere?"

"This is it!" Stef said, her voice breathless. "We did it. Becca, we did . . ." Her voice trailed off as she faced Becca.

"Why didn't you tell me?" was all Becca could manage.

Stef's jaw hung slack as her eyes flitted down the page open in Becca's lap. She didn't respond. Just stared at the photo of Molly Mauler next to her dad's final resting place in the intestinal tract of a giant snake.

"Why?" Becca repeated.

"Would it have mattered?"

"Yes!"

"Seriously?" Anger flashed in Stef's eyes, and the combative Stef that Becca had first met in her high school parking lot returned in full force. "You're going to get all victimy over this? The only one it should matter to is me."

"You lied to me."

"No, I didn't," Stef snapped. "I just didn't overshare."

Coop raised his hand like he was in elementary school. "Um, what's happening?"

Stef answered quickly, her voice icy. "Becca is pissed off because I didn't tell her that her mom killed my dad."

Coop sank back on his heels. "Whoa. That's heavy."

"Thank you!" Becca cried.

Stef pushed herself to her feet, shoving the scrapbook aside. "You know what? Even if I had told you the truth, you wouldn't have believed me. You never did, not until your mom was literally staring you in the face in that arena. So let's not pretend that it would have made any difference." Stef snatched her phone out of Coop's hand. "It's not like you take anything seriously, right, Becca? Me, the audition, this whole fucking trip."

"That's not fair," Becca said. She stood up, fists clenched by her side. "You have no idea why I'm like this."

"You're right," Stef said. "I don't. And I think I'd like to keep it that way." Then she turned and started to walk down the hill. "I'm out."

"Not so fast," a voice said from the shadows.

Becca and Stef both froze, turning slowly. Standing behind the same oak tree from which Stef had watched Ruth's funeral a month ago, was Victor Merchant, Alexei, and a half dozen of his men with guns drawn.

Victor stepped forward into the morning light. "Now, are you going to hand those books over, or are we going to start shooting people?" Then he burst into laughter as if he'd just made the funniest joke in the world. "Oh, who am I kidding? We're going to shoot you anyway. I just wanted to see the looks on your faces."

"Why not just shoot us now?" Becca asked.

"You always have to be the smart-ass," Victor said. Then he shifted the aim of his gun at Coop and fired.

"No!" Fiona cried as Coop hit the ground. He groaned, grasping his left thigh. Fiona grabbed her discarded scarf and wrapped it around his leg, cinching it tight, and though his continued moans were agonized, Becca was thankful he wasn't dead.

"Happy?" Victor asked.

"You've made your point," Becca said, not entirely sure that he had. But at the edge of her vision, she saw Stef's hand—cell phone tightly gripped—creep back behind her body, where she could shield the phone from Victor's view while still being able to see the screen.

The photos Coop had taken of the scrapbooks. She was sending them to someone.

Becca eyed Stef, not daring to let her gaze linger for too long lest Victor's attention should be drawn to what she was doing. Her thumb moved quickly over the screen, whose brightness was camouflaged by the light of the brightening sunlight. Becca wasn't sure if it was Twitter or Instagram or just plain old e-mail she was planning to use, but whatever it was, she needed to buy Stef some time.

"Did you really do all of this for some small-change FundMyFun money?" Becca asked, forcing herself to sound brave even while Coop writhed in agony in the dirt a few feet away. Fiona held his head, stroking his brow, and stared at Becca like she was batshit crazy.

"Shut. Up," Fiona said through clenched teeth.

Becca tried to shoot her a look that said *Trust me*, but she was pretty sure she just looked constipated.

"I don't care what you think of me." Victor shook his head. "That's the beauty of being an adult."

"Did you care what Abe Bronson thought?" Becca said, grasping at straws.

"Oh, Abe. It was never about the money for him. Not really. Money just got him what he wanted. I stayed out of it, except to check in on the investment." Victor sighed, his face aglow in blissful nostalgia. "Abe sent me the master passwords for Alcatraz two-point-oh, knowing I'd probably never use them. Not until the very end, at least. That's how I knew to get the Russians involved. Abe didn't really care about that either. He was happy as a clam as long as he was dressed up like Prince Slycer, disemboweling women."

Coop groaned louder, and Becca wondered which pain was more severe—the gunshot wound or the reminder that his dad was a sociopath.

"Sorry, kid," Victor said, turning to Coop. "This is what you get for wanting to be famous. You should really leave the TV crap to the Merchants and the Bronsons of the world."

"Wait, what?" Becca said. The words flew out of her mouth before she could stop them.

Victor sighed. "I meant your friend shouldn't get involved in stuff he doesn't understand. Leave it to the professionals."

But Becca knew exactly what Victor meant. *The Merchants and the Bronsons of the world.*

Coop was right: Victor had no idea who he was.

This was her chance. At least to distract Victor long enough for Stef to get those photos loaded.

"Coop!" Becca laughed. It almost felt genuine. "He has no idea who you are."

Coop's pale, gaunt face was slick with sweat, but through the pain, he was able to shoot her a glance as if to say *What the hell are you doing, crazy lady?*

"Stop," Victor said. "Whatever it is you're trying to do, it won't work."

"I'm surprised you didn't recognize him from the beginning," Becca continued, "the way you recognized me."

Victor's eyes darted back and forth between her and Coop. "*You* look just like your mom."

"And so does he," Becca continued. *God, I hope I'm right about this.* "But I've heard that his baby-blue eyes are all Abe Bronson."

The name had the desired effect. Victor's cocky smile faltered, the barrel of his gun drooped for an instant, and he stepped forward, staring down at his partner's son.

"You've got to be kidding me," Victor muttered.

Coop gritted his teeth, hand still clamped onto his wound. "I don't think we've ever properly met," he managed. "But . . ." He glanced at Becca, as if trying to figure out her plan. "But I've known all about your little scheme from the beginning."

Don't press your luck, Coop. They needed to stall for time, not show their hand too quickly.

"Oh, really?" Victor was intrigued but not convinced.

Fiona picked up the strain. "The police should be here any minute."

Victor paused for a moment, then bent forward at the waist and slapped his knee with his free hand. "Man, you guys. Nice try. You had me going for like a hot second." His voice popped into a falsetto, mocking Fiona. "'The police should be here any minute.' That's, like, the best movie cliché ever."

"Just. Wait," Coop said. His speech labored against the agony of his wound.

"Now that you pointed it out, you do look a lot like him," Victor continued. "But I don't give a shit. You already signed over your shares of the company, so, meh." He raised his gun again. "Less talking, more shooting."

"Stop!" Stef yelled. She held her phone over her head, thumb poised over the *send* button. "I have photos of the scrapbooks loaded up to post on Twitter. Even tagged the *BeltBull*."

"You're bluffing," Victor said, while craning his head to try to get a better look at the screen.

Becca stepped in front of her, putting herself between Stef and a bullet. "The question is, can you get to her before she gets to the entire Internet?"

"Fucking kids and your social media. Don't you realize that no one reads that stuff?" Victor was the one bluffing now, trying to play this off like it was no big deal, but Becca knew better. If they were going to die, at least they'd make sure the world knew the truth first.

"Goddammit." Victor signaled to his men, and one of them bolted down the hill behind the oak tree. "I didn't want to do this, but you're leaving me no choice."

An engine revved in the distance, and Becca braced herself to see Mandeep's steamroller crashing up the hill. Instead, a white van rounded the curve on the road below. It stopped in full view of Becca and her friends, then the side door slid open. Lying on her side on the floor of the van, bound and gagged, was Rita.

FORTY-TWO

BECCA WASN'T SURE WHETHER SHE WANTED TO LAUGH OR
cry. Her mom wasn't dead. At least not yet. But how were they going to
get out of this?

"Let me hear her," Becca said, grasping at straws. "I want to know
she's okay."

"Get the phone from your girlfriend," Victor said calmly, "and then
I'll let you, your mom, and your friends go."

Did he think she was a complete idiot? "Let me talk to her. Now."

"You're trying my patience, kid." Despite the complaint, Victor
snapped his fingers and the guard in the van pulled the gag roughly away
from Rita's mouth, smearing what was left of her clown makeup.

"Don't give it to him!" Rita screamed. Her voice was hoarse and weak,
but her words were anything but. "Don't believe a fucking word out of
his mouth."

Becca had never heard her mom swear before.

Victor rolled his eyes. "Why is everybody in this town so fucking
dramatic? It's like a soap opera twenty-four/seven." He waved at Rita, and
the guard lifted the gag back into place.

It looked hopeless. Coop had been shot, Rita was in Victor's power,
and despite the fact that Stef was holding her finger over the launch

button, it seemed a hollow victory if she and everyone else Becca cared about ended up dead. Becca was trying to cycle through the various outcomes, when she heard something in the distance.

Is that a siren?

Becca wasn't sure whether or not Victor heard it too, but suddenly, his impatience kicked into high gear. "What'll it be, kid? Give me the phone, or do I have Ilya start shooting your mom in a variety of painful yet nonlethal locations?"

Becca took a deep breath, letting her shoulders sag with the exhale, hoping her body language read "resignation." Were the sirens getting louder, or was that just her imagination? Not that it really mattered. Becca wasn't sure it would save her mom and her friends, but as long as she made Victor pay, that would have to be good enough.

She turned and snatched the phone out of Stef's hand. "I'm sorry." But she wasn't looking at Stef when she said it. She was looking at her mom.

"Becca, don't!" Stef said, but Becca already held the phone out to Victor. Without letting him see her do it, she hit the *send* button.

"Put my friends in the van and give Stef the keys," she said. "Then I'll hand you the phone."

He wouldn't know that she'd already posted the photos. At least not yet.

Rita screamed through her gag, but Becca ignored her. "Do it!"

Victor hesitated, weighing his options. Making sure those photos weren't posted was clearly his first priority if he was even thinking about cutting a deal, and all his posturing earlier had come to nothing.

"I'm serious, Victor," she said, her thumb still poised over the button as if she hadn't already posted. "Let them go and you get the phone."

A flurry of excitement erupted behind Victor as his guards spoke rapidly in Russian. The wail of sirens was now impossible to ignore. Holy crap, were they going to make it?

"What?" Victor cried as Sergey spoke to him rapidly. He spun back to Becca. "You lying bitch!" Uh-oh. Someone was monitoring Twitter. Becca stood frozen as Victor raised the gun, aiming right at her.

The sound of the gun firing and the impact of something on her side seemed to happen simultaneously. Becca felt her body falling and assumed she'd been shot. Maybe that's what it was like—a painless fall where your body didn't even register that it had taken a bullet. But when Becca crash-landed on top of her mom's coffin, she was pretty sure the bullet had missed her. The pain where her elbow struck the coffin lid was worse than anything else.

Then she looked up and saw Stef leaning over the grave.

She pushed me out of the way.

"Stef!" Becca cried. Sirens wailed from somewhere above, but Victor and his thugs were still out there, armed and willing to kill. "Stef, get down!"

Stef teetered, her body unstable; then she pitched forward into the grave.

Becca caught her, breaking her fall with her own body. Stef's chest was damp, the shirt sticky as it clung to her skin, and as Becca lowered her down onto her back, she realized why. The bullet meant for Becca had hit Stef.

"Oh my God!" Becca touched Stef's face, leaving bloody fingerprints on her cheek. "Stef . . ."

"Shh!" Stef said. She tried to smile, but her lips contorted in pain. "Talk too much."

"Stef, you have to hang in there, okay?" Becca felt Stef's side for the wound, pressing her hand against it to try to stop the bleeding.

"Hang in," Stef repeated. She shuddered, her body in shock.

"Yeah." The tears flowed down Becca's cheeks, obscuring her vision, but she didn't want to take her hands away from Stef's body in order to wipe her eyes. "You can't leave me. Not now."

"Be fine," Stef managed. Her eyes searched the grave for something, and Becca realized she couldn't see. "Becks?"

Becca pressed her cheek against Stef's, her lips against Stef's ear. "I'm here. Right here. I'm not going to leave you."

There was commotion up above, and Becca could hear people running around. Then Jackie's voice.

"Where's Becca?" That's why the police had arrived. Jackie and Mateo must have gone to Becca's house this morning, seen Victor and the Russians poking around, followed them, and called for help. Never before had Becca been so grateful for Jackie's nosiness.

"She's okay," Becca heard Fiona say. "But we need an ambulance ASAP."

Help had arrived. Would it be soon enough to save Stef?

"There's an ambulance coming," Becca said, fighting back the sobs. "They're going to get you to the hospital. You'll be okay."

Stef shook her head, and Becca felt her heart crack wide open, all the hope she had left spilling out of her. "Becks . . ."

"Yeah?"

"Sorry."

"It's okay, it's okay."

"Wanted to hate you."

Becca sniffled, stroking Stef's asymmetrical hair away from her face as a sickly pallor washed over her skin. "I think you did there for a while."

"No."

"Maybe a little."

Stef laughed; then her body seized up in pain. Becca held her tightly until her muscles relaxed, but her breathing was ragged.

"Not like them." Stef's voice was little more than a scratchy whisper. "Never like them."

"I know."

Then her eyes darted quickly to Becca's face and looked right in her eyes, seeing her. For the first time since Stef had been shot, Becca thought maybe things were going to be okay.

"Becca, I think . . . Love you."

Becca smiled. "I love you too."

Stef returned her smile. She was so beautiful. So wounded and tough and beautiful on the inside too, and Becca wanted to hold her like that forever until they were both old and wrinkly and lived in a giant house with forty cats. But with her eyes wide, her lips smiling, Stef's body went slack in Becca's arms.

BELTWAY BULLETIN

POLITICS—US Edition
December 24, 1:15 pm ET

James and the Giant Impeachment
by Adrienne Quiñones

To say that the last forty-eight hours have been a roller coaster
ride would be like saying that Mount Everest is "kinda big." After
the explosive photos were leaked to the media via Twitter, the
originals later recovered by the FBI and submitted as evidence in
the impeachment trial, the ever-obstinate leader of the not-so-free
world refused once more to resign, forcing Congress to invoke
Article II of the United States Constitution against a sitting president
for the first time in the history of the republic. With photographic
evidence showing the president, the Russian ambassador, Gavin
Xanthropoulos, and several of Alcatraz 2.0's former executioners
at a private party, hosted by The Postman himself, we almost
didn't need the appearance of new witnesses. But it was after their
testimonies that the Senate moved for an immediate resolution.

Victor Merchant, longtime collaborator with former television producer Abe Bronson, was the first. Testifying in exchange for a reduced sentence in the *Who Wants to Be a Painiac?* case, Merchant placed the president of the United States in a meeting between himself, his former partner, and the Russian ambassador two months before the Alcatraz 2.0 plan was formally presented to Congress. He swore under oath that the Russians had partially funded the operation, and that the president himself, in the guise of a shell company called TP, LLC—a Russia-backed corporation previously reported on by *BeltBull*—was a personal shareholder.

Then Abe Bronson Jr., also known as Abe Cooper or "Coop," still recovering from an injury sustained during the *Who Wants to Be a Painiac?* debacle, testified that his late father, Abe Bronson, was in fact The Postman.

In a unanimous vote—the first time the Senate has agreed on something since they took up the budget bill after the last government shutdown—the Senate voted to remove the president of the United States from office.

Almost immediately, the deputy secretary of the Justice Department filed criminal charges against the former president, forcing him to relinquish his passport.

The upcoming criminal trial should be a reality show worthy of its defendant, but hey, at least he's not president anymore.

Meanwhile, several arrests have been made in the related case of *Who Wants to Be a Painiac?* after the Merchant-Bronson production proved to have ties to the same Russian company that was behind The Postman. Merchant and sixteen others—including ten individuals tapped as the "New Painiacs" and several Russian nationals—were arrested in conjunction with fourteen deaths in Los Angeles. Streamed live to a group of crowdsourced funders and pay-per-view fans, the real reason behind the scheme appears to be Merchant-Bronson's crushing debt in the wake of the Alcatraz 2.0 shutdown. Now that Abe Bronson has been outed as the mastermind behind The Postman, the money trail has been easy to follow. The details of Victor Merchant's plea deal have not yet been made public.

So where does that leave America? The soul of our democracy has been deeply rattled by the events of the past year, so much so that many critics think the moral fiber of America will never recover. But I disagree. If anything, the darkness in which we allowed ourselves to be lulled to sleep has now been exposed for the danger it is. We all have a responsibility not to let it to happen again.

How?

We speak up. We trust the press. We resist and resist and resist. America has seen trying times before and it will see trying times again, but our democracy is worth fighting for—then, now, always.

Please send feedback to the author @TheRealaquinonesBB.

FORTY-THREE

THE ONLY THING WORSE THAN A FUNERAL RIGHT AFTER Thanksgiving was a funeral on Christmas Eve.

It had seemed like an insult at first. Like Stef's grandparents were trying to sweep her death under the rug quickly and quietly so they could enjoy the holiday, but when Becca saw Stef's family at the funeral—her grandmother's face drawn with sorrow, her aunt and uncle bowed with tears—she realized that Stef had been greatly cherished by her family and they were traumatized by her loss.

The turnout at the cemetery in Escanaba was massive, undeterred by the frigid temperatures and proximity to Christmas. Stef would have thought the entire thing ridiculous, as she loathed attention, but then, funerals weren't really for the dead, were they? They were for the living.

And the living that surrounded the grave site on Christmas Eve morning showed the scope of people whom Stef had touched.

Rita, her arm bandaged from her gunshot wound, stood behind Becca with Rafa, who, utterly confused about what was going on, kept asking "Whose funeral is this?" Jackie and Mateo had driven down from Marquette. Coop and Fiona—one on crutches, the other with her arm around him—had flown in directly after Coop's testimony in Washington. Even Dee, Nyles, and Griselda were there, accompanied by a curly-haired Latino man with youthful eyes and too many worry lines who might have been Dee's father, and a small army of bodyguards.

Becca had expected to see all of these people, but there were so many more. Faces Becca didn't know. Hundreds of them. The story of what Becca and her friends had done had circled the Internet like wildfire. The Fed-Xers declared that Stef Ybarra was a martyr. A hero. And with the corruption of The Postman fully exposed, the Postmantics, if not exactly experiencing a change of heart, at least kept their mouths shut. There were no protests at Stef's funeral, no violent clashes between the pro- and anti-Postman factions. Just people from all over the country who had come to pay their respects.

None of which made up for the fact that Stef was dead.

Her funeral was Catholic, but the priest read almost the same exact prayers Reverend Hamlin had recited at Ruth's graveside. The big difference for Becca this time? She had no problem crying.

"When our earthly journey is ended, lead us rejoicing into your kingdom, where you live and reign forever and ever. Amen."

"Amen." Becca's voice broke as she responded.

Becca stood rooted to the ground beside Stef's open grave as the priest crossed himself, offered a whispered word of comfort to Stef's grandmother, then slowly walked toward the cemetery entrance, where a mass of cars lined the streets of sleepy Escanaba. Stef's grandmother sobbed openly as she placed matching bouquets on both Stef's tombstone and that of Stef's mother, who lay beside her.

But Becca's brain only vaguely registered the movements around her. As she stared down at Stef's coffin, all she could picture was the scene at the Marquette cemetery, Stef's head in Becca's lap, her skin turning a sickly shade of grayish brown, her eyes open but unseeing, as her life slowly drained away.

How was Becca supposed to go on without her? Stef was her first everything, and the hole in her heart left by Stef's death would never heal, never go away. Becca knew she had to cherish the gift of life that Stef had given her, but how could she when the pain felt so overwhelming?

"It gets easier." Rita's voice was soft in Becca's ear, and normally, her mom's words of comfort would have fallen on more receptive ears, but Rita's role in all of this still stung. The realization that one of her parents had been a serial killer was bad enough. But that the other was complicit? Becca could never look at Rita in the same way ever again.

"I don't want it to," Becca said through gritted teeth.

"I know." Rita stepped into Becca's view. She looked as if she'd aged ten years in the last ten days. Her usually vibrant skin was sallow and dull, her coat was cinched so tightly at the waist that Becca could clearly see how much weight she'd lost, and her eyes, though as wise and as firm as always, were tinged by a deep sadness that hinted at permanency.

Good.

Investigators into the *Who Wants to Be a Painiac?* debacle had deemed Rita's actions—as well as those of Gucci's mom and Gassy Al's brother—to have been under duress after Victor had threatened to expose their identities to the Fed-Xers. The good news was that Rita wouldn't face jail time, unlike the New Painiacs, which meant Becca and Rafa wouldn't be scooped up by Children's Protective Services. The bad news was that Rita had been placed on administrative leave from her job at the university pending an ethics investigation. So who knew what their future held.

"She'll always be with you," Rita continued. "Just like your mom is always with us."

"Always with us," Becca repeated. Her mom. Molly Mauler. Yes, that would stay with her forever.

"Someday . . ." Rita's voice trailed off as her voice cracked. "Someday I hope you'll understand. And forgive me."

It was a miracle that Rita was alive at all, and that Stef wasn't Becca's second funeral that week, and somehow, hearing her mom say it out loud broke down the wall that Becca had erected between them.

"I love you, Mom," she said, slumping into Rita's arms. She felt her mom wince as Becca accidentally grazed her wounded arm, but she didn't push her daughter away, instead holding her fiercely to her chest.

"I love you, too. I'm so sorry."

They clung to each other as the crowd dissipated. The wind felt colder now, whipping off the lake with renewed ferocity as the wall of people that had surrounded the grave site were no longer there to act as a break.

"I'm cold," Rafa said. "Can we go home?"

Becca broke away from her mom and turned to face her little brother. There was something comforting in the fact that he had no idea what was going on, no idea of the horrors his mom and sister had endured. And Becca didn't want him to. She'd done all of this to protect him and keep him safe, and the fact that he seemed blissfully ignorant about everything was the one bright spot Becca could hold on to.

"Go wait in the car with Mom," she said, forcing a smile. "I'll be there in a minute."

Rafa sighed. "Fine. But I'm taking shotgun."

Becca waited until her mom and Rafa were out of earshot, walking back toward the entrance with Jackie and Mateo, before she crouched down by Stef's open grave.

"I said so many horrible things to you," Becca whispered. She didn't need to speak loudly, but she did need to say the words. "And you always forgave me. I'm sorry I wasn't a better friend. A better girlfriend. You deserved so much more than me."

She could practically hear Stef's voice in her head. *No, I didn't.*

"I will never forget you, Stef. And I'll never forget why you died. Why I'm here and you're not." The tears were flowing again, and Becca found it difficult to keep her voice at a whisper. But she had one more thing to say.

"I can't promise you much," Becca said. "Just like I couldn't protect you at the end. But I swear to God, I will make sure the people who did this will pay for it."

She took a ragged breath, steadying herself. "I'm Molly Mauler's daughter, after all."

THE END

ACKNOWLEDGMENTS

Sequels are tough. These people made this one less so:

To the amazing team at Freeform Books, starting with my editors, Kieran Viola and Eric Geron, as well as Kelly Clair, Cassie McGinty, Dina Sherman, Marci Senders, Mary Mudd, Molly Kong, Sara Boncha, Seale Ballenger, and Emily Meehan. Mouse power.

To the tireless folks at Curtis Brown who, as always, had my back at every step of this process, especially my killer agent, Ginger Clark, but also Holly Frederick, Tess Callero, Sarah Perillo, and Jonathan Lyons.

To the Wolfpack, whose immense contributions to both this book and my sanity while writing it earned them the dedication: Nadine Nettmann, Julia Shahin Collard, Jennifer Wolfe, James Raney, and Brad Gottfred.

To Valia Lind for help with all things Russian.

To Melanie Hoo Swiftney for her Michigan expertise.

To Caitlin O'Brient Bauer of Royal Digital Studio, promo goddess, for her tireless efforts on behalf of this series.

And lastly, to my Johns, who make every single day better than the last.